THE VALLEY OF MASKS

Praise for *The Alchemy of Desire*

'A startling work of Nabokovian fiction'

– *Hindu*

'At last – a new and brilliantly original novel from India'

– V.S. Naipaul

'One of the most attractive Indian writers in English of his generation, he writes with a great deal of raw energy, inventively employing images which are at once sad, haunting, horrendously comic and beautiful'

– *Times Literary Supplement*

'This Indian masterpiece is like a voyage down the Ganges, long and infinitely pleasurable; the only thing that worries you is getting to the end too soon'

– *Figaro*

Praise for *The Story of My Assassins*

'An instant classic … far, far better than anything I've ever read by an Indian author'

– Altaf Tyrewala

'Intrepidly conceived and ingeniously executed, *The Story of My Assassins* casts an intimate, often humorous, but always unflinching, eye at the squalor of modernizing India. Combining a fierce political imagination with a tender solicitude for the losers of history, it sets a new and formidably high standard in Indian writing in English'

– Pankaj Mishra

'Few English novels from India are as finely textured and true-to-life as *The Story of My Assassins*. A marvellously observant writer, Tejpal knows India's elite and underclass alike, and he weaves their stories together seamlessly. The narrative voice seduces and the novel is full of laugh-out-loud lines. But *The Story of My Assassins* does not just entertain. It enlightens'

– Manjushree Thapa

'A devastating tale about political power and its malignity. With his ferocious new book, with his compelling writing, Tarun ensures, hopefully, that Indian exotica will never sell'

– *Financial Express*

THE VALLEY OF MASKS

Tarun J Tejpal

FOURTH ESTATE • *New Delhi*

First published in India in 2011 by Fourth Estate
An imprint of HarperCollins *Publishers*
a joint venture with
The India Today Group

Copyright © Tarun J Tejpal 2011

ISBN: 978-93-5029-046-0

2 4 6 8 10 9 7 5 3 1

Tarun J Tejpal asserts the moral right
to be identified as the author of this work.

HarperCollins *Publishers*
A-53, Sector 57, Noida 201301, India
77-85 Fulham Palace Road, London W6 8JB, United Kingdom
Hazelton Lanes, 55 Avenue Road, Suite 2900, Toronto, Ontario M5R 3L2
and 1995 Markham Road, Scarborough, Ontario M1B 5M8, Canada
25 Ryde Road, Pymble, Sydney, NSW 2073, Australia
31 View Road, Glenfield, Auckland 10, New Zealand
10 East 53rd Street, New York NY 10022, USA

Typeset in 11/14 Adobe Garamond
Jojy Philip New Delhi 110 015

Printed and bound at
Thomson Press (India) Ltd.

FOR TIYA AND CARA

Morning dew, summer gales, passion fruit – the sum
of all enchantment and promise

For Peter,
wishing you
the best.

12/8/[...]

THE LAST NIGHT

This is my story. And the story of my people.

It is not a long story. Some men would tell it in the time it takes to drink a glass of bittersweet Ferment. And then there are those who would tell it in such detail that barrels would be drained dry and they would not arrive at its end. I am in between – too confused to be too short or too long. I was not always so. Once I was a man of opinion and will and purpose. Men turned to me for fixity when their hearts and minds wavered. Once.

Today my crisis is time. I have just heard the whistle of the nine o'clock train, and know the sand is running out of my hourglass. What a beautiful sound the whistle of a train is! When I first heard it I thought it the cry of the biggest bird in the universe. Then I saw the man-made beast, and I heard it chatter and I heard it sing, and I fell in love with its voice. These months past how often have I crept up the embankment and sat by the sharp stones, caressing the iron veins, placing the lobe of my ear on their hardsmooth cool to hear the approaching throb of life from far away. I have been amazed at how indifferent men are to the beauty of a train's voice, how they will not even give pause to their conversation when its soaring whistle shrapnels the air. But this too I have learned, that all beautiful things are not considered beautiful by all men. And perhaps one must be glad for that.

How easily I digress! How much I have changed. How much become like these men I have come to live amongst. Distracted and seduced by anything that may chance by. And perhaps one must be glad for that.

Yet, today, my only two virtues must be focus and words. They must be like the nail and the hammer, banging away in ringing unison till there is no further to go.

Today my crisis is time.

In a few hours it will be midnight and the Wafadars will begin to close in. Already they must be stirring, limbering their muscles with push-ups and chin-ups, testing their fists on unyielding walls, whetting their double-edged daggers on wet stone. Now they will be unrolling their goatskin belts to clean the sacred chonch: each of the eleven hardwood pins capable of perforating an artery with minimal fuss, emptying one of blood like a leaking cask. Soon they will shave their scalps till they glisten like the underside of freshly stripped bark, and then each will oil his skin till it shines like a duck 'n wing and slips like water. When the exertions are done, they will sit in a tight circle – three, four, five: never have more been sent – and they will each quaff a dram of Ferment and clasp hands on either side and close their eyes, united deeply in their purity and in their purpose.

In that moment of coiled stillness, they will know that nothing they pursue will ever elude them or the fatal insertion of the hallowed chonch. Life must be made to ebb away slowly, giving one a chance to repent. It is the gift of men, different from the oblivion of animals. Death by the chonch is a courtesy – of one man to another.

All this I know. As one knows the lines on one's toiling palm.

I know the Wafadars will find me. I know they will show me no mercy, for mercy is flab. Each of them can without assistance undo fifteen men. And tonight there may be five of them. And me – for all purposes, there is just one of me. I know I will not see another dawn, and if my luck is fully run, never hear the whistle of another train. There is one that arrives from the capital at two in the night, but between midnight and two lie two long hours. The Wafadars need less than a minute. If there are five of them the cask will leak like a ripped sieve.

And yet I feel no fear. Once I felt it, and I inspired it. Fear was the paper on which every day of my life was written. Though I did not see it – just as one does not see the tree that has become the page under one's scanning eye. At the time, I thought my life was bliss. Each time I imagined the unblinking eye of the True One, I was swept with gratitude for the grace and purpose that had been granted unto me. Unto us.

Now I know better.

I know the minds of men, everywhere, are like mango pulp. They can be squeezed into a glass or a spoon, or even be splattered on a plate. If a man will not take charge of his mango pulp and put it in the right place, someone else will. I have learned that most men are happy to leave their pulp in the care of others. I have also learned that the world has seen grand pulpmasters, some impossibly noble, and some responsible for gutting the entrails of a million. In the eyes of these men lie knowledge and madness. The knowledge that men yearn for a greater purpose; and the madness to find for this yearning a door and a space.

It's time for a cup of tea. Some months ago I needed it a few times a day. Now I need it by the hour. A galloping addiction; a welcome one. Strange to think I had never tasted the brew till recently. More calming than Ferment; more aromatic than the Vapours. I don't drink it the way everyone here does. I take no sugar, and I don't taint the dark hues with even a drop of milk. When I look into the cup – allowing the sweet steam to scale my nostrils and caress my eyes – I can see in the rich translucence moving mysteries and hidden stories. Such as seem to surround most men here.

The steps give perilously, and creak as if they will break. They are also narrow. A fat man would have to slant his body to make progress. And when you reach the last, at the bottom, you have to bend low lest you damage your brow on the thick beam that holds up the first floor. The pinewood – chir, from the hills above – is old and gone to black, all its grain blurred. Everywhere. The walls, the floor, the stairs, the doors, the window frames, the planks under the tin roof. All the edges appear mouldering and rotten, and little holes have opened up even in the rafters. But I know if you ran a simple plane on it – anywhere – a taut new skin would emerge, fresh, shining, golden. The miracle of wood: priceless in its ageing and forever young, capable of being reborn a hundred times. And yet, in this town, nestled in a damp crease of the Himalayas, men prefer to seek out brick and concrete. So typical to admire the hard, to imagine it is more substantial and more enduring.

So it is that this house is bracketed by blocks of brick-and-concrete. They are new and climb up straight, box on box, till the town planner will be challenged no more. Across every opening, from top to bottom, is a crosshatch of iron grilles, painted in hunting green. At night the front door is protected by a steel shutter. These houses are built to withstand the assault of a battalion of thieves. And to combat marauding djinns there are the painted pots – demon faces in black and white – slung across the shining forehead.

The neighbours joke that it is these strong shoulders that keep my – our – house from collapsing. Pappu, the young man who runs property around this place, once came to me, parking his big red car at my door, and said, 'Uncle, this house looks like a mosquito stuck between two butterflies. Give it to me and I will give you back a butterfly and some money.' He wore big dark glasses which he kept taking off to polish with the edge of his red tee-shirt. On his large fingers were enough rings to marry off an aisle of a church.

Pappu does not know what I know. That not just brick and mortar, even rock crumbles when the earth moves. The only thing that can sway like a tree and hold its perch is wood. Pappu does not know what I know. That beneath the majesty of these oakskin mountains, in whose shadow we all crouch, run restless nerves that can stir without warning. Pappu is too young to know that it has happened in the past, and when it has, the bricks and rocks of men have been fragile as glass in a child's hand. The only thing that has swayed like a tree and held its perch is wood.

In time I have understood that Pappu does not know because men have taught themselves to bury the bad news and pass on the good. It is the way they go on. By telling stories not of the perils ahead but of the waiting oases, with springs of sherbet and doe-eyed houris. In a short time I have understood that at every step of his life a man buries and leaves behind loss, sorrow, deprivation, failure: misery so deep it can make a hole to the very centre of the earth and beyond. The man who does not master the routines of this burial becomes so weighted as to be incapable of moving a single step. He perishes where he stands.

In a farm near this town lives a turbaned farmer who as a young man saw his ripe wife mastered by a mob and his two sons and a daughter carved into pieces before being roasted. It was a tangential settling of accounts, as often happens with men. A great leader had been gunned down in the faraway capital. In this case I think the arithmetic was 4,000 ordinary lives as the price of one great one. I am told this was a fair equation. Sometimes a great life can demand a settlement that runs into tens of thousands. But the young farmer was unreasonably distraught. He took scraps of cloth from the slaughtered bodies and stitched them into a vest for himself. He wore it day and night and never took it off. He put his hands on his holy book and took a vow to kill, or to die. Twice he was picked up by the police to cool him off. In a few years his farm went to ruin, and he became a fugitive, shunned by all. Then an old priest – a trained singer of hymns – visiting from the holiest of shrines, tutored the man on the rites of burial. He helped him dig a deep pit and to cast his sorrows into it. Once the soil had been tamped down firmly, the young man remarried. Now I see him on Wednesday mornings, driving his blue tractor-trolley to the vegetable mart, his two young sons strewn among the cabbages and carrots, the white patkas on their heads unfurling in the wind like the tail of a tree pie.

In this too we were different from these men. We did not grieve. And we had no sorrow to bury because we had no sorrow. Out here men have hope and fear, and the elaborate imagination of hope and fear. We had certitude. We knew everything. The here and the hereafter; the good and the bad; the dangers and the delights. And we knew the right way to deal with everything.

In this house, on days, I feel I have been left stranded between two worlds. I am of one, and I am trying to arrive in another. It has proven more difficult than I thought. A man can become new things in a new place, but if he has travelled far from where he first learned to walk he can never again be whole. Always when he puts his hand inside himself he finds yawning gaps that make his fingers stretch and ache.

I, too, on some nights, wake with a start, from a dream of yearning for the face that was once my life. Then I reach into Parvati, and in the warm solace of her unhooked blouse, in the curve of her heavy flesh, I know the impulse to be dangerously false.

I like the room we sleep in. It is small – very small – and it forces a small bed on us. A small, single bed. In the beginning Parvati would throw herself a light mattress and blanket on the floor, next to the bed, half under the bed. Each time I woke – which I did on the hour – I would peer down for reassurance and all I would see were the contours of her round face, the rest of her sari-wrapped body a curled blob under the blankets. When I finally persuaded her to share my bed I discovered a kind of peace.

I fitted myself into her curves, held her firmly under her neck and around her belly, and ceased to wake like a watchdog. Parvati's body has been addictive, a profound sedative. I can no longer sleep without it. In the afternoon when she does not wish to sleep, I coerce her to lie with me till my nerves have stilled and sleep has seized me. Even so I am aware of the amputation when she gently disentangles my arm and tiptoes away. And, always, I wake in panic, calling for her. She slaps her forehead and calls me a foolish schoolboy. But I know she is always pleased.

When her daughter left the house, she suggested we move down to the larger room on the ground floor. I declined. I was scared of creating more room – giving her body a chance to drift away. In any case, even though the planks continually groan, I prefer the first floor. The house is old. No one is sure but they say it could be close to a hundred. Yet everyone – save Pappu – says it is safe. Solid workmanship, they say. It will last another hundred years. On that I would not bet, but in this town I have not seen another house I would care to live in.

This house – my house, our house – sits on a plinth of heavy stones. If you care to look past the furry moss and the bursts of grass, you can see how beautifully – and painstakingly – the stone has been dressed, in perfect slices, no seam out of true. And, inside, it boasts the last remains of thick iron latches and twelve-nail brackets. Just outside the front door, between the street and the house, grows a semul so tall you cannot see its top till you have walked away a distance. It is a many-armed giant, with countless hands and countless fingers. For much of the year its fingers are crooked in admonition and in warning. But for some weeks in the waning winter they become gaudily laden with the gift of red flowers. From my perch on the first floor I can lean out the window and gather them in. And later, when the pods burst, the breeze picks up the cotton fluffs and sails them into the house. They get stuck to everything and like puppies roll on the floor and try to sneak into our sleeping room which lies just beyond.

Parvati complains in her sweet mumbling way, but I cannot get myself to shut the window. For some reason it brings on a panic of old memories.

This window – stuck into the middle of the façade like an open mouth – is my favourite place. It has a broad sill on which you can sit, with your feet dangling out, or in, or braced against the opposite wall. I would spend every waking minute at this window were I not afraid that I would be seen by as many of the endless passers-by as I crane my neck to see. It's a delight that has not paled on me. The

sheer variety of creatures that wind their way past. In each I try and
imagine the embedded story. But it has been important that I attract
no attention here: the same man endlessly at the same window does
not make for discretion.

Now it matters no more.

I have been found, and my time is run. I have not had the courage
to tell Parvati. When I go back up with my glass of tea, I will stop
in our tiny room where she sleeps, and I will take out the folded
letter from my pocket and place it under her pillow. She will not
wake. The creak of the floorboards, the rustle of the bedclothes, the
opening and closing of doors, the hiss of the kettle downstairs, the
occasional squawk of nightbirds, the soft hammering of the nightjar,
drunken voices from the street, the roar and rumble of trucks, the
sweet song of the last train, the music from any black box – nothing
ever breaks her sleep.

All these noises are – have become – part of the landscape of her
night. For me they are alien. I come from a country of deep silences.
These sounds keep me awake, and I contribute to them. As I sit at
my small table, with its smooth green baize top, close to my window,
I leave the connecting door ajar so I can keep turning to see her
reassuring silhouette. I never turn in until I have heard the voice of
the two o'clock train, and sometimes, by the time I do the rites of
dawn are already afoot. Newspaper boys wheeling past tossing their
rolls; milkmen on motorcycles, their large tin cans clanging; brisk
bowlegged old men and women working their arms as if dragging
back their youth; boy servants taking out the dogs of their masters;
young men in cheap track pants, jogging with high knees; and,
pleasingly, the sweet whistle of the five o'clock shuttle returning to
the capital.

As the dark ticks its time, speaking its garbled tongue, and Parvati
slumbers, I read.

I read, and I read. Till sleep smothers me I read every scrap I
have been able to lay my hands on. Of all that I have discovered
journeying in this new world, it is this that I find most compelling:

that men write so much! In so many tones and voices, espousing and denouncing, celebrating and lamenting, agreeing and contesting – with such passion and feeling, such wit and intellect, with such cartwheels of prose, such somersaults of the imagination. It is not as if we lacked in passion, but ours was a straight-flying arrow. Here it is an exploding bomb, the sound and light and shrapnel flying in every direction. Can passion be so diffuse, so splintered, and still possess meaning? In this place I have learned that it is best that it is so. If not diffused, men's passions easily grow themselves into a rabies, repelling the water of all reason. Of this perhaps I know more than anybody in this town. Or in any other.

I read. To the soul-stirring baying of the unowned dogs, I read everything I have been able to purchase and purloin. Newspapers and magazines, books and journals, old and older. Often I find myself poring over even the paper packets in which Parvati brings home the grocery. Once a week I go to the Chawdi Bazaar and with what little money I have I buy reading material by the kilo. Old discarded printed paper in all shapes and sizes; yellowing, fading, tearing, detached from its glue and binding; heaped in dusty piles under a makeshift shed, lashed together with plastic and twine – all of it priceless, all of it crammed with words.

The trader, with the nose of a vulture and legs of matchstick, wants to know the name of the ragpickers' market where I ply my trade. When I tell him I take them for myself, to read, he says, And I am a koel singing from the highest tree!

How beautifully he puts it. Even in mocking me he produces beauty. A koel singing from the highest tree! In my land such a line would be frowned upon, would be seen as an excess. Here the anarchy of voices produces poetry on the street. It is an extraordinary thing.

I cart every piece of printed paper to my room because every written thing here has a story to tell, an idea to sell, a picture to paint. Even the advertisements, even the columns where marriages are bartered. It enchants me. In my time here, on tattered pieces, I have discovered thoughts and provocations that set the body and mind on fire. The ceaseless chatter of this world is nothing short of wondrous.

I pour the tea and it jumps and spits. Before taking a sip, I inhale its aroma. The ginger is deliciously pungent. Parvati says I crush ginger into tea like the rest of them pour milk. I love the way it hits the roof of my mouth and roars through my nostrils. The small kitchen is orderly and clean. There is not an unwashed spoon in the sink. No matter how long and wearisome the day, Parvati will not turn in till she has put every plate, pan, tin and container back in its place, washed the cooking slab, mopped the floor, collected the leftovers and left them out the back door for the foraging cats and dogs. Even now, as I take my first scalding sip, I can hear the scuffling of paws and maws outside. When there are no leftovers I have seen her create them so that the animals will not go back with nothing. Parvati is a woman of few words, but I am ever humble in her presence for the selflessness of her labours and the generosity of her spirit. No wonder she sleeps without stirring, while I struggle to find the door into an untormented rest.

Again I digress. So easily I digress. So much of this world has rubbed off on me. But today I must take care. I have no time. It is true – and I have learned it here – that there are endless stories to tell. But today I must tell the one that I alone can. If I do not do so, it may never be told.

Men must know what I have to tell; men must think about what I have to tell; and men must act on what I have to tell. At the same time I fear my story may pass for a fiction. Men may read it and not heed it. They may take it merely as a tale – a compelling one, sure, but one that does not exist beyond the paper it is written on.

That would be a great tragedy for my people, and for the men I have come to live amidst. It has happened before. Other Dagadars, deserters like me, before they were hunted down, had tried to tell the story, shout the story, scream the story. They were ignored, dismissed, laughed at. In the face of such disbelief, a few of them had run deranged by the time the Wafadars got to them and opening their veins, dripped them dry.

In the valley we heard these stories as instruction, about the deserters who had been run mad by the world out there. The Wafadars would narrate accounts of how, when they closed in on the Dagadar, they found not a derelict brother who had run away but a frothing lunatic. At least one was found in a decrepit mental asylum hiding under a broken table in a damp room. The flesh had shrivelled on his bones and in his hands were two little stones which he was softly tapping together. It was told to us that tears welled in the eyes of the rescuers as they reached for him, unrolling their goatskin belts.

There was another one, whom we all knew and admired, who had legs strong as logs of wood. He had travelled far, six districts away from the foothills, and the pursuit took over three years. Finally he was tracked down to the city jail. The local police had incarcerated him after he had made a repeated nuisance of himself at the newspaper offices, insisting on telling his story which is also my story. The Wafadars said when they got to him – having effortlessly scaled the ten-foot walls laced with barbed wire – he embraced them in relief and begged for the redemption of the chonch. They reported that as life began to flow out of the sacred pinholes, the penitent admitted it was a deep folly to seek anything in this world of men. It was a flawed and cruel place, selfish, uncharitable, doomed. He had betrayed himself and his people by attempting to escape. In going away he had understood the truth of everything he had always been told.

So it was said.

It is possible this account was accurate, and it is equally possible the Wafadars made it up. I do not know. I only know the truth of what I have lived and seen and felt. I can only tell what I know. What I know is, it is as nothing for a Wafadar to scale high walls and enter guarded spaces. A Wafadar is nothing like an ordinary man. He is shaped in a peerless mould, of both spirit and substance. In the dark, he is a bat; on a tree, he is a bird; in the water, a fish; on the wall, a lizard. In the open, he is a stone. Behind closed doors, a shadow. He can run for hours without breaking for breath, and stay motionless for days without flickering an eyelid. The limits of his strength are the very limits of the human body. He can snap a neck like the stem of a grape, and break a man in two on his raised thigh. In battle he is an insect: swift, relentless, capable of going on and on even as his bones are broken and his limbs hacked. A Wafadar is not dead till he is fully dead, to the pulling out of his very last breath – and till then he is a fiend capable of chaos. And yet he is not all about physical prowess. The core of his superiority is an inner calm. He moves not in anger, or in revenge; he pursues neither pleasure, nor personal gain. He kills in mercy, not in spite. He is filled with deep passion but it has the stillness of a meditation. He is the motionless air in whose womb sleeps the tornado. From his mastery of his emotions springs the phenomenon of his deeds.

He is pure in purpose; and in his action an artist.

I should know. As few can.

There are noises on the street. Laughter; high-pitched exclamations. This is what enchants me the most about the men of this world – their gift for merriment at the oddest hours, in the oddest situations. Easy ribaldry and empty laughter. Among my people it was a dire sign, of emptiness, of foolishness. To say something that meant nothing, that was only intended to provoke amusement, showed a loss of compass. With the Wafadars even a smile was a weakness.

Someone is laughing so hard it is ripping open the night. Leaving my tea, I go to the front room and part the threadbare curtains. Beyond the semul, under the streetlights, there are four men bent over in desperate laughter while a fifth does a dance in the middle of the street, jerking his hips, one hand on his head, the other on his buttocks. These are men returning from the evening show at Delite Talkies at the end of the bazaar. They are singing a song loudly, in chorus. Soon another one joins the dancer, mimicking him; then another does the same; in a minute, they are all in a line, thrusting and jerking and singing down the street.

My guess is they are not drunk. They are just blessed with the gift of the empty moment. I lack it totally. It is the burden of my inheritance. Out here I find it displayed in the bazaars and tea-shops, by old people and young, by rich men and poor.

Suddenly they will say something and laugh – in different ways, loud or low, long or short, from their belly or the eyes, clapping their own hands or someone's shoulder – suddenly they will say something and laugh and it will be like rain in the desert, altering the world. When I see men laugh I see them shed of all fear and bitterness, of greed and cunning. A laughing man seems like a bird between trees. When I see a man laugh I see him radiate light. Sometimes I think if all living men laughed together, at the very same time, their radiance would obliterate the sun.

The Wafadars never laugh. Perhaps that is why they are like shadows in the dark, so difficult to see.

If I had to choose between gifting my people unthinking mirth and unsmiling wisdom, I know without doubt which I would pick.

The gift of the empty moment: I do not have it, and this is not the time to think of it. I have a story to tell. A story whose telling may yet vindicate my life. And, on the very outside, I have six hours to do it. As I pick up my glass from the kitchen I hear the scuffling still going on outside. Most nights Parvati puts out enough offal to feed waves of animals. If, as most men believe, there is a law of karma, Parvati will be born a queen in her next life.

I pause in our little bedroom at the top of the stairs. I am always surprised by how tiny Parvati can make herself. A foetus in a sari, scrunched up to take the least space it can in the universe. The embodiment of unwanting.

I take out the yellow envelope from my pocket – postmarked with lions, sealed with self-glue – and weigh it in my hand. It is heavy for a letter. And yet it is nothing, a mere five pages written on one side, nothing more than a litany of apologies and gratitude. I have not tried to tell her my story. It might bewilder her and pain her. She is a simple woman. She has offered me her companionship and trust unconditionally. I don't think she really cares where I come from and what my past is. I do not doubt she will grieve for me. But I know she will not let it overwhelm her. She has more resilience and philosophy in her daily toil than men of letters acquire in a lifetime.

All I am trying to do is to somehow let her know how grateful I am, and to somewhat manage her sense of alarm. Often the Wafadars leave nothing behind. My bloodless body may be borne all the way back, or simply buried on the outskirts of the town. I do not want her to think I abandoned her; nor that something terrible has befallen me. I want her to understand what she best understands – that I have merely lived out my karma.

She cannot read too well, and of course she cannot write. So I have been painstaking, keeping the words simple and shaping them boldly. I push the envelope under my pillow, leaving a corner jutting out like an animal's ear. Then I take out the small bundle of big currency notes from my pocket, yank off the rubber-band, and count them once more. Not a fortune but enough to abet her life for a while. I am still not used to the idea of money but I have come to understand its meaning in the lives of men here. And I am thankful I had a skill to barter. Zubair Ali, the old man with the white skull cap in whose workshop I have earned these valuable pieces of paper, always wants to know where I learned to chisel. His boys, fine carpenters all – some no more than eleven years old – can saw and plane and hammer wood in straight lines and angles, wedges and scissors; they can groove and joint and skirt and hinge, but not one of them can sculpt a block of wood into the head of an eagle or a lion's face.

I can find cantering deer in tree trunks and make flowers bloom on short planks. As a child I was trained to do it. Most of us were – to work wood or stone – since both were in abundance and we were not to leave any hour empty. Here it has proven a lifesaver, a livelihood. Zubair's clients have simple affectations. A carved headboard for a bed; a table with the paws of a tiger; a cabinet with clusters of grapes running down its side; chairs with backs on which birds chirp. Zubair does mainly furniture, but once word got around that I had skills, a new demand arose.

So I began to conjure up their gods and goddesses. So many these people have, and how well they manage them! Such a division of spiritual labour. When we first learned of it as children – under the tall Bodhi tree – it sounded like an absurd frivolity, in keeping with the other failures of these men. But here I have sensed in the multiplicity a weight and a purpose. I cannot still genuflect to them, nor seek from them random benedictions. But no longer am I indifferent to their life or their meaning.

The most in demand at Zubair's workshop was Ganesha – and I enjoyed him the most. The flapping ears, the four benign arms, the sweep of the trunk, the luxurious belly, and the two tusks, one slightly broken. Occasionally the client paid enough to even put a rodent under him. Though it was not his faith Zubair saw the creation of each Ganesha as a sign of good luck. And soon I began to feel the same. In confirmation, with each Ganesha we saw Zubair's business flourish, till he was struggling to make deadlines and I was earning more than I needed for the running of the house and the buying of superannuated paper.

I worked hard – often twelve hours a day – till my fingers ached and my eyes were red and my shoulders locked. I didn't mind the labour. It was in me. And I was impelled – from a deep place within that I had no idea existed – to provide all I could for this slumbering woman whose selfless embrace had given me a peace and a passion I had never known. Zubair paid well, and I stashed it away, for this day, for this night. Without doubling the rubber-band I roll it onto the straight notes and stick the lot under my pillow, next to the letter, one corner sticking out. With its two ears, the pillow is now a supine animal.

I am tempted to caress Parvati's smooth round face. But that could lead to other things, detain me. I need to settle down, to work. I am trying to draw from one of the simple and profound things I have heard of here. The message of the song divine, the book they call the Gita: men must act, in the right way, with no thought to success or failure. Everyone here knows it, even Zubair and his callow boys.

Though, from what I have seen here, it seems to me that men have drawn exactly the opposite lesson. If I were to identify the one god to whom all men genuflect, it would not be goodness but success. To me it appears that the two poles of human life between which men must stumble, the two opposing deities they must embrace and resist, are not as is widely believed, good and evil, right and wrong. They are success and failure. Success. That is the one true religion. Its holy trinity is power, money and adulation. And in its catechism are contained many unsentimental things: cunning, cruelty, betrayal, violence.

And yet it would be unfair to be so sweeping. I have only to look at Parvati to know the existence and beauty of goodness. I feel heady in its presence. When I stand in the kitchen and see her bustle about – her body plump, her skin fair, her hair tied tight, her feet in flat slippers, her sari hitched high, her forehead adorned with a red bindi, her eyes kind, her smile warm – as I see her chop and cook and clean, as I see her find and manufacture offal for the orphaned cats and dogs of the world, as I see her rush out to help someone who has called in a crisis of marriage, death, sorrow or injury, as I see her shrink into her bed looking to occupy the least possible space she can in the universe, I feel humbled and exalted and I know there is goodness in the world, and I hope its scales are heavier – much heavier – than those of success.

She does not know it – and would laugh in embarrassment if I told her – but it is she who gives me confidence in myself, inspires in me the resolve to tell my story. If I did not see the goodness in her, and how it holds up the world, I would not be impelled to labour at my table. I would attempt to flee, to hide. And that would be wrong. And futile. My ordained task, my karma, is to tell my story, and the story of my people, and as I settle down at my small desk and look out the window at the waving arms of the semul and the lamplit street beyond, now empty of all pantomime, as I settle down and switch on my machine, I understand that it is in the fate of men to carry mysterious burdens. And I understand that the unspoken goal of every life is to shed as many of its burdens as is possible before its time is done.

It is nearly nine-thirty. A few hours are all I have. The Wafadars will come through this open window. Or they could flow soundlessly up the stairs. It is pointless to attempt a barricade. One moment I will look up and the room will be full of their shadows. They may decide to speak to me or, in their mercy, drain me empty without a word.

That I will be dead before the night is out is almost certain.

The only thing that matters is what I can tell while I am still alive.

THE FIRST OF EVERYTHING

His origins are shrouded in twirling mists and swirling stories. Some say his original name was Pitamber, some claim Gopala, others Narayana, Lakshmana, Mahadeva. In idle conversations other names have been tossed up too, like Nachiketa and Kartikeya, Mohammed and Abraham, even Thomas and Francis, but most believe he was actually named Aum, the very first sound of the universe, befitting of who he was, the very first of everything.

You must understand all these speculations were made under one's breath. All inquiry into the past was discouraged. It was the written rule. The past was over. Interpreting it, analysing it, imagining it in different ways was a dangerous thing. There was an account of the past, the truth of it, and it was available to us all. No further conjecture was necessary. He was Aum, the very first sound of the universe, the very first of everything.

The story said he was born in a unique settlement in the far north, where the great mountain ranges tear into Central Asia, where the boulders are bigger than elephants and the men tall and bearded and untamed and wild-eyed like jungle beasts. Fed by an eternal spring, his village nestled between two towering cliffs and was green with grass and flowering trees. From the moment you woke to the moment you slept your ears were filled with birdsong. The women's skins were milk and their eyes blackest coal. The men they spawned had sinews of stone and unbowed heads. They knew neither fear nor avarice. They neither enslaved nor succumbed.

It was a hallowed spot. Surpassing men of legend had graced it, blessing its air and soil with their words and their presence. Nanak, Kabir, Adi Shankaracharya, the Prophet, and earlier still the Buddha, the Mahavira, and the one they called Christ. It was a place of miracle and wisdom, without a parallel in the universe. Great warriors too had broken hoof here. Genghis Khan, Taimur the Lame, Mahmud of Ghaznvi, Babur, Ranjit Singh, Banda Bahadur, Shivaji, and the armies of Napoleon and Robert Clive. In their fleeting sojourn, it was said, all these conquerors had been touched by a surge of compassion and mercy.

The story of the past said it had been prophesied that in the eighty-eighth year of the nineteenth century in this mystical spot a great master would be born. In him would bloom to its fullness his unique ancestry. In him would flow both the blood of the wise and the blood of the warrior. He would be a saint, and he would be a soldier. In a word, he would be a god. The shelter of the good, and the scourge of the ungood.

The story said that by the end of the year of 1887 every woman in the settlement from fourteen to forty filled her belly with hot seed in a glorious bid for immortality. After all there is no creature more blessed in the world than the mother of a great master. In the year of 1888 as the globe hurtled towards chaos, convulsed by invasions and wars, disease and destruction, merriment and mayhem, as white men crushed men who were not white, as the idea of god became a narrow one, in that marked year twenty-one children were born in the enchanted hamlet. Of these, thirteen were girls and eight were boys. Of the eight boys, seven were dead before a day had passed, while one glowed with a vigour that seemed beyond all eclipse.

This was not the first sign that the chosen one had arrived. For months the foetus had spoken through its mother's mouth, chanting couplets of rare illumination. The unlettered mother, who tended her champing sheep on the grassland, had rushed in terror to the apothecary. On hearing the awaited one's voice emerge from the young shepherdess's panicked mouth the graybeard had fallen to the floor, and burying his forehead in the divine pubis sung the glory of the omnipotent lord. From that day the girl's mud-and-thatch hut had become a site of pilgrimage. No one returned disappointed. The foetus spoke all hours. In many tongues, of the East and the West. The other twenty mothers cupped their swollen bellies in deep sadness, aware that they were empty of all glory. The apothecary, stroking his long beard, gave them cheer, telling them it was a rare fortune to be even the companion of a master. The life they carried inside them was already blessed. A master belongs to none, he said, but to those who follow him.

The night he was born the entire settlement was camped around the mother's hut, huddled in blankets, the dancing feet of fire all around them, and high above them a presaging procession of shooting stars. The midwife said it was the first time in her life she saw a delivering mother smile serenely. He gave his mother no pain and he emerged the other way around, landing on his feet. Nor did he wail as newborns do. The first sound the waiting village heard was a resounding AUM! It rolled over the valley, bounced off the mountains and echoed around the world. Aum!

The very first sound of the universe, befitting of who he was, the very first of everything.

As was meet, he became the desired of all. He had not one mother but eight. The seven women who had given birth to dead sons redirected the milk of their love to him, bathing him in adoration, letting him suckle their swollen teats, filling him with the power and passion and purity of the source, eight times over. One mother can endow eight sons with vigour. Eight mothers pouring primal energy into one son bears no cosmic calculation.

This is what the story said.

As he grew into a luminous child – his hair thick and black, his skin golden, his eyes blue like the summer sky – his closest companions were the thirteen girls born in his year. Like the eight mothers, each of the thirteen adored him. Every spare minute they ran to him, and he filled their ears with fine words and wondrous thoughts. He had begun to speak as a foetus, and as he grew into a boy the beauty of his speech was like that of the harsingar tree in October. The words fell from his soft lips like perfect flowers, redolent of beauty and perfume, and itinerants passing through the valley were drawn to his hut to experience the enchantment.

After a first encounter, the visiting preacher from the nearby town said, As the camel lives off his back, this boy will live off his words. He will make men believe they can walk on air.

Like his words, the boy was exquisite of structure, the nose and chin chiselled, the limbs slim, the fingers tapering. But the eyes were a kaleidoscope. When they were soft, they made the women melt and weep. When they were hard, grown men felt their knees buckle. The eyes were full of knowing. The chief of the settlement – whose turban rose four tiers, and whose body bore sixty-six battle scars – said, I don't look into his eyes when I meet him. I feel I have walked out of my house naked.

Before the boy was ten he had learned everything the settlement could teach him. Reading, writing, the legends, the scriptures, history, geography, mathematics, theology. He had to hear anything once to know it forever. It was said he was born with all the world's knowledge – it had only to be tapped and it rose potent and complete, like a flaring cobra at the charmer's prod.

Nor was he a mere scholar. Despite his delicate appearance he could move a sword like lightning in his two-handed grip. The dexterity rode on nerve. With a barely discernible sway he could elude the slash of steel, and the strongest counter-blow could not wilt his arm. But his chief weapon was not nimbleness, nor nerve, nor stringy sinews. It was his gaze. Unblinking, mesmeric, commanding. Without fear; full of certitude. Like a single-eyed animal of myth, he compelled his assailant to do what he willed – to strike where he was waiting for him, and to leave himself open where he was to strike.

It was no different with his followers. From the time he suckled at sixteen different nipples he had a gaze that commanded compliance. Inevitably – as with every great master – his first disciple was his mother, or rather his mothers. There is no mother in the world who does not have the measure of her child. Every mother knows, even when she cannot articulate it, her child's gifts and failings, its body and soul, the trajectory of its destiny. Just as one knows how much weight one's arms can carry and how fast one's legs can run. Seeing him look up at them from their milking teats, each of the eight knew they were mere vestibules for the passage of greatness. There was nothing they could teach this boy with the basilisk eye. They were here only to learn at his feet.

At the age of nine he gave his first sermon. His eight mothers sat on the floor and he on a wooden stool. In his hypnotic voice he asked them to think about things they had never had the leisure or the courage to contemplate. The purpose of life; the nature of men and women; the meaning of their toil; tradition and the new; sin and virtue; god and religion; the miracle of birth; the mystery of death.

The sermon was only the asking of questions. Simple questions, but with answers so profound that the questions too became impossibly profound. His tone was exalting – full of deep knowing, beyond all questioning. And he held the eyes of all eight of them in the very same instant, so each felt he was speaking to her alone. In time the tone would grow even more profound – more all-knowing, beyond all questioning. In time he would be able to hold the eyes of not eight or ten but of hundreds and thousands, all in the same instant. In time, each time he spoke, every listener would think he was speaking to them alone. His words and his gaze each one's intimate possession.

This is what the story said.

To be honest I do not recall when I first heard the story. In this I was not alone. The story swam all around you like water about a fish. It was what you lived in. There was no time in your life you were not aware of it. I am sure I suckled it in from the teats of my mothers. Yes, mothers; we all had mothers. It is what the master had decreed. It was how a man, with the first suck of the milk of life, began the slow journey to complete equality, consummate oneness. When you drank every day from a new breast, when you clutched, each day, with your tiny hands varying flesh, you began to learn the art of collapsing the differences that plague men.

In his boundless wisdom Aum knew the great undoing of the human race was its vanity. Its individualism: its selfishness and its greed. It had to be excised. We knew the axiom. To wish to possess is to be possessed.

I think I know who my mother was. But I could be utterly wrong. It wasn't that our features matched – it was never possible to know such things. Nor that anyone ever hinted it to me – that would have been blasphemy. It was just that in the motherhood there was one slim one who held me as I have never again been held in my life. Not by the black-eyed one; not by Parvati.

In the three hours each day that we were given access to the motherhood – it became one after we turned six – she always sought me out for the longest possible time. And though extended displays of affection were discouraged, she always managed to envelop me several times before our time was up.

As we wandered about being held and caressed, getting our nails trimmed and hair snipped, being taught how to clean our teeth and wash our face, wear our clothes and lash our sandals, as we shouted and played, she would seek me out and pluck me away from my companions.

Pulling me into a corner of the large shed she would drop to her knees and clamp her arms tight around my body, the fingers splayed to get as much of me as she could. She would tuck my face into her warm neck, filling my head with the warm scent of her skin – the memory of which can still fill my heart with howling winds. Then she would press me to herself and release me, press me and release me, as if she were trying to inhale me and exhale me, make me a part of her very breath.

I cannot tell you the shape of her nose or the slant of her eyebrows, but I remember precisely the smell of her breath, the smell of her skin, the texture of her thick smooth hair, and the sound of her crooning voice, as she pressed me and released me, and I clung to her as one would cling to a raft in a raging river. Without real hope, but with desperate relief.

I can also tell you her collarbone was sharp. It dug into my cheek. Often she would press me in so tight and for so long that my cheek would get a dent and my breath would stop. I think I was happy to have my breath stop as long as she did not stop holding me.

There were days when she was not there – later I would learn there were often more urgent tasks at hand. And those were terrible days. As everyone rushed about, creating mayhem and being corralled, I would go from mother to mother hoping to spot her. In truth by then my heart would have sunk and I would know I was not going to find her. For were she there, I would not be looking for her; she would have found me in the first few minutes.

After all we were still small children, not yet fully equal, still easily identifiable. Even though the motherhood was enjoined to steer above the narrowness of genes, to be wisely unbiased with its time and affections, I could sense there was a kind of pattern to the mothers and children.

My close companion Arjuna – there were never less than six Arjunas in the home – who first taught me how to eat an entire apple without snapping the thread of the core, was always picked up by this tall mother who feverishly massaged his head with oil and stuffed his mouth with soggy almonds she'd secreted into the pockets of her thick tunic. I can't tell you how she looked but at the time she was easily the tallest in the motherhood. And as Arjuna began to outgrow us year on year, I knew for certain that every child had one mother who was more of a mother than the other mothers.

The doctrine of Aum was clear. All mothers were equal, and

equally precious. And all children were equal, and equally precious. To choose one over another, to let emotion cloud judgement and fairplay was to fall from grace. It was a failure to live up to your higher self. It was to become like the beasts out there, in the other world, following no rules but those of greed and possession.

So we loved all our mothers. Before we went back we stood in line and embraced each one. And each in turn ruffled our hair and patted our heads. Some even kissed our foreheads. But there was only one who clasped me to her body as if she were breathing me in and out, whose collarbone left a dent in my cheek, whose skin filled my head with a fragrance that has never ever gone.

At the time I did not acknowledge this. We knew all the mothers were the same – even if they smelled different and felt different. Sometimes we would start to whisper about this in our bunks when the lights were off, but then we would abruptly stop, aware that we were allowing our lower selves to seize control of us.

We knew from the sublime life of Aum that contrary to the abject history of the world, the lower self could be vanquished completely, as long as one took to the task early, and never gave up. Each of us was determined never to let Aum down.

Some days I am a bit confused about my memories of my childhood. I thought I was happy. Content, cared for, happy. For the nine years I was in the home – from the age of three years, when I was taken from the cradle, to twelve, when I was sent off to the barracks – I never felt any sense of dismay. In my years the population of the home ranged between fifteen and twenty, as new ones arrived from the cradle and older ones left for the barracks.

The home was like a centipede. The first section was our bedroom. In it were arrayed twenty-four wooden bunks, opposite each other. None of them belonged to you. And they all belonged to you. The simple rule was, you could not sleep in the same bunk two nights running. The ideal was to ever be unattached. Inevitably it had to begin with the mother – and then the bed. It was not as if someone monitored us. Once the lamps were off and the Pathfinders had left, we could, if we wished, have slept in the same bunk every night. No one would have known. And it's not that one would have been penalized as if for a crime. But we never did it. We understood the deep principle behind the instruction. And we wished for nothing more than to be worthy of Aum.

The next section, a slightly smaller room, was for the body. In it were horizontal iron bars, vertical ropes, hanging mud-sacks, weights of stone. Whenever we were not doing anything else – eating, sleeping, studying – we had to be exerting our muscles. Pushing our bodies to climb, carry, endure. We all knew that a fine roof without strong walls is doomed to collapse. Unknown to us, we were also undergoing our first auditions for the legion of the Wafadars. No one knew better than Aum the value of spotting and moulding purposefulness at an early age.

In contrast, the next section of the centipede, for the mind, was a spare room with polished cedar floors and no windows. It was patterned in clean, straight lines with twenty-four flat rocks. They were large, about a foot-and-a-half high, and impossible for us to move when we first encountered them. Their surface had been deliberately left uneven and rough. When we sat on them cross-legged, our ankles at our hips, the sharp angles cut into our buttocks and our bones. To begin with we would twitch and shift while the Pathfinders looked at us with the contempt we deserved. There was no way we could discover a comfortable fit – since, as with the beds, we were expected to pick a different one each day.

For a long time we suffered. Two hours on the rocks each day: one in the morning, one in the evening. None of us complained, but we suffered. Our thighs and bottoms ached unbearably, and it was difficult to go to the toilet, to walk, to sleep.

I had a trick. When our Pathfinder told us to close our eyes and empty our minds of everything, I would think of Aum – tall, serene, radiant, with a flowing beard, and kind eyes. Next to him would be the mother who buried my face in her sweet fragrance and sharp collarbone. Now I could see her face. It had fair skin, fawn eyes, and a smile sweeter than anyone had seen among our people in the longest time. This mother – let me say it, perhaps my mother – had a light hand on Aum's waist as Aum joyously flung me up in the air. As I went up there, floating away happily in the clean wide open, I forgot all pain and discomfort and the rough stone under me was nothing but a nest of feathers.

The mind room, appropriately, was taken even more seriously than the body room. No one was permitted even a minute's reprieve from its daily regime – unless you were too unwell to get out of bed. Minor ailments were discounted. The whole point of the room was that an evolved mind could override ordinary suffering and distress. The Pathfinders would say: these are nice smooth seats, give yourself time and even beds of nails will leave you unaffected. We never got off the rocks till our time was done – even though the cramps and sores were often excruciating. It would have been too shaming.

By the time we were eight we were spending four hours a day in there. And we knew by now how right Aum was. Once the mind was made supreme, there was no discomfort, no pain, no aches. We could now sit on the rocks as if they were water. An hour would go by in a blink. The Pathfinder would clap his hands sharply twice, and we would open our eyes, and I would realize the session was over and I had not moved a hair. By now I had stopped using the image of Aum and the sharp collarboned mother to distract me. Now I could in a moment blank out completely, make my mind a white sheet without a single ripple, vanish into a world without sound, colour or suggestion. Now when we finished, I rose from the rock as if from a chair, without a strained muscle or a sore bone.

To be fair it was not equally easy for everyone. Sahadev – the only Sahadev in my first years at the home – used to groan most nights, muttering in pain. He was a thin boy with oversized hands and feet, and for some reason was not too supple. He could not touch his toes without bending his knees, and each time he had to sit on the meditation rock he needed help to lock his ankles at his waist. On a few occasions, unable to master himself, he cried out in agony in the middle of a session and had to be helped by the Pathfinder.

The rest of us took it as a collective disgrace. We all felt diminished by his lack of fortitude. Not one of us offered him sympathy when he wailed and wept in the dead of night. In fact, even though it was a vulgar thing to do, many voices snapped at him in admonition. The roughest was the oldest Bhima at the time – in his last year at the home – who would say in a slow baritone, Only your bones are paining right now. Do you want me to make your flesh pain too?

Some nights I would be sleeping next to thin Sahadev, and when old Bhima's gravelly taunt carved up the night I could sense the moaning boy struggle to still his voice. For a long time after, wracking sobs and muffled sniffles would break the air. He was shameful. By the time he was nine we knew he'd been marked to be sent down.

The next segment of the centipede was smaller still and consisted of two rows of cubicles that faced each other with a broad corridor running between them. All the cubicles had windows that opened onto the trees and the forest. The corridor felt like a ravine because the rows of cubicles were set on a platform two feet high. The cubicles on the left – ten of them – were holes-in-the-floor with wooden swing doors four feet high. On the right the rooms were fewer – only eight – and therefore a little bigger. They were without doors and each had a steel bucket and a mug. These rooms looked like troughs because across the threshold ran a low wall two feet high. When we bathed and washed our clothes it ensured no water splashed into the corridor.

The theatre of our daily ablutions had been placed right between our sleeping–meditating areas and the dining hall because Aum in his deep wisdom understood how by creating a disgust of their own bodies men had become dangerously twisted within themselves. We were free and pure and clean and so were our bodies. For an hour every morning and evening we would all be naked in there, overhauling our bodies and its passages. And yet, by the time we left the ablutions hall you could sleep in there and spread your food out on it. We egged each other on to swab every last inch. Any stain pointed out by a Pathfinder made us cringe in humiliation.

The end of the centipede was the dining hall, and at a slight distance, through a roofed veranda, lay the kitchen. There were three dining tables – wooden, low, with backless benches, fit to seat about ten each. The cooking staff was meant to eat with us. It was Aum's beautiful principle of equality. We all trooped into the kitchen – with its clay ovens and woodfires, the smells of spices and meat, and the cooks and helpers with a film of oil wetting their skins – we all trooped in and brought out the food and laid it on the tables. A Pathfinder then read out the Catechism of Worldly Appetites. We all repeated it, with our hands on our bellies, fingers intertwined. Then we ate and chattered without restraint.

Though they were meant to divide themselves among the tables, the cooking staff tended to sit together. For some reason they always ended up at the table of the youngest inhabitants of the home. In keeping with the ideal of brotherhood, no one rose from the table till everyone had finished. Then we carried everything back to the kitchen. The final clean-up – like the initial cooking – was left to the staff.

The Pathfinders told us it was crucial to understand and establish the great principle of equality. Its use and practise was finally a matter of pragmatism. It was beyond all contention that all men were equal. But it was also true that by talent and temperament men were made for different tasks. It was an abiding foolishness to put a fine cook to working the plough. The land suffered and so did the table.

The idea of equality – pure and complete equality – had to bloom riotously in our hearts. We had to believe in it and to commit to it. Once we did so, we were in the clear. What happened in the physical world around us was of no consequence. It was a mere working of things, a creating of necessary processes.

We understood and we believed.

We understood and we believed everything we were told. There was so much beauty to it, so much truth. Aum had dug into deep and eternal springs and we were fortunate to bathe in the waters and drink of them. From the first day of our lives we knew we were the chosen.

As I narrate this – at this small table, the dying night street just beyond – I see not the huge semul but an even more magnificent tree: a gigantic deodar, under which we studied every day. Its benevolent branches fanned out on every side like a hundred wings, and it rose more than a hundred feet high and was said to be many centuries old. It was an old tree even when Aum first found it. He had named it the Bodhi – intuiting it would soon become a canopy for daily enlightenment. A twenty-minute walk from the home, it sat on high ground, a wide circle of flat around it. The final ascent was thirty-three steep steps, and you were always winded when you reached the top.

From there the eye could track the length of the valley, following Amrita, the sprinting stream, all the way to the other end, where it vanished under the ground, and where the patrolling shadows of the Wafadars fell across the mouth of the narrow twisting pass, day and night. To the left and the right the ranges rose so tall that the white of the snows merged into the white of the clouds. When the sun rode high it burnt the eye to look at them. This was an expanse unbroken by human feet. The rare animals that moved there were the high mountain goat, the big cream cat, and the shuffling ox with the long hair of a crone. There were also demons there, but we knew they were afraid of us.

To the left and behind us rose a wall of rock so sheer you could drop a stone from its top and it would hit the valley floor without a deflection. When you stood at its bottom and craned your neck you understood scale. As an ant to our Bodhi, were we to the cliff. It had never been scaled. There had been attempts – each one fatal. It was not a verdict on the climbers, but on the brittleness of the rock. It lay in layers like slices of bread, and at the slightest pressure turned to shrapnel. All around lay smashed rocks, from tiny pebbles to gigantic boulders. If you risked its hard beauty you had to do so with one eye on the fractured ground and one on the unstable face above.

The bowl of the valley, in every direction, for most of the year, was a palette of greens and yellows, purples and reds. From mid-March to early-November the trees were in leaf – some in brilliant flower – and the orchards lay heavy with fruit. Tall grass, vegetable ears, cabbage rows, stalks of corn – different patterns and shades of green crisscrossed the valley.

As I tell of it I realize I may be failing to convey its true size. The bowl was enormous, sprawling, twice as long as it was wide, and even from a vantage point you could not discern men or movement at the ends of it. From where our home sat – near the Bodhi – it was two days' walk to the mouth of the valley – to the twisting underground pass that few had seen, that connected us to the other world.

When the sun was weak we sat cross-legged, on the ground outside the shade of the Bodhi, as the Pathfinder walked up and down filling us with the illuminations of life. When the sun was searing we stayed close to the mammoth trunk, in a half-circle around it, while the Pathfinder sat on a carved slat of deodar wedged into the trunk.

There was a beautiful discipline to the classes. Only one person spoke. No interruptions were allowed, no arguments. Aum's axiom was that first one had to learn to listen. To sit still, and to listen. Talk was easy, talk was cheap, and talk was what everyone wanted to do all the time. Early in his luminous life the great seer had intuited that the world out there was in a miserable chaos because men had lost the ability to hear. From the moment the larynx learned how to make words out of sounds, the music of their own voice beguiled men.

The secret of the great masters was that they could hear all the time. They kept their ears wide open so the wisdom of life could pour in ceaselessly. And they knew how to keep their mouth closed for long spells – so that it stayed in, deep within, where it could roil and mature and become a thing of surpassing value. The ear an open funnel; the mouth a closed tap.

The stories were told to us – they were all around us. Of how Aum would go silent for hours, for days, for weeks – just listening. To his followers, to the wind in the trees, the chirring of insects, the fluttering of butterflies, the crackle of fire, the shuffling of horses, the growls of wild animals, the mewling of infants, the gurgling of streams, the patter of rain, the whisper of snow, the creaking of wood, the cracking of stone, the collision of clouds, the growing of corn, the turning of the Earth. To every whisper of the universe.

The stories were told to us. They were all around us.

How he would suddenly say – his eyes drinking in everyone else's: did you hear that? And then: did you understand what was said?

And everyone did – flutter and patter, gurgle and collision. That was the miracle of Aum. In his presence everyone became twice who they were, and sometimes more. Men and women found they could hear things and think things and do things they had never imagined possible. The miracle of Aum was not that he was extraordinary. The miracle of Aum was that he made everyone around him extraordinary. So it was said.

We found it easy to listen. The Pathfinders spoke with such passion and eloquence. We were told all about the other world, from the nine books of Aum. Dictated by the master himself, these were not spiritual texts or abstract sermons. They were gems of information and learning; they contained the distilled knowledge of the other world. Its history and geography, its patterns and workings. The stories of conquests and violence and cruelty; of hatreds and bigotry; of murder and torture and rapine; of enslavement and persecution; of greed and possession. Of the destruction and degradation, of both men and nature.

We understood what Aum had first understood. In the world out there, men were neither free nor equal nor moral. They were driven by shallow impulses which made them dangerously selfish and dishonest. Every code of conduct was honoured in the breach, and every single one of them was oppressive of another.

The seed of this inferno was the need to possess.

The seed of this inferno was the word 'my'.

Me. Myself. Mine.

In the world out there, Aum had understood, every man was driven by 'my', every man was a raging inferno.

THE BROTHERHOOD

In our world there was no 'my'.

So much you must have guessed by now.

Each day as we sat under the Bodhi and opened our ears like funnels to suck in the wisdom of the Pathfinders, we understood the truth and beauty of everything that had happened in our lives so far. Why we had the names we had. Why we had not one mother but an entire motherhood. Why we had no fathers, and why we would never need any. Why brotherhood was a greater concept than parenting or children. Why one day we would look the way we would look.

My name was Karna. At the time I'd no idea who had named me. Much later I would come to believe it was my mother. Or the person I believe was my mother.

In my years at the home there happened to be only two other Karnas. One was leaving for the barracks the year I came in, and a new one appeared – with sky blue eyes – only two years before I moved on. Obviously Karna was not a popular name. But there were two which were even less popular, Nakul and Sahadev. In my time there were only two Nakuls and just the one Sahadev – the timid one with the inelastic body who used to moan in pain every night.

This was the one act of proprietorship the mothers were allowed – the giving of the name. There were six to choose from. By far the most popular was Arjuna. It was inevitable. Anyone who knows the Mahabharata knows the allure of the peerless archer. Not just the greatest of warriors but also a handsome lover and a seeking philosopher. The jibe was, if Aum had been given a choice, he too would have named himself Arjuna. Every night, as I slept in my bunk, sleeping around me were Arjunas of different ages and sizes.

A respectable second was Bhima. Clearly there were enough mothers who found honour in the strength and forthrightness of the strongest of the Pandava brothers. To those who know the great story, Bhima is not just a glutton and a breaker of bones. He is also the redeemer of insults and pledges, and the unabashed protector of the pride of Draupadi. He is not a man to be crossed. He is a merciless slayer of demons and demonic men.

My name did not figure even in the third place. This belonged to the embodiment of truth, the incarnation of virtue: Yudhishtira, the eldest of the legitimate brothers. A man vexed with the conundrums of right and wrong; a man who never set down a foot without making a tortured reckoning of the entire moral-ethical universe. A man born to be king, but almost too forgiving to be one. The brother who would outlast all the others, carry the last burden, know the final truths. He would not naturally have been a popular choice, but it seems many mothers glimpsed in him some shadow of Aum.

I – my namesakes – ranked a distant fourth. It's curious it should have been so. Given what we all believed in, Karna was an exemplar. Born out of wedlock, firm believer in equality, paragon of loyalty, majestic warrior, exceedingly honourable and recklessly generous. I could not see it then, but much later I understood that the rejection of Karna arose from the anxiety of the mothers. Even though they could never claim their spawn, even though they knew that no child belonged to any one parent, even though they knew better than to fall prey to cheap superstition, they blanched at touching their offspring with any trace of bad luck. Karna was glorious but also ill-starred. The mothers, in the only act of ownership given unto them, screamed out their protective instincts.

I like to believe that my mother chose the damaged name because she saw in it the story that set it apart. Karna, master of the world, and not of it. Karna, oldest of six illustrious brothers, yet not one of them. Karna, born of the highest, yet reared among the lowest. Karna, cheated of trust, yet constant giver of it. I like to believe that if I eventually turned out different, it had something to do with that first intuition of my mother.

I suppose you have figured it out by now. With his faith in the glory of brotherhood, Aum had picked the greatest brothers in the annals of the world to give us their names.

Each of the great brothers had one mother but a different father, all at a far remove. Just like us. One motherhood, and many different fathers, whom we would never know. All the great brothers happily shared a wife, and never made a woman a bone of contention between them. Just as we would, when our loins matured and the sap of life pulsated in our veins. Each great brother selflessly defended the others, letting no blandishment of power, money, women or glory diminish his commitment to the others. Exactly as Aum had enjoined us to do.

So there was the brotherhood, and there was no 'mine', and there were all of us, namesakes of the great Pandavas – till we were eighteen and had graduated from the barracks.

As Aum had wisely understood, as Aum had wisely decreed, at every stage of our lives the gear was shifted to take us up the ladder of enlightenment. From the cradle to the home had been about breaking the narrow bonds of maternal possessiveness and understanding the principle of universal brotherhood. About learning to train the mind, about mastering stillness upon an uneven rock, and making one's ear the widest funnel in the world. It had been about soaking oneself in the idea of equality, killing the instinct to ownership. Your bed was not yours, your rock was not yours, even your name was not yours – any number of others could blazon it.

The home was also about tuning the body. Transcendent thoughts were fine arrows that had to be kept in a robust quiver. A second-rate quiver could never carry as many fine arrows through the journey of life as Aum wished each of us to. There were quivers in the home that were broken or infirm. Great care was taken to fix them. There was an Outstanding Scholar's policy. Instead of embarrassing the brothers who could not measure up, they were pulled out and sent to a separate facility where Pathfinders could shower them with special attention.

In my time at the home several boys were moved to the special facility. Some needed work on their mind, some on their body, and some on their emotions. Occasionally it was also a matter of conduct. You did something so shameful that you needed to be removed for intensive counselling so you didn't infect the others. It almost happened to me when I was nine. A dark, terrifying episode that I – from fear more than cunning – somehow managed to hide from everyone. But decades later its shadow was to fall across my life in ways I could never have imagined.

When I was nine there was a Bhima – a year older than me – who I really liked. In fact – and we were not supposed to think like this – he was the boy I was closest to. His mother had named him well. He was big, fat almost, with plump thighs that rubbed against each other when he walked. He also had extra flesh on his chest that shook like breasts when he bathed. Of course no one said anything to him, in jest or jibe. We were careful never to be like that. But I know the older boys had contempt in their eyes when they saw him naked, and when they saw him struggle to keep his perch on the rock.

His body was a big vessel, so he ate a lot. The kitchen staff found it distasteful, as did the Pathfinders. Everyone was bred on Aum's spartan tenets – frugal diets, lean bodies. We all knew the story. Aum's every rib could be counted from twenty feet, and he never ate more than two meals a day. The flock was free to eat meats and spices, but the master confined himself to fruits and light cereals. We knew no germ had ever breached his defence, and not once was he felled by fever or by disease. It was said he never put on a year – even as others grew old around him – right till the moment he was last seen.

Away from all of us, in private, gently, the Pathfinders counselled fat little Bhima. He would have to learn restraint. Just have to. I had to only look at the confused eyes in the round face to know someone had been trying to mend his ways. He told me everything. He was older than me and bigger than me, but he looked to me for reassurance. It was a wretched thing to do, yet he contrived to sleep close to my bunk, sit by me in the dining hall, and even to get into the ablutions hall the same time as I did.

I felt guilty not discouraging him from this possessive conduct, but I really liked being with him. For all his size he had a soft voice, and if no one was around he would try and hold my hand. I would play reluctant, but the truth is it felt good, his fleshy hand – always a little damp – and he tended to clasp me tightly with it. Sometimes he would do it under the dining table, sometimes reach across the bunks in the dark. It was inadvisable. Not because we would suffer admonition. It was just that we were letting ourselves and everyone else down.

Several times I did think of impressing upon him the principle of detachment – of how we needed to step back from each other. But each time we were alone, I saw something in his eye that said to me I would shatter him if I suggested any moving away. To be fair, I did not want it to end either. In those days I think we made ourselves into failures – dependent on each other, physically and emotionally.

There were many things little fat Bhima used to talk to me about. How every day on the rock his buttocks got sore and his scrotum twisted. He showed me the self-therapy he had devised – which he applied to himself every night. Parting his podgy legs, he lightly traced his fingertips over his upper thighs and testicles, again and again and again, till all ache had vanished into a sweet sleep. The trick, he told me, was to keep the touch feather-light, skin whispering against skin. I saw him do it – his flesh so angry – and saw the relief and pleasure sweep across his face. In later years I learned it was a technique not just against torment of the body but also of the soul, and I have lost count of the number of times I have used it successfully when sleep has eluded me for one reason or another.

Little fat Bhima told me how the Pathfinders counselled him. Fat was a failure. It was against the order of nature. Aum had understood this. It was the annexing of a disproportionate share of the world. Fat had to be combated, bested. It was a sign of weakness, gluttony, an absence of self-control. It was dishonourable. They were sympathetic. They knew he was fat despite himself. But they also knew he was capable of getting rid of it. They were here to help him shore up his will, cramp his hunger, work his body. Whatever it took. But do it he must.

He was however seized by other things. He would talk to me continually about what he most liked to do. It was what I most liked him to do too. He had a singing voice. When he spoke he sounded merely soft, but when he broke into one of the hill melodies his voice was a rippling brook, rustling tree, rolling thunder. He could pick his voice up and in a moment take it to dizzy heights and then as easily in a moment bring it crashing to the ground. He knew only the four-five songs that we all knew, but he could sing them in different tones – his voice pulling a fresh musicality out of each word. Sometimes, instead of the songs he would pick a line from the Pathfinders' tutorials and sing it into something astonishingly beguiling.

The singing voice had to be kept on a leash. Mostly it was only when we were in the woods, by ourselves, that I got to hear him. It was not as if singing was banned. It was just looked down upon. Rightly, it was seen as an indulgence. Not evil, but merely purposeless, capable of creating exceeding distraction. My favourite Pathfinder – the one with the thin wrists and long fingers – always cautioned fat little Bhima: One. You can sing one song every day, at the very most. Never another!

So he never sang more than one. But he cheated. Without breaking for breath he would run the songs into each other – often looping back, repeating favourite lines, and even adding in the prose lectures of the Pathfinders. Sometimes an entire hour in the woods would end up being one unbroken song. He also cheated by humming. Quietly, whenever he could. He was consummate at it. I could spot the song the moment he started. He said he didn't part his lips or work his tongue, so it wasn't singing. It was true: if you didn't know, you couldn't tell. I could, even from a distance, by the look in his eye. His eyes were happy when he hummed.

Later, when he was gone, I asked a Pathfinder about this and he said, Of course it was singing. We were aware of it, and perturbed by it. Conduct is crucial, but intent is no less. What do you think Aum would have said? Do you think he would have been fooled?

The song I most liked him to sing was about a mother waiting for her son to return from foreign lands. He has gone to work his fortune, and he has been gone many years. Each day of his absence – the mother laments – has been an aeon. She lists the tasks that line her day. They have been unchanging for thirty years since she was married as a young girl. The only difference is her missing son. Her eyes are sore from scanning the horizon; her spirit leaden with ache. Is he well? Does he have a roof over his head? A bed to sleep on? Food in his stomach? Are strangers kind to him? Do they recognize the beauty of his soul? Even her husband is a conqueror laying claim to her body. But her son is herself, carved from her flesh, blood of her blood, bone of her bone. The song ends on a moment of doubt. Has he been perchance annexed by another woman's love? Is it possible he no longer belongs to his mother? It cannot be. It cannot be. It cannot be.

The refrain went:

> My days are too long; these mountains too high,
> Will your feet find their way back before I die?

He never sang this song in anyone else's presence. It was after all an embarrassing one. Full of sentimentality and of shallow ideas of proprietorship. For some reason – and I never acknowledged it, not even to the singer – it filled me with a sweet ache. I would get him to sing it to me when we were in the woods, and his voice would climb up the towering deodars and spread everywhere.

For me, as his voice soared, the mother in the song was always the sharp collarboned one, and I could see her face clearly, and it was beautiful: her skin so smooth and fair, her eyes brown and soft, her mouth generous and kind. She sang with languid gestures of her slim arms. The arms that used to hug me as if they'd never let me go.

The song that he sang in the presence of others was about the soldier patrolling the high borders, stoic in the face of sleet and snow, hunger and deprivation, resolute against invading beast and man. His duty is his honour and his honour is his life. At times he thinks of his wife and children, his cosy home where the woodfire crackles, where the food sits succulent on the table. And then he admonishes himself for his weakness of spirit. Only by doing his duty can he rise above himself, soar above the limits of flesh and body, beyond the limiting ties of family and friends, resplendent on the path of honour.

Most of us liked this song. Occasionally even a Pathfinder would ask him to sing it. Though the one they really preferred was a bouncy one about the pure joys of the natural world: the birds, the bees, the trees, the flowers, the running waters and falling sunlight. It had a loud chorus line that declared:

> Open your eyes, jump to your feet;
> The storm is a caress, the snow a sheet.
> Seek not the coin, nor the crown.
> Men must be pristine and life a breeze.

In the last year that I knew him, little fat Bhima became obsessed with a secret that he shared with me alone, the secret that finally undid him. For some reason he grew obsessed with thoughts of his father – to the point that he felt he knew who he was. He said he had seen him twice, during our treks through the valley. Once a month everyone at the home went for a long march, twenty-four hours, from sunrise to sunrise. We were given a route, but no Pathfinder accompanied us. The oldest boy led the trek, and we all walked in a single file, our food, water and blankets on our backs. The idea was to build endurance, discipline, brotherhood. It was all very humane. It was the prerogative of the weakest member to ask for a halt – to rest or to sleep. Of course no one wanted to be weak, and sometimes we ended up walking till our limbs had become numb.

Little fat Bhima said the first time he saw him, he was standing by a bank of horse chestnut trees, heaving stacks of corn into a cart. My singing friend, my brother, said, I am fat, but he was tall and strong. While his companions were struggling to lift the sheaves, he was effortlessly tossing them up. His shoulders were broad and his neck thick. Do you think I will be like that when I grow up?

The next time he saw him, just two months later, was by the Jhinjheri, the brook that runs diagonally across the valley, emerging from the rocks under the north-western face and finally vanishing into the rocks at the south-eastern end. At its widest it is fifteen feet, and at its narrowest fit to be stepped over. It is easier to trawl for fish than the Amrita because it is shallower and slower. If you are quick you can grab the trout with your bare hands. A Wafadar can simultaneously snare one in each hand while looking away. My friend, my brother, said, He was standing in the middle of the Jhinjheri, in a loincloth, a big net in his hands, sieving the waters. On the banks there were fish flashing silver as they did their last flips. As we marched past, he looked up at me – and you know why I knew who he was? I said: the size, the neck, the arms. He said, No, no, no! I knew because he was humming! Humming so beautifully that the fish were swimming towards him!

I tried hard to dissuade him from this line of thought. Surely he knew it was disgraceful. It was of no consequence who our parents were. To look for them was wrong. But he was weak, more flawed than I could recognize. He said he was trying very hard to not think of him but he could not keep his mind from wandering. Was it possible – did I think it was possible for him to meet with him once?

Just once. I said no. Absolutely no. There was little chance the man was his father. And if he were, it would be even more disastrous. And it wasn't just the fear of others finding out. I didn't think we could look at ourselves in the mirror if we went down that road.

But my friend, my brother, was not to be deterred. From the moment of his second sighting he could talk to me of nothing else. Just once, he kept insisting – to satisfy his doubt, to settle his craving.

I became deeply worried for him. Then he told me he was going to do something about it. Now when we walked in the woods he didn't sing, we just argued. I was outraged and he was sullen. Not just sullen, but also sad. Continually humming the song of the waiting mother. I became weak too. I could not bear to see his unhappiness.

One morning we both pretended to be incapacitated by an acute stomach ache. Something in the dinner. When everyone had left for the Bodhi, we sneaked out of the home and ran towards the grove of horse chestnuts. Bhima's eyes were shining as I had never seen them before, and for once he was able to keep pace with me. We stayed off the main paths, going through the fields and the trees, crouching low all the while.

Not that anyone knew us, but everyone knew as children we ought to be at the home, not wandering around like this. We knew every adult had the right to arraign us and to seize us. The prospect of being dragged back to the home, to confront our Pathfinders and brothers, was a dreadful one. Bhima perhaps had less to lose, but I could find myself strung on a big question mark, all my excellence besmirched, my chances of becoming a Wafadar marred forever.

I had warned him – if at any point there was a risk of being caught, we were both on our own. It was against the principle of brotherhood, but then what we were doing was against the principles of everything we had been taught.

I hissed constantly at my fat brother to keep his bulk behind the camouflage of grass and crops and trees. Soon our legs were muddy and our arms scratched by blades of leaves. We startled birds, insects, little animals and snakes, but miraculously did not run into a single person.

When we found him he was not alone. There were three of them, at a little distance from the grove, squatting on the ground, scything grass for the cattle. They were strung out in a line, thirty feet apart, and moving at an angle – on their haunches – leaving behind small piles of grass. Their sickles moved smoothly making juicy sounds. We waited, kneeling in the grove, behind the tree trunks. I suggested we go back, come again another day, but my fat brother did not even care to reply. His eyes were fixed unmoving on the broad back of the man he thought was his father.

I looked up at the sun. It would soon be above us. We had little time. Suddenly the father stood up, and walking down the angled line began collecting the piles. Soon he was a moving green heap, heading towards us. I shrank lower in the foliage. He dumped his huge load near the grove where the first cut had been made, and straightened up with a loud sigh. Then he looked back – the other two men were cutting away in a widening swathe. In a loud voice, he bellowed, Stop it! Unless you want to cut your way into the next country! The men waved their sickles, and went on scything.

He shuffled a few more steps towards us, I saw his shoulders shake, his eyes close, and then heard the sound of his urine pattering on the grass. I shrank back further, starting to edge away, a bad feeling sweeping over me. I put out a hand to nudge my brother, but he was already out of reach, moving in a crouch towards the man. Suddenly he stood up and said, Father! Jumping back, the man said, Eh boy, who are you? My little fat brother said, Your son Bhima! The man turned his head and shouted, Come here the two of you! Look what I've found among the trees!

The two men came trotting up, sickles in hand. The shorter one had a bad leg and listed precariously. The other had a black cummerbund around his brown tunic. He said, stroking his face, Have we ever seen anything like it before? What do you think it is? The limper said, It crawled out of the trees? Must be some kind of animal. Father said, Looks fat and juicy, but you can never tell how new animals will cook.

I flattened myself on the ground, sliding under the foliage. Through the leaves, I could see them waist up. Of my brother I could see nothing but the back of his round head. The cummerbund said, Shall I gut it right here or do you want to take it back for the others to see? Father said, What is there to see? Either it tastes right or it doesn't! That we will all know soon enough. Easier to carry pieces than the whole.

My stomach had turned to water. I thought I was going to soil my clothes. The limper said, in a nasal voice, But why carry even pieces? We already have the burden of this grass. Maybe we can persuade it to walk along.

My brother had begun to cry. A low whine punctuated by deep sobs. I was now a snake, only my head half lifted. Father said, I say let's finish the job now. I can't bear to hear this sound all the way back. At this my brother blubbered, You are my father! I know you are! The big man guffawed. Father! Never heard the word! Never met anyone who had a father or was a father or wanted to be a father! You are an animal that has crawled out of the trees! And I am the butcher of Jhinjheri! I seize living breath and make it dead meat! Do you understand? And these are my assistants! And these are our carving knives! At this all three of them held their sickles aloft, slicing the sunlight.

I was so weak with fright I thought I had died. Even if I wanted to help my brother I don't think I could have moved a muscle. Suddenly the cummerbund said, Are you alone or are there other animals with you? I dug my face into the mud and closed my eyes. In a crying voice I heard my brother say, I am alone. Just as well then, bellowed the big man, that you have enough flesh on you!

I heard my brother shout Father! and follow it up with a low long wail. When I had the courage to open my eyes I saw the backs of the three men receding in the distance.

I waited till they had vanished from sight, and then I got up and ran.

Long before I reached the home I was empty of all breath and my heart was hammering like stormy rain on our tin roof. I hid in my bed and by the time everyone returned from the Bodhi I had genuinely acquired a fever.

It was evening before little fat Bhima's absence was noted. I pretended I knew nothing. Search parties were divided into threes and sent out – to comb the adjoining copses, the fields, the pond, even go as far as the cradle. Lying in my bunk I began to feel it had been a bad dream, and any moment he would walk in, humming his favourite song.

But as it grew dark, the search parties returned without success. My group was stunned, but the older boys said there had been a couple of disappearances in the past too. The missing boys had never returned. Many strange and macabre stories had been heard – but no firm explanation. A sense of foreboding enveloped us.

At night, at the dining table, all our four Pathfinders were present, and food was put on hold while they convened a palaver. Around the tables everyone held hands to the right and the left, and the oldest Pathfinder – who had folds of age on his neck and white hair on his arms – spoke. What had happened was terrible. It was a taint on all of us. As brothers it was our duty to watch out for each other at all times. Did anyone have an inkling as to what may have happened? Was there anyone here who knew something but was unable to come forward?

I was sure the boys flanking me could feel my hands sweaty and cold, and hear my heart pounding. I knew if any of the Pathfinders caught my eye I would crumple. So I stared unmoving at the boy across from me. I knew what I was doing was dishonourable, but I also knew what I had done earlier in the day was far more dishonourable, and there was no way I would find the courage to own up to it.

The old Pathfinder said he was going to make the process easy. Everyone was to shut their eyes – except the one who knew. When he clapped his hands I screwed my eyelids down till they hurt, and did not open them till well after the second clap. I saw everyone was looking at everyone else, and many of them at me – after all I was the last one to have been with him. I struggled to control my expression, acutely aware what a handicap a naked face was.

Looking at me, the old Pathfinder said, I have come to know enough. Tomorrow we will send word to the rest of the valley. Aum taught us there is a lesson in everything that happens to us. I ask all the brothers here to think about what has taken place. We may never learn the truth of what occurred – but that is of little consequence. What matters are the truths it helps us divine. Aum strove all his life to gift us liberty, to make us free men, free men such as cannot be found anywhere in the world. Aum strove, but only our endeavours can make us so. And remember, freedom is a roaring fire – it warms and feeds and illuminates, but it also scalds and burns and makes of everything a worthless ash.

Each day we waited for news of our brother. In our bunks at night, we remembered his sweet singing voice and his inability to sit on the rock. Word had been sent out into the valley. No word came back. At least not to us.

After the third day the Pathfinders, too, said no more. A brother had incinerated himself in the fire of freedom, made himself ash instead of light – so it was.

I kept waiting to be summoned, but no one asked me anything. For weeks I lay awake at night tortured by images of what might have happened to him. Always when I closed my eyes I saw the three men and the raised sickles – sometimes my brother was with them, and sometimes there was only blood dripping from the curved blades.

After the first paralysis of terror, in the week that followed, I considered confessing. Perhaps that would solve the mystery. Perhaps the Pathfinders could track down the three beastly men and somehow extricate my brother, or at least the truth. But soon a month had passed and because everyone had stopped talking of it, the incident had acquired an unreal air. It was a fiction. Nothing had really happened.

In less than three months little fat Bhima – his dulcet voice and his ungainly body – had been forgotten. It was okay. He had chosen to make himself ash instead of light – we had all taken the lesson. I, in particular, had understood how wrong my brother had been. And how remiss I had been in abetting his dubious quest.

From the embers of my contrition rose the flames of an intense new focus on the teachings of Aum. Under the Bodhi my ear became a flaring funnel, and on the rock I became a motionless stone.

There was nothing that could distract me. It was not long before the Pathfinders recognized I was special – a future Pathfinder, or even a Wafadar. I began to get some precious time alone with them – a stroll in the woods, extra discussions after class, a seat by their side at the dining table. I felt heady, elated; full of a purity and passion for the miracle of Aum.

Seeing my intensity, the Pathfinders cautioned me. The home was the crucible but the final test lay in the barracks. It was there that my true worth would be established. There would be the mastering of the mind to rival the greatest monks – how to make it soar like a kite, to dip and to dart, and to be held completely still, suspended mid-air, between heaven and earth. And then there would be the challenges to the body: the endurance, the strength, the skill, the weapons, and the artistry of the chonch.

To become a Pathfinder I would have to develop the mind of a monk.

To become a Wafadar I would have to become an exemplar of it all. Achieve the perfect union of the two, mind and body, till they uncurled as seamlessly one, as do living flesh and bone.

PILGRIM FATHERS

Do not for a moment assume we were unaware of the world outside. That we lived in some bubble of unknowing. Aum had always been clear: he wanted to make us pure out of knowledge, not out of ignorance. He had refined us out of something out there, and he wanted us to know what that thing was. As water must flow over rock to know it is fluid and different, we had to understand the outer world to know who we were.

The force of this learning was unleashed on us when we moved to the barracks. Now the Bodhi belonged to us in the afternoons. After the boys from the home had left we would arrive there, from a long morning of meditation and physical training, our muscles and minds hard and cleansed like pebbles in a mountain stream. The workouts came first – relentless, explosive, exhausting, pushing every muscle to its tearing limit. In order to settle down with a still mind that could envelop the universe, we had to first be drained of all our violent and corrosive energies. Our bodies spent; our minds now everything.

By the time we arrived under the Bodhi, mind and body were on a perfect keel, shining and honed receptacles. As we sat in a semicircle, the Pathfinders – one after the other – would circumambulate the platform, pouring their wisdom into the wide funnel of our open ears.

For our ease, Aum had condensed the knowledge of the world into a mere nine volumes. These were not for us to read. They had been read and absorbed, and were passed down by the Pathfinders. No one knew where the original texts were kept, and in whose custody – it was the surest way of keeping them safe. With his sweeping knowledge, Aum had summarized all the great civilizations known to man. The Greek, the Egyptian, the Roman, the Indian, the Mesopotamian, the Chinese, and from recent times, the Japanese, the Spanish, the French, the British and the American. He had distilled all the big and small religious schools: Christianity, Islam, Hinduism, Buddhism, Judaism, Sikhism, Jainism, Confucianism, Taoism, Zoroastrianism, as well as Shinto, Cao Dai, Baha'I and Spiritism. And he had summed up the achievements of science and technology and medicine. We knew about anaesthesia and airplanes and bombs that could blow holes in the ground the size of our valley. The geography of the world had been explained to us, as had been the different shades of men. We knew the immense countries that flanked our beautiful valley; we knew the waters and lines that divided the world.

We knew the ways of men. How they lived to possess, and killed to possess. How, alone among all living creatures, they bucked the order of things. Plants grew as they were meant to, and animals and insects lived as they were meant to, but men constantly deviated – ever driven by the need to possess power, wealth, women. All things could be expected to follow their order, but not men. They were deceitful with themselves, staying by no rules, making of their inconstancy a constant.

Each day the Pathfinders poured the glorious volumes of Aum into our funnels, and day on day our vessels filled up. But we knew information by itself was nothing – no more than a log of wood. A raw, unmade thing. What you did with it was what mattered. Shape a chair, carve a spear, burn it in fire. Not all the wood in the world became a chair unless you knew how to craft it. From all the gallons of information being poured into us, we had to distil wisdom.

That is what Aum had once done. That is what had made us who we were.

No one I knew had seen the nine books. But there were enough people who knew someone who had seen them or someone who knew someone who had seen them. There was some dispute about who had actually written them – as in, whose hand it was. The Pathfinders maintained it was Aum himself – and that was the chief reason they needed to be protected.

Others whispered that while every word was doubtless Aum's, the writing itself had been entrusted to Ali, his closest companion. This version drew credence from the fact that Ali – it was said – could wield both hands with equal dexterity, flashing sword or quill. To keep pace with Aum's torrent of sentences, the believers said, Ali had scribbled with unflagging speed, with both hands, concomitantly. Every sentence, then, was written in two different hands over two different parchments. To read them, to make sense of them, you had to set the pages side by side, finishing on the right sheet the half-sentence you had abandoned on the left.

I preferred this account. I liked the idea of a puzzle – even if a simple one – that had to be decoded, and I loved the image of Ali working both hands, an eye on each page, as the words sang out of Aum's mouth. Some said even when Aum ceased talking Ali would go on writing because he knew exactly what Aum had to say. That is how close they were.

In my time some suggested it was not always Ali who was the follower and Aum the master. Often it was the other way around. I doubt this was true – except in the sense that every teacher also learns from his disciple. Aum was the One – the only. I think the speculation arose because Ali was four years older than Aum. But the truth is Ali had always been the follower – following Aum's every footstep, from the age of eleven when he first met the master at a village wedding.

Ali's hamlet was a mountain away. When his thirty-strong clan arrived in Aum's village to claim their bride, they were already aware of the existence of a sainted one. Information travels in the highlands on breeze and birdback. For seven years, in the navels and armpits of the mountains, word had hummed of the foetus that had spoken in the womb and entered the world delivering sermons.

On the evening that Ali's curious family came to visit, Aum was sitting outside his hut, under an apple tree richly in blossom. The sun had just slashed itself on the near peak, bleeding a faint redness that cast over Aum a celestial glow. As ordinary men must, in deference, the family bowed low before settling down on the rocks that lined the courtyard. It was beyond dispute: the boy was divine. Sitting cross-legged on a small wooden platform he could have been the Buddha. His eyes were old, yet playful. He radiated wisdom and understanding.

To test him, Ali's father said, Will the winter be a little gentler on us this year? The boy said, with the faintest of smiles, The winter will be what it will be. How we choose to experience it is what will matter. For the farmer the night is a time of repose; for the hunter it is the hour of work. If the wind turns to ice, explore the life that throbs within your walls. Perhaps discover those that you every day see. Ali's father said, What you say are mere words. The truth is, where we stay, in the high mountains, the winter kills us. The boy said, So does life – no matter where you stay – in its time. That is no reason to turn your back on it.

As darkness sucked out the last of the light, the boy's mother emerged on soundless feet and set a taper by his side. The jumping flame caught the boy's long nose and slim face; it shone in his eyes. In later years Ali said, It was the vision of god. I knew it at that moment. I had found the destination of my life.

Ali never returned to his own hamlet. His parents understood. It was a fortunate few who found the canopy of a master under which to live their lives. Sure he was a boy, only seven. But that meant nothing. You clung to a master wherever and whenever he appeared.

Moreover, the choice was not yours; it was the master who chose. Aum, it is said, would say, When Ali walked in he was like the first sun of morning. Is there anyone who turns their back on it?

If Aum was all uncompromising angles and taut surfaces, long and sharp in nose, fingers, limbs and face, Ali was all flowing curves, with the face of an angel and skin of satin. While the wisdom of Aum's voice travelled sheathed in a flaming armour that could melt grown men's bones, Ali spoke in the petal of roses, all perfumery and guile.

Men befriended and adored Ali; they worshipped and followed Aum.

Aum, it is said, ribbed Ali for being popular. You want to be loved – that is your failing. When you seek to be loved you go away from who you are. You become other things, something you imagine someone wants you to be. And it never ends – you are always becoming other things. That is why democracies will end up as failures, no matter how gleefully men celebrate this new dawn. They will always be run by men who will not be who they really are. Shadows will fight shadows; everyone will chase shadows. You, my friend, could be a great leader there.

Aum was never wrong. Ali lived to charm. From the day he peeled away from his parents to stay back with the master, he had the village eating out of his hand, men and women, children and animals. He gossiped with them, played with them, lent a hand in their chores. He also told them about Aum, and led them to Aum. The young master knew that for all his wayward affections, Ali had only one locus. All the other diversions he created because he could not have enough of the master – for Aum belonged to everyone and could never be claimed by just one.

All this was told to the brotherhood by Ali himself. Much of what we all knew about Aum came to us from Ali. From that first moment under the dying sky, by the apple tree in blossom, Ali was in public the shadow of Aum, and each night he slept by the master, at his feet, poised to respond to every suggestion of a need.

Every great master needs one great disciple. Ali was the one. Though there were also others.

When they left those mountains to trek to this high valley that was to be our home – of the born and the unborn – it was Ali who marshalled the men and material, it was Ali who ensured that every word of Aum became our every action.

It was never stated but we all know it: that Aum broke from his own teachings when it came to Ali. Non-possession; equal love; detachment. In the master's profoundly even gaze, we all knew, there was more space for Ali than for anyone else in the world.

Formally, we were never taught in any great detail about Ali. In class, under the Bodhi, the Pathfinders gave him credit for nothing except being Aum's longest and closest companion. Formally, he was even denied the honour of being the master's amanuensis, taking down the volumes. Most of what we learned about him came through casual conversations with the Pathfinders and the older boys who had heard the stories from still older ones.

In the long march to liberation – which came before the devastations of the first great war, at a time when brown men were locked in conflict with white men – in the long march to liberation he had, it seems, played a crucial role. The master, rising from his pre-dawn meditation one morning, had announced it was time for them to leave their village and proceed to a place where they could live the truth and give birth to new things.

The master had read the past, the present and the future, and he knew that men were doomed. Mankind was doomed. He was old enough to know that its redemption would come not from merely knowing the truth, but from living it. In him lay the seed of salvation, but he had to find the perfect bower to set it to grow. From that tree of purity would a million pure saplings spring. One day they would fill the forest; one day they would be the forest. Fully pure; fully redeemed. It would not happen in a year, or in ten. It would take time, but a beginning had to be made. The first seeds had to be protected, the first trees grown.

Already, in the village, and the villages around, foolish men, egotistical men, were being stirred against the truth of the master. Their women were in thrall. Their sons were captivated. The strange boy had grown into a dangerous young man. He had done no harm yet, but he spoke in words that seemed to challenge old ways. It was unclear what desires lay in his deep, dark eyes.

Across the highlands, gruff, bearded, battle-scarred men – whose bloodline had seen off the Greeks, the Persians, the Mughals, the Sikhs, and the white man – were starting to question Aum's charisma. He was too young to be a great teacher; he was too good-looking to be god's man; he did not have the divine touch of the healer.

Sure there were stories of small children who had benefited from his touch, their throats cured of rasp, their lungs drained of infection, their carbuncles dried of pus. There was also the more impressive miracle of barren wombs filled with pulsing seed. But what of Ghaffar who travelled three days bearing his eleven-year-old son on the back of a donkey, his stomach swollen with a tumour? The boy died with Aum's hand on his forehead, leaving Ghaffar wailing like a baby. What of Imran's mother who came in her son's arms, all her limbs unbending with ache, and Aum's gentle caress failed to unlock even one? And what of Gyan Chand's father who could not recognize his son any more, whose mind had become a blank slate – on which the young master failed to inscribe a single word?

For every voice that extolled Aum, one was stoked to discredit him. The master made it more difficult for himself by dismissing the idea of miracle cures and holy healing. It was shamanism, trickery – the work of the devil, not of the gods. Looks, bodies, ailments, place and time of birth were all determined by the workings of the divine principle. There was a karmic arithmetic to it.

When you reckoned at the till of the shopkeeper you knew precisely, to the last coin, the value of your transaction. You did not try to cheat and swindle. If you wanted more you just went away, worked harder, and came back with more money. At its simplest, the divine principle was plain arithmetic. It gave unto you the life you had already earned. To get a better one, you had to simply work harder – to live with greater purpose, greater grace, greater love, greater purity.

Seeking the miracle cure was attempting to cheat the divine principle. In the long run it meant annoying the great policeman in the sky. Men, among themselves, could get away with fraud and perjury and criminal excess. In the account books of the universe there was no sleight-of-hand possible.

But since the impulses of men are complex, their affairs an intricate matrix of values, judgments, conflicting situations and moralities – since the calculus of the divine principle cannot always be easily decoded, a master is needed.

That was the call of Aum, to provide clarity to human endeavour, to illuminate the true path. Not to siphon out pus and put poultices – that was the task of medics and quacks. A true master is a mender of souls, not a juggler of ailments.

Aum knew small, foolish men had been seeding ire against him. Soon they would begin the harvest. Through millennia great masters had been quartered and crucified by the vulgar and the unthinking. You did not carry out a dialogue with rampaging boars. You merely got out of the way. He had to move on from the old and the decaying. He had to gather the faithful and travel to a place where new things could come into bloom.

There is apparently a detailed account of the long march to liberation. No one I know has read it, but everyone knows someone who knows someone who has. It was written by one of the thirteen girls who were born along with Aum in that hallowed year. It goes without saying that all thirteen of his birthmates left the village and their families to follow the master. They were one with him, the same milk coursing through their bodies.

The one who wrote the story of the march was called Alaiya. She was so beautiful that even the women coveted her. So it was said. Her hair was black and long and fell like a cataract; her eyes were the same, coal-dark and liquid; her skin was milk; and her mouth so full, it stirred hopeless visions. But she was no fainting damsel. Her limbs were strong, her heart stout, her voice stentorian. In that great walk of a hundred days, she walked just behind Ali, who walked just behind Aum, and was one of the few who did not once falter.

According to Alaiya, Aum knew precisely where they were going. There was no fork in the path where he dithered, no hamlet at which he asked for directions. The discipline of the walk was simple: they walked when Aum walked, and they stopped when he stopped. Some days the master would keep going for sixteen hours, and some days he would just lie on a knoll of grass and look up at the sky.

When they left their homes – in the hour after midnight, in the darkest cycle of the month, the wolves howling their grief to the universe – there were one hundred and eleven of them. One Aum, and the rest his people. The youngest was Arif, all of nine, and the oldest was Baba, over fifty, with a snowy beard that touched the ground when he sat, forcing him to throw it over his right shoulder. Many in the train were fleeing oppressions – of marriage and caste, of power and poverty. In the grace of the master lay all succour.

For the first twenty-four hours they did not break step, for food or ablution. Aum wanted them to be beyond several horizons by the time the villages and hamlets assembled a pursuit.

In his infinite wisdom Aum knew men are not content to merely see the backs of their detractors. They want them brought to book. When a man looks at his neighbour, he wants to see himself – in all his fears and anxieties, in all his smallness and failings. Men can genuflect to greatness if it comes from afar; up close, they want to nail it to the cross. The master knew they would be pursued; and if caught, made to bleed so everyone could see that all men were the same, none greater than another.

True to his apprehension, late on the evening of the fifth day they saw the pursuers. In a long thin thread the pilgrims of the new world were strung out on the top of a ravine when they heard from deep below the sounds of neighing horses and arguing men. Kneeling at the edge of the drop, two hundred and twenty-two eyes looked down and saw a few score armed men breaking saddle to bivouac. There was grass down there and a muttering stream. On horseback, the pursuers were less than a day away. There was no hope they would lose track. A thread of two hundred and twenty-two limbs leaves behind a trail a blind man can follow.

The pilgrims did not panic, because their master did not panic. Moving everyone away from the lip of the precipice, Aum convened a conference. The question he posed was simple. What would the pursuers, who had ridden hard for days – their muskets and swords slapping horse flanks – do when they finally came upon them?

The pulpit was first ceded to the beauteous Alaiya who spoke in a voice that could have moved the stars. Down there were beasts. They cared not for wife or child, for love or compassion, for ideas or aesthetics. They only understood crude possession, blind tradition, foolish honour, and bloody revenge. Had they not seen it all their lives? Had they not suffered it all their lives? Without a doubt, when their hooves bore down on the pilgrims of liberty, they would command summary death. Surely each one of the pilgrims knew that these men would give no quarter to friend or relation, woman or child. Could anyone sitting here – under the raining stars, in the lee of a great master – could anyone imagine a single beat of mercy in the hearts of these barbarians?

A ripple thrilled through the anxious flock.

And now the master, sitting on a rock shaped like a camel, his long black hair catching the moon, posed the next question. What is it they ought to do?

At this Ali rose, his cherub's face without a crease of consternation, his loose dress flapping in the wind. Even in a moment of mortal crisis he spoke to charm. After the thunderstorm of Alaiya, his voice was the cool morning breeze of the oasis. There was beauty in the world, he said. In this great beauty there was fragrance. There was wisdom. There was love. But none of it came without endeavour, none of it came without a price. If you had the fortune to gain it, you had to not only celebrate it, but also to guard it, enhance it, enshrine it.

Soothing as a feather, Ali said everything he was saying he had learned from Aum. The beauty in the world was shrinking because men who cherished beauty equated it with softness. Men imagined beauty was a fragile virgin that must remain untouched by blood and sinew. Men wanted the infinite pleasures of beauty without paying for any of its pain.

Such men were fools. With their phoney softness they were killing beauty. By lacking a sword arm, by lacking skin thick as armour, by lacking a will immovable as a rock, they were ceding the keep of beauty to men who set no value by it. Men who felt threatened by it.

Beauty liberates men. It gives them wings – of music, words, imagination. Men who do not like free men, men who do not like men to experience abandon – such men do not like beauty. They wish to contain it, to tear its wings out. These men cannot be fought with sweet words and fine gestures. These men are not to be persuaded or appeased. These men have to be looked unblinking in the eye. To preserve beauty requires a heart of fire and flesh of steel. It requires passion, not compassion, courage not coyness, hardness not softness. It demands a readiness to go to war each time words fail.

Look! Look down into the depths of the ravine, at the moving eyes of the woodfires. Those men down there were against beauty, against free men. They were riding hard, day on day, to destroy both. Aum knew – as ever – what he had to do. But what did the rest of them think? What would they like to do?

Eyes flashing, like a roll of thunder, Alaiya spoke from where she sat. Did they wish to fight for beauty and freedom? Or would they like to run in the hope they could outpace the iron hooves of the barbarians?

That night as the moon ripened to its fullness and burst and shrank, and the sieve of stars leaked pinheads of light, the pilgrims of freedom laboured in the defence of beauty. All along the edge of the abyss they arrayed an arsenal of rocks. With a strength born of passion puny men and women carried loads they could never have imagined. Forming chains they tossed the stones from hand to hand in the rhythm of drums. When every limb was exhausted, the master took over. With an ease that could only be divine, Aum finished the task, effortlessly moving giant boulders that others could not budge. So it is said.

Then, as the rest slumbered, the master kept watch. When the first line of grey broke the horizon, he put his hand on Ali who put his hand on Alaiya who put her hand on Rubaiya who put her hand on… till all one hundred and eleven warriors of beauty were awake. Peering into the abyss the master waited for the first flint to strike. To assault a sleeping enemy was to rob oneself of the pleasure of a fair triumph. Generations later, it is a rule the Wafadars still never flout. As orange glows burst in the darkness below and shadows began to move, Aum raised his hand and dropped it, and in the heave of a hundred free shoulders a thousand rocks took flight.

The noise was deafening – horse, man and debris all at once. Some of the big boulders took down a train with them, and the pilgrims did not stop till every last pebble had been hurled. When the sun emerged and scampered down the slopes the pilgrim–warriors saw their attack had been devastating. Nothing stirred below, and above them the carrion birds had begun to wheel in narrow and narrower circles.

The destruction of the posse was so complete that the legend of Aum and his soldier–saints radiated over the mountains. There were no fresh volunteers for a fresh pursuit, and some of the families whose members had left to become followers of Aum marvelled at the transformation that had been wrought. Now they whispered: perhaps it was true, he was a great master.

Since no one who'd left ever returned, over the years, and then over generations, the mystery became a myth. In some stories he was a sorcerer, in others a magician, and in many simply a divine being. In most tellings he had literally given wings to his followers and flown them to another land. Over the high mountains, beyond the boundless plains of Hind, across the dark deep waters, to a place from where there was no return.

In truth, the journey was gruelling beyond anything the pilgrims could have imagined. On days they snaked their way through such high passes that nothing could be seen but the white of snow. Not a tree, not an animal, not a blade of grass. At other times a valley of stones would lie in wait, to slash their feet at every step. Sometimes the sun would be in such a fervour it would roast the rocks and peel their skins. Ever so often the mountains turned so brittle that one feared to breathe lest they crumble.

Always Aum led the way – and in his hand would be one end of a rope to which each follower held firm, secure that the master would never let them down. Often, as the climb became too arduous and the limbs of the pilgrims disobedient, the master reached inside his depthless resource and yanked them along like strips of paper flapping on a string. In the last days, in the account of Alaiya – which has been read by people known to people I know – this is precisely how it was. The master, alone, pulling his people to the valley of new beginnings.

The question is sometimes posed – in confidence, between brothers who understand it does not constitute betrayal: did all the pilgrims arrive at the promised land? Some believe some died on the way; some believe many died. The truth is no one did. So we know, from the Pathfinders. Each of the one hundred and eleven pilgrims was led through the Pass of all Hope by the great master himself.

In the telling of the beauteous Alaiya, one moment Aum was walking at the head of the undulating snake, so tall and full of grace, and the next he was gone. Instantly, his people exploded in a roar of panic. Without him they were nothing. Just lost children, with no meaning and no purpose. These many weeks it was only the sight of Aum that had kept the blood stirring in their fatigued limbs. Wild-eyed, they wailed his name – which was the first sound of the universe. Aum. Aum!

To the left the land fell away into a deep gorge where the beads of huge rocks were threaded by a rush of silver water whose noise carried all the way up to the narrow shelf where they stood lamenting. To the right, rising steeply above them, were giant deodars, thick together, their fanning arms entwined. These were ancient creatures, their skins dark, their girth the span of two and more men. If you bent your neck back till it would go no further you could see the line where the deodars ended and the white snows began, blinding and sheer, all the way into the clouds, the peaks glimpsed only in rare clear moments.

It happened late in the afternoon. The sun was on their backs, and they had been trudging for hours, in the rhythm of ants, each one's place in the line fixed, each one's hand firm on the magic rope, when the master suddenly vanished at a bend on the dizzy trail. As Ali's cry and Alaiya's cry was picked up and relayed, the line broke and the pilgrims fell into a wailing heap. Many held hands and peered into the tumultuous gorge in wordless dread. Others stared into the dark trees fearing the shadows of undreamt demons. But there was nothing – the master had evaporated without a trace.

Alaiya was the first to counsel calm. Her thick hair tamed by a blue scarf, her eyes on fire, she spoke in her ringing voice, commanding everyone to squat where they stood. As they did so, cupping chins and cradling knees, she asked them if they were offal, unworthy of the master. Having brought them so far, having borne their burden day and night, through snow and stone, storm and starvation, did they think he would abandon them now? Or did they think he had just slipped and fallen – having kept them all, for months, steady on their feet with his unwavering hand?

Was this the quality of their faith?

What if Aum was testing them?

They would have failed before the test began.

Ali spoke too. As always, to charm. He could understand how they felt. For a moment he'd felt bereft too. Like an abandoned child. But he was not going to keep wailing. The moment had passed; the fear was gone. Though he could not see the master, he could feel him holding his finger. Could they not feel the same? Did they not feel themselves protected and overseen? Should they not just calmly wait here for the master's return, or for a sign from him that would show them their path?

Reassured, the pilgrims, one by one, settled down to wait. Some cradling heads in laps, some back to back, some prostrate, staring up at the failing sun. No one spoke; the river deep in the gorge roared without a pause. Ali and Alaiya climbed into the deodar thicket, their swords unsheathed, and disappeared from view. The air became colder, and then even colder. Soon it was keening through the woods – louder than the water.

The blob of pilgrims shrank tight into each other, struggling with their nerves. They all reached for their weapons when there was a scruffing in the trees. But it was only Ali and Alaiya returning, just as they had gone, swords unsheathed. Ali looked at the host of desperate eyes, and smiled. You don't find the master, the master finds you!

When the moon rose it was big and close, putting a coat of shiny silver on everything. The rock faces shone, and the high snows gleamed. Sporadic animal sounds broke out, their source a mystery. Alaiya put together a detail to watch the forest-line. She herself paced the shelf like a big cat guarding her brood. Ali stood at the precipice and began to sling stones into the gorge. He did it deliberately, with a full swing of his arm – waiting for the stone's imagined drop into the raging waters below. To nine-year-old Arif, he said, He will arrive with the one-thousandth.

Fittingly, the first to be shown the promised land were Ali and Alaiya. So it is said. As the faithful slumbered, as the moon fell from its zenith, as Ali cast the one-thousandth stone into the roaring abyss, the master materialized by their side. Wordlessly he led them into the ancient deodars, and walking around a giant boulder the size of a hut, he turned sideways and disappeared into a slash in the stone that was weeping water.

The chosen two followed in the darkness lit by the glow of the master. After ten feet of breath-choking tightness, the passage opened up. The jagged stone walls were wet with damp, and around their feet, to the ankles, was the rustle of warm water. The master's touch had unfrozen the spring. In Alaiya's account Ali and she felt they were floating in a dream. Slowly they drifted down and down, through a long winding passage, lit only by the master's glow, water murmuring at their feet, and when they emerged out into the open they were standing on a wide smooth platform, and spread out before them, in the blue light of the dying moon, was the map of paradise.

They woke the flock while it was still dark, and an exhalation of joy ripped the air as the pilgrims saw the lean silhouette of Aum framed by the deodars. When one inquired where the master had been, Alaiya thundered, Will now the cat preach to the lion? Aum conjures worlds. Prepare yourselves to get the answer no question ever asked!

Once again Aum led the way, and each one went through the primal wet crack, sideways and wordless. To those at the end of the line it seemed the mountain was silently swallowing up their mates. Inside, they held each other to keep their footing, and quailed at what new trial the master had in store. The only solace was the warm water at their feet, and Alaiya's voice calling out instruction.

After an indeterminate time, walking down, the line was suddenly brought to a halt. A master always knows the moment. Every pilgrim, every believer, was to be given his full epiphany. As each one emerged from the Pass of all Hope, in the very first moment of daybreak, Aum was waiting to hold their hand and share with them their first sight of the magical valley.

It was an oblong bowl whose ends could not be seen, except as a rim of high mountains. In that breaking light it was clear this was a place that had been carved by angels. As Ali said, This was created for Aum – to be the crucible for all new beginnings. From where the pilgrims stood, well above the floor of the valley, they could see many shades of green and gold and magenta – lush forests of every hue. As they looked on, mouths open, crowding the stone platform, holding hands, linking arms, they saw the first soft rays of the sun begin to cascade down, painting a glint on the giant snakes of water rippling through the valley.

Alaiya said it was then that Aum spoke. Standing tall, an exclamation mark of wisdom in a world of foolish men, his black beard full and long, his eyes deep and unblinking, he told them they had arrived at their home. It took a mere glance to know it was a marked place. And here they had a destiny, a task – to create surpassing beauty. Pure beauty. The beauty of purity.

Aum said, in a voice that filled the immense bowl to overflowing, that men could be whatever they wished to be. They had fled a big world where men had chosen to be small. In this smallest of worlds they would forge the template to make men big once more. When you look at each other, the master said, do not see brothers and fathers and mothers and wives. Do not see ordinary people. See who you truly are. You are the warriors of the pure; you are the priests of beauty; you are the chosen.

At this moment – recounted the magnificent Alaiya – the sun broke out in all its glory, bathing the green valley in light and warmth and joy, drying their skins and igniting their hearts, and in that instant they knew, beyond all doubt, in that strange mix of pride and humility that surges in the finest of the species, that they were truly the chosen.

And Aum the unquestioned master.

THE FACE

At sixteen they put the face on me.

At the time everyone got the face at sixteen – later the age was cut to fourteen. At the time there was only one face for everyone – later one more would be introduced, and then just before I left, there was the addition of another. None of this was an aberration. Someone who knew someone who had read the books of Aum said this was precisely how the master had wished it.

On the eve of the big day, was I expectant? Or was I fearful? Perhaps a bit of both. Though in my case it may have been more of the latter. Of all the rites of passage, this was the most important. It enjoined a sacred covenant. Once the face was put, you could take it off only in the dark and never in anyone's presence. And you ensured that you never caught a reflection, in glass or in water, of how you once were.

I tossed in bed the entire night, as did the three others on the day's roster. Especially restless was good-looking Arjuna – with the chin of a conqueror and the eyes of a saint – who sneaked into the bathroom for one last look, again and again.

Tomorrow everything would change. We were going to become adults. We were going to become one of everyone. And finally we were going to enter the world of women. That, perhaps, more than anything else, made the initiates sleepless and sweaty. In the barracks, in quiet corners, the older boys had often joked that that alone was worth it all, even getting a pair of buttocks welded to your face.

In my case I have to say this was not entirely true. There were thoughts other than a woman's body that torched me. I was ashamed it was so, but I simply could not staunch the dread that filled me at losing my face forever. Never again would I look in the mirror and see myself. Just as I did not know who my father was, and could only guess at who my mother was, I would slowly forget what I once looked like.

To counter these thoughts I dug deep into myself. I flagellated myself for my vanity. This desperate attachment to what was mine. If I could understand the logic of not owning a mother or a father, why was this so difficult to absorb? Given my agitation, it was clear how right Aum had been. In his infinite wisdom, the master had understood that equality was not just a word or an attitude, it also had to be a face. The quest of the pure was an inside-outside thing.

By the time I fell asleep it was morning. But by then my mind was clear: this was to be my last moment of agitation about my face. Never again was I to shame myself with such thoughts.

When we reached the last shed of the workshop – more pretty than the others, rows of colourful flowers girdling it – the old man, the ustaad, and his assistant were ready and waiting. This was my third visit in the last month. The first time when I had sat down on the wooden stool, he had said, without levity, Do you want to look like him or me? His assistant had said, equally without humour, Think well before you answer.

The old ustaad had told me to stare unmoving at a pair of deer antlers on the wall. From the corner of my eye I had tracked the white hair on the old man's wrinkled hands as he measured my face from chin to top, across my brow; and then across my ears, my nose, and my mouth. Then there were endless fine measurements. Of my mouth – shut and open fully; the nose, the ears, the jawline; and the eyes – wide, closed, open. He used a measuring tape, and the two of them worked in rhythm – the ustaad spitting out the numbers and the assistant going huhh after each scribble.

My only preparation for the appointment had been to shave my head in the morning. Now as I sat there bare to the waist, the assistant oiled my scalp and face with brisk hands while the ustaad worked a wooden ladle in the thick mix that they would soon pour on my head. For my own future comfort I stilled every muscle as they patted down the green coagulate, teasing out my eyes and mouth and nostrils with firm fingertips. It smelt nice, of leaves and wet earth. In a moment I had entered the perfect meditation on the rock.

I had no idea how long it had been – ten minutes, an hour – when the assistant tapped my shoulder. It took some effort to crack open my eyes. The assistant caught my shoulders from the back and the ustaad wiggled his fingertips at the edge of the stiffened mix around my jawline and in one jerk had the mould off.

The assistant came around and nodded his approval. They didn't show it to me. When I asked to see it, the ustaad said, Why? The sooner you forget it the better. He was more brutal with Arjuna. Tracing his fingertips over his conqueror's chin, he said sharply, Feeling bad? Well it's for men like you that Aum created this. A man must be what he does, not what he looks. Then, gesturing at me, he said, Otherwise men like him may as well dig a hole in the ground and bury themselves.

Without showing us the moulds he had made he took them through a door at the far end into another room. I was not sure what these were for, but I did know the first act of tediously measuring our features had nothing to do with the second one of making an impression of our faces. The reason for the first we all knew. But no one could explain to us the purpose of the green moulds. There were whispers that they were used for maintaining some kind of a record. There was no point asking the ustaad. He would have cruelly snubbed us.

The ustaad was over seventy, and let it be said that in our land of equals if there were any that were more equal, he was the first of them. The reasons were many. Some said he was a pilgrim father who had joined the long march as a boy. Others said he was a favourite of Aum, and that's how he had attained to this key post. The uncontested truth is he was a magical craftsman, the most important ustaad in our land. To cross him was to risk terrible distress. He was after all the keeper of the face. By micro millimetres he could put a rub on your skin, or a crimp in your nose, that would make a hell of every living moment. No matter how the ustaad behaved you never took offence.

The second visit had been the trial fitting. The assistant put the face on, and the ustaad stood to a side watching intently, the index finger of his right hand slowly rotating inside his right ear. I can never forget the panic of the first moment when the face touched my skin, momentarily obliterated sight, and then settled on the bridge of my nose. My initial reaction was — it's cold, it's heavy! The old man put his rough hand with slim fingers on my forehead and tilted my head back. It was strange to see the ageing rafters of the shed with a kind of shell cutting all peripheral vision. Looking at the fluidly intercut beams and the grooved planks I marvelled at how magnificent my people were with carpentry. The assistant took his hands away. Now the face was held up by nothing but its own contours and the angle of my neck.

Stand up! barked the old man. I did, spine arched, head thrown back. I walked slowly, up and down, balancing my untethered face, my hands ready to catch it if it fell. I got a slap on my arm and the order to straighten up. I brought my chin down slowly, very slowly. The face held. There was no question: the old man was an artist, his sculpting so perfect it rivalled nature's. I thought: what responsibility it is, to give men another face!

Now, on my third visit, I was on the same stool, gazing at the same antlers — after another tormented night of dread and longing. With a light oil the assistant gently massaged my face; then wiped his hands dry on the buzz of my scalp. I sat stone-still as in our meditations. There was no panic this time when they put the face on. In fact there was a surge of relief. I suddenly realized, in some strange way, since the trial fitting, and its feel against my skin, I had been missing the face. As if I had had a moment of completion, and then again a truncation.

As the face settled on me, flowing over every rise and dip of nose and cheek, along my jawline and around my ears, I felt the surge of relief become a wave of elation. The two of them – maestro and apprentice – worked deftly and wordlessly, smoothly tucking in the rubberized skin under my hairline, and expertly cauterizing the excess behind my ears and at the base of my neck.

In a final check the old man ran his fingertips along the seams of the face, found nothing out of true, and stepped back. Then he barked, Say something! I said, I am happy to look like you. I felt the stretch as I spoke, as if someone had dehydrated my skin. For the first time he seemed to smile. Good. Since I am as good-looking a man as you'll ever see. Seeing me flex my jaw, he said, You'll get used to it. It's like anything you wear for the first time. In ten days you won't remember you have it.

I said, Do you have a mirror here?

He said, Fool. Just look at me.

I was completely taken aback by how I felt. By the time we returned to the barracks I was beginning to feel light and happy. A deep sense of belonging and security was brimming up in me. The face had made me one of everyone. I was a seamless part of the whole of us. The burden of I, me, myself was gone. I was filled with an abiding sense of strength and confidence and camaraderie. Once again I was struck by the sheer wisdom of Aum. How right he was in obliterating personal vanity, the individual ego. How liberating its absence was. How wrong I had been in my torments.

Now when I looked at my brothers who were not yet sixteen I saw deformities. Nose and eyes, mouth and skin, eyebrows and teeth, all screaming for attention. Each one making an abject, shallow statement; each one demanding to be considered, to be evaluated. How ugly they were. How insecure, how uncertain, how shaky in their pretences.

I thought of Arjuna, who'd got his face alongside me, and remembered how all these years his conqueror's chin had got in the way of everything he said or did. In his own eyes, and in the eyes of those who looked at him, it brought on a skew. Now it was gone. In one redeeming day, all foolishness was gone.

Four days later, for the first time, we were taken to the Serai of Fleeting Happiness. In the barracks, and as far back as the home, whenever the boys had talked about acquiring the face, it was this moment they had most dwelled upon. We all knew what happened there. We all knew that the regular explosions in our bodies – so full of ache, so full of pleasure – had only one real succour. Those who already had the face always returned on Sunday mornings with a sense of settled calm that not even the morning meditations on the rock fully achieved.

We were also aware of the intense anticipation with which the older boys woke on Saturday mornings. In a strange paradox you saw them, through the day, become happier and lighter, yet coiled and tighter. The change was in the tone of their voices – most of them began to talk more, talk more speedily, at a higher pitch, with greater friendliness. A very few went completely quiet at the night's prospect. You could almost touch the excitement. And those of us who did not yet have the face were filled with envy, curiosity, longing.

We woke that morning, all three of us – Arjuna of the conqueror's chin and the short Arjuna who had arms like a monkey – as if from a night of no sleep. The moment the rafters lightened I got off the bed, crossed my ankles on the stone floor, put my wrists on my knees, and began to chant the name of the master, the very first word of the universe. Aum, auum, auuum.

In no time, both the Arjunas were on the floor too, doing the same. In no time we had stilled our raging minds and softened our raging flesh.

Aum, auum, auuum.

All night we had burned, our bodies coiling and writhing. For the last many days we had been holding ourselves in for the initiation. Each hour, each day, the torment had grown. But we knew it to be a part of Aum's lesson. To know restraint before you knew excess, and then to know restraint again after you had tasted excess. Later in the morning – to prepare us for the evening – the Pathfinders would talk to us about it.

Excess and restraint – it was the dance of life, the master had said. But a good dancer must always be in control. Even the most abandoned dance had its rules, its steps and beats. Throwing limbs about was hysteria, not dance, just as lying supine was lassitude, not meditation. The beautiful life was made up of a fine rhythm. That rhythm was not mere anarchy – or individual eccentricity – as was imagined out there in the other world. It had a music – divined and set by Aum.

Great pleasure is a great blessing. But it is also the edge of a precipice that can kill its seeker.

The Serai of Fleeting Happiness consisted of four large hexagonal rooms set like the petals of a flower. The path leading to it was its curving stalk. It seems Aum himself had designed it. The transitory beauty of the flower; and its endless renewal. There were twelve of us – three of us new. We huddled among the older ones, weak with anticipation and anxiety. Till now the veterans had been shoring us up with advice and encouragement, but now they seemed to have gone silent, each focused on what lay ahead.

There was a big wooden knocker shaped like a teardrop hung outside the front door. The teardrop had to be only thwacked once and the heavy door opened. To this day my first hours inside the house remain a daze.

There were doors. There were couches. There were chairs. There were beds. There were wooden lanterns. There were shadows, moving and unmoving. There were fragrances intoxicating the air. Sticks of burning incense. Claypots exuding vapours. And there were madonnas – many, too many of them, moving with the shadows.

I looked without looking, my limbs robbed of their sinews, my senses reeling. There was the ripple of voices. Soft ones, as I had not heard since the cradle.

In no time there were older boys twined around women like jungle creepers around an oak. Everything around me was moving. Hands, legs, fingers, mouths. Some voices were now mere sounds. Just two of us stood in the middle of the room – Arjuna of the chin and me – swivelling our necks, trying to shrink ourselves. In the near corner we could see short Arjuna of the long arms working hard to become a creeper too.

It was mere minutes but I felt I was stranded at a banquet where everyone had been invited to feast but me. Soon the oaks and creepers began to vanish through doors. Astonishingly, some creepers had wound themselves around two trees. Most voices were now only sounds. I turned around to the front door, wondering if I should get out, clear my head, come back with a sense of purpose. I sensed a movement behind me and when I looked, Arjuna the conqueror was gone, just another spineless creeper in a corner now. I felt as I once had years ago, during that dread morning with doomed Bhima, prostrate in the forest, paralysed by fear.

A shadow by the wall said, The slower they are to start, the more obsessed they end up. From the same place, behind the arc of light thrown by the lantern hanging from the rafter, another voice drawled, Aum said, If a man has been hungry for too long, he always hesitates at the first bite. I could see nothing, and I was shaking. The first voice said, Aum also said she earns great merit who feeds the hungry. The second voice said, Is it time then for us to collect great merit?

As I entered the dark space of the two voices, shadowy hands seized my body. I have spent a lifetime trying to disentangle those first moments, without any success. Almost instantly there was an explosion of sensation. The two voices were witches of giving. Their generosity filled my flesh so tight that I became desperate to burst out of it. All sounds had died except my own. My eyes were closed and I was howling like a jackal of the night. More than four hands, more than twenty fingers, more than two mouths – I felt there was more of everything than there really was. I had become a flaming meteor of pleasure, desperate to tear out of my aching skin. And then I detonated, became a shower of white light, and nothing.

Yet the journey was not done. Another lick of liquid skin, forty more hands, two hundred more fingers, twenty more mouths – the meteor blazed on till I became a continual shower of white light, and nothing.

It was how the entire night went. All around me my brothers howling like jackals, as the shadows flowed with their liquid skin from one to another, witches of the greatest giving. At some point before daybreak I became one with Aum. I arrived at a place so tranquil it was beyond any meditation. All the petals of the flowerlike house were now still. Even the musk of pleasure that hung so heavy in the air had ceased to move.

The sun was at midday as we meandered back to the barracks, fields on one side and forest on the other. Hardly anyone spoke. One of the older boys had asked us, Happy? We had nodded. He said, Good. There'll always be more. But forget it once it's over. Don't become dreamers.

In the shade, among the trees, blue and yellow butterflies flitted around. Even in the daytime the undergrowth was humming loud. On the other side the fields were young with corn. I had to stop myself from floating. It was so easy to become a fool. A few moments of pleasure, a few moments of well-being, the march of dark rain-clouds, a flock of migratory ducks in flight, the new green of leaves being born – any trivial, fleeting thing could excite fantasy.

We knew from the Pathfinders that this was how it was in the world out there. Most men were petty fantasists, their sense of purpose and

purity easily lost. Their minds like grasshoppers, waiting to jump at
the next distraction. Aum, the lamp of all wisdom, had described it
to perfection. Chiefly, it was three things that did them in. Lust of
the material, lust of the sensual, and lust for superiority. All of them
involved conquest of another, not of oneself.

In the world intuited by Aum, decreed by Aum, the first and most
important conquest was always of the self.

Each weekend I gladly became a flaming meteor of pleasure. But I
remained resolute. Even as I howled like a jackal – and heard my
brothers howling around me: in fact, especially when I heard them –
I was aware that the body must never be allowed to bend the mind.
I understood what the master had understood. The body had its
needs and its joys, and these were legitimate, and must be indulged
and burned. Yet the mind had to remain resolute. Uncompromised,
undiminished, by the sentimentalities the body provoked.

We knew that in the world out there irrational fantasia distracted
men and excessive sentimentality made them vulnerable to every
untruth. Great verities, great principles, great moralities were
sacrificed at the altar of sentimentality. The story of man was littered
with the entrails of such blunders. To be pure was to be non-attached.
It was to be aligned to principles greater than the petty needs of
men. It was the ideal each of us pursued. Especially in the Serai of
Fleeting Happiness.

We were all equally resolute. Each time one of the boys found
himself getting too close to a shadow who made him howl louder
and longer than any other, he centred his energies and worked to cut
her out. The best way to do this – the barracks had discovered – was
to speak the crisis aloud. The moment you named the attachment,
put it out for debate and description, for derision and ridicule, it was
leached of all its potency. It remained nothing more than a cursory
stop for fleeting pleasure.

This cauterizing of infatuations was part of the weekly routine.

There were two hours set aside every Sunday evening for the brothers to air their attachments, name them, tame them, be rid of them. It was easy to get attached. I had felt the tug in my very first weekend. I had felt like cleaving to my two shadows, the two witches of giving, each possessed of hands and mouths without count. Both had black hair, down to the waist. The eyes of one were the waters of Jhinjheri, and of the other the warm soil of the fields.

As I lay between them, I turned my head from side to side, filling my mouth with their yielding flesh. The two of them trailed their fingers through places in my body that produced sensations I had never known. For the first time since the motherhood, I felt a woman's breath on my skin. And I became aware of its power to intoxicate beyond the finest Ferment.

At that moment, despite the warnings of the Pathfinders, despite the warnings of my brothers, I felt a tenderness begin to power through me. I became filled with the need to say soft things, to squeeze soft hands, to gaze into soft eyes. I knew how dangerous this was. I struggled to rein myself in. I was aware of the shame that would fill me when I confessed to my brothers that I had stumbled at the very first step.

The wait to the next Saturday was excruciating. I had to work to master myself, find the heart of meditation even when not at meditation – in the class, in the fields, in the workshop. At every moment, I found the dark-haired shadows with blue eyes and brown eyes, with soft hands and softer mouths, waiting for me. During meditation too it took some time before they could be pushed out completely, and the mind stilled.

As was expected of me I told my brothers about it. They understood. They said it would take a few weekends and a passage through different shadows before it began to settle. They said the first explosions of the body always generated the maximum sentimentality. It was how in the other world, out there, men and women fell prey early to perilous stupidity and never recovered. What they then tried to paint as virtues – constancy, love, devotion – were merely a delusion of the body. Inevitably, it passed – but not before it had made a shambles of everything.

Aum understood the mind, the heart and the body. And he knew well how each could subvert our true selves. Make us less than we were.

Even so when I went back the next Saturday I found myself looking for the same shadows, and when I saw them I wanted to reach for them. I noticed they were older than most of the others. The one with blue eyes was perhaps not too far from getting a face and being granted permanent motherhood. For a moment I thought she wanted me too – something in the way she looked at me. But I tore my eyes away and went into the other room where many of my brothers had already become creepers. Some oaks had more than one creeper tangled around them, and some creepers were tangled with more than one oak.

I found a young one sitting in a corner and addressed her boldly with my hands and mouth. It was my first lesson in the limitations of youth. She was not without expertise or enthusiasm, but she was a little rough and low on pleasure. The night passed in howling but I was aware I had been served poorly – for the future – by the special wonders of my initiation.

In the coming months all such concerns would be rendered irrelevant. Like my brothers, I'd end up twining myself around every oak, and I'd find that while the shape, size and girth of each might differ, they were all made of the same material and fundamentally fit to be used for the same thing. In fact to have no idea what would fall to one's lot each weekend created a sense of edgy anticipation.

I am sorry I have omitted explaining something important – the madonnas of the Serai were not like us. They did not have a face. The limitless one, the knower of all things, Aum, had understood it was impossible to cure us of the seductions and sentimentalities of the body unless we were exposed to the challenge of many. In time any man can become immune to the allure of one face. The triumph of the pure was to acquire an indifference to the charms of a thousand.

Thus it was that the most beauteous of girls were earmarked early for the educations of the Serai. Scrupulously tutored in the rites of pleasure, even the newest novice in the Serai – a girl of fifteen, with tendrils for hair and the flesh still thickening on her limbs – had a profound knowledge of both pleasure and a man's body. If she wished she could make a man – or men – howl through the night, again and again. Aum wished them all to be virtuosos, so we would test ourselves against the greatest of pleasure and yet remain uncompromised.

But just as with us, it was not merely about what the body must do and can do, more about what the mind must know and understand. Like us the women too were embarked on the road to freedom. Aum said that in the world out there men over millennia had forced women to make exclusive temples of their bodies. By declaring her body sacred they had shut it down – all its needs, energies, possibilities. So a woman spent the prime of her life contending with her body and lost out on all else. What was divine about a woman, said Aum, was not her body but her inner force. When a woman allowed her body to flow in the untrammelled way a river does, she became free of it. The body was now just another need, like thirst and hunger and sleep. To be routinely dealt with. No more defined by her body, she could open the portals for her true inner force – the primal energy that women alone possess – to come powering through, illuminating and enhancing the entire world.

In the way it was with Alaiya.

Be clear then, that in the Serai of Fleeting Happiness, it was not just us going beyond the imprisonments of the self, it was also the women. Through the thrashing of limbs, through the infernal howls, we were all moving towards an ideal that the master had set for us.

For some reason, none of this proved true for Arjuna of the conqueror's chin. Contrary to appearance he turned out to be woefully weak. To begin with he suffered greatly with the face. At all times you could see him feeling it with tentative fingers, tracing its contours. He would peer into anything that caught his reflection, and move his neck to catch himself in different profiles. It was abject.

One night I woke suddenly to see him sitting at the edge of his bed, clutching his face and sobbing. I was appalled. The fool had learned nothing in all these years. I called out softly, then hissed, hoping he would stop. If the others woke it would become a night of cringing shame. Instead his body began to shake with louder sobs. I got off the bed and slapped him. So hard that he fell off the bed.

In the dark a few voices muttered. For a moment I was afraid. I thought he was going to jump up and hit me back. And he was big, taller than all of us, with wide shoulders. Instead he just curled up in a ball and began to cry. I became nauseous. Nothing! He had learned nothing! All the wisdom of Aum had flown past him like wind under the wings of a bird. It was men like him, full of weakness, who threatened the vision of the master. I kicked him, and my toes caught him in the crack of his buttocks. He gave a loud grunt, rolled over, and lay still.

The next morning I cornered him in the woods after meditation. He was limping a little and trying to avoid my eye. I thought, he can cripple me with one blow but he is such a coward. I knew then – and it has never been proven untrue – that size has nothing to do with strength. I demanded an explanation for his sordid conduct.

He was all scrunched up, his fingers nervous on his nose and mouth. He said he was unhappy. He didn't like the face. He wanted his old one back. I almost hit him again. This is your face! I hissed. There is no other! You are unhappy because you have understood nothing! You are unhappy because you haven't understood why you've been gifted this beautiful face! You are like the men out there – trapped inside the circle of your own selfishness! In the vanity of your own face! You bring shame on yourself and all your brothers!

The fool began to cry. I kicked him once, twice, three times. Each time he yelped, sending the crested bulbuls fluttering from the trees. I said, I knew a boy once, at the home. He thought he wanted

to find his father. He thought if he found his father his life would
be perfect. Then he thought he had found his father. I saw what
happened to him. You want to know what happened to him? The
father he thought he had found picked him up and quartered him!
We never again heard about him! You think you have a lovely face?
Well, he thought he had a lovely voice!

As I saw him cower I understood what Aum had really been up
against. My father, my face, my voice… Mine, myself, me… Men
untutored, men left to themselves, men not challenged to seek their
true depths, such men were only animals, pursuing nothing but
shallow vanities.

This idiot was so tormented by the loss of his old face that he fared
poorly even at the Serai. In the beginning he sulked, attempting to
hold his body back. The shadows of the Serai, however, knew how
to commandeer and consume even the most reluctant. But within
minutes, each time, he managed to slink back into his shell. As the
rest of us howled like jackals I could see his big silhouette slumped
in a chair, motionless.

Later his tack changed – for the worse. He embarked on the
absurd road to sentimentality. Every week he would go to the Serai
and attempt to forge a relationship. I would see him in a corner
trying to talk to one of the girls. If she slipped away he would look
to corral another. I tried to talk to him several times – kicking him
as I spoke – but he appeared to lack any quality of self-examination
and correction.

Then some months later everyone began to notice he was spending
all his time with the same girl. She was very young, had red-black
hair that fell to her shoulders, and a shy smile of crooked teeth. I
don't think she had been put to mothering yet, and when I asked
around of my older brothers – some of whom had howled with her
several times – it was confirmed her belly had not been distended
even once.

Every Saturday evening, from the moment he entered the Serai,
he would isolate her in a corner. While the rest of us twined and

untwined ourselves around different oaks, the two of them would hold hands and rub faces. Even when they howled, I noticed, it was different from us. It was low and intense and murmurous. Also, they talked. It was not possible to hear what they said, but you could see them talking. It was impossible to imagine about what. I could never find anything beyond three sentences to say to any of them.

As I saw him do this, I began to fear for him. He was turning into a bigger fool with every passing day. He had been with me in the cradle and the home. There were no signs then of the coming foolishness. In fact, the Pathfinders really liked him. Some called him an intellectual, a Pathfinder in the making. Others looked at his strengthening limbs and said he would go even further; one day he would be a leading sentinel of the faith, a great Wafadar.

At the time I looked up to him. He was the first among us to master all nine books of the peerless one, and he could discuss them with the Pathfinders. So good he was, so ahead of all of us, that sometimes they left it to him to lead us through the catechism. I was proud to be his friend. I wanted to be Ali to his Aum. To stay by his side, cherish him and guard him.

And then, one day, I got an early warning that all was not well, that his mind was beginning to capsize. Two years earlier, one Saturday evening, when all our older brothers were at the Serai, and we were walking through the woods next to the Jhinjheri, he said to me, without looking at me, Sometimes I think about life out there. Wouldn't you like to go there once? I said, If you become a Wafadar, you will. He said, No, not as a Wafadar. Just.

I was nonplussed. It was not something that had ever crossed my mind.

That night as we lay in bed I said to him, in a low whisper, What made you think like that? He said, I was just wondering. I said, You know what Aum has said. Even a few drops of oil in water make the water impure. And once the two are mixed, they can never be unmixed. He was quiet for a long time. I was almost asleep when he said, And what if you don't mind some oil in your water? I said in a hiss, Then you are no longer pure. You don't belong with the pure. You are oil and water, no longer pure water. You deserve to be thrown away.

Next morning I felt him avoiding me. But I had not forgotten what he'd said. I cornered him. He always called me Karna-bharna – what you do is what you get. I didn't mind it. He said, Karna-bharna, I am only doing what Aum said, thinking hard. I said, No. You are thinking loose. You are doing what Aum said you must never do! It's what men out there do – think loose, live loose! And thereby bring to ruin everything! Each man out there is digging his own shallow hole of thinking – and finding nothing but worms! The whole world has been pockmarked and still there is no gold of wisdom! You know that the one and true master has dug deep for all of us, deeper than anyone ever can, and he has found the mine of infinite wisdom. The rest of us have only to travel down that shaft. We have to dig, but only in his footsteps!

I felt exalted by my own words. I had said it well. I felt one with the beauty and glory of Aum. I felt worthy of the unequalled one.

Arjuna of the chin was, however, trapped in a bog of ignorance. But the world has so many of everything. Trees, birds, plants, animals. Why should it have only one mine of gold, one mine of wisdom?

My anger spiralled. Yes! But is the wood of every tree firm and good? Can you eat every plant without tempting grief? Does every bird fly equally high? There is one great mine of truth and wisdom, and the master has found it for us! You discover the sun once, you discover the moon once, you discover gravity once. Then you move on, taking it as a verity. Only fools keep looking to find what has already been found.

He was looking away. I caught his conqueror's chin and yanked his head around. I knew then, two years before we got the face and gained entry into the Serai, that he had begun to slide down a slippery slope.

I said, The truth has already been discovered for us. We have only to follow it and celebrate it. Not rush about all our lives, looking for something that is right in front of our eyes.

DEGRADATION

If you started at sunrise and walked steadily along the banks of the Amrita as it ran down the centre of our valley, you reached the other end by sunrise the next day. At the start of its journey, the divine river tore out of the wall of brittle rock at the bottom of our land, and fell with a thunder of spray into the wide pool of stones below. Anyone standing under it had their skull and bones smashed in mere seconds. At the close of its journey, Amrita vanished into the ground, again with an infernal roar, just under the Pass of all Hope, which was secured day and night by the peerless Wafadars. If you fell into the waters here you disappeared into a netherworld from which there was no return. There were stories of intruders who over the decades had been thus dispatched by our great guardsmen. It was said that in the world out there men dreaded the weeping crack in the mountain for none was said to have come back, dead or alive, from its wet embrace.

In the time of Aum, the river had been decreed a marker. On one side lay the Realm of Learning and on the other the Realm of Doing. Since the all-knowing master knew that absolute freedom was based on absolute discipline, he had left us with delicate norms. With good reason denizens of the adult realm could enter our side but we were never to cross the liquid boundary. Just as a tree cannot bear fruit before it has matured, a boy cannot become a man before his time.

In the wisdom of Aum this time began at eighteen. It did not mean each of us crossed over to the other realm at this age. We had to be ready; we had to ripen with fruit. Many of us took time. In the barracks some of our brothers were well over twenty years old. The Pathfinders worked extra hard with them. A few of us, of course, would never make it. There are trees on which the fruit will never bloom. It does not mean they are without a use. These brothers were absorbed in running our realm, in helping at the cradle and the home and the barracks; in the kitchens and in the woods; in the fields and in the training workshops.

It was the infinite beauty of Aum's vision – the perfect equality and anonymity of just one face – that no one ever suffered the humiliation of inadequacy or rejection.

Alone among the brothers born of my year I was picked for the crossing when I turned eighteen. I had to present myself to the jury of Pathfinders – five of them – under the Bodhi at the precise moment of first light. It was the sacred moment – when Aum first unveiled the promised land.

I was not nervous. Each day at the home, each day at the barracks, I had endeavoured to be worthy of my people. I had burnt into my brain every word of my teachers – the nine books of Aum, the narratives of Alaiya, the stories of Ali; every injunction, exhortation and wisdom of the timeless master. In the presence of my gurus I had been nothing but a giant ear.

In meditation I had achieved a rare perfection. In a moment I could still every cell of my being, make my mind empty as a desert, stop the beating of my heart, and enter a zone of perfect calm, beyond life and death. At such a time fire could not scald me, nor snow make me numb.

As for my body, it was not big, but I had pushed it and pushed it till it was second to none. I had understood that like the mind the body too has few limits. It can keep going long after you imagine it can go no further. So I'd never stopped. Hours after the training sessions were over and everyone had repaired to the barracks, I would keep running, keep climbing, keep punching, keep swimming, keep exercising, keep twirling the sword and the stave, keep at every drill of defence and offence, over and over.

Every hour that my brothers took off I would use not just to hone my sinews, but also to school my senses to match those of a forest predator. I would wander the woods at a rapid pace with a tight blindfold over my eyes and my elbows close to my hips – willing to suffer injury if I could not master sightless navigation. For months I bruised and scarred my body, but I refused to relent. And then slowly, a third eye began to open in my forehead. I began to sense – like a dark physicality – trees and bushes and dips in the ground. I would be walking in the complete blackness of my blindfold and through the blackness suddenly I would know there was something ahead and I would swerve.

In time my hard work in the woods woke in me greater animal gifts. Not only did a third eye open in me but also a third and a fourth ear. In the open I could hear the crack of a twig and the rustle of a leaf from hundreds of feet away. Even the feathery paw of the big cat – which cannot be heard even when it is seen – did not escape me. At night, lying in my bed, I knew everything that each brother of mine was doing. Sometimes, in distress, I would push the sheet into my ears to shut the sounds out.

This was not acumen to be developed in the barracks. This was the rarified territory of the Wafadars. But that was where I had always dreamt of going. And it was never too early to start to prepare. As I presented myself before the jury under the Bodhi, I was sure I had left nothing to chance.

I was the first to ascend the platform where I had imbibed knowledge and wisdom since I was a small boy. No fingertip of light had touched the horizon when I heard, amid the scruffing and chirring of birds and insects, the footfalls of the gurus. Silently, without exchanging a word, the Pathfinders settled down on the five rocks arrayed in a semicircle. This was solemn business. There was no greater step in any life than to cross into the realm of doing.

I sat on the ground, cross-legged, ankles at the waist, bare but for my loincloth. I knew the pre-dawn breeze was icy, because there was a time when I'd huddle against it. Now I felt nothing. I had two weapons, my mind and my body. I could shut it out with either. I used just my body; my mind focused on the test ahead. The Pathfinders were in their tight pajamas and double tunics, their feet in deerskin slippers. For the occasion, each wore a short, two-eared cap on the head.

We waited in silence. When light drew its first line in the skies, one of them said, What is the source of all light?

I said, The truth.

He said, What is the source of all truth?

It is Aum.

Another voice said, And what is Aum?

Aum is the truth that resides in me.

And what are you?

I am a soldier of the truth.

Why does the truth need soldiers?

Even the gods need prophets.

Prophets do not take up arms.

True prophets do. There is no other way.

No other way for what?

To take on the armies of untruth. The great battle demands not just words but also warriors.

What do you know about the armies of untruth?

In the world out there, each day, the armies of untruth multiply. On their standard is emblazoned – me, mine, myself. Their holy book is the song of greed and possession. Their vision is dangerous and impure. They are the opposite of everything that is god.

And what is god?

God is giving, god is grace, god is courage, god is non-possession, god is sharing, god is equal. God is the pure. God is the truth. God is Aum.

If god is Aum and Aum is the truth that resides in you, are you too god and are you too Aum?

No! Aum is the ocean, Aum is the air, Aum is the soil. I have a tiny bit of it, but I am not it. None of us are it. None of us can ever be it. It is, and can only be, Aum: the fullness of truth, the distillate of purity.

And you are content merely to be its soldier?

I am honoured to be its soldier. I am exalted by it.

And so it went for more than two hours, without a moment's pause. Before I would finish answering one guru, the next would begin. They came at me from every angle, using logic, rhetoric, cunning, and had I not been so steeped in the truth of Aum I might have stumbled. I knew many of my brothers had, some mirage of doubt giving them the trip. It's what the jury probed you for. The presence of one locust of doubt, the smallest locust of doubt, could swiftly multiply into a million. In no time the spirit of the faithful could become a tattered fabric. For the pure there was no greater threat than the locust of doubt.

How could you embark for the realm of doing if you were not yet done with the realm of learning?

The light grew behind me, eating into the circle of darkness beneath the Bodhi. All the five faces in front of me were one face, every eye still.

The inquisition did not pertain to truth, purity and god alone. It tested my knowledge of the nine books of Aum – with their stories of the world – and of the tales of Ali and Alaiya, and their account of both the master and the great march. I was asked odd questions about the cradle and the home and the barracks and the face and the Serai of Fleeting Happiness. Also about our valley and my brothers, about Arjuna of the chin and fat Bhima who used to sing. The questions followed no pattern – anyone can block the expected arrow. Finally I was asked about the Wafadars. Long before you become one in the flesh, you had to be one in the spirit.

The sun had taken the dew off the grass by the time the jury dismissed me. I left full of confidence, but far from certain. I knew of exemplary brothers who had not been given the nod. Sometimes even the best of us fail to see the chinks that enfeeble our armour. We do not possess the microscopic eye that can spot the germ of doubt.

I knew it, and in a few days it was confirmed to me. I was unequivocally of the pure.

I bid goodbye to my brothers in the barracks with great love but without a trace of sentimentality. It was an abject failing, the great master had taught us, in anyone, but especially in a soldier and in a saint. In the world out there men were continually sick with sentimentality. For their children, their parents, their spouses, their lovers, their friends – some in a vague, weepy way for all living things, plants, animals, everything.

The world out there, we knew, was full of faux masters who actually encouraged such foolishness in their flock. They bred a weakness that pulled away from the truth. In this they were aided by a culture that celebrated sentimentality. Men could not see for the tears in their eyes. They could not speak for the lump in their throat. It was a strategy of enslavement: sentimental men were easily controlled, easily manipulated. For the sake of sentiment, a man will abandon the true path in the blink of an eye.

The first thing I learned when I crossed into the realm of doing was how little I had so far learned. The difference between theory and praxis is greater than that between a seed and its tree. I thought I knew all there was to know about the ego, non-possession and the body. Under the Pathfinders, in the firmness of my resolve, I had mastered them, and set them aside. Yet, in the very first weeks I found myself confronted by them all.

Instead of being welcomed into the camp of the Wafadars, to be trained to be a jewel among jewels, I was taken by a squat brother – who spoke no more than five words to me – to a farmers' kitchen, and put to toiling in the scullery. To begin with I was not even allowed to go near the food or the cooking. All I had to do all day was to scrub and clean the pots and pans, the plates and glasses, the spoons and ladles. In eighteen years, through the cradle, the home and the barracks, this had never been asked of me, and I had no facility with it.

Rising well before dawn I had first to carry buckets of water from the Jhinjheri – two at a time, balanced on the ends of a stick – and top up the wooden trough in the kitchen backyard. If I had not done the dinner dishes at night they would be waiting for me, heaped high. The choice was mine. Stay up and finish them before the grease and gravy had congealed, or retire in time and labour harder next morning. Whatever I chose, everything had to be cleaned, dried and put back on the shelves before the cooks arrived.

The washing was done at ground level, and one had to squat between the sink and the water trough, working both arms continually. After I soaped and rinsed each piece, I had to half hop forward to place it to dry on a slatted table. Later I had to scrub each one spotlessly dry. As I ran this routine several hundred times, several times a day, I began to understand how different it is to bend the mind and push the body for lofty reasons rather than for something so prosaic.

In a few weeks with growing self-disgust I realized that the irritation and fatigue creeping up on me was a clear sign of how unfinished my education was. I was far from living up to Aum's selfless ideals. And I was far from being a master of my mind or body.

Ruthlessly, the cooks tested both all day. They would keep sending back scores of dishes for re-washing, some with barely a discernible daub. Often I felt one of them deliberately splashed some curry over a stack of plates just as I was getting up to straighten my back. If I ever asked a question I fetched either a stony silence or a barked insult. None of them called me by my name. A few called me boy; the others referred to me as an insect.

I would scarcely finish the breakfast heaps – wash, dry, put them back – than the cooks would start to shout for me to scrub the floor of the kitchen. Then there was the laundry, including the tunics and grimy vests of the cooks. By the time this was done a fresh line of pots and pans would begin to arrive as lunch got under way; and then by afternoon there would be such a pile of dirty dishes that more than half would be heaped outside the sink. Some nights I could barely lift my arms by the time the dinner debris began to roll in.

In the early weeks I was often so infuriated I wanted to lodge a protest, to inform someone that something was terribly amiss, that I had been sent to the wrong place, that someone needed to check with my Pathfinders. The problem was I didn't know whom to ask. The thickset brother who'd brought me here I never caught sight of again, and the cooks were brusque when they were not insulting. Each time I tried to engage them in a conversation they rubbed the air with their hands and pointed me to the trough.

The dining hall was out of bounds for me, so I didn't know who ate there, and if they were more open to a dialogue. The thickset brother – who had picked me up when I crossed the river – had made it clear to me, in the five words he spoke, that I was to stay here till he came back to fetch me. In the meantime I was to do whatever the kitchen demanded. Wordlessly, one of the cooks had shown me a narrow bunk in a room in which firewood was stored. It was an old shed, at a remove from the kitchens, its windows blocked by big logs. Light entered only in slivers and pinpricks. The chopped pieces of wood lay everywhere, not stacked like the logs but heaped like sand. My bed – the lower one – was clean, the mattress and duvet folded at one end. The upper one was overloaded with an assortment of pots, pans, and containers of salt, sugar and tea leaves. All night, through my weariness and distress, I could hear rodents and other insects scraping and grinding above me. It was not uncommon for them to go bounding over my unstirring body.

Many times each day I told myself I was being tested. It was the way of Aum, the way of the pure, to never see oneself as a finished project, to never rest on one's accomplishments, to always push the frontiers of mind and body, to continually examine the spirit's resolve. Just as the face made us all equal beyond the vanities of fleeting beauty, beyond the comparative anxieties of nose and lips and eyes and skin, this daily humiliation at the scullery was designed to run a steaming iron over my ego. To flatten its false ballooning, to remind me that all of us were equal, and that even one destined to be a Wafadar must have the equanimity to clean the offal of mere farmers.

I told myself this all the time, but as the weeks rolled by I went from anxiety to wise acceptance to being convulsed by anxiety once again. As I lay in bed every night, my arms aching, the nails of my fingers jammed with the grime of food, my nostrils assailed by the dank odour of the shed, my trained ears alert for the rustle of a snake or a scorpion, I was hit by waves of panic.

Was I the victim of someone's mistake? Someone careless who had forgotten that I existed, or where I'd been sent? I knew all information in the valley of the pure was on a need-to-know basis. A principle designed to contain the self-aggrandizing delusions of so-called free societies, where everyone assumes a pose of great knowledge without possessing any. Was it possible the brother who'd sent me here had since been dispatched on another assignment? Or perhaps he'd suddenly passed on to his next life. And no one even knew I was here, a man marked by the Pathfinders as a future Wafadar, now scrubbing dirty plates from dawn to midnight.

A few times I considered running away. It was not difficult. The kitchen backed into a stretch of thick woods, full of deodar, pine, oak, cedar, surai and morpankhi. The picket fence at the boundary was a mere four feet high, the stakes sharp at the tip to keep the animals out. Of course it was nothing for me. I could take two steps and jump clear of it – perhaps even do it from a standing position. And there was no animal in those woods that could get the better of me, even in the black of night. I was not yet a Wafadar, but I was also not a scullery boy. In fact I knew if I wanted I could walk out the front door and all the cooks put together would not be able to hold me back.

And yet I was intuitively aware that would be a blunder. For even as I worried that I had been mislaid in transit, another part of me was sure I was under scrutiny, undergoing some rite of passage. Its true meaning would be revealed to me one day – beyond what I already assumed: the negation of the ego, the assertion of the equal dignity of all labour. I fretted because these were values already deep in me. I did not need to scrub dirty dishes endlessly to re-learn them. The big cat kills when it needs to eat. It doesn't kill just to practise how to kill. It carries the perfect impulse in its every follicle.

Yet I held my hand and stayed with the task.

Soon I gave up trying to speak to the cooks, and reaching inside myself for old lessons, began to work on centring my mind till it became a beautiful white space unblemished by anger, irritation, weariness. Now cleaning the greasy dishes became an act of joy, a wonderful cleansing of the world. I felt it as a fine dance, the rhythmic choreography of pouring, scrubbing, pouring, drip-drying and shining. As each used piece passed through my hands and was born anew – ready to do fresh service – I felt a sense of satisfaction, even pride, fill me. The cooks and their brusqueness no longer enraged me. Once again I began to feel worthy of Aum, my mind pure and still, my resolve undiminished.

There was a soaring story unfolding here. Perhaps I did not know all of it, nor ever would. But I had a role to play in it. I had to ensure my character held fast. After all, one delinquent can undo an epic.

Late one night I was woken from my sleep by the sound of footfalls. I closed my eyes and listened. Beyond, in the woods, were the hard hooves of a wild pig and the feathery paws of a few jackals; and much farther, a deer was rubbing its antlers on a tree. Around me, in the shed, was the busy traffic of rodents and insects, and just outside, the stop-and-start rustle of a wolf snake. In the middle distance, coming from the cookhouse towards me, was the pad of human feet. There were two treads, one light, the other heavy.

I opened my eyes: a thousand darts of moonlight punctured the shed. When the door was pushed open I half-closed my eyelids. Behind the two men standing in the doorway the night was silver-blue. As they stood there trying to penetrate the shed's darkness, I could see their faces were in need of a fresh coat. I could not tell who they were. One of them was broad and short, the other tall and thin.

My heart was pounding, but in a moment I had stilled it. Fear is the only animal in the world that grows by feeding on itself. We had been taught that in the world out there, the leaders of men had an entire science of fear with which they kept other men in thrall. Aum said, when as a seeker in his teenage years he visited the ancient city of worldly departures set by the mighty holy river, he was told by everyone that he must feed and furnish the priests in order to earn good karma. When he asked who had said it should be so, he was told it was the decree of the priests themselves!

Aum said he left the city where divinity flowed like water with a weeping heart, forever convinced that men use fear to make a commerce of the sacred. He said men used power, money and god to stir the demon of fear in other men. The great master said that in many ways the dominant universal emotion was neither love nor hate nor greed. It was fear. And yet, said the peerless one, fear was nothing. It was not a line on the ground. It was merely a line inside a man's head. All a man had to do was to walk across this line inside his own head and he was free forever. Free of the empty terrors that men conjure up for each other.

The short, broad man said, You are awake?

I could smell the Ferment on his breath. A pleasant, bittersweet aroma, of apples and cloves. We all had to drink it four days every week, a minimum of two fingers and a maximum of eight; and once a month as much as your belly could hold. Aum had taught us that each brother must know intoxication, yet always be outside of it.

The body must know every ecstasy – as its divine right – but it must always be commanded by the mind, its sole overlord. I drank two, never more, and it made me content.

Without moving, I said, Yes.

He said, What is the difference between a cook and a Wafadar?

I said, Of occupation.

He said, What else?

I said, Nothing else.

He said, Who is the greater?

I said, The cook, when he is pure with the fullness of Aum, is greater than a Wafadar who is not. But in truth, they are equal, none greater. Each merely answers to his calling.

Now the thin, tall man spoke, his voice a deep baritone. What is the body?

I said, The body, if not an instrument of the pure, is only a vanity.

He said, For what do the pure use this instrument?

I said, To pass through fleeting pleasure to the true purpose beyond.

He said, What is the difference between the body of a cook and that of a Wafadar?

I said, Nothing – except in their purpose.

He said, Is one more sacred than the other?

I said, No. Each merely answers to its calling.

The short, broad man said, Why do we wear the face?

I said, To kill the first and greatest source of unequalness.

He said, But looks are the gift of life.

I said, No, they are its greatest curse. A decoy and a distraction. They are the crucial test set by divinity that all men fail. In the garden of looks bloom envy, ego, anxiety, covetousness, vanity, bitterness, lust and despair. In the garden of looks bloom the seeds that first destroy the brotherhood.

He said, What then of the body?

I said, Freed of the monumental falsity of looks, the body becomes an unfettered instrument of the pure, wedded to nothing but its greater purpose.

He said, To whom then does the body belong?

I said, Always to the brotherhood, to its true purpose.

He said, Is this true for our sisters too?

I said, In spirit and in principle, yes.

He said, If the body is the brotherhood's and the mind Aum's, what is it that is our own?

I said, The pure know they are like the air – which is everywhere and is forever giving of itself. Does the air need people to survive, or is it the other way around? Even the unwise know the answer to that.

The other man said, So the pure belong to everyone?

I said, No, only to the brotherhood and to Aum. But like the air, they serve everyone – without discrimination.

As we spoke, the short, broad man had pushed the door shut, damming the chill wind that had been lacerating the shed. The moonlight went dead too, and in the one moment it took for my eyes to adjust I realized he had taken off his tunic and was unknotting his pajamas.

The baritone said, You have learned your lessons well, boy.

I said, Else it's not possible to fjord the Amrita. The realm of doing opens only to those who master the realm of learning.

The other man was now standing on one foot, pulling the pajamas off his feet. His legs were thick as trunks of pine. His belly swelled free of his undershirt. The shadow between his legs was long and fat.

The baritone said, But surely you know that the chasm between learning and doing is much more than the width of the Amrita.

I said, It is that very chasm I have set out to cross.

The short, broad man was now sitting on the edge of my bunk and had put his hand under my quilt. I caught it by the wrist. He was burly but my grip was iron.

The thin, tall man said, In the realm of doing is also the learning. You know what Aum said – each brother brings to his brothers the fruits of his experience, sharing them equally, without avarice or ego.

I said, As the great Arjuna did his beloved wife Draupadi, with each of his four brothers. He who learns from his brothers, he who gives all unto his brothers, attains to the pure and enhances the pure.

He said, You are not here to learn the washing of dishes.

I said, I am here for more.

He said, Every general must first be a soldier, every guru first a disciple.

I let go of the wrist, and like a released serpent the hand struck my body. I closed my eyes to enter the tranquil white space that always lay within me. The wild pig was now nearer the fence, while the foxes had moved deeper into the forest. Rough fingers were unknotting the strings of pajamas.

The tall man said, Beyond the body begins the wisdom of the soul. As Aum taught us, you have to burn through the body to find the true path.

I said, Those who imagine they can ignore the body and move beyond are fools. The body has always to be reckoned with. Else like lice in the scalp, it allows no calm. Its itch waxes and wanes but never disappears. You scratch and you bleed, you scratch and you bleed, and the scabs form and open, and form and open, and instead of an instrument of fleeting pleasure the body becomes an adversary dragging you back each time you try to go beyond.

The baritone said, The only way to move beyond the body is to burn through the body. The pleasure is a mere passage.

I opened my eyes. His legs were thinner than the broad man's arms. The shadow in his middle was moving. The hand under my quilt was hot and damp and relentless. The tall, thin man sat down near my head and began to caress my hair. Both of them smelled of food and spices – like the dishes I washed all day. I did not recoil. It was a test. They were only cooks, but they were my brothers.

I nearly gagged when my mouth was taken. The broad man had vanished under the quilt. His face was cold on my skin. Soon I found myself on my stomach. I closed my eyes, reaching for the white space in me. As I was diffusing in its tranquillity, a burning stake tore through it, and I heard myself moan. All the white lay shredded incarnadine. Each time I put my white space together the burning stake would shred it. Yes, this was a test. I dug deeper within myself, deeper than the night, deeper than the pain, deeper than the stake, till I had found a pool of rippleless white in which I could fully drown myself.

The two things became my day and my night: the scullery work and the pleasure of my brothers. I understood fully now why I had been sent here. In the realm of doing, selflessness and equality had to be understood not just as fine principles but as lived actions. There was no dish in the cookhouse that did not pass through my hands dirty and emerge shining, and there was no worker in those kitchens who did not show up at the shed, one night or the other, with his body burning, and leave in the morning beautifully calmed.

Of course I suffered. It would be a lie to say anything else. There were nights when three or four of my brothers would arrive at the shed, badly aflame. The purging, the passage through pleasure, would last for hours. Each time it was a challenge to find the white space. I'd dig and dig, and would be still digging when the raging moment had passed. The nights that no one came by were rare, and they too left me sleepless, as I waited unknowing for a footfall, a nudge at the door.

There was no question, I was being tested. I was being steeled.

This became even more obvious to me when some months later I developed a virulent infection. The pain tore through my bowels, wringing my insides as you would a washed piece of cloth. An angry swelling made it impossible for me to sit, and even to lie on my back. In the woods, in the morning, I had to squat against a tree trunk, clutching my head, biting my lip, tears rolling down my cheeks. Afterwards, when I stood up, my legs shook like leaves in the wind.

Then came the fever. It felt as if fire had been set to my skin. My eyelids burned, and no matter how much water I drank my mouth remained parched and numb. I lay on my stomach, feeling the heat radiate from my body, my clothes damp with sweat. Without the quilt, I burned and shivered at the same time; with it covering me, I felt I would explode in a panic. So I put it over my midriff and stuck my feet out.

To begin with I did not stop working. It was a test. Aum had taught us that the limits of the mind and body lie way beyond what men imagine. Centring myself, shutting out the pain, I made my way to the back of the cookhouse every morning and laboured all day at the dirty dishes. The work arrived in cyclical heaps, and in between, I curled up next to the water trough and rested. Each time the spasm struck and my innards were twisted and my bowels throbbed I curled up into a tight ball and wept.

For many days I was proud of myself. I told no one of my affliction, and asked for no concession. Even at night, as my brothers arrived, I bit hard into my forearm, drawing blood, but sought no mercy. I knew Wafadars – like dauntless insects – kept fighting even after their limbs had been chopped off. Some of my brothers even remarked that I was hotter and more pleasurable than before. Then one day the fever took hold of me like an eagle does a rabbit, and shook me and shook me till I thought I was going to die.

When I could no longer even roll off my bed, my brothers came to nurse me. By now the fever had invaded my brain. I do not know how many days I drifted in and out of consciousness, but each time I came to, the shed door was open, the light was flowing in, and my brothers were looking at me. A few times I tried to get up, in panic that my scullery work remained unfinished, but I could not move a single limb, not one muscle.

In my delirium I thought I was being visited by the slim mother in the motherhood, and once again as she held me close her sharp collarbone dug hard into my cheeks. As she cradled me I felt I was safe and could sleep without anxiety that the dishes were unwashed.

I also heard the sad song of fat little Bhima. But I could not see him. He was standing on top of a mountain, with his back to me, but his voice filled the entire valley. I saw three big men with glinting scythes walking up the slope towards him, and I shouted to him to warn him, but he could not hear me and I could not save him.

And then I saw Aum.

I woke one night and found the shed was bathed in a luminous silver radiance. His hair and beard were long and the colour of snow, and his white tunic flowed like water to the ground. The light glowed from him, but his eyes were so deep I could not look into them. He put a hand to my forehead, and without opening his mouth said, My son. The voice seemed to come from everywhere, from all directions. I began to weep with emotion.

I knew then for certain that everything was a test. My degradation, the endless scullery work, the annexation of my body by my brothers, the rampaging onslaught of infection and fever – everything was a test, decreed by Aum, on the journey to purity and freedom.

HIGHER TERRACES

The alphanumber I picked for myself was X470.

I had no idea I would be given a choice, but I was offered three numbers, and I picked X470. The other two on offer were from the L series and the H series. I was influenced by the fact that the greatest living Wafadar of our time was an X.

We had heard stories about XX7 at the home and in the barracks. He was indestructible. He was the equal of a thousand men. He was the perfect warrior, and the perfect monk. No one knew how old he was. Some said he was a hundred and had been trained by Ali and Alaiya themselves. By getting two of his alphanumbers in my name, I felt I was somehow getting close to him.

Already I had decided that if I became a Wafadar I would take the alphanumber XY7. Only the Wafadars were allowed two alphabets and one numeral in their alphanumber. All other brothers had one alphabet and three numerals.

We were all equal, we were all brothers. But even among brothers there is a regard for the more than equal.

As with getting the face, I felt a sense of relief when I shed my name of Karna and became X470. It was a testimonial to my adulthood; to finally belonging to the realm of doing. I had been right. The scullery work, the pleasure burden, the raging fever, had all been a test. The new name was the reward, the badge of approval.

Many of my brothers from the barracks – out of habit, out of sentiment – continued to call each other by their old names. But I was resolute. If someone said Karna I refused to respond. In fact with deliberation I walked off in the opposite direction.

It was the teaching of Aum: new worlds could not be realized if the old were not shed.

I must make it clear it was not easy. It may seem as if I managed to walk through and past everything with nothing ever clinging to me. This is not true. I too had my moments of dangerous weakness, with the incubi of faux love and affection, of attraction and attachment, raging to seize control of me.

At the cookhouse, when the fever first ravaged me, testing me, there was a brother, C963, who nursed me back to strength. From the hair on his arm I could tell he was much older than me but not yet old. It seems he had volunteered to stay by my side. Each time I swam up from the hot dark depths, gasping for breath, beset by hallucinations, I found him waiting on the shore. He daubed my burning body with a cool flannel, and squeezed the juice of a tangerine into my parched mouth. It was in his strong arms, clinging to his neck like a baby, that I was carried out of the shed, so my body could do what it had to do.

Every brother does all he can for his brothers. But C963, it was clear, was doing more. In the hell of those weeks, there was not a single moment he was not by my side; there was not a single distasteful thing he did not readily do. I can still feel his hands – smooth and gentle – massaging my skin, bringing succour to my aching muscles.

When I was able to stand he would hold me by the upper arm and take me for short walks. He gave me the first bath by carrying canisters of hot water to the shed. While I squatted on a large stone, he poured the water over me and scrubbed me, asking every few moments if I wished for more or less of water or of scrubbing. Later he dried me with care, and put me back in my clothes.

By the time he leaned me back into my bed I was faint with exhaustion, but also overcome by a new kind of emotion. I found myself not letting go of his hand. He began to slowly stroke my forearm. I looked into his brown eyes and I wanted to embrace him, pull him down next to me, hold him close. But I passed out, and when I woke it was dark, and he was not by my side.

He was standing in the open doorway, looking out. From the thin slice of night sky visible to me I could tell it was just before midnight. I had been asleep twelve hours. I wondered if he had slept at all. C963 – how fine his name sounded. No rough edges, so full and rounded. For the first time I realized how slim and tall he was. He stood there motionless, as if waiting for someone to arrive, and I lay there watching him for a very long time. Had I trusted in my limbs I would have crept out of bed and embraced him from the back.

Every moment of their lives the pure must feel gratitude. But as Aum had taught us it must never be an individual thing, never for a person. Our gratitude must be for the grand plan of the cosmos, the great design of things. It was this apprehension of the infinitely large that led to the negation of the ego; that continually validated the ideal of non-possession. Aum said, It is the study of the stars not the catechism of religions and classrooms that makes men humane. Astronomers never kill or claim – priests and historians do. We had been taught that, on the other hand, gratitude for the individual created the play of the ego. It set into motion transactions of emotions that created selfish units and destroyed the brotherhood.

I must confess, in my weakness, I forgot all my learning. I called out his name in a soft moan, and when he rushed to me, I held his hand and pulled him down till my face was in his neck, and his entire body – so slim, so supple – was entwined with the length of mine. What I felt at the time I could not fully comprehend then, and

I cannot fully describe now. I felt alive and exalted and grateful and desirous and calmed and stirred. All at once.

I held on to him long after the urgencies were over – something I had never done before, not in the barracks, not in the Serai. And then before I knew it, the urgency came on us again. And when it had passed, still did I cling to him.

The next morning when he went away to the cookhouse I lay in ache and emptiness, every moment an age. With a great struggle I crawled out of bed, found the canister of water and cleaned myself scrupulously in preparation. Twice, approaching footfalls quickened my blood, only to disappoint as other brothers from the kitchens came to bring me food. I became almost sullen at the deception. Then as I lay in bed watching the day die through the open door – the light first perishing in the woods beyond – I heard a tread, light of heel. C963! It was how he walked, on the balls of his feet.

For years after I was abject with shame at the way I felt and behaved in those months. By the time he showed up at the doorway I could not breathe, and my heart was so loud it filled my ears. When he knelt by the bed to test my skin for fever I put my hands around his neck and pulled him down and did not let go till he had fitted his body perfectly into mine.

In the dark, lying faithless on his arm, breathing him in, with my eyes closed I described to him the unfolding life in the woods. The snuffling wild pigs, the grazing deer, the sniffing jackals, the foraging nightbirds – each whisper and scuttle of the feeding life. I was thrilled to dazzle him. He had not even a passing acquaintance with the faculties I'd already trained myself in. For him, a cook in the cookhouse, the Wafadars were men who walked on water.

His waist was so delicate I held it all night.

In the morning when he left I was filled with a yearning, and simultaneously with a great self-disgust. I knew I had failed the master and myself. I knew I was allowing myself to ache for something more than the need of the body. Through the day I was riven. At one point, squatting outside the shed, I found myself writing his name in the mud with my finger. C963. The flowing curves, the promise of fullness. I was doing it in a trance, and when I suddenly woke to it I was so appalled that I scrubbed and stamped it in a frenzy of revulsion.

And yet as night fell and through the cacophony of nesting birds I heard the heelless tread I became completely breathless and light in the head.

Day after day I wrestled with ache and self-revulsion, and one morning a new deceit sank its hook into me. When my brothers came to check on my progress, bringing me breakfast and medicine, I found myself pretending to be more infirm than I was. Though the strength was back in my limbs, I lay there as if unable to rise, and when they spoke to me I answered in moans.

As the sun turned dark, C963 arrived on the balls of his feet.

When I had done this many days, one morning the cooks brought in the apothecary, a man clearly ancient even through his young face. With bony, shaking fingers he palpitated my stomach, chest and neck, prised open my eyes and nostrils and mouth, examined my genitals, and bent and straightened my limbs. Then he patted my forehead twice and went out. My brothers followed him. When they thought they were out of earshot, the apothecary said, His time is up. The germ has seized his insides. Any day now it will begin to feed in a frenzy. He may last a week or a year but his time is up. In our world or the other there is no antidote for it.

I was devastated. I lay in my bunk all day swinging between rage and despair. My trek to glory had not even begun. I had not yet touched the threshold of my true calling. Surely the purpose of my life could not have been a base scullery and this rodent-infested shed. Surely the excellence of my years at the home and the barracks were not meant to end in this nothingness.

Then as the afternoon wore on I began to think of Aum, and Ali, and Alaiya. The odds they had faced, the perilous journey they had undertaken, the new world they had discovered and designed. I saw the founding fathers and mothers, one hundred and eleven of them, stretched out in a thin but unbreakable line on the knife-edge of the highest of mountains, resolute in the truth. As I saw them march, their heads set against the icy wind, my rage began to subside and my despair to dispel.

Surely the spirit of the pure was more powerful than the strongest germ. Surely the knock of death was merely a gauntlet thrown to life. Surely the mind of the chosen could bend an apothecary's diagnosis.

Minute on minute a new courage began to dance through my veins. As evening fell, I rose from my bed and walking to the very edge of the yard, with a strength I had not felt in many weeks, I jumped over the four-foot fence and went into the woods. Tearing off a strip of my undershirt I tied it around my eyes, and centring myself till I was nothing but my senses, I began to rapidly walk.

Almost instantly the old purity and potency filled me. Negotiating the forest sightless was the only challenge to live for. On my success in mastering my senses rested the success of bigger things. The diminishments of my time at the scullery, the nightly invasions of my body by my brothers, the frivolity of my attachment to C963 — all of it sloughed off like the skin from a snake.

I strode with precision and without doubt, my third eye open once again. Always, at the last moment, the mass of a tree loomed hard and dark in front of my bandaged eyes and I was able to swerve and survive. Often, there was another and another and I turned and twisted and veered and swivelled, now and then grazing my shoulders and cheeks, but never faltering, never crashing.

My third and fourth ears were wide open too. I could hear every animal padding the forest floor, every insect strumming its limbs, every bird settling its feathers, and at the back, far away, the sounds of the cookhouse.

By the time I got back to the fence and took off my blindfold I was coated in a thick sweat. Immediately I fell to the ground and did two hundred push-ups without breaking for breath. Then I went to the tank and fetched a canister of water and standing naked outside the shed let it run ice-cold over my head. It was my first proper bath in weeks and standing there under the night sky, wonderfully warm after the chilled water, I felt fully alive once more.

That night, C963 tried to cradle my head and sobbed, saying, I heard about the apothecary. I slapped his arm away and flung him out of the bed. Instead of getting angry, he lay there, solicitous. I understand, he said, in a soft voice. But don't worry. It will be okay. Rising from the bed, I picked him by his shoulders and pushed him out the door. He resisted, but he was only a cook and I a Wafadar-to-be.

He said, I will be by your side, till the very end. I will take care of everything.

Banging the door shut on him, I said, If you come here again I'll break your bones.

I was still trembling when I lay down. What a fool I'd been! How could I ever dream of being a Wafadar if I fell to every trap that lay in my path? What was the point of mastering the ego by washing a mountain of dirty dishes if it took me only a moment to slide down the endlessly slippery slope of infatuation and attachment?

Had not Aum taught us that more men are undone by soft words than hard battles?

The memory of the things I'd been saying to C963 brought on a wave of nausea. I'd been tested and I'd been found wanting.

I knew he had not left. I could hear him outside the door, shuffling his feet. After a while he pushed at the door, but I had thrown the bolt. A little later, he knocked softly with his fingers; then sharper. Then he began to slap the door and call out to me in a tight voice.

It made me think of him moaning my name as we lay in bed. So wayward I'd been. How far I'd wandered from the path of pleasure. He was now beseeching, telling me I should not be so full of despair, begging to be let in. I jumped up and ripped open the door so suddenly that he fell to the floor. In one movement I caught him by the back of his tunic and threw him face down on the bunk and brutalized him, not for pleasure but in fury and in punishment. Each time he tried to say something I banged his head against the bed, and even as I was done I pulled him to his feet and shoved him out the door.

I slept well that night, my body and mind calm. I had pulled back from the very brink. Aum clearly had his hand over me.

It was depressing to discover C963 was a bigger fool than I had thought. Day on day he kept returning, imagining I was acting out of the despair produced by the apothecary's verdict. His intimate words made my stomach churn. I was violent with him. I cursed, punched, brutalized – but he took it for other things, not the rejection it was, and kept mewling softly.

Nine days later, in the evening, I took him into the woods and broke his neck. He was still talking softly about his feelings and my future when I caught his head at the forehead and chin and turned it all the way around. It made a satisfying crack.

You died because you allowed yourself to, not because the apothecary said so. After I had laid him down on the ground gently and righted his head – how long and slim his body was – I thought of removing his face to see what he had been born to, but I desisted. Even in death the sanctity of the face was inviolate.

I carried him across my shoulder and placed him neatly outside the threshold of the cookhouse. Within minutes a great uproar erupted as the news spread and everyone came tumbling out. It peaked when I informed them that the broken neck was my handiwork. No one knew what to do, and they backed away from me, muttering. They were my brothers but I could see why they were only cooks.

I walked back to the shed, and standing naked in the dark I emptied a canister of cold water over my head. My skin sprang alive, and a joyous mood of liberation filled me. I felt I had cleansed myself of a terrible taint. I felt wonderfully strong. I knew now that everything – since I crossed the Amrita – had been a test, including C963.

A few hours later I heard many footfalls coming towards the shed. Since the bath I had been sleeping, with a rare calm. I waited, lying still. A sharp voice called my name. I did not recognize it. When I opened the door there was one brother standing in front of me, and some distance behind him, another six, their arms folded across their chests. As brothers do I embraced him on either side, touching my shoulders to his. He was taller than I was, and his face was in perfect condition – not like ours at the cookhouse, which were all in need of repair.

Pushing me aside, he walked into the shed and sat down on my bunk. His head almost touched the disused bed on top. I stood in front of him, aware that he was a brother more equal than others. The moonlight cut a lopsided rectangle on the floor.

He said, Tell me everything.

I did not spare a single detail. Not conceal a single thought or feeling. Among the pure, few things were worse than to not give trust. It took a while, but he didn't interrupt me even once. Outside, the six brothers stayed as I'd first seen them. When I'd finished breaking C963's neck, brought his body back, and returned to the shed, I stopped. I could hear the wild pigs near the fence. A whole family was scouring for food.

In his sharp voice he said, Did you do right?

I said, I believe so.

He said, To kill a brother?

I said, The idea is always bigger than the man.

He said, Why is that so?

He had the manner of someone who's been demanding explanations all his life. The cooks must have rung a very big alarm bell somewhere.

I said, We live to serve the truth, not men. The truth is unchanging, unbending, a constant. Men can falter, fail, lose their way.

He said, He was much older than you…

I said, The truth has nothing to do with age, shape, size, experience. It is a slippery fish in a raging stream. You can stand in the water all your life and never grasp it. And even if you do you could lose it in one moment of negligence. Before you know it your fingers have loosened and it has swum out of reach.

He said, It seems he cared for you. Very deeply.

I said, I did for him too. But not more than I care for the truth of the brotherhood. I could not bear to see his decline. As we know a dead brother is better than a diminished one.

I was not sure if he was there to arraign me or laud me. But I felt no apprehension. I felt strong. I knew I had done right. I had acted on the tenets of Aum. If for some reason unknown to me, punishment awaited me, I would cheerfully embrace it.

Standing up and walking towards the door, he said, But only the brotherhood is the judge of that. He walked past the men waiting as he'd left them, and they followed wordlessly in his wake like a loyal shadow.

I slept poorly. I examined and re-examined my actions. I thought what I had done was right. But perhaps I had been precipitate. Perhaps there was a different way of dealing with C963's abjection.

To centre myself, to cleanse my head, I went into the woods before dawn, tied the blindfold around my eyes, and walked. When I came back the sun was peeping over the peaks, my clothes were damp with sweat, and I was calm.

Outside the shed stood two brothers from the cookhouse. They had come to take me away. They waited while I bathed, and tied my few clothes in a tight bundle. Brothers have no other possessions. I took one last look around the derelict shed and was ready to go.

For the first time since I arrived here more than two years ago, I once again went through the kitchens, the dining hall, and out past the communal rooms into the front yard. Everyone turned to look at me.

The brother waiting for me by the gate was not tall but the set of his shoulders and the sculpture of his forearms made it clear he was not a man who cooked or cleaned. The way he held his body announced he was not a farmer either. I felt myself thrill as I realized he was probably the purest of the pure, the most loyal of the loyal, a holy warrior, a Wafadar.

We walked for six hours without breaking for food or water, and in that time my escort did not speak even six words to me. He walked ahead and I had to be brisk to keep pace. We went through woods of dark oak and sunny pine and orchards of apple in early bloom; forded gentle brooks and rushing streams; walked past fields of corn and potatoes, with scores of brothers working the crop lines. Every now and then I could see, far away, in the crease of the mountains, the silhouette of sheds, sending up fingers of smoke.

It was not easy to tell, but I had a sense we were walking in the direction of the Pass of All Hope, along the run of the Amrita, though I spied it only a few times, shimmering and speeding in the distance. This was my first taste of this part of the world, and I was filled with excitement. It was glorious to be out of the cookhouse and the shed, to be in the company of a warrior, and to be headed – hopefully – to where I belonged. I wanted to share my elation with my escort, to learn all I could about him, and to tell him all about myself. Each time we passed a group of brothers working the fields, each time I saw large sheds, each time I saw horses and livestock, I tried to provoke a conversation. I wanted to know where we were and where we were headed. But it was pointless. I could have been addressing a wall.

Later I felt shamed by my conduct. How could I ever hope to become a Wafadar if I lacked all restraint? How many times would I have to blunder before I understood the simple principle of self-containment? Men who warbled like birds were infirm beings hunting for affirmation. They could not be trusted with either trivial detail or eternal truths.

After six hours of walking the valley floor, I realized we were close to the foot of the mountains. Since we were walking through oak forests, it was not possible to clearly see the slopes. Then we came to a roaring stream that was crashing down from the rocks above and powering through a deep gulley into the trees below. It was the Jhinjheri, close to its source. Its fury sent shards of water high into the air, drowning out every other sound. Across its hundred-foot span lay the trunk of a pine, notched every six inches for traction. Running some six feet above it was a thick rope. The spray sailed through the bridge and rope ceaselessly.

Without breaking step or looking back, my escort stepped on to the pine trunk and kept walking. Nor did he bother to grip the rope. In a flash I knew I was under scrutiny. I did the same, with a quick shuffle adjusting my step to a shorter, surer one. The spray drenched me immediately, but I didn't look down, I didn't reach for the rope, and I didn't let fear touch my heart. In that one moment before I put my foot on the log, I had decided I would rather plunge to my death than be unworthy. If all my preparations of mind and body had still left me short, then it was best to perish.

I must admit to some pride. When my escort reached the other bank and turned around, I was right behind him, and I saw the surprise ripple his body. Later I would learn this was a test many had failed. Some had hesitated far too long, others had been smashed to death on the rocks below. It was called the trial by water, and it was widely acknowledged that only the pure made it without mishap. From that point we began to climb steeply. Within minutes we had entered a dense deodar forest and the huge ancient trees towered above us, blanking out the sun. Underfoot, the mulch was heavy and damp. The path we followed was barely discernible.

By now the roar of the cataract had faded, and we were moving through a deep silence. The occasional swifts darted past, and a great green barbet tore the quiet. My escort may not have suspected so, but I was keenly aware of the forest. I knew there were men lurking everywhere, from the moment we had crossed the angry stream. I had not been able to spy a single one, but that is how it is with the Wafadars. Sunbeams in the sun; shadows in the dark. The thought of them around me, invisible, soundless, watchful, thrilled me as nothing had in my entire life.

More than an hour later – the incline arduous, making my heart thump, reminding me of my sedentary time at the scullery – more than an hour later, we suddenly burst out of the dark forest into bright sunlight. It was late afternoon, and we were standing on a wide flat terrace, most of it neatly hoed and set to cultivation. Like an outsized stairway, step upon step of large terrace climbed up to another treeline far above.

Without pausing to regain breath my escort walked to the wall of the terrace and began to climb to the next. At the far end of the first terrace I saw a couple of wooden cabins, and men moving about. So it was for the first five terraces – cultivated rows and wooden cabins at the far end – and then we came to the sixth and the ground was flat and unbroken and the building was in the middle and not at the end, and it was not a wooden shed but a stone house, large, with a porch, and two chimneys sticking out of its head.

Inside, the man sitting on the chair had my face but it exuded an air of authority I had never seen in any of the Pathfinders. For more than half an hour, while I stood in front of him, he just looked at me without saying a single word. I don't know what he was reading – my body, my face, my temperament, my nerves – but I took it as a test, and stood unmoving, unblinking. Then he got up, opened the door and left, and did not come back for two hours. I stayed where he had left me. I knew by now it was a test.

Settling back into his chair he said, in a slow voice, What is the most valuable thing in life?

I said, Aum. The vision of Aum.

He said, And what is the least?

I said, My life.

He said, And what of the life of your brothers?

I said, They are far more valuable than mine.

He waited, and I added, But they are of far less value than Aum and the vision of Aum.

He said, And what is Aum?

I said, Aum is the truth. The inviolate truth.

He said, A Wafadar lives only to die. Why would anyone choose death?

I said, Death comes to us all. But to die for the truth is to be freed of one's karmic covenant. It is an opportunity. A Wafadar knows he lives if he lives and he triumphs if he dies.

It was dark by now, and the high slopes were alive with a million chirring insects and stirring animals. Every word I spoke would decide my fate. Since I first heard of the Wafadars as a child I had wanted to be nothing else in my life, and every minute of every day had been a preparation.

He watched me for some time. Then he got up and left the room, saying, Words are mere grass. Only action is fruit.

Nothing more happened that day. In the night I slept in the wooden shed at the end of the first terrace. The two brothers in there said nothing to me, and gave me some place on the floor. The hardness of the wooden planks didn't bother me but I had to crush a few scorpions before I settled in.

Next morning I was taken back up to the sixth terrace, to meet the same brother in the same room. All day he interrogated me intermittently. I stood in front of his desk unmoving, while he came and went, quizzing me to some random design.

I was questioned on facts – Ali, Alaiya, the long march; details of the other world, its history, geography, obsessions. Under the Bodhi I had been an unfaltering student, and there was nothing I did not know.

I was questioned on the abstractions of ethics and morality. Again and again he presented me a situation, and asked me to conduct myself through it. Many of these had to do with pleasure and the body. It was easy to see why. He obviously knew of my terrible failure at the cookhouse. C963! I'd break his neck again if it were possible.

Many of the dilemmas he posed had to do with conflicts of loyalty: between brothers; brothers and desires; brothers and the truth; desires and the truth. I think he knew every last thing about me. One situation he put to me had to do with a boy who sang too much, and was driven to hunt for his father. When the singing boy had been taken away by his supposed father who had a glinting scythe in his hand, and I had witnessed it from my hiding place in the thicket, he asked me what I would do now when I went back to the home.

I began to cry. It is true – my shoulders shook, and my nose began to run. Through my tears I told him everything. I had erred. I had sinned. I had let down my brothers, the Pathfinders, Ali, Alaiya, Aum. I was not worthy of standing here; of even dreaming of becoming a Wafadar.

He said nothing. He let me wail on till I was spent. Then he got up and left the room. By now my heart was so heavy I could scarcely stand. In my cowardice I had shamed everyone. They had trusted me, and each time they'd asked the question in the home and I had not answered, they had known I was lying. I could see now why I had been sent to the scullery; why I did not deserve anything more.

When he came back, he said, What should you have done?

I said, I should have spoken. From the moment my brother began to stray from the true path I should have informed the Pathfinders. Beguiled by the bird, I lost sight of the forest. I forgot it is the forest that harbours the bird, not the other way around. And at all times it is our first duty to protect the source rather than the seeker. I was weak, a coward. In truth I should have acted, on my own, to slice off the wings of my misinspired brother.

He said, You did none of this. What should your penitence be?

I said, Nothing is enough. My trespass is fundamental. It strikes at the very heart of our purity. And with each day that I have kept silent, I have compounded my sin. I can see that in Aum's peerless vision I am the kind of man who undoes great things by his fearfulness. No punishment is too great for me.

I felt the truth of what I was saying in my very bones. I wanted to immediately do something that would make apparent my bottomless remorse. An act of expiation beyond question: like jumping off the bridge into the killer cataract, or simply slitting my throat where I stood.

As if he were inside my mind, he said, You are thinking of dramatic things, like martyrdom. There will be time for that – but in the pursuit of Aum's vision, not in its flouting. Dramatic mistakes do not always demand dramatic atonement. When a bowl of honey has an ant in it we remove the ant, not throw away the honey. Sometimes a mistake only confirms us in what we must never do again.

I waited, sensing there was more to come.

He said, And what is it that you must never do again?

I said, Never put men before the idea.

He rose from his chair and embraced me, lightly, but as a brother, and said, You bow never to me but always to the vision, and then walking past me, he opened the door and left the room.

The next morning when I went up he was not in his room. I went to the edge of the terrace, found a large rock shaped like an egg, and sitting down on it, began to meditate. As my thoughts died I could hear the sounds below me – all the way into the forest – and above me, upon the hallowed terraces. In the flats I had walked through there was the sound of soil being ripped and raked, and the occasional idle word of the toiling brothers. Above me were mostly the whoosh of men's breath and the geometric slicing of the air with cold, sharp steel. I had never seen it, but I knew it was the sound of the Wafadars practising their poems.

All my life I had dreamt of this. Spending hours every day, mastering the metre of complicated moves. Any capable Wafadar is a master of at least six to eight different poetic forms. The simplest consists of only a few repetitive strokes: right blow, left blow, right blow, left blow, jab, jab, swipe. At the end of it, you can have a concussed body at your feet or a decapitated head – as you choose. Even ordinary warriors – like us at the barracks – can manage this simple lyric, but without anything approaching true grace and speed. A Wafadar can do it in his sleep, with one hand, as pure instinct, just as a bird takes wing at a sudden report. An assailant will be spreadeagled, on the point of death, before a Wafadar realizes he is joined in battle.

The more evolved poetic forms involve twists, feints, blows, jabs, swipes, flights, pivots, somersaults and pirouettes in complex patterns that take years to master and daily practice to keep sharp. Every day of the year a Wafadar spends four to six hours memorizing his poems, repeating and repeating them till they are like his breath.

Every movement of every form is precise, and each poem answers to the unique demands of the adversary. There are poems to take on three combatants, five combatants, and even ten and more. There is a poem to neutralize adversaries on horseback. There is one to be used against firearms; another to pulverize a mountain bear or a big cat. There are some that are meant to disarm and disable; and there are others that are intended to unleash sheer death and destruction.

In the main there are twenty-four poetic forms, but dexterous Wafadars are known to creatively push the metre of each of them to fit unexpected situations. The truly accomplished warriors are masters of twelve to fourteen forms, making them almost indestructible, in fair combat, by man or beast. A rare maestro has gone further, up to seventeen and eighteen – XX9, for example – but no one yet has commanded all twenty-four, the last of which allows you to withstand a hail of bullets, drop an elephant with a blow, and stop the charge of a small army.

As I sat on the rock with my eyes closed I could hear scores of poems being furiously written in the wind. There were no sounds of clash of steel, or roars and grunts of effort and aggression. That's the domain of ordinary soldiers. A Wafadar practises with himself, against himself, in supreme serenity. In battle, he does not react; consummately he sets the script and the adversary can do nothing but follow.

I do not know how long I sat in a reverie, immersed in the poems – aware that this could be as close as I would ever get to my life's dream. But I had spent the night steeling myself. I would not let a rejection be the end of the world. I was a son of Aum, a soldier of the pure. I would do, as best as I could, whatever was ordained for me. The greatest house is held up not by the roof, but by the stones that lie at its base.

A soft tread informed me my moment of reckoning had come. When I went in he was sitting unmoving with his hands folded over his lap. He asked me what I had been doing all morning. I said I had been sitting on a rock listening to poetry. It's never possible to be sure but I think I saw the mood in his eyes change.

It was then that he asked me to choose my name. One letter, three numerals. For a moment I was despondent. Was it then final? Was I not to be a Wafadar? Had all the hopes of my journey been in vain?

When I did not speak, he said in his deep voice, Till you prove yourself worthy of two numerals and one alphabet.

THE ROMANTIC BETRAYAL

I was still walking on air when the two brothers who shared my shed – on the lowest, the first, terrace – returned from their day's labours. I told them my new name, my alphanumber, and they loosened up and took me into their fold. I well understood their caution of the night before. It was meet, no different from how I would be with a newcomer. Every brother owes his every brother all cooperation, pleasure, even his very life – but intimacy and friendship have always to be earned.

As we lit a small bonfire by the shed – the forest of towering deodars just below us – I discovered they were as curious about me as I was about them. The reason was simple. I was going places as they never had; I was going to become what they never would.

As we roasted a crested pheasant on an open pit, they told me their stories. They had arrived here, in the highlands, three years apart, seeking the prize I sought. That was fifteen years ago, and they had been met by the same guru who had interrogated me. He was as masterful then, and more acerbic.

One of them said for a long time his bowels would loosen each time he came into his presence. The other said, Make no mistake. Even today he is no ageing great Helmsman. He is one of the legendary Wafadars of his time. As we speak, he could pass between the three of us sitting here and we would not know. With one hand tied behind his back he could toy with the three of us for hours and we would not be able to best him.

Slowly turning the glistening pheasant with the iron rod that pierced its heart, the first brother said, They say at his peak he was a master of seventeen poetic forms. At the time of the Romantic Betrayal, he was magnificent. It's difficult to believe it now, but for a few days it had seemed the traitors would carry the day. Then ZZ9 – that's his alphanumber – took over. He was like the raging wind – unseeable, untouchable, but battering the turncoats everywhere.

The Romantic Betrayal? I had never heard of it.

Testing the succulence with a sharp stick, the brother said, It was before our time. But when we first crossed the roaring cataract and came up to this terrace, it's all that everyone spoke of. It had already become a parable of rise and fall, of honour and disgrace. The Wafadar's name was QT2, and they said he was so superior, so gifted, that he was flying close to the sun and his wings were bound to burn. He was the youngest Wafadar ever. He crossed the bridge at eighteen, and was awarded two letters and one numeral before he was twenty. So luminous was he, so loved of everyone, that he was never sent to a scullery or the fields, or the orchards, or the foundry, or the workshop, or the piggery, or the stables. From the barracks he came straight here, and in a few years he'd become the equal of the greatest. You see those giant deodars. He could scale any of them in the blink of an eye, and move through their tops as a raven does. He was wiry as a whip, and moved faster than a lash. In battle six Wafadars could not contain him, and when he filled with fury he could lay low a dozen. At the time he was given recognition only for fourteen forms, but they say this was only to lend some modesty to his precociousness. His prowess already put him close to seventeen. There was talk he could end up at twenty-one – something no one had ever accomplished. You see these terraces?

I looked up. The terraces rose like giant steps, and woodfires pulsed in the dark. I could not see the terraces beyond the first eight or nine, though the sky was light grey in the light of a half-moon and it showed the trees on the mountain peak like short hair on a head. Beyond, the stars were thick and close.

Pulling the rod off the fire, the brother peeled a strip of the pheasant's roasted flesh, tasted it, nodded, and put it back to burn. Like us brothers, all Wafadars are completely equal, but some are more equal than the others. As you go up these terraces you come to greater and greater Wafadars – the peerless Helmsmen. Everyone said QT2 was destined to go to the very last, just below the clouds, just below the peak – which no one has seen, except he who has ascended to it.

I said, How far have you been?

He gave a short laugh, and in the light of the flames I could see his face was in need of repair. The nose had chipped and there were stains on the left cheek. No further than you have! he said. Just the sixth terrace – from where ZZ9 controls the interface of the upper and the lower worlds. It is exactly as it should be. The Wafadars are the purest of the pure, and each of us must strive to keep it that way. One drop of poison sullies the clearest pool of water – and then everyone suffers. If we wanted, the three of us could this minute start climbing and climb to the highest terrace. But what would we gain? All we would do is to ruin the purity of our own clear water. Has not Aum taught us that we destroy the best in us when we destroy the best amongst us?

I was stirred by his words. I hoped I would find in myself the same grace if I failed in my quest to become one of the purest of the pure. The forest was fully alive now. I could hear the scuffle of a bear. In these parts the bears feared men. Too many of them had been brutalized by the Wafadars.

I said, What happened to QT2?

They'd both torn a strip each off the burning pheasant and were chewing on it. You know what Alaiya always said. After they craft a perfect picture, the gods smirch it. Even when they cast the perfect man, they flaw him. Perfection challenges the gods. It deranges the possessor. Aum alone is the exception. The gods made him for a purpose…

Interrupting him the other brother said, A woman. QT2 was undone by a woman. The Wafadars have their own Serai of Fleeting Happiness, up the stream from the bridge, on a lovely grassy motte surrounded by horse chestnut trees. There is a wide veranda around it, and in it are hung, in big wooden cages, birds of such colour and feather as you can rarely glimpse. Out front is a pond shaped like a flower, with fish in it so red and golden that they coruscate in the light of the sun. This beautiful house is called by a different name. The Kiln of Inevitable Impulses. A Wafadar does not pursue something as banal as happiness, even fleetingly. But he does need to burn through what the body must burn through…

Licking his fingers, the first brother said, Maya. Her name was Maya. Of course she was beautiful. Each madonna there is. The finest of all the Serais of the valley arrive at the Kiln – for a Wafadar must taste the greatest seductions in the world and remain immune to them. But they say she was much more. Her black eyes and rose mouth played in a dance whose promise lay way beyond flesh and pleasure. The look that makes kings forsake kingdoms and men to lose their sense of purpose. The look whose promise can never be given words, nor ever be redeemed. We are much too mean to know this look, but they say a man in its thrall craves nothing but a moment of acceptance, the warmth of a word, the mercy of an embrace.

Sniffing at the bursting aroma of the pheasant, the other brother said, The thing is she was just a novice. She had recently arrived at the Kiln. Before her subversive potency could be detected and she be removed, QT2 had been snared. That look, the maddening brew of profound innocence and profound knowing. Maya. She was the perfect flaw for the perfect man. From the first moment QT2 burnt himself in her, he began to unravel. A Wafadar does not live by ordinary discipline. He is meant to set out his own. It is for him to take himself from a higher to a higher and a still higher state. In the barracks you were permitted the Serai once in a week. But a

Wafadar can repair to the Kiln many times a day, or not ever for a year. There is a surpassing beauty in this, in the Wafadar continually mastering himself.

Their words had brought on a fever in me. Finally I had arrived at the arena of glorious actions. I was pacing up and down, between the black abyss of the forest and the snapping flames of the fire. Both the brothers were on their haunches, steadily stripping the charred bird. It was easy to see why they had not ascended the terraces.

Given his peerless gifts, the Kiln should have been no more than a cookhouse for QT2. A bodily need, an inescapable compulsion, swiftly sated. But as Aum said, we are most tested not in our bodies but in our minds. QT2's mind laid him the simplest trap – of attachment – and he fell down the hole so deep that he could never crawl out.

By now both brothers had stopped their noisy chewing, and were holding their knees and looking at me. At last they were caught up in the power of the story they were telling.

It was more than a month before the murmurs began. QT2 was visiting the Kiln every day. Worse, he had not laid his hands, or eyes, on anyone save one young girl. Worse, much worse, he spent many hours whispering to her. Those who guide the paths of the Wafadars are profound men. They understand the chemistry of passion. They know it is more combustible between some people; and they know that the logic of this combustion is not knowable. But they also know that a man's passion is like a fish – it can sometimes go still, only to move again. It is the women that are a problem, tending to shackle their bodies to their souls. And that is why they are kept moving, from Kiln to Serai to cradle, and are regularly set to mothering so their bodies cease to go hunting with their souls.

I marvelled at the elegance of the words. These men had failed to become Wafadars, they ate fowl without a gesture to refinement, yet how finely they understood the concepts of honour and nobility. How pure they were.

I said, So they let him continue?

For a while. But when they discovered the fish was simply refusing to move, they carried the news up a few more terraces. Then to their utter alarm it became apparent that not only was the fish not moving, it was now warning off other fish from entering its realm. The truth is this bodily attachment is not unknown. Every now and then a Wafadar will succumb to it – in embarrassment and in shame. Then quickly he will right himself and move beyond. It is in a way one of the tests of enlightenment. It is the reason the most beauteous of the valley are sent to the Kiln. But with QT2 matters swiftly worsened. Soon he had dug a palisade around Maya, and no brother was permitted to lay a finger on her. This news was carried up a few more terraces. Up there they know everything, but choose to hold their hand till there is no choice. In their boundless wisdom they know that every rustle of a leaf does not presage a storm.

I said, Have you ever seen them?

Chewing a bone, he said, We don't see them, they see us. As it ought to be. They are all great Helmsmen, made in the image of Aum. And among them is the one we call Gentle Father. It is his guiding hand that keeps us true and pure.

The hair on my body was standing now. I looked up at the terraces and felt the grace of our mentors flow through me. I said, Yes, I understand. But did no one tell QT2 he had lost his way?

Of course! Again and again. To begin with, his brothers, who would often visit the Kiln with him and saw his deranged conduct. Some may think it was because they too wanted to burn in Maya – and who could blame them for that! But it was not so. QT2 was extraordinary. They all held him in esteem. They all saw him as more than an equal. He was destined for the highest terrace. Eventually the great Helmsmen arraigned him, gently, urging him to recognize he had gone too far. QT2 said nothing. This was taken for contrition. Then a few weeks later the news came that nothing had changed. QT2 had laid claim to Maya even more vehemently, and none were allowed to approach her. Curiously the complaint came not from QT2's brothers but from Maya's sisters, who were offended at the shameless exclusivity that had been established for her. Anyone less luminous and the great Helmsmen would have moved ruthlessly. But now a new tactic was initiated. Instructions were sent to remove the flower that was maddening the bee. And that's when all hell broke loose.

I said, What happened?

In an abominable move no one could have imagined, QT2 ambushed his flower as it was being taken away, and made off with it into the deep forest. The real horror however was that QT2 was not alone in this despicable escapade. He had managed to poison the blood of four of his brothers. So now the great Helmsmen had to deal with not one but five Wafadars – and as you know, one is the equal of ten, and five are a virtual army.

I said, Why did the four others corrupt their souls?

Both of them it seemed were waiting for the question. They said in a chorus, It's a mystery that's never been properly settled. Maya was not for them. They had nothing to gain. There was no reason for them to risk their place among the finest of the fine. The accepted conclusion is they were brainwashed. You must remember that QT2 was a very clever man, and his strength and skill lent more power to his slippery words. To justify his terrible descent into lust and possession, he incited in them a philosophy of exclusive love and free will. He told them it was the birthright of every man to live as he chose, and love as he chose. By now he was in the grip of romantic derangement. He said the space between two people in love was sacrosanct and no other had the right to trespass in it. He made it sound like the law of god. Only slaves and animals, he declared, were without free will – and they were neither. And what, pray, was the manifestation of this glorious free will? To disobey our great Helmsmen; to tear at the spirit of purity that is our purpose and our being!

I was in shock. I said, All because he wanted a woman?

That's it. The woman. Nothing more. The traitor built a whole theology to justify his awful failure, and persuaded four of his brothers to believe in it. Such things are known to happen continually in the world out there – where men construct elaborate philosophies of anger and violence and possession out of their greed and ego, and persuade thousands to follow them. It was everything that Aum had turned his back on, everything that he had tried to cleanse.

I was beginning to see how close to hubris we all skirted. A little learning, a little skill, a little praise, and we began to see ourselves as masters, ready to rewrite the book of life. Ali, Alaiya, a hundred great Helmsmen had with scrupulous care put their feet into the footprints of Aum, but QT2, in order to possess a mere woman, swollen with vanity, had thought nothing of running out sightless.

I said, How was it sorted out?

Sifting the ashes for last bones one said, The hunt lasted for weeks. It was a situation without precedent. Wafadars against Wafadars. Most men cannot even understand what that means. It was like panthers stalking each other, all shadows and claws and fangs. QT2 and his band were deep in the forest and moving location by the hour. The first group of eight young Wafadars – mere apprentices, in their first year – that was sent to bring them in was ruthlessly humbled. Each limb of the eight was broken in several places. Those who saw say they came back crawling, up to this very terrace, like insects on their bellies. QT2 had isolated and trapped each one, exhorted them to join him, and when refused, broken their bones one by one.

I said, He didn't kill them?

That would have offended his own comrades. You must remember they were all brothers till a few days before. But thereon things spiralled out of control. A day later, three more young Wafadars slipped away and joined QT2. The great Helmsmen realized it was no longer about one man losing his way over a woman. Now it was about men succumbing to their basest instinct, of possession. Me, myself, mine. Now it was shaping into an assault on Aum's very vision, on the great good that was their life's endeavour. Soon a mere urge to carnality would be shaped into a philosophy of art and aesthetics, politics and power. The great Helmsmen knew how in order to indulge simple desires men often construct elaborate organizations and high-sounding ideas. They could see impressionable young Wafadars about to be sacrificed to QT2's base passions.

I thought of the world out there. How fragile it was, built on the shifting egos of men, vulnerable to the whimsical desire of any one man! I could see the miracle of Aum's enlightenment.

One of the brothers had come back from the shed with a flagon of Ferment. A tiny wooden glass – four fingers deep – was tied to its neck. They both filled it to the rim twice each and threw it down their throats. Eight fingers, twice the cookhouse quota. It was then offered to me. I poured and drained my customary two fingers, and was buoyed by the aroma of apples and cloves.

The onslaught was immediately stepped up. The next group of Wafadars – older, seasoned – that went in brought back two of the rebels and strung them up, naked, by their ankles. That tree – can you see it?

Two terraces above us, in the far corner, grew a huge deodar with one strong arm stretched out over the terrace below. No doubt, it was a hangman's tree.

I said, Dead?

No. As brothers, we must always give the other a chance at redemption. You know a Wafadar can kill in the flutter of an eyelash, but he only does so when there is no other answer left in the world. Two of the smallest chonch were applied to their calves, and they began to empty, millidrop by millidrop, the blood travelling so slowly over their upturned bodies that it coagulated on the skin before it could drip to the ground. They were secured at the wrists and the thighs and the knees, and watched every moment – for you know how impossible it is to keep a Wafadar down. That night a war of the shadows raged as the rebels mounted assault upon assault to free their bandsmen. Those who stayed in this shed at the time told us it was akin to watching a battle of djinns. The moon was half that night, and all around the hangman's tree was the sound of the wind being sliced by lightning-fast warriors. When the sun rose the two renegades were still hanging upside down, still alive, with lines of deep red striating their bodies, but around them lay a dozen slashed warriors.

I was looking up at the hallowed site. How consummate it must have been! I wanted to be there too – parrying, feinting, striking. My shoulders clenched, as did my fingers.

It was then that ZZ9 was summoned. He was not yet a great Helmsman. He was chief of the guard at the Pass, and had already led a few missions into the other world. Five of the guard came here, thundering on their horses, ZZ9 at their head. All the young Wafadars were lined up. He picked ten, tested them, and rejected four. He then announced that QT2 was his; and for the rest of the rebels there were now two Wafadars each. To press more into action would be a disgrace. By now a few days had passed and the upside-down rebels had been run over by so many blood lines they were virtually encased in a red shell. Of course they were not dead. It takes a lot more to kill a Wafadar than mere torture. Once his team was ready, ZZ9 cut down the rebels and sent them to the Reformatory. They didn't need bait. They were not going to sit and wait. They were going to hunt down the impure with the strength of the pure. The pursuer moves on courage; the pursued on fear.

I said, How old was ZZ9 at the time?

Thirty-five, maybe forty – difficult to tell. Those who saw him then say he literally radiated energy. His muscles moved even when he stood stock still, and he could appear and vanish in the blink of an eye. He fought with short swords, one in each hand, and he was a master of the fifteenth poetic form, a unique manoeuvre called the kachchua, the tortoise. Rotating at one spot, he could twirl his swords at such blistering speed that he became encased in an armour, a tortoise inside his shell. Nothing could pierce through – no sword, no spear, no arrow, not even a bullet. He could sustain this manoeuvre for almost an hour, and hold off three score men.

I said, Have you seen him at it?

We haven't, but we know some who have. All you can see, they say, is a wall of flashing steel. Anyway, that evening the ustaad came by and touched up the face of ZZ9 and his hunters, and as night fell they ran towards the forest-line and vanished. Those who were watching said, in the passage of a moment, half of them had gone up the trees, while the others had vanished into the undergrowth. For three days everyone watched the forest-line with growing anxiety. Even the great Helmsmen were on edge. It was not possible that QT2 could carry the day, but suppose he did. So much was at stake. One woman, one act of possession, could end up as the keystone that collapsed the roof.

The other brother pulled at the chillum he had just lit, gave a clearing cough, and said, When on the fourth day, with the rise of the sun the hunters returned, there were great Helmsmen waiting on every terrace, all the way up. It was a sight never seen before. Not one man was standing, save ZZ9. And his skin too was slashed open in countless places. With one arm he was dragging the pulverized bodies of his bandsmen and the rebels, all yoked together along one rope. He collapsed into the arms of the brothers as they rushed to greet him. It was many days before he came to and could speak – the others lay in delirium for weeks, hovering between life and death.

What happened? My imagination was on fire.

Every brother has a different account. And that is not surprising. A Wafadar in battle is a flying bird, a darting rabbit, a striking snake, a bat in the dark, a squirrel in a tree, a panther in the grass, a scorpion in a crevice. He moves at a speed the eye cannot follow, and devastates in ways the mind cannot comprehend. Two Wafadars in combat against each other – rarely known – is like drawing pictures in the air. Only the two know what's being done. The rest see only the blur of limbs.

They were enjoying this. I could see they had done it before. Told the greatest story of their lives to novices like me. They were passing the chillum to and fro, and the sweet smell of the ganja was thickening the air.

One version says the first encounter took place in the air, as both sides flew through the trees. Like ravenous serpent eagles they ripped at each other, and when they had swept past there was not one whose skin was unbroken. And so it was that entire night, dark shadows tearing through each other high above the ground. If you were an ordinary man standing underneath, you would know nothing but the loud rustle of leaves and the whoosh of the wind. You know Wafadars give utterance to neither triumph nor injury. By morning there was not a single combatant who had not taken a blow.

In the day they stalked each other through the undergrowth, warriors – once brothers – who knew every move of the other. QT2 arrayed his five bandsmen into two fighting animals – one a domukhi, a two-faced one; and the other, a teenmukhi, a three-faced one. You perhaps know this is one of the fundamental fighting formations of the Wafadars in which they move with perfect harmony back-to-back – two, three, four, more – insulated against all surprise, capable of taking on a simultaneous assault from every direction. Inevitably, ZZ9 did the same. He set up his men as three fighting animals, one chaumukhi, one teenmukhi and one domukhi...

The other brother said, putting an ember into his chillum, It is a fearsome sight. The birds go still and the animals cower when a chaumukhi, a four-faced beast, moves through the forest. Even the big cats and mountain bears piss in fright.

The first brother said, On that day the forest shrank into hiding as these five many-headed animals stalked each other. Each time they crossed paths, steel, skin and blood flew. I am sure you understand that between Wafadars numbers are no real advantage. A rock is a rock, big or small. And when rocks clash, there is no immediate advantage to any of them. As captains of their bands, ZZ9 and QT2 had stayed away from the protections of the multiple beast. Their honour demanded they best each other without resort to subterfuge or support.

The moon was sinking fast. I brought more wood from the shed and put it on the fire. I wanted every word of this tale of glory and hubris. As a potential Wafadar, there were lessons here for me.

Sucking on the chillum, the brother said, Through the day the captains did not clash with the beasts. Even the greatest Wafadar can come up short against the many-headed one. The only way to destroy the animal is to somehow break it up. Prise its faces apart and take each on, one by one. When these many-faced beasts fight each other, that is what they try and do. There are elaborate tactics for it. But they are known to every Wafadar, and therefore of little use. And I am sure you understand that the more faces the beast has, the more formidable the challenge is. When with a mighty effort you destroy one face of a chaumukhi, it closes ranks and becomes a teenmukhi, still an impregnable three-faced beast. When again with great endeavour, you destroy another face, it closes ranks and becomes a domukhi, still an impregnable two-faced beast. Think now of the naumukhi, the nine-faced one, and how impossible it is to subdue it. Think now, that in theory, the Wafadars can conjure up a saumukhi, a hundred-faced one, and you have some idea of the impossible challenge of the many-faced animal whose every face is the same.

I was in a daze. This was complexity beyond anything I'd ever imagined. A beast with endless faces, whom no adversary could ever fully destroy.

I suddenly remembered. What about the woman?

The woman was of no consequence. The flaw lay in our brother – she had merely drawn it out. In fact she had in a way done us all a favour by isolating the rot in our midst. ZZ9 was clear. The woman would not be harmed. She would be returned to the Kiln. Their task was to beat sense into the twisted heads of the rebels. In the first instance, ZZ9 called out and urged a surrender, promising a short penitence and reprieve. At this it seems QT2 issued a loud counter, exhorting the righteous to come over to his side, promising them a pride of place in the new order of creativity and freedom which he was going to create. When ZZ9 rubbished this, saying QT2 should not attempt to give grand epithets to the pursuit of pleasure and ownership, all dialogue was off and combat was joined.

A low whistle sliced the night. Immediately one brother began to pull out the big pieces of wood from the fire, while the other fetched a canister of water and splashed out the flames. Sizzle and smoke exploded, and as quickly died. I could sense similar activity up the other terraces. It was time to turn in. The mornings began well before sunrise. When we'd settled in, I said, Go on.

The brother in the lower bunk, still pulling on his chillum said, Through the day the many-headed beasts clashed, drawing blood, hurting bone, but failing to crack the other open. In the night they all went up the trees, flowing through the branches, mauling each other in lightning skirmishes. The next morning they were back on the ground. This time QT2 arrayed a single beast, a panchmukhi, and ZZ9 unleashed a naumukhi. The forest emptied of every animal, big and small. The combat was so intense that the beasts were set to twirling, like giant wheels rubbing against each other to the sound of singing steel and flying sparks. At the end of the day there was blood everywhere, and yet none had yielded a hand.

I said, Why did ZZ9 not do something?

The brother in the upper bunk said, It is the way of the leader – to wait for the right moment. Too early, and you risk taking over the role of your followers, leaving them untested; too late, and there may be nothing left to redeem. So ZZ9 waited, letting his men test their worth. But then, that night QT2 went too far. As the warriors took to the trees, the young traitor began to call out to the Wafadars. Moving from deodar to deodar, he began to declaim to them the meaning of love and to recount the stories of free men. Remember he was mercurial of wit, quicksilver of tongue.

They say that night he was like a sorcerer – his disembodied voice full of sincerity and passion. In an ingenious strategy of duplicity he praised the glory of Aum, the truth of Aum, the purity of Aum, while lamenting Aum's betrayal by the great Helmsmen. The cunning rebel said, just as Aum had broken with his people to follow the long road to the valley of the pure, it was now their duty to do the same. It was their task to reclaim the lost truth of

Aum. No longer were the great Helmsmen and the Pathfinders its true guardians.

I said, Surely ZZ9's Wafadars scoffed at such blasphemy?

Never underestimate the deceptions of a dark night and the persuasions of an infatuated man. Real wisdom is a function of age. Just as the most virile tree will not bear fruit till its time has come, a man will not know the true weight of any word till he has been bent under its burden. In the final reckoning, the cleverest young man is merely that – the cleverest young man. Not the wisest.

Next morning when the great Wafadar prepared to array his men for battle, he found he had lost two of them to the night's sorcery. The numbers were now even. Enraged by the desertions, rattled by a sudden vulnerability, and wanting to keep his men together, ZZ9 made the tactical mistake of creating only one beast again, the seven-faced, the saatmukhi. QT2 sent forth a chaumukhi and a teenmukhi, and through the day, whirling rapidly, they tormented and tore at the single animal. By night, even as ZZ9's men nursed their injuries and doubts, the wily QT2 began to bait them again with dangerous fictions of love and free men.

That night ZZ9 realized that just as every immutable principle of the world has an exception, the Wafadar too had to know when the moment had come to step outside the code – only so he could protect the code. At least once in his life a Wafadar must not be a cool mountain wind but a raging forest fire, scorching the earth to save the earth.

Yet again I was struck by the soaring eloquence of my brothers. I had known it of our Pathfinders and of their lessons of Aum. But these were just brothers who put the hoe to the lower fields all day, pulled out and cleaned roots and vegetables, and brought in the wood for the nightfires. They were everyone's equal, no less than any other, but their tools were toiling limbs, not complex tongues. Now listening to them, I realized why Ali and Alaiya had grown as luminous as Aum. To live in the shadow of greatness is to have it settle on you like a skin. Toiling in the terraces below the great Helmsmen, my brothers had become magnificent beyond their station. I resolved then that I would never leave these slopes, even if the ultimate prize was not to be mine.

The next morning, the rebel numbers had swelled to nine. The sorcery of the dark was proving lethal. In fact it was because of the Romantic Betrayal that the great Helmsmen realized the subversive potential of decorative words. They understood that words were witchcraft and, wielded by a juggler, could turn the head of even the most sound brother. It was then that the Gentle Father passed a law that forbade conjurors of words from entering the ranks of the purest. It is good, my brother, that you speak sparingly and do not emblazon your speech with finery and fire. The Romantic Betrayal taught the great Helmsmen that men who speak like the gods often wish to dethrone the gods.

In a display of arrogance, confident of overwhelming the remaining defenders of Aum, QT2 now sent forth a naumukhi. But powered by truth, the pure are dauntless. Even as ZZ9's panchmukhi resolutely took on the nine-faced one, the ground was about to shift beneath the rebels. Badly wounded yet whirring like a bee, the panchmukhi took the fearsome naumukhi to the precise spot where ZZ9 lay buried under the forest floor.

In the last hour of dark the peerless warrior had entered the earth to await his moment. As the naumukhi twirled, drunk on its superiority, the great Wafadar exploded from the soil like an uncorked djinn, right in the heart of the nine-faced beast, his two short swords slashing swifter than lightning. By the time the beast turned its nine faces inward, ZZ9 had ripped open so much skin that he stood bathed in the spurting fountains of severed veins. As nine pairs of hands fell on him, ZZ9 unfurled the fifteenth poetic form, the kachchua, and became encased in an armour of flashing steel that nothing could pierce. The beast was now in disarray – the attack had come from within, its only vulnerable flank. The beast was constructed to take on external attacks, but now it was being gutted from the inside. And the moment it turned inwards, scrambling to protect its soft belly, the panchmukhi began to tear the flesh off its back. In no time the dreaded animal stood unhinged, reduced to nine battered rebels struggling to save their lives.

I realized, in the dark, my mouth had fallen open. Such a battle I had never heard of, not in the home, not at the barracks. I said, And QT2? Where was he?

Caught unawares! He'd been watching, sanguine in the power of his words and the strength of his fearsome beast. The suddenness of the massacre forced him to leap in. But the carnage could no longer be stemmed. ZZ9 had now entered the zone in which a great Wafadar goes beyond all containment. In his anger, QT2 did manage to brutally punish the panchmukhi, but he was no match for the raging ZZ9 who tore him up with his short swords as he had his traitorous men. The cut of a saw in high motion runs deeper than that of a stationary one. And they say, so great was ZZ9's fury that he kept whirling for a very long time after every single warrior had fallen, the betrayers and the loyal.

The other brother said, No one saw it, but try and see it. Amid the giant deodars, all alone, a whirling ZZ9. Finally, slowing to a stop, he lay down and he slept, hour on hour, for the first time in four days. Waking at midnight, he yoked all the men together with one length of twine, and dragged them back. As the sun rose and the great Helmsmen lined the terraces, they saw him emerge from the forest, painted incarnadine, a warrior of the faith, the glory of the pure.

I waited for a long time before speaking. I could see it all – the transgression and the taming, the sinner and the soldier. I wondered if life would give me a chance to prove myself, like ZZ9.

And what happened to Maya?

Soon after the triumphant return of ZZ9, a loud scream shred the sky. As everyone looked on, a slim figure emerged from the forest, stumbling and falling. It was the woman, withered of her great charm as a poplar is at the first blast of winter of its leaves. She lay where you now lie, my brother, and the great Helmsmen came to see her.

You know Aum has said that the beauty of most women is that of a flower, vulnerable to the whimsy of too many things – a twist of the weather, a turn in the soil, a passing hand, a crushing foot. The effulgence of such a woman cannot be trusted beyond the moment. There is the rare woman whose beauty is a tree – more stately with time, defining the landscape, succouring the weary, giving shade to the traveller and firewood to the cold, joy to the child, security to the old, giving suckle to the bird and to the bee, holding in place the earth and holding up the sky, unshakeable in its purpose, generous when alive, generous when dead. Such a woman was Alaiya, and rare is such a one.

One look and the great Helmsmen knew this Maya was nothing more than a mere mountain flower, crushed by the first rain of snow. A crushed flower can be punished no further. The girl was full of penitence. But she needn't have begged for mercy. She was already forgiven. With a single glance, without hearing a word, the Gentle Father read her decay.

I felt I could stay awake all night listening to these wondrous brothers. Finally I was in the amphitheatre of great questions, great conflicts, great warriors. I thought of my own romantic contretemps at the cookhouse and was filled with shame. How close we all came to abjection! It was time I understood that the line between glory and disgrace was thin as the scale of a fish.

I said, And QT2? And the other traitors. How were they punished?

Punished? There was no further punishment that could be handed out to them. They were the fallen. From being the jewels of their people, they had become the dung. A man has glory only because other men see in him that glory. Now everyone saw in these once-puissant Wafadars only weakness and greed and betrayal – such as men in the other world harbour – deserving of nothing but contempt.

But what happened to them?

I felt the brother from the lower bunk enter my bed.

In a way, you can say, they were all forgiven. You know Aum taught us that the pure must not be weakened by sentiment, but he also taught us that the pure must not be weakened by anger. Their bones broken, their honour shredded beyond repair, they were all dispatched separately to different parts of the valley, to cookhouses and farms and orchards and foundries. Our brothers still, but no longer worthy. Thus ended the Romantic Betrayal. In the Kiln a covenant was sealed: every sister was to constantly guard against another being seized by infatuation, and was to do everything she could to keep her sisters from ruin – even if it meant alerting the great Helmsmen.

And ZZ9?

Now the brother from the upper bunk was at the edge of my bed too.

He was brought back from the Pass and made protector of the great Helmsmen, and in a few years he had become a great Helmsman himself, and then he took charge as the mediator of the upper and lower terraces, and each time a buzz filled the slopes everyone knew that ZZ9 was practising the fifteenth poetic form and had become encased in an armour of singing swords just as he had once before, in the middle of the towering deodars, in defence of the peerless pure.

THE DRAIN INSPECTOR

Parvati moans, and in a flash I click off the machine and am at her side. The slice of light from my room cuts across her face, revealing her gentle mouth that is twitching. There is no question: she is more beautiful than anyone I saw at the Serai or at the Kiln. I have come to believe that it is not skin and bone that create beauty but knowledge. And I knew nothing about any of the scores of bodies I had continually burned myself in. Most of them offered urgent gratification, but I cannot remember any of them calling up in me the word beauty.

Parvati always sleeps the sleep of the blameless. These moans come from a rare bad dream. She tells me about them. They are always to do with her daughter, whom she loves more than herself, and who is married to a man she can never be sure of. They live in a town three hours away, where he is a drain inspector with the local municipality. He always smells rank, and he drinks copiously to numb the stench.

Some days, when it involves the clogged pipes of a high official, he too is forced to go down the manhole. Because he is an officer – well, almost one – he does not enter the sewer bare-bodied as his men do. He has a khaki dungaree, which he keeps at his workplace. Parvati's daughter tells Parvati that it is stiff with years of grime and stands behind the door unaided. Its odour, she says, could concuss an entire village.

On days he goes down the manhole he does not eat. He drinks a bottle of rum and beats his wife, and sometimes his children too. Each day, the daughter and Parvati, in their prayers, importune the gods to keep the pipes of important people unclogged.

Parvati says the man who fixed the marriage did not tell them the prospective groom would be going down drains. They were told he had two different degrees from college, was very intelligent, and possessed of a secure government job as an inspector. It gave him free quarters, of brick, with piped water, and he had an old scooter.

Of his brilliance there is clear evidence. He buys two daily newspapers, in two different languages; and he reads books, many of which he keeps by his bed. If you talk to him when he is reading, he nods without looking up.

But Parvati says the brilliance is tragically flawed. Each day he risks losing caste – which to begin with is not a high one. He breaks bread with the sewermen, sits them in his living-room when they come to meet him, and forces his wife to serve them tea and biscuits. One day when he discovered she was using a separate crockery for the sewermen he foamed like a lunatic and smashed every dish in the house. Then he beat her and beat her, admonishing her all the while for being a witch who treated other humans as animals.

Where I come from, men were dubiously equal. And here I find they are dubiously unequal. I struggle to understand what I should think.

I place my hand on Parvati's greying hair and keep it there till the last moan has died out and her mouth has ceased to twitch. Under the quilt she is tiny as a sparrow. Tomorrow I will not be here to listen to her recount her nightmare. Perhaps it is of her daughter being dragged down a dark manhole and being buried there forever by her raging husband. It is the most frequent one. The other one that recurs is of the daughter being ravaged by scores of dark, bony, naked sewermen while the son-in-law reads a book and silently nods.

Since I have left my chair, I decide to go down to get myself a mug of tea, even though my break is not due for another ten minutes. If I did not discipline myself, I would be hurtling down the stairs every five minutes. Not simply because I love the brew, but more to escape, for a few moments, the challenge of finding the right words for the waiting machine.

It's a small black box, gifted to Parvati by the drain inspector. You can feed it the sound of your choice and it will play it back for you. She listens to it early in the morning when she combines her cleaning of the house with the chanting of prayers, and then she listens to it in the evening when she takes a break from the kitchen to have a cup of tea. The morning sound is a rhythmic chorus in praise of her gods; the evening one, songs from films full of dancing words. I, on the other hand, cannot stop experimenting with the unimaginable range of its voices.

Outside Delite Talkies there is a small kiosk that sells cigarettes, paan – which I have come to love – and many odd wrapped and unwrapped confections. The weedy man with a drooping moustache inside this wooden box is always in a flurry of painting, stuffing and folding wet leaves, and selling sticks of cigarette which he pulls out of packets using his unstained knuckles. He is from the antique city by the holy river, where he says the gods first appeared before they went anywhere else in the world. This man – who must have been born cross-legged because he sits so all day – is my music master.

Never, for a moment, does he stop humming. As he briskly vends, asks and answers questions of his clients, carries on long conversations, and chews steadily on endless triangles of paan, the hum stays unbroken. I would have imagined it impossible were I not witness to it several times each week. The hum has many registers, from one so soft that it is the buzz of an unseen insect, to piercing high notes that impel him to raise his hands and shake his head.

In rhythm, through the hum, he tells me that the difference between a maestro and a paan vendor is only a few crucial notes, and where he comes from, the eternal city, everyone is connected to both. He reels off names of legendary pundits intimately known to his family, names that twist my tongue. When I make a query, he laughs and says, Not priests, my friend, not priests! Priests are just petty crooks. I am talking about the true men of god. The pundits of music. Who utter the true sound of the true one. When you hear the raag malhar sung by a maestro you can feel the rain falling on your skin. Then he picks up the hum, cracks his throat, and produces sounds of such astonishing reverberation that my mouth falls open.

I understand almost nothing of the dissertations he freely gives me on music that he says is so powerful and ancient that if rendered perfectly it can blank out the sun, make rivers flow, turn tigers into pussycats, and still marauding armies. I simply take what he gives me, from his back shelf, in cellophane wrap, and feed it to the black music box. Then I play it and play it and play it till its sound has entered my skin as water seeps under the pores of a drowned man. Each time I am astonished by the new rhythms I discover.

Parvati complains, in her good-natured way. She says I am bringing home wailers, as if there has been a death in the family. I tell her to keep listening and she will find beauty. I tell her what my music master in the kiosk tells me. Is it the fault of a delicate cuisine that the pig does not thrill to it?

The drain inspector takes a different view. He says – through angry lips – that men are made into swine by denying them music. He says it and I immediately know the truth of it. I finally understand why the fat friend of my childhood yearned for his father. It was because he had music in him. Today I know that men without music are men without emotion. Music is the fire that thaws emotion and lets it flow. Today I understand the profound significance of the fat man and his voice. And I am filled with sorrow.

There is so much music in this place that I have come to. Of every kind. It flows out of houses and it beats out from shops, it envelops the carts of street vendors and it fills out cars, it winds through the choking lanes of Zubair's basti and it trembles the walls of Delite Talkies. Coming from a country of deep silences I am constantly aware of it. Men here move through it as if it did not exist, or take it for granted like the trees and the air.

This world is overflowing with music, and it unlocks all the emotions of men, making them lurch and leap like a bounding mountain stream.

I go down the narrow stairs feeling for and finding the switches. In the kitchen, though Parvati has left it spotless, there is the rustle of roaches running for cover as the bulb explodes into light. As the water boils I open the window at the back and peer through the mesh. It is a sight that never pales on me. Dozens of dogs and cats – and if you peer long enough, hairy rodents big as puppies – working their maws through the heaps of leftovers put out by Parvati. Often there are also nightbirds, cows, goats, the occasional wandering pig.

Each day she generates the refuse not just from her own kitchen, but also inveigles it off the neighbours. Often, with fascination, I watch her scrutinize what they've dumped on her, from cooked food to pulpy fruit and mouldering bread. She palpitates it, sniffs it, and then neatly heaps it up on the stone slabs she has placed just beyond the narrow gutter that trims the kitchen. What she deems inedible she ties tightly in a thin plastic bag and leaves under the sink. It is my task then, at some point, to throw this irredeemable package into the steaming garbage dump at the end of the street.

Preparing this repast is the last thing she does at night. She believes it is not enough to collect good karma during the day. She hopes that as she sleeps, with every bite the beasts take, her cosmic counter will tick purposefully on.

Tonight there is a big black pig struggling to participate in the feast. Every few minutes the dogs bark him away, but resolutely it returns and grabs what it can in its snout before being chased away. The dogs are dumb. Two of them could keep the pig at bay, but each time all of them – more than a dozen – round on it, snarling and charging. While they are away the cats step in.

I watch for a while, and soon the dogs tire of the bullying. The pig now works the margins, pulling out what it can. I turn back to my tea, hearing its boil rattle the pan. I throw in some sticks of clove to go with the mashed ginger and cap the pan with a steel plate, leaving it to concoct. I go back to the window. The pig is now shoulder to shoulder with the dogs. The cats are statues – on the windowsills, the walls, the water drum, the old cycle.

The first sip fires my tongue. Then the aroma storms my nostrils and I am happy. The drain inspector – whom I grudgingly like – asserts that tea must be drunk boiling and in a series of seamless sips. The glass must never be put down till the last drop is drained. If it is, it must be abandoned. He is true to his word. When he visits, every few weeks, he keeps Parvati on her toes. It is strange to watch her bustle about, full of deference, catering to his every whim, even though she doesn't like him. Till she hears his stammering snore rattle the room below us, she keeps awake, in case he needs something.

When, with irritation, I ask her about it, she says he's the son-in-law. There is no such thing as doing too much for him. The key to her daughter's well-being is in his hands alone. And there is nothing more precious in the world for her than her daughter. Then she rounds on me. Which paradise in the universe have you come from? Do you not have daughters and sons-in-law there?

In the short time I have been here I have discovered that in this world there is simply too much love of one's children. It seems to take precedence over everything. Even wise Zubair – lord of carpentry, relentless toiler – constantly carps about his son's failures at the premium school he attends. Once, when I suggested he ameliorate everyone's misery by putting his boy to working the wood rather than cramming books, he raised his hands to the skies and declaimed, May the all-seeing, all-knowing, all-mighty one claim me to his side before I make of my son something so mean!

At times like this the memory of Aum floods my being.

With Parvati it took me time to realize things were deeply complicated. The primary reason she finds it difficult to warm to her son-in-law is his caste. He is a whole caste and a quarter lower than her. She is sure the only reason he agreed to the marriage was to gain purchase on a higher rung. Her own reasons she knows only too well. Her daughter has a bad leg. The left one. It is atrophied with polio, and drags behind the other. Sometimes she has to help it along by using her hand, and when she sits she has to settle it carefully like a piece of cloth.

Parvati says her choice was clear: a destitute husband of the same caste, or someone of means from the lower orders. Tormented at the thought of making the wrong choice, she left it to her daughter. When the matchmaker presented the proposal of the drain inspector, the girl said, Let's keep going. Then the two met in the small living-room on the ground floor of this house, and that evening the girl said yes. The mother said, Your children will lose caste. The daughter said, He reads books. The mother said, Will they make up the caste?

Parvati had collected a mountain of things to give to her daughter – linen, jewellery, utensils, furniture – but the groom rejected them all. Only the clothes on her back, he declared. Parvati says she plunged into panic. It was clear her daughter was marrying a crank. The daughter said, He has principles. The mother said, You marry a man, not principles.

Now she has put away all these things for her granddaughter, who is a mere seven. Parvati thinks it unlikely the next-generation son-in-law will also trip up a mother's generosity with principles.

The drain inspector is all bones, a skeleton with skin stretched over it, and he is dark as the rum he drinks – endless glasses, rapidly, with splashes of water in it. When he visits we sit in the tight drawing room and he talks in such a torrent that I have to struggle to keep myself from drowning. At one level I am happy for this: if he broke breath to make inquiries of me he would certainly become suspicious.

The caste theory outrages him. He says he had made up his mind the moment the matchmaker informed him that the suggested bride had a minor shortcoming. It was made out to be a negligible limp.

But when he came here he found a fully dysfunctional leg. It only reinforced his determination. Among us a handicapped woman is a dead woman. You may as well set fire to her. Then he laughs in a manic way, shaking his head and rolling his black eyes: But it's not all virtuous. Don't think I am an angel. She had a lovely face. So smooth, so fair. I thought at least now the coal of my children will be washed in some milk.

I cannot tell Parvati, but the truth is the more I see of the drain inspector the more I like him. He talks rough, and he talks too much, but I sense in him a kind of honour. A code that is personal, and not the accepted practice of everyone else around. I have tried to make out a case for him with Parvati, but the caste thing always gets in the way. When I question this attitude of hers and contrast it with her kindness to animals, she says, Am I marrying my daughter to animals? Am I having grandchildren from animals? Do I break the law between men and animals? There is an order to the universe. Only fools and sinners ignore it.

No man can leave the clutching fingers of his past behind. Sometimes when I hear the drain inspector roar and rage I am transported back to the valley. He wants equality. He wants efficiency. He wants an end to exploitation. He wants the extermination of the elite. As he talks the words begin to drum in my head and the blood pounds in my veins.

Then I ask him gently why he beats his wife, and he becomes maudlin. He sucks in the rum and says, Because I am wretched. Like all men I too am weak. When I see her disgusted by my sewermen – purifying the dishes with drops of holy water, fumigating the room with incense – something explodes in my head. She, who has known the disgust of the world for her crippled leg, how can she have no feelings for the misery heaped on these people? Think of a job that cleans the world and takes it on its own skin. Think each day of going home not knowing if your flesh will burst in a forest of boils or peel off like wet paper.

I say, gently, But why beat her?

He says, I am ashamed to say it but the fact is I feel good when I am doing it. I feel I am somehow beating some of the bad things out of this world.

When I talk to the daughter she says she just can't stand the smell. It's only that. The rest she has managed to get past. The cleansing, the fumigation – everything has to do with the smell. She says, He is a good man. He is right to beat me. I should be able to control myself. But I can't. It is like having your head inside the latrine. When I go in to give them tea I have to hold my breath. And for hours afterwards I cannot bear to put anything in my mouth.

In turn, the drain inspector rages. That's good, that's good. That's why I bring them home. That's why I want to take them everywhere. To the superintendent's house, and that of the commissioner, and the chief medical officer, and the executive engineer, and the college principal, and the sugarmill owner, and the minister, and every upper-caste man in my town, and in every town. I want each one of them to feel their head is inside the latrine. I want them to hold their breath, and to vomit, and to be unable to eat anything for hours. Let me tell you, it never gets easier for my men. Even if you are born to it, even if you live it every day, you never get used to the smell. All shit smells like shit. And it always smells like shit. There are days my men too cannot eat. You know why all my men are drunks? Because they are trying to drown the smell! To erase it for one fleeting moment.

She says, But why does he punish me? Life has already punished me with a bad leg. The drain inspector explodes. He bangs his glass on the table, and jumps to his feet. At such times it is easy to forget he is a matchstick of a man. I could snap two dozen of him across my knee without breaking a sweat. His fury makes him big: A bad leg! A bad leg is not a bad smell. You can live with a bad leg, you can eat with it, you can sleep with it, you can sit amongst people with it! A bad leg may blight you, but it will also get you pity and consideration. Even marriage with an inspector! A bad smell only gets you disgust and rejection. Only a bad smell will sit with another bad smell; only a bad smell will eat with a bad smell; only a bad smell will marry a bad smell. Let me tell you, even now I struggle to master my nausea when I am with them. That's why I do not wash my overalls. I keep them in my office so I may never forget the smell. Let me tell you it's I who have made those men smell bad. It is my one-legged wife who has made them smell bad. It is you and my mother-in-law who have made them smell bad. All of us, all the people you see wherever you go – we have all made them smell bad. And we should know what we have done to them. And unless the smell invades our nostrils and the nausea rises in our throats we will never know what we have done.

I listen to him and I am moved. And once again – as I do here all the time – I struggle to understand what is right and what is wrong.

Suddenly the drain inspector begins to sing. A low, melancholic song, with eyes half-closed, about the injustices of men which are backed by the injustices of the gods. I lean back in my chair. When he finishes he picks up his glass, holds it to the light, and says, If we did not have song, we would all be killers.

The light makes the dark rum a happy orange. Failed love would make us kill, failed luck would make us kill, failed justice would make us kill. Anger would make us kill, envy would make us kill, idealism would make us kill, sorrow would make us kill. But we are saved by song. We sing and we hear song, and we understand and we forgive, and our great unhappiness slowly drains out of us, like pus from a boil, and we sheathe our knives and bury our axes, and we are saved.

I am rapt. Such eloquence his fury generates.

He bought the black machine for Parvati so he would not be deprived of song when he came visiting. When I first arrived here she would keep it covered under a lacy white cloth, and the day her saturnine son-in-law was expected, uncover it and dust it till it shone. Then the inspector began to educate me on its use. Play, forward, rewind, eject. Loud, louder, loudest.

For me it was a startling discovery that I had a ready ear for it – given that I had spent my life set against all song. When I said this to the inspector, he snorted and said, Everyone is born with song. It's like a sense of right and wrong. Like dharma. You don't have to go looking for it. The sorry fact is most people spend their lives burying it. Their sense of right and wrong, and their ear for music.

Once he started me on it, it became like the reading – a voracious appetite that fed on itself. I wanted to try out every kind of sound that was there. I chanced on the religious chanting and film songs that helped me draw Parvati to the machine. And then the inspector introduced me to the master in the kiosk, the cross-legged seller of cigarettes and paan, and I began to understand that music was not a road to be followed from one point to another, but a wide open field, stretching in every direction, beckoning us to endlessly meander.

I also discovered – as with the words – that there was so much of it reverberating in the world that if I lived to be a thousand years and then another thousand, I could not taste it all.

As I walk past the tiny lump on my bed I smile at the two ears – of money and missive – that stick out of the pillow. I know she will be unhappy about both. She will speak of it to her daughter, who in turn will tell her husband. It will then fall upon him to join all the dots and examine the picture that emerges.

For all my fondness for the drain inspector I am uncertain about his response. He is a talker; he seldom cares to listen. Will he have the patience to sit for hours by this machine and hear my uninterrupted voice tell my story and the story of my people? And if he does, will he trust it for what it is, or will he imagine it to be the feverish fable of a man fleeing an old woman and seeking to excuse his flight?

Often have I heard him rage about the absurd stories men invent to justify their excesses. He says the world is awash with myths invented to unfairly serve the cause of those who made them up. With him it always comes back to his sewermen. Those who claim high caste, he says, have over the centuries conjured up libraries and epics to drive his men into dank and invisible places.

I trust no story of any revelation, he says, nor any man who tells me he knows something unique. A bad smell envelops me immediately. And instantly I feel someone trying to push my head into the latrine.

Yet I am grateful there is a man like the drain inspector I can leave my tale to.

Maybe he will sit back quietly, examine the mystery of my sudden arrival, my many small ignorances, my occasionally uninformed conduct, my final dramatic disappearance – and putting together the pieces, arrive at a place of trust.

I sit down again at the small desk, press the rewind button, and softly play back my voice. Yes, it is thin and lacks body, and some of my pauses are so long one might imagine the Wafadars have already arrived. But to me it sounds sincere. I have tried to speak with slow, firm deliberation, and before I started I made a plan, writing it down on a piece of paper, so that I would not meander.

I got the idea of discipline from the same article that started me down this road. It was a piece in an old paper that came out of a yellowing pile I'd bought many months ago. The headline was 'Don't be afraid to write your story'. Immediately I felt it was addressing me. And when I went to the top of the paper, looking for the dateline, I found it was more than four years old. I took it for a sign.

The author said everyone in the world was entitled to tell his story. No one's story was without consequence, no man too mean to be denied his space in the annals of the world. Anyone's story could become the reason for someone else's salvation. In an image that I liked, the author said every story in the world was like the perfect pill for someone's affliction. By helping fill up the world's pharmacy of tales we would be doing our bit to alleviate pain and suffering.

The hour is etched in my mind. It was very early, the world holding its breath for one last moment before exploding into action. I was sitting at my desk in front of the open window, watching the light strengthen, watching the restless birds play with the giant semul. The milkmen had not yet clanked down the road, and I was still waiting for the first thud of the newspapers. Parvati had given me my first mug of ginger tea and gone for her bath. Randomly I picked a paper from the old pile lying on the floor. Swiftly I skated through the news, read the opinions on matters long dead, and then came upon the weekend supplement dressed up in vivid colours – and there it was, waiting for me, a full, long page. Don't be afraid to write your story.

When Parvati came back with my second mug of tea, and then with the day's newspapers, I did not even raise my head. I missed the sunrise too which I have rarely done in my entire life. Even after I had finished reading it twice I did not put it away or get up from my chair. My head was on fire. This was the reason I'd got away; this was the reason I was here; if, as is said, every life has one true purpose, this was mine.

Anybody, everybody, could tell their story.

More than anybody, everybody, I had a story to tell.

I would place my pill in the world's pharmacy of tales. And hope it would, in time, succour the anguish of some, or many.

Having given a reason to write, the author then went on to outline how it could be done. If you could make your language eloquent, wonderful. If not, then simple prose ought to be the goal. The story was always more important than the syntax. If you possessed the skill you could start your story anywhere – from the middle, the end, anywhere. If you did not, there was no ignominy in telling it in a straight line, like a railway track, from beginning to end. Were you afraid you did not know enough, even about your own story, to be seen as credible? The name of the tree outside your house, the history of your community, the law that you broke? If so, you could work to find these out; and if this was beyond your exertions you should without shame declare it in your writing as the tree-whose-name-you-do-not-know. If you did not lie to them, most readers would forgive you. Even the great writers were full of vast ignorance. The act of writing was not only one of bestowing but also one of discovery. And remember every story has its unique soul, and unless the tree is your story's soul you must not allow it to impede your progress.

So there it was. Without fancy words, without great skill, without profound knowledge, you could still tell your story. Just one simple exercise needed to be undertaken. In a notebook, each day, you ought to, as in a grocery list, write every point that you wished to include in your story. For days, for weeks, for months, perhaps even for years, the man who would tell his story must diligently note down his ingredients. Every incident, every person, every emotion, everything – number them one, two, three, four… And then as he begins to write he must keep cancelling out the items in this catalogue. One day, if he ploughs on, the grocery list will be gone, and in its place there will be a story, his story – his unique pill in the pharmacy of the world's tales.

I read and re-read the article, shaking with excitement. Then I put it down, closed my eyes, and tried to think about it. But the agitation only grew. Finally I got up, laced on my shoes, slipped out the front door, and began to run. Exiting our street I took the main road that runs straight out of town all the way to the motor-parts shops and the green fields beyond.

I did not jog, I ran, pounding the tarmac, surging past the morning cyclists and the schoolboy athletes dressed in shiny tracksuits, past the horse-carts going from the railway station to the nearby villages. Soon I was galloping past green fields with mist still clinging to them in gossamer sheets even as frisky birds punched holes in it. Every time an arthritic truck rumbled by I was pushed off the road, but I did not break step. In fact, occasionally I took it as a challenge and picked up speed to keep pace with the vehicle. Once, I grabbed the chain of the tail-guard and sprinted alongside the truck till the helper, leaning out the window, began to scream at me.

It was a while since I'd been in training, but this was nothing for me. Eight kilometres hard running to the next village, and then eight back. I could have done it twice over, but I was aware it was a mistake for me to let on what I was capable of, and I always took care to stay inconspicuous.

In the early days I had blundered. Late at night at Delite, emerging from a poorly attended show, I had broken the arms of five boys who were tormenting a young couple. They were slapping the man and fondling the woman. When I asked them to stop, one of them said next in line was my wife and I ought to rush home and fetch her. Then they pushed their hands under her clothes and she whined like an injured dog. I caught the shoulder of the man who was pushing his hand in and yanked him out. He turned to strike me and I broke his arm. His wild scream I cut off with a sharp slap that concussed his senses. In a few minutes they were all on the ground, moaning.

The young couple was cowering. By now a group had gathered. It is always so here. In the blink of an eye a mob materializes. Closing in slowly, it was muttering and querying and abusing and shaking its fists. I thought, this is the bahumukhia, the many-faced beast of this world. It is untrained, undisciplined, but no less dangerous than ours. Its many faces may look different, but at such a time they are all the same. Of course, I was not anxious. An old and deep instinct was beginning to move in me. No more than two dozen men. I could have broken all their bones before they could lay a finger on me.

Then I suddenly saw, through the moving heads, the nonplussed expression of my music master, craning from his kiosk to see the fracas. In that moment I knew I was risking everything that I had come to cherish. This many-faced beast had no idea of my prowess. It would be foolish of me to display it. I was once the elite of a cadre that has no equal. As effortlessly as I broke bones I could become a shadow. In a moment I was gone.

For weeks after, Parvati told me a diabolic djinn had visited the cinema. He had molested a woman, broken the bones of many men, and disappeared into thin air when assaulted by a mob. A hundred people had seen it. Now a police post had been established there; along with a holy fakir famous for taming djinns and putting them on a leash.

For many weeks I did not venture near Delite. I had blundered badly. If my pursuers got a scent of the story, they'd know in an instant where I was. Seeing me, a month later, my cross-legged master said, You vanished like the djinn. I was worried. It was a reminder that I was now in a world where people were randomly – and perilously – curious about things peripheral to their lives.

When I came back from my run my mind was made up. After a very long time I felt myself full of purpose. That very day I bought myself a lined notebook such as is used by schoolchildren here, and leaving the first page blank, I began to write up the laundry list of my story. I did as the article had instructed, numbering the ingredients, committing no more than five entries to a page. In the first week itself I had crossed fifty; a month later I bought myself another notebook.

Though I enjoyed the cataloguing, it was not easy. Every entry was like a sharp hook dredging up the debris of painful memories. At times after I'd written a single line I would sink into a reverie that was not broken for hours. At times I found myself crying for myself – and I found in it a kind of relief, an unexpected relief. Very quickly Parvati understood I was not be disturbed when bent over the children's notebook; and that there were things in there that were best left unquestioned.

Inexorably then, as the days passed, the entries came in slower and slower. And from the great energy and assurance with which I had started I moved to uncertainty and confusion. It was strange. I began to struggle with the hardness and certitude of the word – precisely what had excited me about the writing earlier. I became unsure whether the notes I was making, the story I was attempting, had any real meaning. More accurately, I knew it had some meaning, but what was it? Could I be so presumptuous as to write a story whose meaning I did not know?

Soon I fell into despair. I was sure now that the author of the article had never managed to write his own story. It was easier to inspire endeavour than to practise it. As the words died on me and my mind raged in turmoil, I found renewed solace in music. For hours on end I would sit back in my chair and listen to the splendid array of sounds I had bought and collected from the kiosk master and the drain inspector. The range of instruments and sounds that poured out of the machine was so bewilderingly wide that I found it almost difficult to believe they had their origins in the same animal. Defeated by the word, rejuvenated by the mellifluous notes, I came to believe what my cross-legged tutor always said. If there was any evidence that man was unique in the vast universe, and that there was a god, it was music.

I had not been writing my notes for weeks – sapless as a dead tree, not a leaf of inspiration pushing through – when I had my first real scare. It happened at the kiosk. By now I had concluded it was too difficult a task to disentangle my story, and each time I looked at the notes, lying on the paper like rows of dead worms, I knew I did not have it in me to twist and turn them into anything resembling a coherent narrative. The article in the paper had given me a false idea of my abilities. I could do many things that men here could not. But I did not have it in me to recount a tale – even if it was mine, and urgent – whose meaning and truth continued to elude me.

It was in such a mood, of vague stasis, examining cellophane-wrapped discs at the kiosk in the early evening, in the momentary lull before the afternoon show vomited out hundreds of heated viewers and sucked in even more, that I suddenly felt a cold snake crawl down my spine. I turned quicker than lightning. For any other man there was nothing to be seen except the languid bustle of the bazaar, but I saw the shadow of a shadow slide past the old peepul near the parking lot and I knew the sand was finally beginning to run out of my hourglass.

In the time it took the cross-legged master to look up from the paan he was folding I had vanished. For days after, I stayed inside the house, sitting back from the window, at an angle, watching the street. It would be a lie if I said I was not afraid. And yet it was not fear as men here know it – of loss of limb or life or property. It was a nameless dread. As if I were at the lip of a bottomless abyss, and once cast into it I would be lost and alone forever. Not alive, not dead, and no one in the vast universe aware of my existence.

I clung to Parvati, in sleep and awake. It was the only thing that calmed my terror. Holding on to her small, round body, feeling the beat of her heart, looking into her peaceful eyes, I felt I was safe. At night I discovered a way of dragging her heavy leg on to mine, pinning me down, nailing me to the bed. Her goodness would protect me. Nothing in the logic of the world could be as malign as to wish her harm, or to those that she loved.

A week later, my panic in abeyance, aware that I'd always been aware that I would be eventually run down, I ventured out to the workshop. Zubair was worried. I apologized and said I would henceforth be erratic in my appearances but would finish all the assignments that had been set out for me. He probed no further. He was used to private griefs derailing the arc of his workers' lives.

I was working on the bust of a Buddha for the headboard of a bed. It was a new thing here, Zubair told me, this interest in the Buddha. When he was growing up no one in these parts ever mentioned him except as a kind of curio, preaching denial and detachment. Now the educated and the rich were embracing him. Zubair laughed bitterly and said that was how it was here – you embraced the man and forgot his ideas.

After I had copied a few I'd understood the trick of the Buddha lay not in the curls of hair or the long earlobes, but in his smile and in his eyes. How you curved them determined the serenity he radiated. The first few I chiselled were grim, demanding compliance. Then I mastered the gentle slope of eyelids and lips, and I have to say that though I had learned to be suspicious of manufactured tranquillity, I found that even in the flurry of the workshop – amid the mess and the noise – he began to generate a calm that was difficult to describe.

And so I was bent over, squinting, tapping delicately at my chisel to pull god out of the wood, when I felt the cold snake on my spine again. I made no sudden move. This time I stayed as I was, tapping the wooden handle without allowing the blows to go through, while my eyes swivelled in every direction. And there it was again, the shadow of a shadow sliding past the stacked-up planks of teak and cedar. I held the pose – tapping ineffectually – for a long time, but it was gone.

Later, knowing I would find nothing, I carefully reconnoitred the area. Zubair noticed and said, Looking for something? I said, A ghost. He said, Is it looking for you too? I said, I think so. He said, Then go home and wait for it. Let it do the hard work. As I turned to leave, he said, Do you know how to vanquish a ghost? I said, Tell me. He said, There's a spell for every ghost. Find the one for yours and it will disappear.

That evening I took the long route home, past the old police station built of narrow bricks, with a stable by its side where the policemen now kept buffaloes. Once again I was the peerless warrior of the high valley. Every sense was alive, and I slid like a shadow through the streets, not more than a fleeting daub on a wall. I did not enter the house through the front door, and Parvati gave a start when she suddenly saw me materialize in the little alcove upstairs where she sat knitting a cardigan.

I made myself a big mug of tea and sat in the living-room with the lights off. Without a doubt they were beginning to close in. It could be a day away or fifteen. The shadow I had not seen but sensed was probably a scout. They would not come for me underprepared. Once they were certain they would make their move. I knew how they thought. They were of a tribe whose notions of fear and failure had been buried long ago.

The next morning, a Saturday, the drain inspector arrived with his family. While Parvati and her lame daughter huddled in the kitchen in a kind of communion beyond all understanding, and the two children watched something noisy on a television set downstairs, the inspector and I sat in my little room on the first floor, looking out at the street and drinking amber rum. The inspector was in a great fret. In the last week he had moved to a major decision. He took out a cassette from his pocket and popping open the black machine slid it in.

Listen! he said.

I thought he had brought me some new miracle of music, but what came surging out of the machine was the drain inspector's voice. I looked so flabbergasted that he laughed. In the machine, he was speaking with even more rage than usual. If it was not made equal and just, he was threatening to tear down the entire world. He said this in many different and evocative ways. After each telling, men shouted and roared. Twenty minutes later, the world torn down to wild applause several times, with a loud click the machine stopped. In the silence, he looked at me for a response.

I said, You are very angry.

Not enough! Not enough! I want to become angrier! And angrier!

Then he told me he'd decided in order to clean the gutter he had to leave the gutter. He had had an epiphany. He had understood something fundamental. In each of the vast vehicles of the world only one person mattered. The one with his hand on the steering wheel. Perfect nuts and bolts, perfect engine, perfect tyres, perfect seats, perfect passengers, perfect everything did not mean a thing if the hand on the steering wheel decided to drive you into a ditch, or not drive you anywhere at all.

He was resigning from the employ of the government. The papers had been submitted. His goal was to become the government himself. The sewermen had a kind of radical party. He would head it, and soon they would tear down the world. And build it anew – just and equal. I had just heard his first speech. The sewermen were in a delirium of enthusiasm.

I was not paying attention to his manifesto. I only wanted to know how one embedded one's voice into the machine. He explained it to me with impatience. In the night, when everyone was asleep, I sat at the table and read into the machine from a book, and then played it back. It was eerie, the way my voice floated out at me. I heard it several times, at several noise levels, and was appalled at its atonality. My awe for the miracle of music – the sheer suppleness of the singing voice – deepened further.

And yet again I found myself thinking of the fat boy.

Sleep eluded me that night. The resolve of the drain inspector and the mechanism of the recording machine – both things had reignited my need to tell my story. I knew that earlier, the challenge of the writing, word on word – a task for which I had no facility – had stalled me. Just making the laundry list had been exhausting. Now I pulled out the exercise books and read them. And immediately I was glad for the notes. Yes, there was a story to tell. Perhaps an important one. A critically important one.

Perhaps more important than most other pills in the pharmacy of the world's tales.

Now as I settle back into my chair, and prepare to push the button that will bring on a small red light that tells me the machine is ready to embalm my words, I again realize how remiss I have been in becoming dejected. How out of shallow despair I have risked losing everything. It's not important whether I understand the entire meaning of my story or not. Someone will, sooner or later. It's the principle on which men must operate. Do what they ought to, in the faith that someone else will do what they ought to.

I have arrived at this house, in front of this black box, so I can tell my story. The sand is running out fast. Soon there will be implacable shadows of shadows slipping in through the crevices of this old house.

I set the empty mug on the windowsill beyond the table. Not a leaf of the semul is moving. It is time to continue. It is time to push to the finish.

ORIGINS

It did not take me long to earn the trust of ZZ9. It was because of my passionate devotion to the training. I loved it, and was always seeking for the limits to be pushed further and further. We were allotted four hours of sleep every day, and I found even that too much. Always I would be awake half an hour before fall-in time, while my brothers would be scrambling till the last minute to get themselves together.

In the first year it was only about the body. The greatest warriors are finally masters of the mind, but the mind has to be housed in a peerless body. It is the water that nourishes not the vessel, but if the vessel is not firm the water will not hold.

At three in the morning we would start to run, through endless paths in the forest, up the slopes and down, by the dying light of the moon, stilling the hearts of predator and prey. It is not easy to imagine, but twice I have seen my brothers slap a big bear out of their way without breaking step. And more than once I have seen a big cat shrink back in dread as we pounded past. Some days we would run till the sun rose in the east, mounted the heavens above us, and sank in the west. We would run till it was the only thing our limbs knew – and keeping them at rest was a torment.

Let me not speak for everyone. That is one lesson – having come away – I should have learned. That no man can, nor ought to, presume to speak for all men. Though that is how it was with us, in the valley, at all times.

We were five of us, all brothers, and no more than two would become Wafadars. This we knew. The purest of the pure must also be the strongest of the strong. We slept in one small room, on the hard mud floor, next to each other. I loved my brothers. When I looked at them I saw not just a face that was my own, but a spirit that was exactly mine. When I held them close at night I felt our bodies would blend into each other.

I would have gladly stepped aside for any of them. But that would have been a betrayal, a slide into the abyss of the self. Our sworn duty was to give to our people the best among us. We had to push each other till the purest rose to the top, and became the warrior of all of us. None of us was to give any quarter, ever, to another. Never, ever, were we to bring out the weak in the other. Softness, niceness were luxuries, vanities. Our goal was the well-being of the brotherhood, not of any single brother.

As the weeks rolled by, and the regime became more strenuous, there would be days when one of us would stumble. That was when we were most tested. The temptation to stretch out a helping hand to a brother who shared every moment of your life, whose body touched yours as you slept, the temptation was overwhelming, but we fought it.

One evening, when we had already been running for twelve hours and had to run for another six, R215, who was ahead of me, suddenly crumbled at his ankles and fell into a dry gulch. A warrior, he did not cry out in pain or for help. I could see he had landed amid rocks, and if his bones were broken he would be hard put to pulling himself up the steep slope. I turned around to look at the brothers behind me for some gesture, but they were looking at me for the same, and in that moment we knew we could not stop, we must not stop. Weakness was a rot. Once it set in, it would spread to everything.

R215 was not there when we returned to our shed six hours later.

And he was not back when we woke well before dawn, ready to resume running. When we informed the Mentor of the body what had happened, he did not say a word. He spelled out our day's regime – run, swim, run, swim, in alternate cycles of three hours till the moon came up – and we were off.

While the running arena was the deodar slopes, the swimming was done in a five-hundred-metre stretch where the Jhinjheri bubbled through a small plateau in the forest before falling in a roaring splash to the valley floor. We had to enter the water at the lip of the fall and swim upstream till we came to its source in the rocks, then float back, and then swim back up again. A thick rope was strung across the water at the fall, and if you missed grabbing it when you floated back you would be smashed on the rocks below.

All this may sound most exhausting and dangerous, but it was not. Men do not know the possibilities of the body. After a few hours of running or swimming, the limbs acquire a life of their own. They need no exertion of the spirit to keep them going. Sometimes when we stopped, after hours and hours, I felt a fret at not being allowed to go on. I was always aching to discover how impossibly far one could go.

We expected R215 to be back when we returned that night, with the moon well up. But he was not in any of the rooms that were our abode – the cookhouse, the sleeping shed, the meditation room, or the bathroom. When one of us asked the old man who cooked for us, he said through his face which was no older than ours, I have seen a thousand of you come and go.

We stood warned, in shame. Even when we settled into our beds on the hard floor, we held our tongues. Sentimentality was as bad as cowardice. In fact, it was often the source of cowardice. R215 ought to make it back on his own – he had the mind and body for it. If he didn't, well, he didn't deserve to.

They brought his body back two days later. It had bloated a little, the skin smudged black and blue. One could see he had broken his knees when he fell, and clearly his resolve was not greater than his smashed knees. But one thing was remarkable, and was like a sign. While parts of his body had been eaten away by wild animals, the face was unravaged. The face – my face, our face – had deterred fang and claw. Even in death the power of the brotherhood shone strong.

Before he was taken away to be buried in the Family Garden, the cavernous pit of final togetherness which is every brother's eternally equal resting place, ZZ9 asked the four of us if we were sad. We said no. Why not, he asked. We said because our brother had succumbed attempting to become the best he could, for all of us. He said but was it not every brother's duty to protect each brother? We said, no, the duty was to protect the brotherhood, not the brother. By focusing on the brother we were likely to lose sight of the brotherhood. It is what happened in the world out there.

Me, mine, myself. Man over mankind.

Were we, he said, willing to be similarly abandoned? Yes we were, we said, all at once, no shadow of doubt darkening our minds.

We suffered no further depletion in the first two years. By the end of it our bodies were capable of feats we could not have imagined in the home or the barracks. Our stamina was limitless, and the strength in our limbs beyond measure. We could do endless push-ups on a single finger, and endlessly pull ourselves up with a single hand. If we locked an arm around anything, man or beast, nothing could unlock it. A single punch could slay anything, man or beast. The four of us, together, could kick in a stone shed in minutes.

We also became as arboreal as we were terrestrial and aquatic, capable of scaling the tallest trees with the speed of squirrels, and of moving through their tops like loose-limbed monkeys. The Mentor would clap his hands and we would be gone, a small rustle in the high branches marking our passage.

Sometimes for days we were ordered not to alight at all. We had to eat, drink and perform our ablutions in the trees. Soon we were able to blend into the bark like jungle cats, and sleep hanging from branches like the black bats of night.

We also learned to leap. On the run, without breaking step, in a single bound, we could jump more than twenty feet. We did this daily over deep crevices. We knew the catechism. If you looked to fail, failure would embrace you. The blood and bones of fearful brothers stained the rocks everywhere.

At the end of the year we were offered an exit if we did not wish to continue. Actually that was an option available to us at any time. In the brotherhood everything was voluntary. But of course no one withdrew. In fact it was a proud tradition that no brother had ever backed away once on this path. Yes, many had been crippled and many had died, but no one, not one, ever, had lost his resolve.

Aum had taught us there was a price to be paid for the glorious life, and that was something each of us was happy to do.

Everything we had achieved in the first two years was ruthlessly tested in the third. As ZZ9 said, Even a dog is a fierce animal till it meets a panther.

A Wafadar had to be fashioned to be superior to any beast he would ever encounter anywhere. And to be prepared against every surprise.

By now we had muscles and lungs, shoulders and limbs, fingers and feet that were infinitely capable, but did we have the ears and eyes, the instincts and intuitions, the sixth and seventh senses that made a warrior indestructible?

This was the year in which we killed all complacence. Never again would we be unaware of the most infinitesimal movement around us, every beat of a mosquito's wing; never again would we sleep without being awake. It was a year in which every day, every hour, every minute we were challenged. Snares, traps, surprises were set for us everywhere. While running we could be tripped, flung into a ditch, hit by a falling log. In the water we could be snarled in nets, impaled on wooden stakes, hit by falling boulders. The tops of the trees were similarly unsafe. Any branch could be a sawn-off one; the thin green serpent that struck like a lash, swelling your joints like a pumpkin, could be waiting behind each leaf.

Poisonous vermin were insinuated into our bedding, and our door left open to rampaging animals. The food could be poisoned, the water laced with venom. We knew the stories. Brothers, for a moment of laxity, had died in every kind of way. Each death had imbued the collective memory with a new caution.

We learned the hard way. Our bodies were pummelled, smashed, the flesh torn, the bones broken. We had access to the apothecary all the time, and he patched us up time and again. But far more than the apothecary, we had to depend on the Commander of the Senses to save us from destruction.

No one knew how old he was, but it was accepted that he was the oldest among the great Helmsmen. The man in the cookhouse, whose own age was a mystery, said the Commander was already old when he, the cook, was still a boy. Aum himself, the Commander had learned at the feet of Aum himself. It was the reason he was so consummate. At regular intervals even the great Helmsmen submitted themselves to the Commander – for a man's senses are not mastered once and for all time, but have to be continually duelled with.

For the Commander, the body was nothing. Everything was the mind. He spoke to us in a low rumble that seemed to come from somewhere under the ground. After you had been listening to it for a while, it was like a spell.

As we sat completely naked, our legs crossed, our wrists on our knees, our eyes closed, the rumbling voice taught us to expand our consciousness till it filled the world and straddled the entire universe. Till we became one with Aum. At such times I could feel a myriad planets whizzing around me like tiny gnats, and the sun was nothing but a glow worm near my elbow. Entire galaxies passed under my armpit, swept over my navel, and disappeared around my waist. The deep silence of space was lit by nothing but my inner radiance. Everything emanated from me. Everything was me.

As we lived out our fullness, the Commander's subterranean voice would start to shrink us. Soon I was nothing but a speck on the ground, a grain of dust. Every leaf of grass towered over me like a giant deodar. I scurried for safety as big beastly ants moved past me on hairy muscular legs, their big jaws quivering with menace. A monstrous serpent, its hide thick and scaly, made a slow undulation. In one movement it could smother a thousand of me. Then, suddenly, all fear vanished as I was shrunk further till I was too small to be seen or touched, too small to be eaten or crushed.

At either end of my consciousness I was taken beyond fear. That was the goal. I had to know both omnipotence and oblivion, and know that both were simply me. Always, I was everything and nothing.

The Commander did it to us again and again. Made us omni and then nil. It was a kind of mental tempering, like craftsmen do with swords. Hot fire, cold water – repeatedly, till the steel shines its toughness and is beyond the touch of hot or cold.

Besides fear, the Commander tutored us in the pathology of pain. We learned it was the minds of men that filled them with pain long before it actually occurred. Yes, there was something called physical pain, but it was only a fraction of what men ended up suffering. Fed on fear, the prick of a thorn ballooned into the head of an axe. The man whose mind was pure and strong would feel nothing for a long time, till the pain actually broke his body. Soon I was able to look at my skin as the bark of a tree, unmoved as it was scraped, cut, punctured and scorched.

All this arose from an incredible stillness of the mind. I had worked on it in the home and the barracks, but now the Commander took it to another level. I had trained myself to hear and to sense by silencing my inner noise and by practising with the blindfold. But this was about developing an intuition that was as solid and reliable as eyesight.

Day on day the Commander shut down every rustle inside our cranium, emptying our brains of all movement. As we became hollow and still, vast caverns without a single mote of thought drifting through them, incredibly, a hundred eyes began to open up all over our bodies. In the back of my head, down my spine, on my shoulders, on the top of my head, on my knees and elbows, my toes and fingers – suddenly I could see all around me, in every direction. And not just eyes. A hundred ears bloomed all across my body too. With every eye there was an ear. Sitting there, eyes closed, mind empty, I could see and hear everything happening around me for hundreds of feet.

In the beginning we could sustain it only for a short span. Soon, the wisp of a thought would float through the head; then another; and another. Each one would shut down one eye and one ear. In no time a growing buzz would smother our new senses.

The Commander's low rumble would then remind us that the problem with men is that they think too much. He taught us that every thought is a lethal arrow; every argument, a flashing sword. In the world out there men failed to be purposeful because they were at such bitter war inside their own heads. As the arrows flew and the steel clashed, as the din of battle rang inside his head, it was all a man could do to hold his poise. There was no way he could forge ahead with meaning and with resolve.

This was not the way of the pure. There was no noise inside the heads of the chosen. All their arsenal was pointed in the same direction.

And sure enough, as we aligned the weaponry in our head, as we stilled the buzz of thought, the eyes and ears on our body would begin to open. Soon, aided by the hypnotic rumble of the Commander, we were able to sustain this miraculous state for hours on end. It was like being in a trance where one is completely empty and at the same time completely aware of everything.

Each day after he had finished disciplining our minds, the Commander would tell us a story. Most times it was about Aum or the pilgrim fathers. This was the moment I waited for. It stirred me to hear how the great fathers, bone weary after the long march, had been instantly rejuvenated by the sight of the promised land. How by the sweat of their brow and the iron of their will they had shaped the valley for the mighty tasks of the future. How day on day the land was tamed, the forests mastered, the waters harnessed.

Aum was everywhere – Ali and Alaiya by his side – ranging over the uncharted territory, reviving with a mere touch the flagging and the fevered. The Commander said as a small boy he had once received a pat on his head from the luminous one, and more than eight decades later the energy of that moment still beat in his veins.

The Commander said just as we were doing now, he had heard the stories of the early years from the great swordsman Amar. The Commander said though he was already old, Amar had such strength in his arms he could bring a wild horse to his knees with a twist of his wrists. Amar told them – just as the Commander was telling us now – that each evening, after the sun had died, everyone gathered by the Bodhi to sip at the source. Always, first Ali spoke and then Alaiya, while the unequalled one sat, as we sat now, legs crossed, wrists on knees, eyes closed.

The two great guardians spoke of quotidian things, of the work done, and the work remaining. They reminded the flock of its unique destiny, and extolled its virtues of fortitude and purposefulness. Then they narrated the stories everyone was waiting for – of Aum's divine feats. How with a gentle push he had felled a gargantuan deodar that was blocking their progress; how, as a child plays with pebbles, he had rolled giant rocks into the racing Jhinjheri to form a path for the flock; how he had nudged aside wild animals, panthers and bears, with an admonishing hand.

Then, said the Commander, Amar told them the peerless one would open his eyes and start to speak. Till this moment many would have been fidgety, playing the games of dancing fingers and darting eyes that small children play in the midst of adults. Now all movement would cease. A voice with the timbre of thunder but soothing like a summer breeze would start to wash over all of them.

Aum would tell them the secrets of life and death. He would tell them the story of man, so flawed, so full of cowardice and deceit, so full of ego and possession, so full of weakness and venom, so full of misery and grief. To illustrate this he would tell them the story of Jaya, the greatest epic of the world.

Three thousand years ago the most magnificent of men strode the earth. They had strength, courage, beauty, learning. They also had wealth, power, breeding and intelligence. They were knit tightly in ties of family and love, of loyalty and honour. They asked the big questions of right conduct and right action, of dharma and karma. They tried to understand cosmic cause and effect. They taught themselves to claim the world, and to as easily renounce it.

And yet, and yet they failed.

Why?

It was the question that haunted Aum. And in order to apprise his flock of the daunting challenges that faced the pure, he recounted the stories of these grand men and women who floundered despite their magnificence. Among them were kings and warriors, priests and teachers, queens and princesses. At the very end, the lot of each was only loss and sorrow. Everything they had pursued was turned to ash. Not in the final negation that is death. But in the final negation that is the soul's defeat. Even those who won the great war of their desires knew only the taste of ash on their swollen tongues.

The Commander said even as a boy, hearing this story from Amar, who had heard it and lived it at the feet of the unblemished one, he had been fired by an excitement that made his hair stand. The names rang in his head all day. Bhishma, Drona, Arjuna, Bhima, Karna, Duryodhana, Krishna, Jarasandha, Satyaki, Dhristadyumna, Ekalavya, Abhimanyu, Vidura, Shakuni, Dhritarashtra, Draupadi, Kunti, Gandhari, Ghatotkacha, Ashwatthama, Yudhishtira. Men and women of such fire and such force that they were the equal of the gods.

Amar listened to these tales without paying heed to why the luminous one was telling them. Till one evening, sitting under the star-crowded skies, wedged between scores of bodies, his coarse blanket tight around him, he suddenly began to realize what their true purpose was.

It was the day, Amar said, that he began to grow up. Now he understood that Aum was not extolling those mythic men. His purpose was not to praise their strength and their beauty. On the contrary, he was wondering at their shortcomings and failures. In telling the epic of Jaya he wanted his flock to focus on what undid men, even extraordinary ones. After he finished the day's narration, he would proceed to ask questions about it. Anyone from the gathered family of the chosen could volunteer an answer.

Aum would say, So who do you think is the most magnificent character in Jaya?

In one voice, many would say, Bhishma!

Aum would say, The old patriarch. Really – why?

Several voices would say, He lived for others, never for himself. In the prime of his youth he took a vow of celibacy for the happiness of his father, and never gave it up. And with that he renounced his right to be king.

Aum would say, Do you think he did right?

Someone would say, Absolutely. It was a selfless act so his father could marry the woman he loved.

Aum would say, Should he not have thought of his people, who saw in him their ideal king?

There would be silence as everyone tried to balance the scales.

Aum would say, Did selfish love – of his father – make him forsake his real duty?

Someone would say, But he sacrificed his happiness and his throne for the happiness of his father!

Aum would say, Could it have been an act of poor judgment? A sentimental bowing to his father's covetousness. His father was old, he had known enough pleasure all his life; should he not have been thinking beyond it? Should not the young Bhishma have guided his father into wisdom rather than pander to his inappropriate desire?

Someone would say, quietly, Perhaps young Bhishma was driven by love.

Aum would say, Love? Or something else. Could it have been vanity? My celibacy. My throne. My sacrifice. My father. My place in legend. Was it essentially about himself and nothing else?

There would be silence as everyone tried to pull their opinions inside out and examine them.

Aum would say, Though she was betrothed in love to another, Bhishma abducted Amba for his half-brother, who then rejected her because her heart lay elsewhere. When she went back to her betrothed, he too spurned her as a soiled woman. She then went pleading to Bhishma to marry her and save her from ignominy, but he too pushed her away. In despair she killed herself. Was Bhishma right in rejecting her?

Someone would say, Well, he had to be true to his dharma – his oath of celibacy.

Aum would say, And what of the dharma to protect a guiltless woman whom he had wronged? Was it his vanity that made him think only of his own splendour and nothing of the woman's distress?

Someone would say, There is a lesser and a greater dharma...

Aum would say, And in this case, tell me, which is which?

When a long time had passed, and everyone had seen several stars burn across the sky, Aum would say, When Dushasana dragged Draupadi in and tried to strip her of her vestments, Bhishma was present in the palace hall, but he did nothing. Was that the conduct of a wise and great man?

A feeble voice would say, No, it was not. But his dharma bound him in loyalty to his king. We know he was in agony but could not interfere.

Aum would say, in that voice of thunder that was soothing like a summer breeze, His own little dharma, always his little dharma. And was there no dharma towards a woman's humiliation, and the disgrace of his entire people? Was he following some immutable cosmic law? Or was he just calculating his own little stature?

Someone would say, There is a lesser and a greater dharma…

Aum would say, And in this case, tell me, which is which?

The flock would quietly uncramp its legs, and listen to the wind in the trees and the fluid chatter of the Amrita. The moon would be moving above them, and in the dance of the torches the luminous one would look the god he was.

Aum would say, It was the war to end all wars. On either side stood arrayed the greatest warriors the world had ever seen. It was a war between right and wrong. It was a war between cousins. The cousins had one great grandsire…

The flock would exhale, Bhishmaaa…

Aum would say, Yes, Bhishma. Four score and ten years now, his beard trailing below his chest. Bhishma, long entrusted with the guardianship of his grand-nephews, with their upbringing as princes and men. On whose side do you think this old man of mighty arms and moral lustre should have fought?

Someone would say, On the side of the right. On the side of the five great brothers.

Aum would say, And did he?

The flock would exhale, Nooo…

Aum would say, Why did such an old and wise man fight on the side of the wrong against the right?

Slowly, someone would say, His dharma made him loyal to his king…

Aum would say, And what of his dharma towards the people? Was it not for him to stand by what was right, to fight for what was right, to give to his people rulers who were in the right?

Someone would whisper, There is a lesser and a greater dharma…

Aum would say, And in this case, tell me, which is which? His loyalty to a king or his loyalty to a people? And if this old man could not understand which was which, why did he fight at all? If he could not lend his strength to the right, he could have at least kept it from the wrong. Why did he not?

Someone would say, Perhaps he could not turn his back on his duty. Stand by while his kin drew their bows and swords and fell on each other. To act was then the written code, each warrior's bounden duty.

Aum would say, Duty or vanity? Which do you think it really was? Was he following the higher code of action, or is it that he could not bear to be left out of the historic moment? He was offered the command of the army as a gesture – an offer due to him as the oldest but meant to be refused. But he took it! Is it that, even at four score and ten, his sinews aged, his bones brittle, he could not resist the pomp of standing at the head of ranks of majestic warriors?

The pause would fill the night as a ripe fruit fills its skin, waiting to burst.

Aum would say, And you know what the consequence of the old man's vanity was. It meant for the first ten days of the great battle – of a mere eighteen days – they lost the mighty arms of the greatest archer in their midst. Insulted by the old man, magnificent Karna refused to fight as long as the old man remained on the field. And the old man fought as only an old man can – with a wavering heart and fatiguing limbs. He served his king poorly, for his heart was inconstant; it lay with the enemy. By the time the old man fell and the real battle could begin, he had already ceded the advantages of his far superior army.

By now we would be in a trance. The very thought that the Commander as a small boy had heard this story from Amar who had seen and heard Aum say all these things was impossibly stirring. The Commander's face was no older than mine, but what an old and deep place he had come from. He would explain to us, as the timeless master had once explained to our forebears, the true meaning of the stories and the interrogations.

Why was the great Bhishma, forsaker of personal pleasure, peerless patriarch, revered over several millennia by countless millions, in the end a tragic failure, presiding over an age of tragic failure? If he was so wise, why could he not hammer out justice and prevent a holocaust?

If he was so splendid, why did he oversee the complete ruination and destruction of his house and clan?

Me, mine, myself.

The answer to all these questions lay in the ego.

The Commander told us what Amar had told him. How Aum, the flawless one, day on day, would unspool each great person's story to show them how men undid themselves and all that was worthy in the world. And with the telling of each story, day on day, the flock came to understand the perils of me, mine, myself.

It was from this understanding, this question of the corrosive ego that the answer of the face finally arose. Vanity began with that first look into unmoving water. When the first face was made it was made in the image of the unblemished one. To begin with, in his infinite grace, Aum was pleased that everyone should look like him. If the idea of equality was to be a glorious tree then it was imperative its roots ran to the core. The master and the pupil: seamlessly same.

Soon, however, the faultless one realized it was a vanity – of his own – to have everyone adorned with his face. And so the face began to change. The ustaad of the time first gave it Ali's eyebrows and eyes, and added to it Alaiya's rich mouth. Now when you looked at it you saw a vision of all three. This too was not acceptable to the matchless one. Walking with the ustaad, he would point to one of his children and say, His nose, his nose is full of purpose – give the face his nose. Or he would see a cleft on a chin, and whisper, That might lend it the perfect look of determination. Try it.

And so each day new features were added and old ones removed. The ustaad worked under the big rhododendron – where the workshops stand today – with its fretwork of branches protecting him from sun and squall. When children crept up to spy on him – the home was still not set up – he would look up from his crouch and say, Stop bothering me. I am crafting your future.

The incandescent one would carefully examine each fresh attempt and ask for some change. In a few weeks every recognizable trait was gone – the face had become something utterly original. Late one evening, with the sun long gone and the restless flames dancing on tall torches, and the flock shuffling its limbs as it settled itself, Alaiya stepped up to the platform and asked for four volunteers prepared to instantly sacrifice their lives for the true path of the prophet.

The first one to stand was the man they called Camel. He was tall and stooped and slow of mind, but in the long march had carried on his back every tiring child and woman. By the time Ali embraced him, three others were already standing. The Commander said Amar told them that he sprang to his feet too, but sitting at the back amid the shadows, he was only spotted later.

As Alaiya led away the truest of the true, the flock waited in quiet unknowing. The ways of Aum were mysterious. He saw what ordinary mortals could not. How easily, one morning, he had embarked on a long march to the end of the world.

In every heart was a mix of dread and anticipation. Would the master ask of them what they were unequal to? Would they let him down? Or would he open new doors of perception through which they could all travel on light feet?

The moon was up when the first stranger appeared before them. His face shone, and every muscle in it was set and unmoving. It was the visage of purity and purpose. Amar said every member of the flock sitting there, man and woman, young and old, felt themselves thrill. Amar himself felt a bolt of lightning shoot through his body. The Commander said, hearing Amar, he'd felt the same bolt. And we, hearing the Commander, felt ourselves no less on fire.

Amar said in a moment there was another and another and another stranger in front of them, and they all were the same, and the wind whipped the light of the flames over their smooth cheeks and unblinking eyes, and the flock of the faithful exploded in a spontaneous cry of ecstasy that filled the valley and shook the skies.

Aum!!!

The very first sound of the universe, befitting of who he was, the very first of everything. While Aum was the first one to wear the face, Ali had been the second, and then the Camel and the other three bravehearts. In the ensuing days and weeks every man of the flock acquired the splendid face, became one with the effulgent one. The face now represented the best of us. It was greater than all of us. It was the sum of all our parts. It was the symbol of our equality and of our brotherhood. It was clear as the waters of the Amrita that we were the pure, unique among mortals, chosen of the divine.

A WAFADAR

At the end of three years no rejections needed to be made. There were only two of us left. One of my brothers had lost his right arm in a moment's lapse. Moving through the trees he had put his hand into a snare. He had fallen to the forest floor while his arm, plucked out of its socket, dangled by the tree. You can tell how good he was by the fact that he landed on his feet and immediately tried to climb back up the tree to retrieve his arm.

The other brother had succumbed to the prick of the chonch. The apothecary had been training us for months with the hardwood pins that are every Wafadar's most lethal and sacred weapon. A Wafadar is supposed to know the secret of every tube of blood in the human body. On the first day of our instruction, the apothecary had said a Wafadar with his chonch had to be skilled as a leech. He should be able to drain the blood out of a body without the body getting to know. The greatest Wafadars could make perforations so small and so accurate that a man was emptied of his blood and dead before he realized he had been pricked.

Yet it was not really about killing. It was about controlling perfectly the damage you wished to wreak. Mastery of the chonch meant you could drain a man in mere minutes or make his life ebb away over weeks, half-drop by half-drop. You could make a victim deaf, or just blind – or just half of either. You could wither away only one leg or just one arm.

The thinnest of the eleven chonch was fine as a hair, its insinuation into the skin subtler than a mosquito bite. The thickest was fit to dig a hole in the heart big enough to make the blood spout like a spring and beyond all suturing. The nine pins in between were of varying sizes, in length and diameter, the longest capable of entering at the navel and emerging through the spine. Each set was the product of months of hard labour, and each chonch was tempered by coatings of resin and trials through fire. Even the goatskin belt into which each chonch was perfectly fitted was superbly contoured to be worn on the body like a second skin. And that is what every Wafadar was enjoined to do – wear it always like a skin, and take care of it in similar fashion.

To begin with, the apothecary taught us on diagrams. There were a hundred charts done on parchment that opened up every secret of the body, the last lingering of every nerve, the last journey of every drop of blood. Initially it seemed impossible to comprehend this chaos of coloured lines that lay beneath skin and bone and filled them with life. Then the colours acquired meaning. Red for the arteries; blue for the veins; black for the capillaries.

Soon we began to understand that of these thousands of lines, we had to first master only a few dozen. It was basically a tree, with scores of branches and numberless leaves. To disfigure a tree you had to hack at the branches; to kill it you had to go for the trunk. There would be reason to work the leaves when the goal was slow and prolonged disfigurement and death, leaf by leaf, nerve by nerve. But that would come later.

For the moment we set aside the leaves, those filaments of blood and nerve that caressed the skin everywhere, and worked to become consummate destroyers of trunks and branches, able to swiftly puncture the thick red lines with any of the eleven chonch.

One morning as we returned from a quick four-hour run through the forest, the apothecary was waiting for us with a brother laid out on the ground before him. The brother's face was in disrepair, fraying at the nose, and he was breathing heavily, in jerks. His eyes were closed. The apothecary said parchment was not flesh, and you could not taste fruit by merely sketching it.

We stripped the man of his garments, and he was not very old. The hair on his chest was still dark. The skin at the neck was taut, but the limbs looked wasted. The apothecary said this brother was a martyr. Struck by a debilitating ailment of the lungs he had chosen to gift his life to the brotherhood, for the education of the new Wafadars, the warriors of the pure.

Under the sharp eye of our tutor we took turns piercing the brother's body. Though his limbs jerked each time we put in a chonch, he did not open his eyes even once. He appeared to be in a kind of stupor. In a few hours we had found and perforated most of the thick red lines, and our brother's body was rich with daubs and stripes.

At every step the apothecary told us how much pressure we must apply, how deep the chonch must go, how long to wait before pulling it out. After weeks of puncturing rough parchment it was a pleasure to pierce real flesh, to feel the skin break, the first slow dot of red appear.

The brother took three days to die, and in that time we perforated his body in a thousand places. The apothecary ordered us to be relentless, to test our knowledge in every way possible. The sacrifice must not go to waste, he said. Remarkably, the brother did not wake once. Not even when I, on the third day, pierced his right eye with a sharp jab – for the ear, you had to essay a slow, firm slide. All he did was to jerk and moan.

Later the apothecary – a short man with fleshy forearms – stood over the dead brother and with a long stick pointed out all the things we had done wrong. Missed targets, messy entries, inaccurate pressure, wrong chonch, delayed withdrawal – it seemed we'd done hardly anything right. And this, said our tutor, was a man who was barely alive, who could not move, who could not retaliate.

Two days later there was another brother waiting for us, serving up his body for the brotherhood. The apothecary said some people had to sacrifice their lives in times of peace so that others might do so in battle. This brother was younger. His kidneys had failed. He too was in a stupor and did not wake once as we riddled him with our chonch. Yet again we felt the pleasure of a living body, living skin, living blood.

On the third day, when he was dead, our tutor once more stood over him with a stick and pointed out our failures. We had done better. But we needed to be neater. Minimal splashes; aesthetic entries and exits. Unmessy death. The chonch was an art form.

Mere killing was easy. There were scores of different weapons. A Wafadar did not even need them. He could snap necks all day just as women pluck flowers. But the aim was to give to the end of life a fitting sanctity.

That was the meaning of the chonch, and of its mastery.

After that, over the next two weeks, there were two more brothers, as deeply comatose, whom we honoured with a far more skilled performance. When we were done the bodies looked beautifully embroidered. The apothecary gave us no praise. And ZZ9 in his weekly audience said, the true test lay in carving a running fish not a still one.

A few days later we understood what he meant. Assembling in the morning after our run we found our tutor leading in a man tethered by a rope. There was a black hood over his head and his hands were lashed behind his back. The ankles too were tied together with twine and he was hopping to where the rope tugged him.

When the apothecary pulled off the hood we were startled. The man did not have the face. He was not of us. A bandana had been run across his mouth so he could not speak. On his forehead was the lump of a blow. He was unshaven and his eyes were wild. Clearly a savage – from somewhere out there, the other world. I was riveted by his ugliness. The big nose, the pits in the skin, the hair in the ears, the fat lips, the bushy eyebrows.

When our teacher pulled off his bandana the savage fell to his knees mumbling for mercy, the drool dropping from his mouth. He spoke our language – the language the founding fathers had brought with them – but he spoke it like a barbarian. The moment his hands were cut free, the savage flung himself flat on the ground, clutching at the apothecary's feet, whining to be forgiven. It was disgusting, the abjectness – clear evidence that men out there were without honour.

Pushing his hands away, the apothecary said, don't be so alarmed, you are free to escape. And he leaned forward and cut the twine around his ankles. The savage stood up unsteadily, flicking his wild eyes at each of us. He was wearing tight pajamas and a loose short tunic. I felt the blood in my body begin to move.

Go, hissed the apothecary. Run! If you can get away from these boys then you have your freedom. The savage stayed in a crouch, swivelling his eyes. The apothecary said, I promise you they will not start for an hour, so go, claim your freedom! And he hit him with the butt of his dagger and the savage took off like a deer startled by a big cat.

In a few minutes he was in the forest and lost to sight.

The apothecary picked two of us and spelled out the rules. The savage had to be brought back dying but not dead, and the only weapon to be used was the chonch. No hands, no legs, nothing – just the chonch.

When the hour had run out, our tutor gave the nod, and we were off in a flash. T242 took to the trees while I sprinted along the forest floor. True to his nature, the savage had run without guile or grace. We could have followed him with our eyes closed. Though I was running fast, each time I looked up my brother was pacing me. In fifteen minutes we could hear him; in twenty he was within eyeshot. He was tired, running in a stumbling panic. Not worthy of two of us.

I looked up and touched my ankle. The next moment my brother had swooped down on the savage and before he knew it stuck a small chonch deep into the vein of his left calf. The savage yelped like a stricken animal and turned to protect himself, but by then my brother had vanished into the trees. It was my turn now. I came up on him on soundless feet, and had pushed my chonch into his right calf and slipped away before he spotted my vanishing shadow. He began to bay in fear and twist and turn as he ran. It was amusing to witness: how men fear what they cannot see even more than what they can.

Diving like an eagle my brother perforated the back of the fugitive's knee with the eighth chonch – the favoured of most Wafadars, like a small dagger, easily plunged and withdrawn. The savage wailed, trying to lash out with his right arm. By then I had run past him, unseen, and punctured the back of his other knee. Now he was running screaming and waving both his arms.

I gestured to my brother and in a moment we had exchanged places. This was nicer. Most Wafadars prefer the trees. The view is commanding, and the freedom to manoeuvre unmatched. I flowed through the branches easily, staying over the savage, wondering at his desperate animal self. When my brother signalled I went down in a slow loop, turning in the air twice, and landing on the balls of my feet I stabbed the chonch between the moving buttocks of the savage, and even as he fell shrieking, I was gone, back up the trees.

He had seen nothing, and he was now rolled on to his back, alternately panting like a dog and crying like an infant. In a while he struggled to his feet and began to stumble on again. Within minutes I saw my brother – running so low and so fast he was a veritable snake in the grass – flash past him, piercing him between the buttocks exactly as I had.

Wailing, he backed up against the broad trunk of a deodar. In a trice I was on top of him, looking down at his trembling head. His legs had given way, and he had slumped to his haunches. Suddenly my brother was next to me, and we were sitting perched like two eagles examining an insect. The insect was sniffling loudly and moaning for his mother.

It was pathetic. We could have gently dropped a chonch and skewered his brains, but that was not the idea. We had been given six hours to bleed him. And we had to take him back dying, not dead. This was a test of our skill, not our destructive power.

We waited, more motionless than the leaves. Starting at every sound, looking around frantically, the savage was examining his wounds. He gave a loud groan when he found the small chonch in his calves and pulled them out. The blood began to ooze and he quickly dug for fistfuls of mulch to pack the wound. He slapped some on the back of his knees too, and also pushed it between his buttocks. Then he closed his eyes to feel the relief of the damp soil.

Flowing down to the lowest branch, my brother inverted himself, hanging upside down by his toes till his face was right next to the savage's head. Then he gave the laugh of the high mountain woodpecker. An eerie cackle that unwinds in a long wave. The savage sat up in panic and turned his head, only to find the beautifully frozen features of my brother inches from him, upside down. He screamed in crazed terror and ran into the trees, with another long cackle from my brother chasing him.

We were toying with our task because it was so light. But it was not amusement. It was work. We gave him fifteen minutes to run, and then we were again upon him. In the next four hours, working with restraint, we closed one eye, opened one eardrum, put a chonch – the fourth – through his nostrils, sprung a vein in each arm, and one in the abdomen. We were careful not to touch any of the big red lines. One mistake and he would be gone. A ridiculously easy task would end in disaster.

By the time we picked him up to take him back he could barely stand. We had done well, I thought. Apart from crippling his body, we had unhinged his mind. He was mumbling in a kind of delirium. When we laid him in front of our tutor, he was a rag doll, all his parts out of alignment, and even his good eye only half-open and unseeing.

The apothecary examined our work carefully, asking questions.

Why had we chosen this chonch and not that? Why had we chosen to pierce this part and not that? Was this not too deep a wound? Whose handiwork was the eye? The entry was not crisp enough. It was true – a running fish is not the same as a still one. Each of us had to point out our individual efforts. Fortunately we'd managed to match them perfectly, neither moving one perforation ahead, since this was a joint task not a contest between us.

As the assessment proceeded I looked at the face of the savage and was once again repelled. More than the punctured eye and congealed blood it was the pit and flab of the skin, the crudity of the nose and mouth, the rage of hair everywhere – cheeks, nostrils, ears. Involuntarily I ran my fingers over the smoothness of my own face, our face, and I was filled with gratitude for the brotherhood.

Then the tutor said, Okay, who'll finish it now?

Before I could move, my brother had dropped to his knees and put a chonch through the big red line in the throat. The blood spurted in a sharp thread, and jerking his head the savage gargled in it a few times before falling back. The limbs twitched once or twice and then they too were still.

Later, after we had burnt him, we sat down to make our expiation. Led by the apothecary, we chanted the invocation:

In the path of the pure, endless challenges are sown.
May our limbs be sturdy; may our hearts be stone.

I felt power and purpose course through me as I chanted. And we did not stop chanting till a profound peace had settled on us all.

The next savage was given to the other two brothers. It didn't go well. He was burly, and he decided not to run. He found a shallow groove in the mountain-face and tucked himself in there. As their hours ran down and he did not emerge, the brothers were forced to follow him into the narrow space. He threw rocks at them, and kept them at bay with a stave. It was not as if the savage was a match for them. In an unfettered situation they could have walked in blindfolded and broken him into a hundred pieces. But now they could only wield the chonch.

Eventually, in the sixth hour, their time running out, they crawled in as a double-backed serpent. As the savage attacked the one on top, the one below, brandishing a chonch in either hand, swiftly opened up every small and big red line in the savage's legs, and then pushed the eighth into his genitals. This made him wail like an unholy beast. But coward that he was, he refused to emerge into the open, continuing to thrash about in his little rock hole.

Eventually, all finesse had to be forsaken. By the time the savage collapsed he was a mess, leaking all over. He did not survive the journey back. When they laid him out in front of our tutor he was a damp and dead bundle. Using his short stick, the apothecary went over each perforation, pointing out the chaotic handiwork, while the brothers stood abashed at their failure. Once again I stared in revulsion at the dead face. The small puffy eyes, the fat nostrils, and hair everywhere, so animal.

Finally straightening up, the apothecary asked, What do you think they did wrong?

I said, Failed on both counts – failed to make the deadline and killed him.

He said, You are right. What should they have done?

We all stayed silent. It was not for us to declare these things.

With his blood-smeared stick he wrote in the mud. Choice.

Looking up he said, A Wafadar always possesses clarity, always knows what to do. You should have decided: break the rule of time by waiting till the savage crawled out, or break the rule of life by going in and swiftly dispatching him. This garbage that has been brought back is the consequence of vagueness and indecision. The butchers from the cookhouse would have produced such work.

That evening, after burning the savage, we chanted the expiation for much longer than usual. We had let down the apothecary. Our limbs needed to be stronger, our hearts made of sterner stone.

The next few savages over the next few weeks were mastered with increasing assurance. The savages kept changing – thinner, sturdier, older, younger – but two things remained constant. The first was their abjectness, their craven fear for their lives. The second was their sheer ugliness. From the moment they were brought in till we burnt them I could not take my eyes off their coarseness. It seemed inevitable to me that men so unpleasant looking must be unpleasant in every aspect of their lives.

The apothecary tested us with different tasks. With precision he would outline what parts he wished immobilized, how much damage done. Then it came down to one warrior hunting down one savage; then it became one of us hunting down two. Of course, the basic rule remained unchanging. You used the chonch and nothing but the chonch. It was the tool of deliverance, ordained by Aum himself.

In a few months we had become so proficient we could bring back a savage, inches from death, on whose body you would be hard put to find the fatal aperture. Sometimes that alone would be the task set for us. And when we were back, the apothecary would call the old man from the kitchen and ask him to locate where the wound lay.

The apothecary said, Out there men live in terror of death. Their terror multiplies when they cannot tell its cause. Often, with your chonch, you will have to deepen the mystery of death – and its terror. Fear makes men irrationally pliant.

The next step was to master the chonch blindfolded. So we could work it in the dark, our fingertips reading a body like eyes. The years of early self-training paid off now. Pursuing the savages through the forest, a thick cloth tied across my eyes, I could do this better than anyone else. In fact I even found it more gratifying. Shutting out all sight heightened my concentration, made me more purposeful and accurate.

The apothecary said, Maybe I should blind you permanently.

This was however far from true for M442. I saw the slight tremor in his skin each time the blindfold was tightened and he began the chase. The cloth shut off sight, but nervousness, I knew, muffled all the senses. It was no surprise then that he put his hand into the snare and left his arm on the tree as he crashed to the ground.

When we finally picked him up – a day later – he was lying in a pool of congealing blood. We could see he had tried to climb back up the tree to retrieve his arm – which now swayed gently in the wind. After the apothecary had applied packs of poultices, brothers from the infirmary took him away on a stretcher, leaving at a brisk jog.

The apothecary said, He had it coming. I feel relief each time one of you stumbles. It's best you don't make it, than go through imperfect. He will not grow another arm, but he will grow old to understand he was unworthy of being a Wafadar.

The other brother who did not make it erred at the final test of the chonch. By now each of us had worked through half a dozen savages, as well as many dying brothers who'd sacrificed their bodies for our education. The final challenge of the chonch was against oneself.

One morning the three of us stood in a line as our tutor called out the run. In three minutes a hundred clear perforations in the right thigh. The test lay in avoiding every big red line, and as many small ones. Afterwards, with his short stick he made the count. The skin had to be properly punctured for a score. Our thighs were damp with blood, and we had to keep wiping them with a wet cloth so he could see clearly. More than ninety each: acceptable.

Then it got more difficult. No part was left unembroidered. Abdomen, belly, arms. As the size of the chonch kept varying, and the speed of the test escalated, it became a call to the utmost skill and focus. By now we were slippery with a thousand leaks. Mostly they were from the very fine tendrils that lie everywhere just beneath the skin, so swift to open and shut their tiny red mouths.

After each set we would wipe our skin as the count was made. Each time T242 would be the first to finish, the first to be examined. We were working with the sixth chonch now and had just finished scoring our chests with as much caution as speed. The sixth was capable of bursting the heart. I felt our tutor was beginning to disapprove of T242. A hint of arrogance seemed to have entered my swift brother.

You did the best you could, for the brotherhood. Not to prove yourself better than your brothers.

For the last test, the apothecary set out a sequence. The first to go was T242. Kneeling on the ground, in three minutes, with the seventh chonch, he had to make twenty-five holes in his neck. Anyone but a Wafadar would be hard put to make five. My brother went off like an arrow out of a bow. I think it was the seventeenth jab that pierced the fat red line. We saw the spurt, and it did not ebb. Of course my brother kept going, and I think the twenty-fifth made a second breach.

The apothecary said nothing. He looked at me and I dropped to my knees and started. I married speed with precision, closing my eyes, seeing every red line clearly as if I had peeled open my skin. One part of my mind kept the time, the other counted the injections. When I finished, the apothecary gestured to the last of us, who began immediately.

The rivulets from my neck were running down my chest and back. T242 had by now slumped to the ground and had clamped his throat with both his hands, the blood seeping through his fingers. Our tutor had not even glanced in his direction. When he had finished with his last pupil, he turned to the first to start tallying the score. Using his short stick he tapped away T242's clutching fingers and began to examine his handiwork. The blood was still pulsing from his mistakes, but more gently now. His eyes were almost closed. The examiner pointed out the two fatal apertures, then turned to us, and with the point of his stick went around our necks.

Later, when we had laid out our brother, the apothecary said, Did he deserve to die?

We said, in one voice, Yes.

He said, What killed him?

We said, The ego.

He said, But he was excellent. Why should perfection not have an ego?

We said, Because perfection is the absence of the ego.

He said, Is there a name for it, this perfection that is the absence of the ego?

Thrilling to our bones, in one voice, we said, Aum!

There was one last challenge to see off. Challenge is the wrong word. Test, inspection, clearance – these are more appropriate. With sufficient effort most people can master the limits of the mind and the body. But to identify the kernel of unblemished purity that is a Wafadar's greatest virtue you need the soul-seeing eyes of the great Helmsmen.

A man has the kernel or he doesn't. Unlike skill and strength it cannot be acquired. Nor is it for oneself to know if one possesses it. Only a master can spy its glow. When all is done, it is left to the great Helmsmen to identify the purest of the pure. To ensure there is no error, for this final moment, one is scrutinized by the Counsel of the Great Helmsmen.

It is a rare blessing to just meet with the Counsel. Even if it decides to not open the last door for you. If you do not possess the unblemished kernel it is meet that you should proceed no further.

Thus I was excited, not anxious. Nothing that was not owed to me would come my way. The audience was in a shed two terraces above the one in which we regularly met with ZZ9 and when I walked in the room was fragrant with incense. Of the five seated on five chairs around a semi-circular table I recognized ZZ9 by his broad shoulders.

Each of the great men held out a closed fist and I kissed the knuckles in acknowledgement that in the first and the last we were all brothers and equals. Their hands were soft with grace, and smelled of lavender.

The one in the middle, who seemed the smallest, said, Tell us about the failures of your life.

I began from the beginning and left nothing out. I had gone through this three years ago with ZZ9, but now I dug even deeper, determined to bring to light every mistake and weakness that had tarnished my life. Not just the actions, which was easy, but every shameful thought that had ever crossed my head. It took a long time.

As I spoke, excavating from my time at the home and the barracks and the scullery, I was dismayed to realize how far I was from being the purest of the pure. Again and again I unearthed in myself moments of unspoken – even unacknowledged – envy. Of brothers who were stronger, swifter, more felicitous in speech; of brothers more readily sought by other brothers, of brothers more keenly heeded by the Pathfinders; of brothers more endowed and skilled in the Serai of Fleeting Happiness. Then I came upon the lies and the lusts. Chief among them was the escapade of Bhima, my singing brother; the grotesque attachment with C963; and before that with the two shadows at the Serai, blue-eyed and brown-eyed.

But worse than envy, lies and lust, as I kept searching the past, I came upon dark and humiliating pathways of doubt. Nothing can be more diminishing for the pure than a wavering of the faith. Even as I spoke I had to look down, so shamed did I feel. I recalled moments under the Bodhi, or in the bunk, when questioning thoughts had sailed through my mind – about the truth of the long march, about the loyalty of Ali and Alaiya, the unfairness of my missing mother, the existence of the nine books of Aum, the justness of Bhima's quest for his father, the life of the madonnas at the Serai. I thought of the time at the scullery, of the drifting clouds of resentment and anger, the stabs of suspicion of what was being done to me. Even these last few divine years had not been blameless. The fleeting pangs at the crippling and death of my brothers. The passing thought that any one of them could have been me.

As I spoke on and on, the great Helmsmen, whose faces were mine, sat unmoving as rocks. With mounting horror I realized that all my life doubt had lain in the undergrowth like a crouching grasshopper, jumping up in periodic distraction. By the time I finished telling my sorry story I was prepared for the Counsel to banish me instantly from the room and the highgrounds.

The great Helmsman in the middle said, What would you do if you were in our place?

I said, Throw myself out.

I meant it.

He said, What has been your chief failure?

I said, To allow, even fleetingly, the shadow of doubt to soil my mind. To allow, even fleetingly, the worm of scepticism to crawl over my skin. From doubt spring all other sins – deceit, lust, envy, ego. Only the doubtless mind can be pure and purposeful.

I looked at ZZ9. More than anything else I did not want to let him down.

The great Helmsman said, And what has been your chief success?

I said, To recognize I have failed each time I have failed. To crush the worm before it travelled too far.

In his wise voice, he said, The world is full of worms. Some look so harmless you pay them no heed; some are so insidiously small you can barely spy them. And what is a tiny worm to a man so big, of size and ego! Yet all it takes is the laxity of an instant, the deceptive fog of pride, for the worm to slip through. My son, the most destructive worm – of doubt – does not crawl on the skin. It buries deep inside, and then it begins to grow. What foolish men dismiss as tiny and trivial, a small pebble, is in truth a rolling avalanche. The one worm, the one pebble, will gather a thousand as it journeys. A single worm will bring on fevers, aches and hallucinations. A single pebble will flatten a village. One tiny doubt will unhinge a people.

Without turning my head I looked around. It was such a bare room. Nothing in it, not one embellishment. Thick rafters of pine, fine planks of deodar, and a big window through which could be seen the lower terraces and the forest below. I understood its message: it was how the pure had to be. Unadorned, uncluttered, functional, drinking from a single source of light, without a distraction, without a single crawling worm of doubt. In the world of the great Helmsmen nothing was without meaning.

I said, I understand, and I am grateful for the understanding.

The great guide said, The sinews of the pure are made of faith. Questions are like crows, showing up everywhere, flapping their black wings, cawing for attention. You do not need to throw a stone at each one. The faithful know there are no new questions. Every question worth addressing has already been asked and answered. The worm of doubt, the crow of questions: ignore them, annihilate them. The path is found. We have merely to walk it. How can rediscovering the already discovered be an act of virtue?

To hear a great Helmsman speak was to drink at the spring of wisdom.

He said, Tell me, if we labour all day every day of our lives will we understand more about life than Aum did? Or about death? Or about the right and the wrong? The ephemeral and the eternal? Should we glory in the infinite illumination of the radiant one, or should we struggle to strike our own little flint? This is the problem with the men out there, in the other world. The masters they have are few and feeble, and them too they ignore. Even when they bow to them it is only from the waist – the head is held high, full of doubt and ego. And so they go in endless circles, the wise and the foolish, none following the other, repeating the same mistakes, learning nothing.

In that moment I became sure this was the Gentle Father himself. His words were so true I wanted to stand up and shout them in ringing echo. I could see him now as a young Wafadar, a hornet of devastation, so full of power because he was so free of doubt.

I said, I understand, and I am grateful for the understanding.

He said, Soon you will wake and you will no longer be a wriggling creature in a cocoon but a butterfly. But beauty is not your karma. Your task is to spread the seed. The wings and the colours are only mere tools.

I felt an incredible surge in my body and knew if I spread my arms I would be able to fly. He said, The destiny of the pure girdles the world. It is our ordained fate to bring order to chaos; love to hatred; justice to the tormented; equality to the unequal; and above all, purpose to the purposeless. The work is on; the work has been on. The unique grace of Aum showers on us, and we must take it everywhere.

I said, I understand, and I am grateful for the understanding.

When I had kissed the fists of all the great Helmsmen – to affirm we were brothers and equals – I walked out the room and slowly made my way down the terraces. As I stepped out my only surviving brother from our three years of training had stepped in. I was sure he would sail through. I knew he was blemishless in his purity and his purpose. As for myself I was uncertain. I had shocked myself with the list of my failures. At the same time I was without anxiety. I knew if I was denied, it would be with good reason, and exactly as it should be.

THE GREAT HORNBILL

I thought there can be no man more fortunate than I was. Not only was I inducted into the ranks of the Wafadars, I was straightaway attached for my year of internship to the great Helmsman who had been my final inquisitor. He was not, as I had imagined, the Gentle Father, but he was perhaps the oldest of the great Helmsmen, and I could see that to be picked by him was a great honour.

After the relentless exertions of three years I found myself in a quieter regime. My primary task every moment of every day was to stay close to the great Hornbill. That was his name. On becoming a great Helmsman each brother took the name of a bird, and while he lived the name could not be taken by another. ZZ9 was the great Serpent Eagle. These names were only used on the upper terraces, and mostly only between these luminous men. For the rest of us, across the sprawling valley, they were all simply the great Helmsmen – each of them as glorious and full of light as the other, each of them capable of protecting our purity and helming our destiny.

As a Wafadar, after all these years, there was little that I needed to be taught. All I had to do to keep my body perfectly honed, I knew, and I daily did. All the rest, the philosophy, the thoughts, the vision, the catechisms – I breathed those and lived those every instant, and had done so for years. Now was the period of profound osmosis – as

ZZ9, the great Serpent Eagle, had told me. By simply cleaving to
the great Hornbill, by living in the light of his radiance, I would
breathe in attributes that can neither be taught nor learned. They
have, simply, to be absorbed.

I felt the truth of it straightaway. I slept by the foot of the great
Hornbill's bed or right outside his door, and I felt calmed and exalted.
If he so much as stirred I would wake and wait to hear his need. To
serve his needs became the passion of my days. It brought me a joy
and contentment I had never known before. At moments I felt I was
serving not a great Helmsman but Aum himself.

The great Hornbill's ways were frugal and without fuss. He lived
in a shed on the ninth terrace. It had four rooms: for sleeping, for
meditation, for the novitiates and for eating. The meditation room
was bare except for a big mattress on the floor. But it had a fireplace
for the days on which initiation ceremonies took place. At the back,
on one side was a small kitchen, and at the other an enclosed yard
for ablutions.

I would wake a few hours after midnight, quietly leave the shed,
and begin to run. Down the terraces, into the trees, for the next
three hours I would pound through the forest as hard as I could. If
an animal crossed my path I would seize the opportunity to practise
with the chonch. I would maim, kill, paralyse, trying out all the pins
from one to eleven. Some days I would strike with such precision
that when I returned the next night the beast I had perforated would
be lying where I had left it, not yet dead but immobilized.

Often I would pass other Wafadars, their bare bodies glistening
with sweat in the night's chill, the belt of chonch tight around their
waist. We would acknowledge each other with a wave, brothers all,
but intent on our own tasks. It would still be night when I returned
to the shed, and standing in the roofless bathroom poured a canister
of water over my head. In the winter it would fall out in shards of
icicles, nipping the skin. Then I would sit on the six-sided rock at
the edge of the terrace, close my eyes, and fall into a meditation so
deep it had no bottom.

I would climb out of my trance only when I sensed the first line of grey in the black sky. In the kitchen I would start the fire, and brew four mugs of vapours, one for myself and three for the great Hornbill. While he sipped the brew I would massage his limbs to stimulate his circulation. Most mornings while I did this the great Hornbill would tell me about his dreams of the night. As was to be expected with someone so realized, his sleep was full of profound visions.

His skin was growing crisp like a dried onion skin, and each morning it needed an infusion of oil to make it supple. As I gently pressed down on his ageing bones he would with long pauses narrate the night's visitations and then question me on their meaning. Often it was easy to find the answer, for each dream bore in itself a deep illumination. But every now and then the symbols were so complex, the line of the story so non-linear, that I would declare myself defeated, leaving it to him to explain its significance.

There was one that came to him repeatedly. It was about a pair of unicorns. One had a body so pure it was blindingly white. But its sharp curving horn was irredeemably black. The other had a body so impure it was black as the night. But its sharp curving horn was gloriously white. In the glade of a thick forest both these unicorns were locked in combat, their clashing horns sparking fire. We had deduced the white was selflessness and brotherhood, and the black was possession and the ego. The riddle was: which of the unicorns was more worthy? The pure body with the ego horn, or the ego body with the pure horn?

I felt the pure horn was the superior. My argument was it was the horn that made the unicorn distinct, and it was the horn that led it in battle and in appearance. If it managed to shine unblemished, though emanating from a body of evil, it was nothing short of a triumph. In a way it was like the pilgrim fathers: emerging exalted from the morass of the outside world. On the other hand, the horn of sin rising out of a body so pure was a signal of a colossal failure. It was like the men out there. Gifted the opportunity of transcendence, but making of it a trifling thing. Like QT2: sprung from this vale of the shining but sprouting the dark horn.

The great Hornbill was not so easily swayed. As I tenderly rubbed the parched soles of his feet, he would want to know, What is it that I saw as the horn? Was it the speech of a man? Was it his action? Or was it his thought? If men born pure developed the evil horn, what was its manifestation?

If I said speech, the great Helmsman would ask, But is it not less important than action? And if I said action, he would say, How can anything be more significant than thought? And if I said thought, he would say, Without the windmill of action and speech, thought is nothing but empty, unseen air.

As I scrabbled for the lessons of twenty-five years, the great Hornbill would pose a counter. Was it not better to possess a big body of gleaming purity tarnished only by a single carbuncle of sin? To have amid vast perfection a small imperfection, rather than a small perfection amid vast imperfection?

While I fell over my words, he would remind me that for the pure – especially the Wafadars – both were unacceptable. In the dream both unicorns were locked in perpetual combat, neither prevailing over the other, because both were blemished. That was the true meaning of the apparition: there was no such thing as the almost pure, and it could never find its triumph. If purity was not absolute, it was nothing.

Listening to him I understood what it was to be an attained being. In contrast my own dreams were floating fragments of nonsense. Most days on waking I could recall nothing but a few blurred images.

Once in a while Aum would come to my master in his sleep. Now the great Hornbill's tone would change. As I kneaded the stringy muscles he would speak even slower than usual. Always the matchless one would have his hand on the great Hornbill's shoulder, in a gesture of surpassing brotherhood. Even in the dream Aum would be effulgent – light issuing from him as from the moon – and his touch would energize the great Hornbill so deeply that the charge would not fade even after he had woken.

And so it was with all the great Helmsmen. Aum came to each of them in their hour of need, providing answers to the conundrums that vexed them, providing divine guidance in all things great and small.

As I heard these things I felt my hair rise and I felt the energy of the limitless one pass through the onion skin of the great Hornbill and exalt my entire being.

In the afternoon, after serving the great Hornbill his lunch, I would practise my poems. This we all did under the watchful eye of the great Serpent Eagle. He would walk up and down the terraces as the Wafadars sliced and carved the air at a speed the eye can barely behold.

I had natural rhythm and I mastered the basic forms quickly. Soon my favourite became the ninth poem. It was usually essayed with a double-edged short sword held in a two-handed grip and was best deployed in a close battle where your back was secure and the enemy came at you from three sides. Each stanza had three lines and each line three movements. One, two, three, strike; three, two, one, defend. Turn 45 degrees, and repeat. And again, turn 45 degrees and repeat. Unleashed at a blistering speed it gave the assailant barely a moment to recover, by which time you had reeled off the other two lines, striking mighty blows, and returned to the first.

Like all the poems, once you had mastered the fundamental metre, you could extend it. When I practised the ninth I always saw myself defending a narrow pass against an army of marauders. One, two, three, strike; three, two, one, defend. Again and again and again till there was a mounting heap of dead and dying bodies in front of me beyond which I could no longer see.

Afterward, with the sun falling, I returned to our abode and poured cold water over my burning body. Then I brewed a mug of vapours for the great Hornbill and gave it to him with two pieces of sweet bread. Once again as he sipped he told me of the dreams of his afternoon slumber. Then he wore his moss-green robe, held my arm, and we walked up to the twelfth terrace. He was not infirm but he was slow. The great Helmsmen were known for their long lives. He could have been sixty or ninety. As he walked he liked to pose impromptu riddles.

He would see a great hill barbet alight on a tree and ask, Is a bird more free than a man?

I would say, looking down to ensure his feet fell at the right place, Most people would say so.

Why?

For it can come and go as men may not. It can hover beyond the reach of man and beast. It can nest where it will.

But can it speak? Does it have a voice that tells its tale, sings its freedom?

That, one may safely say, it does not.

But a man does.

Yes, great one, a man does.

What then brings greater freedom – wings or words?

The bird would have flown by now, and I would not know the answer.

I would say, Tell me, great Helmsman.

He would say, There are big birds in the world that have wings but cannot fly. And there are big men in the world who have words but cannot sing. In themselves words and wings are nothing. This bird may never go beyond this forest nor soar higher than these trees, and a man blessed with many words may never speak the truth nor utter a single line of beauty.

I would say, Then what makes a man free?

Intent, he would say. In life, intent is everything. We are free because we intend to be free. We are pure because it is our greatest

intent. It was Aum's intent that gave him the words that set free the
founding fathers and flew them across the high mountains as if they
had wings.

Another time, he would break step, put his hand on the trunk of a
horse chestnut, and say, What about a tree should a man have?

I would say, Solidity, stability, rootedness.

He would say, looking up at the incandescent leaves, And what
about a tree must a man eschew?

My mind would go blank. I would say, The inability to move...

He would cuff my ears and say, You talk like a cookhouse man,
not a Wafadar. Attributes! We are talking attributes. We are not
discussing if a man can grow leaves out of his armpit.

Tell me then, great Helmsman.

A tree lacks discernment. It gives of itself – fruit and shade –
to saint and sinner. A man must never be so. At all times he must
distinguish between the fine and the coarse. He must give to one
and withhold from the other. This alone is how the world will
be changed: through a ceaseless winnowing of the pure from the
impure. All grain is worthless till it is separated from the chaff. This
is our task, in this valley and in the world out there – all of us who
are the fruit of Aum.

I stayed on the eleventh terrace while the great Hornbill went up
to the twelfth. Even a Wafadar was not allowed to go above the
eleventh unless summoned. Every evening the great Helmsmen met
in a round room around a round table, sipped Ferment, and thought
hard about the present and future of the flock. Often their conclaves
continued late into the night.

I would be waiting at the bottom of the steps for the great Hornbill.
He would grasp my left arm, pat my head, and mutter a blessing.
Though it was acceptable to ask him what had ensued in the round
room – for we were, after all, brothers – it was inappropriate. These
were the wisest of us and the radius of their concerns lay beyond

one's easy comprehension. Yet I did venture to ask once and the great Helmsman was not angered.

In a gentle voice like the falling of winter rain he said the destiny of the pure lay far beyond the high walls of this beautiful valley. A people fulfilled their purpose not by courage and purity alone. Also called for were meticulous planning and ingenious strategy. The pure were a mere handful; the world they had to change was a massive sprawl. It was not a bowl of water whose colour could be changed with a few drops of milk. It was a vast cesspool that could easily drown the pure if they were not careful. Every step demanded calibration. Day on day, year on year, the offal had to be drained. It would take time. A long time. But it could be done. It would be done. The beauty of Aum would fill the world.

The undergrowth had begun to chatter and deep in the forest I could hear the animals starting to pad. Turning his pale grey eyes on me, he said, Do you hear the noise?

I said, I have trained myself to do so.

He said, That is good. First you train yourself to hear everything; then you train yourself to shut most of it out. When the big cat walks through the forest do you think he pays heed to this chirping? His ear is cocked only for the one cough, the half-scuffle, which tells him his quarry is at hand.

I stayed silent.

He continued, Up there in that round room every day the great Helmsmen receive the chatter of the world. The information comes from places you have never heard of, in ways you cannot imagine. In that great noise is the one cough, the half-scuffle that signals the true path. It is this that they look for every single day.

I said, Does the Gentle Father come to the round table too?

Patting my head, the great Hornbill said, The Gentle Father is always with us. When he is at the round table, he is with us; when he is not at the table, he is with us. The pure can do nothing without the Gentle Father.

After I had served him dinner, I would pour two glasses of Ferment while he lay in bed with three pillows under his shoulders. As we sipped, I would press his legs and he would tell me stories. Some of them – about Aum and the pilgrim fathers – I had heard before, but several were new.

Many of these were about the Wafadars and their deeds of valour, in guarding the Pass and making forays into the other world. I heard how my brothers went forth in pairs to harvest the savages for training and for labour. There was one known as the Wolf who alone in his time had brought in more than a hundred. This was a great accomplishment. Harvesting was a complex activity. It involved carting back fully grown men, undamaged and intact. And it was carried out with a sense of justice and of fairplay.

No village could be picked from more than once in a year. It was crucial that no alarms were sounded. The cub that snarls before its time risks being killed even by a pig. One savage missing made a hamlet tremble with fear, drove it to mumble idiot invocations. Too many missing could force it to act. If a posse arrived at the Pass it would mean a bloodbath. It would mean loud bells ringing in alarm – all the way into the heart of the other world.

Few Wafadars had travelled as far as the Wolf to harvest fresh bodies. Beyond the high hamlets lay the villages on the slopes, and further still were the hill towns with their clusters of crooked buildings and chaotic bazaars. Teeming with wasteful men, they were full of noise and dust and rank smells. The Wolf, said the great Hornbill, had walked through many of these like an unseen shadow, noting the depravities, physical and moral. These hubs were open, festering wounds; the men in them buzzing flies. Scavenging, quarrelling, dirty, greedy, cruel. These were places fit to be harvested in their entirety.

The farther he went – all the way to where the plains began and the sun was a ball of fire and the roads deranged with the fury of motors – the more aware he became of the sheer beauty of Aum. Wielding his chonch, month after month, year after year, the Wolf brought in the savages from all over. My master said it was curious to see that those from the towns were filled with the greatest terror. It was as if a greater knowledge of the world had bred in them greater fears.

Once, to test a theory, the Wolf had brought in two brothers. He had picked them up from a shop in a town by a mountain lake full of weeds. All day he had sat by a walnut tree watching them vend their confections, one brother picking and packing, the other weighing and collecting the money. He had seen them rude with beggars and lascivious with young girls. At night, when every potential customer had melted from the streets, they had totted up their takings, rolled it tight into their singlets and stepping out begun to pull the steel shutter of the shop down. As they crouched to turn the locks, the Wolf had banged their heads together, picked them up, each under an arm, and draped them over a mule. When they came to many hours later, many miles from their town, he had banged their heads together again.

Up the steep paths across the high shelves he had banged their heads all the way back to the valley. At some point they had begun to beg and beseech him, whining like kicked curs. In a final flourish – typically – they had pulled out the tight roll of money and offered it to him. The Wolf had banged their heads together harder.

When one of them was produced in front of the great Helmsmen, he was given a choice. To gain his freedom he could best the Wolf in combat or he could take on his brother. Later, the same offer was made to the other. Sniffling, both chose to take on each other.

In the night the Wolf summoned them separately and offered commiseration. To kill a brother was no trifling thing. He would try and make it easy. He gave them pills made from the sap of the thorn apple. The brother would go to sleep calm and peacefully pass on to the other world. In the morning it was clear the vileness of men knew no boundaries. As always the incandescent one had been right. Ties of blood, at the brink of a crisis, come to nothing. The only ties that make men brothers are those of ideas and of belief.

When I asked him to tell me more about the Wolf he patted my cheek. Now I was talking like the men out there. The Wolf was of no importance. What he represented was what had significance. You had to celebrate the message, not the messenger. A thousand Wolfs would come and ago – I could be the next one. But in purpose we would all be the same. Many containers carrying the same elixir.

It was the meaning of the face.

Then he told me about Wafadars who undertook tasks even more fraught than the harvesting. They were known as angels. Their task was to retrieve lost souls. Once in a rare while a brother took leave of his senses and wandered away from the valley. In truth, if he wished, any brother was free to leave the valley and the brotherhood. Freedom and liberty were the pillars on which rested Aum's vision. But astonishingly – unsurprisingly – in all these long years not one brother or sister had wished to do so. Clearly there were no seductions in the world out there that could match the beauty of Aum.

As I leaned forward with the flagon to refill his drink he opened his robe and tapped his thigh. I soaked my palms with oil and went to work. Here his flesh was fuller and less like dried onion skin.

But, he resumed, there was always the odd brother whose mind came unhinged. And in a moment of tragic self-destruction he wandered off into the other world. No matter how deluded or foolish, a brother is always a brother. It was then the responsibility of the angels to rescue him and bring him back home.

The angels were Wafadars who had versed themselves in the ways of the other world. They had its language, and its ways. They could sit in its bazaars and ride on its motors. They could work its currency and decode its newspapers. They always went forth in pairs, and sometimes in threes and fours. They never failed. Mostly they brought back the ailing brother, who was then nursed into a state of well-being. Occasionally they could do nothing but liberate him from his torments.

The angels always travelled with a heavy heart. There is no pleasure in seeing brothers who have lost their minds. Many of the accounts were full of pathos. For example, recently one brother was found in a distant town clinging to a thin, dark woman in a small house by a gutter. He had taken off his face and his mouth was soft with foolishness. He declared he had discovered the joys of matrimony and with demented glee held up a wrinkled baby that he claimed to have made and rubbed its nose to his own with loud gurgles. This was a fairly common derangement, women and infants. Each time the angels had to struggle to contain their nausea.

Many were found trapped in mercantile webs, labouring in shops and eateries, earning petty currency, being treated like slaves. One, famously, was recovered from the dark bowels of a Talkies, crazed by the moving pictures, willing to sweep its filthy floor just so he could stay there. A few, blasphemously, were rescued from tawdry temples and churches, painting marks on themselves and muttering into the air. These were the worst cases, their brains now nothing but thin soup.

One signal case was found in the ancient city by the great river, sitting half-naked on the banks, chanting gibberish and clanging cymbals. His hair matted in ropes had grown below his shoulders; his beard even lower. Two mongrels sat at his ankles, their heads busy with fleas. When the angels addressed him, he began to sing his blessings to them and gave each of them an orange flower, which when eaten, petal by petal, would give them sons who'd bring renown to their names. When the angels said they'd come to take him back, he said, If you are messengers of the god of death, tell him I am not ready yet. I have these dogs to look after. Once he has taken them, he can take me.

My rubbing had roused the great Hornbill's skin. It was gleaming now. His glass was empty and I refilled it. He had closed his eyes. My hand was serving its purpose. I wanted to know more about this unkempt man by the great river. My master said the angels insinuated the chonch and brought him back to the valley, burying the mongrels on the way. He was then produced in front of the great Helmsmen who, always open to examining new information, spoke to him of his new-found illuminations.

But he was a disgrace. He began to chant and sing, slapping his hands above his head and swaying like a reed. He had nothing coherent to offer. He was in touch with the gods he said. Not god, gods. They spoke to him. They had told him he was immortal. The body was only a cloak. He would keep shedding and acquiring new cloaks till he had made himself so impossibly fine that he needed no raiment. To get there all he had to do was to sit naked by the great river and take care of the mongrels.

When asked if he remembered Aum, he said of course he did. In fact he often met him by the great river, by the smouldering flats where the bodies were daily burned. He was just like him, naked and immortal. His task was to look after the cows and to make of their dung perfect round cakes. There were many truths, and many paths to every truth. Aum's was through dung; his own through the curs.

I was in shock. My hands had stopped moving.

The great Hornbill said through all this he kept chanting and swaying, smiling oafishly. At every pause he would declare his love for all things of the universe, including the Wafadars, the brothers, the mongrels, the cows, the dung. It took no time for the council to be confirmed in his complete derangement. In sheer dismay, midway, a few of the great Helmsmen actually stood up and left the room.

I had dipped my fingers in the warm oil and was moving them again.

It was a terrible sickness, said the great Hornbill, and its most common symptoms were these foolish sensations of love and happiness. When probed they revealed no logic. They were only emanations of vagueness and weakness. These afflicted brothers were reminders of the truth of Aum. Few things undid men more swiftly than stupid sentiment. And it was a remorseless foe. It lay ever under the skin, poised to seize control. The slip of a moment, and years of schooling against its quicksilver temptations could come to nothing.

It could leave a fine man praising dung or cooing like a bird to a thoughtless infant.

I remembered the lugubrious air of C963. The neat crack of his neck was the only sweet note in the entire memory.

What, I asked, had been done with the egregious chanter? The Crater of Resurrections – that's where he had been sent. So his broken mind could be mended and his soiled spirit cleansed. I knew of the Crater but I had never been there. It was a special place of healing and repair and was generally out of bounds to everyone.

From here, the higher terraces, you proceeded west through the great deodar forest, climbing at a sixty-degree angle till you had left all the trees behind and gone past the snowline. Then you came upon nine mighty boulders, each the size of a hut, stacked on one another as in child's play. If you climbed the steps hewn into the stone to reach the second level, you came to an opening between the boulders no larger than a man.

All this I had gathered over the years from a hundred whispers. I had never met anyone who had been there. But many brothers knew brothers who had. As you stepped through the dark hole the ground began to slope down at a gentle gradient. Soon it ended in a large cave, fit to house more than two score standing men. At the end of it was a large wooden door, with belts of iron giving it strength. As you stepped through it you had to hold on to a thick rope whose one end was tethered with several loops inside the cave while the other fell into the dark passageway. If you made the mistake of slackening your grip on the rope you were sure to burn your palms raw in mere minutes. For almost immediately the path fell away at a steep angle, plunging down sharper and sharper, forcing a man to jog, and occasionally run, feet slipping and slithering. Just when you thought your lungs and arms could take no more, there came a flat platform, where one could squat and rediscover one's breath.

Four times did this happen – a jogging plunge down a deep tunnel, the rope scorching the palms, the lungs pounding like drums, followed by the relief of a flat platform and the reclaiming of one's crazed heart. Low long-burning lamps adumbrated nothing more than the dark maw of the tunnel, and again and again the passage was wet with rock springs. By the time you broke journey at the fourth platform you were certain you had entered the very bowels of the earth. But now, dropping down almost vertically, a slash of light that cut the eyes suddenly appeared. In no time you were standing on solid ground, a big door in front of you, and on either side of it were slim windows, no broader than a man's palm, cut into the rock, allowing in straight shafts of clean light.

Up to this point all accounts were the same. Once you went through this door they tended to vary. Only on one aspect was there consensus: there was no way to leave the place but the way you had come. The Crater of Resurrections was a deep cylinder, plunging more than a hundred metres, a perfect hole in the ground. When you stood at its bottom, the sky was a fine circle and farther from you than ever before in your life. The walls of the Crater rose like glass, sheer and smooth, providing no purchase to toe or finger. The sun rose here late, and set early. A sense of damp never left the place.

The Crater was big. Some said it housed many hamlets. Others said there was just one set of nine connected sheds that housed the reformatory. Some said there were no more than two dozen brothers in there, undergoing resurrection. Others said there were many hundred. Some said the place was so wondrous it healed the broken in mere weeks and months. Others said, yes it was a magical haven, but the brothers who arrived there were so fractured in mind and spirit that it took many years to put them together again.

Once, at the cookhouse, my insidious seducer C963 had told me lies about the Crater, painting it as a diabolic place. The Crater, he said, was a chamber of trial and terror. It aimed not to mend brothers but to break them. It did not heal the lost, it penalized them. The reason so little was known of what happened there – beyond the last door – was because no one ever came back from there alive.

But I had intuited the truth of things. The no-return stood to reason. As a rule, terminal patients return from the infirmary motionless on the bier. Where could the mongrel man be possibly returned to? Or QT2, who had so heinously betrayed the beauty and blessing of

Aum? What choice did the great Helmsmen have but to guard the Crater day and night? To ensure the deranged and the ailing did not run out and harm themselves and others.

Wafadars guarded the ingress every step of the way. On horseback and foot at all hours they also patrolled the lip of the big Crater, for madness can give wings to ordinary men. Besides, in there were brothers – like QT2 – who had been great warriors and magicians. It was not inconceivable that even with broken bones they might attempt to scale the straight walls, finding a hold for toe and finger where geckos would find none.

It had been done, more than once. Therefore fiery torches burnt around the rim all night, the flames eating up the dark and making huge shadows of anything that moved on the Crater's walls. For deterrence, piles of rock sat every twenty feet like crouching men. An insect crawling up could be sent plummeting back in an instant.

Anyway, I was not so anxious to pursue the facts of the Crater. As a Wafadar it was possible I would one day see the crater – perhaps even guard it. Of course I could have asked the great Hornbill for the perfect description. But that would have diminished me in his sage eyes. A fruit ripens in its time. The pure know that knowledge of all things due to them comes to them when they are ready for it.

THE GIRL WITH FLASHING EYES

As an intern with the great Hornbill one ritual I enjoyed was the initiation by the enlightened. There was no fixed day for it. Some months you'd have three or four of them, and then there were months when there would be none. Even the rites tended to vary, though its setting was unchanging: it took place always in the room that had the fireplace, with big logs pulsing rich orange and the woodchips on top throwing out tongues of hot flame and the big square mattress unrolled on the wooden floor sheathed in a crisp white sheet.

It was my job to prepare the room and to burn the herb oils whose aroma invaded the nostrils and opened up the skin. I enjoyed doing this and would hold my head over the diffusers after I had lit them. The oils were not to be burnt at any other time. Things have a purpose. Outside of it they are an indulgence.

I brought in and lit the logs four hours in advance and with a steady infusion of woodchips worked up the fire till the room was filled with layers of warm air. That was how the great Hornbill preferred it. Then I went and brought in the girl. Mostly they were below thirteen, often just eleven. Occasionally there would be an older one. Men control many things, but not the internal clock of a woman's body. The rule was inflexible. The initiation by the enlightened took place once a girl had begun to bleed. There is no meaning to pulling at the udders of a calf.

As a rule I avoided any extended dialogue with the girls. There was little we had in common. They were utter novices; I, a Wafadar, in the shadow of greatness. They were not forthcoming either. Most of them knew themselves to be at a momentous threshold, in a moment of sacred silence.

Strangely, even when they spoke – though they must have known it well – all they wished to know was what would happen. Since it was not my place to speak of the great Hornbill and his duties, I merely told them they had been chosen to be honoured. Their journey, of fecundity and purpose, was to be set in motion by a great Helmsman. If they were truly blessed, his peerless seed would strike deep, and hold – bringing glory to themselves and the brotherhood.

The prospect of it would make them shiver and tremble and bite their lips. A few actually grew faint, and had to be carried in by me.

The great Hornbill tested himself all the time. To ensure the ritual did not become a soulless chore, nor a moment of idle pleasure, he made me change things constantly, to construct for him a challenge. It was the way of the great Helmsmen – never to make it easy for themselves. Thus sometimes I had to divest her of all her clothes, sometimes leave them all on. And sometimes I had to merely roll them up or down, like a half-peeled banana. Sometimes I had to leave her lying on her back, the fire dancing on her belly like butterflies in the forest. And sometimes lay her motionless on her face, the line of her back the contours of the valley. Sometimes I had to set her on her knees, her head to the floor, like a foraging animal. And sometimes I had to prop her up against the wall, like a stationary plough. Sometimes I had to blind the fire so that she was barely discernible and had to be hunted. I did all of it with scrupulous care, nudging the novices along, often working hard to take them past their paralysis of wonderment.

In the beginning, once I had prepared the girl I would leave the room and go back in only after it was all over. There was always some cleaning up to be done, but that was easy. More challenging was shepherding the initiate back to her senses after the exhilaration of the initiation. Often I would find them in a drool or a stupor, mumbling incoherently, a few of them actually weeping – as they struggled to come to terms with their wondrous experience.

I did what I could, patting them into equanimity, feeding them and putting them to bed. Then I waited for the great Hornbill to wake from his exertions. Occasionally he felt he needed to do more work on a novice. Then I kept her back, for a day or more – till he was satisfied he had done all he could. Else I sent a message to the lower terraces where the escort from the motherhood waited, and she was taken away immediately.

Later the great Hornbill gave me permission to witness the initiations. I had to sit just inside the door, on my haunches, and say and do nothing unless asked. As I looked on my admiration for the great man grew. It was hard work, noble work. Even though it was such an honour, the girl would often not be seized of it. She would wriggle, stiffen, flail her arms, and sometimes make of her fingers a scratching claw. A few actually jumped up to scuttle about the room, hugging the walls, their shoulders hunched like vultures on carrion. One even reached into the fireplace to grab a burning log.

Mostly, by the time he had pinioned them to the mattress and prised open their legs he would be layered in sweat and panting. If they screamed he let them. It was one way of expelling their foolishness. He never hit them – I routinely felt like slapping them – and was no rougher than required. He would say: to know what is good for you, you have to know it in the first place.

As is easy to guess the great Hornbill's labours were not over till he had expunged his seed deep into them. I could see him straining till the veins on his neck were thick as fingers. Sometimes the exhaustion of his effort was so great he would roll onto his back and pass out. I have no way of knowing how many of the girls safely carried back the seed and grew it into magnificent new life. What I do know is the failures were not for want of exertion on the great Helmsman's part.

When he was done I had to be quick. The moment he rolled off I snatched the girl's ankles and held her legs aloft. Then I counted till two hundred, looking down to ensure not a drop flowed out. Often, to be certain, I would not put her legs down till the count had touched three hundred.

Even if the great Hornbill's seed did not strike home each time, the initiation without a doubt was a complete success in the second of its goals: to embark a girl on the glorious road to mothering. While a man may live short or long and continue to seed the future till the day he is buried, only a finite time is given unto a woman. She is a field that is fallow in the beginning and fallow at the end. It is necessary, urgently necessary, therefore that when she is fertile, in the middle, she be ploughed and ploughed with tireless diligence to yield all that she possibly can.

Even though as a Wafadar I had the Kiln of Inevitable Impulses to go to, with its alluring women versed in intricate pleasures, I have to confess I took enjoyment in seeing the ritual unfurl. Something about the way the great Hornbill mastered the girls – with their immature limbs and downy hair – was strangely arousing. The more he was challenged, the more he persevered, the more I was riveted.

Ever so often, seeing my obvious agitation, he would remind me: the final destination of all pleasure must always be restraint. The only reason to suffer pleasure is to be eventually rid of it.

Sometimes he would ask me to keep a novice back for more than a few days. I noticed this happened mostly with girls with darkly black hair. The initiation done, he would over the succeeding days summon them to his room for further work. Walking in with the warm oils and fresh towels I would see him murmuring and slowly caressing their hair as they sat on his lap naked, their bodies from the angle of the door like those of young boys.

It was not just their bodies that were undeveloped. Their heads too were still uncreated. I knew what the great Hornbill was doing. As much as setting their bodies into motion, he was trying to shore up their minds.

I could see how crucial this was since most of them were exceedingly foolish. Though my conversations with them were minimal they were sufficient to leave me exhausted. One girl with black hair, whose shoulders were bony but breasts already ripe plums, was to prove a uniquely exasperating case.

She had flashing eyes but a limp body. When I was preparing her for the initiation, she had the insolence to ask me if I knew what I was doing. I was used to vitriol and tears. This was a new thing – an inquisition. I was so appalled by it I tied her mouth shut with a strip of cloth. She flashed her eyes at me and continued to do so as I readied her, oiling her limbs.

As I laid her on the mattress, she sat up. I pushed her back, holding her down for a few minutes, as you do to a piece of metal to fix its shape – but the moment I pulled away my hand she was up again. At that moment I felt not anger but contempt for her profound ignorance. She was dealing with a Wafadar. I could immobilize her with a twist of my fingers.

All I did however was to grip both her wrists in my right hand till her bones were within a hair of cracking and her eyes had widened in a voiceless scream and then I whispered into her ear all the things I would do to her if she did not behave with the decorum that was the hallmark of the pure. She understood. Now when I pushed her down she stayed down.

Just before the great Hornbill arrived – as always solemn for the occasion – I removed the band from her mouth. She flashed her eyes at both of us but did not move.

And that is how she stayed as he proceeded with the initiation. Limp, unmoving, expressionless, soundless: a fish out of water. He parted her limbs, picked them, bent them, turned her over, put her on her knees, turned her on her back, applied his mouth, his fingers, did everything he could, but she remained unalive, marble-eyed.

At one point so disturbed did he become at her reluctance to be educated that he stopped and sat back on the mattress. His disappointment with her conduct, I could see, had shrunk his very ability to pour the seed.

After some time he pulled on his robe and left the room. On the way out he raised a finger at me. I understood. When the door swung shut, she made to lift herself up. I called out to her to remain as she was. She slumped back, lifeless again. Her limbs lay straight and parted and the hair at her core was spare, the light running through it. Her head lay still in a pool of black hair. All I could hear was the roar of the fire.

I sat cross-legged, unmoving. I could stay like this till the next day if required. A long time passed. Then suddenly she said, moving just her lips, Do you even understand what all this is?

Motionless as stone, she said, Even if you knew, it would make no difference – finally you will be like that old man, wrinkled and infirm, but unsparing of even your granddaughters.

I was trained never to be provoked by idle words. She would learn soon, or no doubt be plunged down the Crater. What would be nicer though was a neat crack, as with C963. It truly was the great Hornbill's grace that he had left her unpunished.

I said, Your mothers would be ashamed of you.

She screamed in hysteria, Mothers! Do you even understand what you say? Can anyone have mothers? One! There is one! A mother! Do you even know your mother? You are so sorry that you could be abasing yourself with your own mother and you would not know!

She was so still that her voice – even with its shrillness – sounded disembodied. By now I had entered a meditative zone.

She said, in a suddenly quiet and cold voice, Let me tell you what must have happened to your mother by now. And you have only one, no matter how many are packed into the motherhood. Just one! One womb from which you were ejected. By now that one womb must be wrung and drained of its last drop of life. A tree so remorselessly stripped of every fruit, flower and leaf that it cannot possibly sprout another. Ready now to be hacked and burnt for its wood. Tell me – were you her first or fifth or tenth or fifteenth? Do you even know whether she bore you in joy or in fatigue or in sheer distress? Perhaps she died as she expelled you! Yes, that too happens all the time!

This kind of dementia was not unusual. We had been tutored to expect it. The way of the brotherhood, the path of the pure is never easy. Its demands on heart and spirit can unhinge the stoutest. At such a time, the mind goes into freefall and begins to rant against all that is glorious. We'd been taught to deal with such madness with indifferent sympathy, unless it threatened to impede the journey of our people.

This black-haired girl I did not see as a problem. The unique occasion had momentarily undone her. Before I assisted in my first initiation, the great Hornbill had explained it all to me. I should be prepared to witness every kind of peculiar conduct. Anger, irritation, outrage; screaming, hectoring, shouting. Also infatuation, delight, ecstasy, abandon. It was a hormonal thing. A body's rite of passage. The girls should not be blamed. They had merely to be handled.

Without moving from my perch by the door, I said, We all die. To die for the glory of the pure is an honour. If that is what my mother did, she fills me with pride.

For the first time since I'd pushed her back down, she moved. Sitting up with a jerk she began to bang her forehead against her palms, shouting, Honour! Pride! Glory! Are you all the same? Do you even know what you say? Your mother is milked dead like an animal and all you have to say is honour, pride, glory!

I got up and picked up the cloth and tied her mouth shut again. The screaming was unacceptable. It would wake up the great Hornbill. She kept trying to shout through the cloth. I pushed her back down, squeezing her wrists till the bones creaked and the tears fell out of her eyes and she ceased to struggle.

I only removed her gag a few hours later when I heard the great
Helmsman rise from his bed. Still flashing her eyes at me, she flexed
her jaw and worked her tongue but said nothing. Though I could
hear the icicles in the wind outside, her skin was hot, with a shimmer
of sweat. I'd kept the room warm, laying on fresh pine logs, and I'd
burnt more oils, making the air thick with perfume. The initiation
was not over till the seed had been planted.

The tread of the great Hornbill told me he was calm and
determined. No quarter would be given. When he found she was
still a dead fish he turned her over and using his fingers went where
the seed will not take. She winced and moaned and raised her arm
in protest. That was it. By coming alive she brought him alive. He
made her moan some more; and each time she spasmed he became
increasingly ready. I was seeing a master at work. One day, if I rose to
the higher terraces, this education would stand me in good stead.

Soon he turned her over and put her ankles on his shoulders. I was
on my knees, following the lesson closely. I could see her eyes were
pleading now. She wanted the great man's seed. As he always did at
the brink he dipped his fingertips into the bowl of oil I had kept by
the bed and meticulously anointed himself. As he plunged to his
task her scream of ragged joy filled the room, then became a string
of grateful whimpers.

When he had rolled over I moved quickly, grabbing her ankles and
holding them up. Looking down the line of her strong legs I could
see she would be a great mother. Her shoulders had too much bone,
but her hips were full with flesh and her belly smooth and wide. The
breasts, already plums, would soon grow to big fruits, ready to suckle
a new child every year.

Silently I counted to three hundred and then gently put her legs
down. I noticed her eyes were glistening. This was normal. Every
girl's eyes welled up, and then they turned over on to their stomachs
and buried their face in their hands, and shook their bodies with

loud sobs. I had been taught to let them be till their emotions had settled.

But this one didn't turn over and she didn't shake herself with sobs. Her legs lay as I had left them, slightly apart, and damp. And though her eyes were wet they had begun to flash again. I kept standing there at her feet to ensure she did not suddenly stand up and undo all the hard work. Exhausted with his effort the great Hornbill was now asleep curled on his side close to the fire, the breath singing rhythmically in his nostrils.

Opening her legs wide, the dark-haired girl said, What about you? Don't you want to be glorious too?

Dropping to my knees I gripped both her ankles in my right hand and pushed her legs back till her thighs were against her plum breasts. Putting my mouth to her right ear I said in a hard whisper, Foolish woman, this is neither the house nor the Kiln! This is the abode of a great Helmsman. It's not pleasure that is pursued here but the path. The valley is the abode of the free but we must never forget we have liberty because we walk the path. Away from the path stalk dark forces that would snatch away from us our every blessing. Remember, once you slip off the path there is no coming back. So clamp your legs and stitch your mouth and be grateful for the grace that now fills your belly!

She proved to be beyond redemption.

The great Hornbill kept her back for ten days – as ever in his compassion giving her one last chance to mend her mind. Each day without giving himself a break he laboured on her body, resolutely summoning up his precious seed. On each occasion I held up her legs and reminded her of who she was and who we were. Then I put her in the small novitiate room where she would lie all day on the bed, looking out through the barred window at the forest and above it the snow, till I took her once again to the great Helmsman for another lesson that would again be lost on her.

The great Hornbill did his best. I saw him try things I had seldom seen him essay. A few times he summoned me to the effort too, to manage limbs and positions. She allowed herself to be manipulated. But it was the willingness of the comatose. It was unacceptable to the master. After all there is no point in seeding dead ground. So we worked to make her come alive – however briefly, in a spasm – so the ordained task could be quickly accomplished.

Each day I had to put poultices on her. With characteristic concern the great Helmsman was clear she must be returned to the motherhood without a blemish on her skin. As I spread the warm ointment I noticed her eyes had neither gratitude nor remorse. Black as her hair, they blazed like burning coal. By the third day, with relief, I realized her mien had nothing to do with us. It was how she was; it was how her eyes were. They were fiery at all times, as if making up for the limpness of her body, which was limp at all times.

On the sixth night of her stay something strange happened. As I settled down at my vigil outside the great Hornbill's room, having cleared dinner – after another day of efforts and poultices – I felt a sudden desire seize me. The pure know desire is like sleep, it comes and it goes – a simple need that must be simply serviced. But as I shrank and expanded, turned and tossed, my desire had an identifiable, unmistakable face.

This had not happened since the very first time at the Serai. I tried hard to replace the dark-haired girl with any of the hundreds of girls I had known, at the Serai, the Kiln, and here. It was futile. I would scarce conjure a face that had delighted me and it would become her, the fire burning her eyes, the challenge slanting her lips.

As the night wore on I became increasingly covetous of seeing her, of being in her presence. I fought it but by morning I was ragged. The first thing I did when I rose, before the pre-dawn hour of four to go for my run, was to unlatch her door, step inside and gaze at her. She was sleeping on her back, her arms folded across her breasts, and the starlight through the barred window caught her mouth cleansed of its challenge and the eyelashes long and closed.

I stood there for too long. I was aware of my impropriety. By now I should have been down the terraces running through the forest. And each moment I stood there the urge to step forward and touch her face intensified.

Later in the day as the great Hornbill got ready to labour on her I found myself unable to look. I stepped out of the room, coming back only when the end was near. And when I had to step forward and hold her legs up I did so with my gaze averted, refusing to meet her flashing eyes.

That evening she did not need poultices but I found myself preparing them and taking them to her. I ignored her look of surprise and her curled lips. No blemish on her milky skin escaped my concern and my ointment. I tried to look at her when she was not looking at me. I was apprehensive she would see something in my eye whose shape I too did not recognize. When I had her on her stomach I gently rubbed her spare shoulders and in moving down with the ointment carefully felt each bone in the line of her narrow back. It was all I could do to keep myself from stroking the pool of thick black hair so unruly on her head.

When I was not done long after I ought to have been done, she said, What? You decided you want it too?

I felt it like a slap across my face. Without saying a word I picked up the bowl and towels and left the room.

That night I was again in a torment. Lying where I lay outside the door of the great Helmsman I could hear each time she changed her position or had her chest rattled by a deeper breath. In fact I found myself willing her to move so I could sense her presence. At one point there was a loud creak and I knew she'd sat up and was looking out at the mountain peaks, the night sitting grey and easy on them.

Silent as a breeze I flowed out of the house and stood behind a pine tree from where I could see the barred window. The moon was already low. It caught in her dark hair and bounced off her fair cheeks. The slopes were alive with the scuttle of small animals and a night bird was calling from the lowest terrace. She was still as a boulder, looking at something beyond the snows. Her lips were light against each other, not as I had always seen them, tight in anger or open in protest. The eyes were different too. Not spitting fire but deep and dark as water in a well.

As I watched, she clutched the iron bars and slumped her head against her hands. I stayed at the pine till she pulled away from the window and lay down again.

That morning I pounded the forest like a man possessed and would have slapped dead any beast had it dared cross my path. When I took the vapours to the great Hornbill I squatted by his side and told him I was floundering. He put his hand on my head and encouraged me to speak. He did not say a word till I had finished. Then he said it was okay. The flesh was always weak and it ambushed us in unexpected ways. Even a great Helmsman was not fully immune to its traps. It was the difference between Aum and even the finest of the pure.

He said sometimes the surest way of escaping the trap was to succumb to it. The pull of the flesh could be like the hunter's net that tightens evermore the more you rage against it. But if you only slacken your muscles you can loosen its mesh. He said I should ease myself of my burden. To not do so would be to give it strange shapes, shapes born of delusion, which in the world out there go by the name of love and are responsible for exceptional foolishness and chaos.

He said I must burn through my desire and my discontent as swiftly as I could.

When I went and sat down by her I did not take off my clothes. She lay as she always lay, on her back, naked and limp, legs slightly apart, and eyes alive. In my anxiety I had piled on too much wood and the fireplace was roaring. Already a glimmer of sweat was beginning to sheathe her skin.

It took her some time to realize the great Hornbill was not coming. On my part, for the first time in years I found myself uncertain. I was not sure what I wished to say to her nor what I ought to do. I sat on my haunches, my eyes averted from hers, looking at her plum breasts but not seeing.

Lacing her hands under her head she said, Ah I see it's time for the eager pupil's initiation! So tell me, how would you like to start?

And she pulled back her legs and parted them wide.

When I did nothing she said, Don't be nervous. One day you have to be like the old man. Doing your duty diligently. Making women out of young girls. Filling the valley of the pure with the purer and the purer.

I knew she did not mean a word of what she said. I had understood her by now. All the anger she had inside her was making her speak a distorted language. It filled her with false words. We had been taught about this at the barracks. The pursuit of purity was a lifelong endeavour. Men and women often stumbled. Every stumbler had to be punished and reformed, but only after being understood.

She too would pay for her distortions and her falsehoods – after I'd arrived at a proper understanding of her. I pushed her raised knees down and clamped her legs closed. She rolled over onto her stomach and said, Ah, like your master – I should have known!

I pulled the white sheet lying nearby and, throwing it over her, picked her up and placed her in the corner away from the fire, her back against the wall. I had wrapped her so she was covered from neck to ankle and her limbs were trapped inside. She could move her head and she was lifting it up now to thrust her chin at me.

Squatting in front of her I said, You like to talk? Okay now talk. Say all you want to. I am here to listen.

The great Helmsmen – steeped in the truth that is Aum – are always right. Men and women never know what they want. They agitate for something and in the moment that it is theirs, they are already looking elsewhere, agitating for something else. Men and women always need to be told what they ought to want.

For a long time after I invited her to speak she remained silent as if suddenly stripped smooth of her thorny words. I waited, on my haunches. She made no attempt to free herself of the cocoon I had wrapped her in. The fire had suddenly flared, catching a hollow log, lighting up the room. Soon it would dim, and demand fresh wood. The room was hot but I could hear the gale screaming outside.

I said again, Tell me all. I am here to listen.

She began slowly, picking her words one by one, looking directly at me, but for the first time without venom in her eye. She said the things I expected her to. She said she was distraught at the girls' home. Each time she visited the motherhood she spent her time hunting for her mother. She did not want to be hugged and patted by every mother: she wanted *her* mother. When they went back home all the girls would talk to each other trying to guess which one was their true mother. All night she would stay awake tormented by this question.

There was one – slim and soft, with hair and eyes black as coal – that she thought was hers. This mother would hold her tighter than any of the others. For a long time she struggled to find the courage to ask her and then one day she did. The black-haired black-eyed mother cupped the girl's cheeks in her hands, looked deep into her coal-black eyes and said, It makes me happy you think that but you must know it is terrible to think in such a way.

Even as she rebuked her she held her tighter. Thereafter, visits to the motherhood only meant the black-eyed black-haired mother. The girl could not wait to jump into those strong arms, and each time the mother held her closer and closer. Running her small fingers on the mother's neck the girl wished she could rip off the face to see if she had her nose and mouth and chin and skin.

Nothing in the valley goes unnoticed. The pure stay the path by checking each other's wandering feet. One day, in the ear of the girl the mother whispered that she had been warned. No longer must they make an exhibition of their feelings. They must embrace other mothers and other girls.

They tried. It was no good. The girl found her hands gripping the shoulders of mothers, keeping them from coming closer.

The girl wept through the nights and it was noticed. She was summoned and spoken to, by a powerful mother whose body was

small, with crisp skin, and hands that curled like claws. Her face was
fresh, the lacquer shining, and she had a deep voice four times the size
of her body. She spoke slowly, telling the girl what she already knew.
The poison of possession first took hold in childhood. If stymied
then it never succeeded in making a comeback.

The girl said, I want my mother.

The mother said, I am your mother.

The girl screamed, suddenly opening her mouth and unloosing
a loud unending wail that only stopped when a hard blow to her
temple felled her to the floor. It was then, through the stinging tears,
that her eyes first began to flash.

The next time at the motherhood she went straight to her mother
and clung to her. The mother whispered caution in the girl's ear,
but the girl seemed not to care any more. When the time was done
and all the other girls had left, the rest of the motherhood came and
prised away her fingers one by one from the flesh of her weeping
mother. The girl said nothing, just flashed her eyes.

For the next six days the girl was sent to the room of inner truths
where the walls were tall and close to you and were unbroken by any
window so that one could look nowhere but within oneself. Lying
on the stone floor you could sense day and night by the line of light
high under the slope of the roof. Each day the small powerful mother
with a voice four times the size of her body, visited her and spoke to
her of the selflessness of the pure and the glories of non-possession.
The girl flashed her eyes and held her tongue.

What she learned in her time at the room of inner truths she never
revealed but when she was taken back to the motherhood she clung
again to the neck of her mother as a leech in the rains to an exposed
ankle. The mother begged the girl to step away else a terrible calamity
would befall them. When the girl asked what could be more terrible
than stepping away, the mother said, Worse than not claiming your
children is to not see them at all.

The girl paid no heed and no one came to interrupt them. As
the girls and mothers mingled, the black-eyed black-haired pair held

each other tight, cooing senseless words full of profound meaning. All the while the smooth and worn face of the mother was wet with tears. In that moment the girl knew the motherhood had relented and given unto her what was so unquestionably hers.

On the next visit she did not spot her mother immediately. As she turned and turned, looking for the outstretched arms, her panic began to spiral. Soon she was rushing from mother to mother, demanding, Where is my mother? To which each one said, I am your mother.

She opened her mouth and began to scream till a heavy slap felled her to the ground. In the room of inner truths once again the small powerful mother spoke to her slow and long of the great journey of the founding fathers, the peerless vision of Aum, and the valour of Alaiya and Ali. She spoke to her of the great infirmities and horrors of the men in the other world out there. She spoke to her of the great task of the pure and the glory of their ways. She told her they were all warriors of the truth and the failing of one warrior was the failing of them all.

Surrounded by high walls, filled with the memory of her last time in there, the girl did not scream. And when there was a pause in the voice that was too strong for the body she said she wanted to see her mother. The voice said the warriors of the pure could not be detained by the dubious ties of family and friendship. Anything that weakened a warrior was to be eschewed. The pure could never be married to one man or woman, nor be the children of any one parent. They were born to their ideals and forever wed to only them.

The room had run cold. I rose and turned over the pulsing log and new flames licked out. Over it I poured wood chips. The fire roared.

In the corner, unmoving, encased in white, she looked like a stuffed bird. Her eyes were finally still. I could see what was happening. As she relived the story of her short life she was beginning to recognize the error of her ways.

She never saw her mother again. She heard whispers that the mother had been sent to the Crater. The girl said she cried every night with a pillow over her face so the sobs would not carry. She said the lesson for her was never to reveal her real feelings, always to mask her true self.

She learned to still her tongue but a kind of sullenness came upon her. At the motherhood she never again embraced a mother. And she never stopped looking for her black-eyed black-haired one. She found it impossible to share the enthusiasms of her friends. A few times she tried to talk to them of the doubts scourging her mind but then she quickly withdrew, aware that she was – dangerously – trying to walk on water.

Often she was singled out for a more intensive instruction in the catechism. She listened to everything that was said about Aum and everything that Aum had said and she wondered. And she mastered the art of moving her mouth to say what was being demanded without meaning a word of it. She had no intention of being flung back into the room of inner truths.

She came to blood late – or so it was believed. The truth is with great craftiness she hid the fact from everyone for a long time. One by one, week on week, she saw her friends leave for their initiation, departing as girls and returning as women. Their wombs now ploughed fields ready for the endless sowing and reaping of the crop.

From each one she extracted an account of the ceremony and with each telling she became convinced she was at the mercy of great unholiness. She tried to test her thesis with her friends but quickly realized they were too deep in the dye to see any of the real colours.

And then one day her limbs were prised open and she could hide the blood no more, and here she was…

The fire had dimmed again but I did not rise to stoke it. Squatting in front of her I thought, what a perilous thing the human mind is. Forever it struggles in a fog. How easily it can make an animal of a shadow and a shadow of an animal. How this wonderful girl had made of purity such a sullied thing!

There was so much I had to teach her. It was as if she were standing on her head and looking at the world. But first there was the understanding to be extracted. I was doing well: fluidly she was telling me the story of her mistaken ways. Once I had emptied her of all falsehood I would pour her brimful with the truth.

I said to her, Do you wish to rest?

She said nothing. I stood up, picked her in my arms and walked towards her room. Cocooned in the white sheet her face, the black hair and the black eyes, lay close on my shoulder. As I looked down at her she looked back at me with contrition in her eyes and I pushed her up till her breath was warm on my cheeks and her mouth open near mine and, as the great Hornbill had hinted, desire powered through me like a summer gale through the valley, sweeping away like loose leaves every untethered thought and idea.

I did not sleep that night and no longer was she a cold fish. By lending her a calculating ear I had unloosed both her tongue and her limbs. She trapped me in them and I did all that I was required to. In the moonlight coursing through the barred window it was clear to me that she was made for the motherhood. The strength and beauty of her body would give unto the faith daughters and sons of the highest order.

As she slept she held me tight. I did not pull away. Her trust would give to me her truths. I watched her nostrils flare and contract, her breasts rise and fall, her black hair paint my skin, and I stroked her back slowly so that all her fences fell. Each time she stirred – as if from a dream – I patted her forehead, pushing back the hair from her face, feeling the eyelashes flutter against my fingertips.

For the first time in years I did not wake deep into the night, hours before dawn. I only rose when through the barred window I saw the slimmest line of grey cut the sky. Gently turning her over and tucking the quilt deep into her body I went out and poured cold water over my head. Just before I picked up the canister I smelled my body and it smelled as it never had before. I sniffed along my shoulders and under my arms and bending double along my waist and thighs. Not once but several times. And then I shook off the intoxication and filled and upturned the canister several times over my body till everything deceptive had been washed away.

After I had woken the great Hornbill with his mug of vapours and given to him an account of the night, I went and woke her too with a steaming mug. Before I left his room the master said, A Wafadar treasures his arrows only so they can perish on the target. An arrow's value lies in its dispensability.

She held me around the neck when I proffered her the brew and rubbed her lips against my ear, whispering intimate things. I placed the mug on the floor and leaned into her and tended to her with the diligence that a Wafadar brings to polishing his arrow.

Those few days – but for my duties towards the great Hornbill – I remained a man in quest of an understanding. She clung to me and her words flowed like the waters of the Amrita. Each time they were about to drown me I staunched their onrush by filling her with myself. This she welcomed moving her limbs like oiled scissors.

When the great Helmsman saw me, he said, Every good quiver has many arrows. Never value an arrow as if it's the only one.

I wordlessly bowed, in gratitude and in reverence.

Soon my role in her life had become clear to me. I was to rescue her from herself. Holding her in the crook of my arm, watching her sleep, putting my finger under her nostril to feel her warm breath, I became aware of my profound responsibility towards her – or more accurately towards the brotherhood. She was of the best and she had much to give. I had only to right her, put her head up and her feet down, make her see the world as it was, not the way she feared it to be.

One evening I was in her room diligently working on her when I heard the great Hornbill call. Swiftly, without wiping the sweat off my skin I pulled on my clothes and rushed to him. He was sitting on the floor in meditation and without looking up he sniffed the air, making me aware of what I had been doing. Then turning to look at me, into the very nakedness of my soul, he said it was time for me to be rid of the arrow.

Wordlessly I retreated to our room and I was trembling when she reached out to touch me. I was in panic. I felt I needed more time to finish the task of my understanding. I considered going back to ask for a few more days but feared it would appear inappropriate. When I told her, a cloud fell across her face and she wrapped her arms around my neck and buried herself in my chest. I put my face into her hair and its smell invaded my nostrils and was never to leave me.

A strange anxiety now filled us. She pulled me down and locked me in her limbs. We had run out of time but we could not hurry. We had things to say but we could not speak. I found it difficult to look into her black eyes. And she looked at me deep and steady as if it were she who was trying to understand me.

On the way down I held her hand to steady her. It was dark; she did not know the terrain. I led her slowly, wishing to finish telling her all I needed to. In the deodar forest around us, amid the scurrying of small animals, was the pad of a big beast. Probably a bear threading his way to the fruit trees below.

A terrace before the last I sat her down on a rock and knelt in front of her and, holding her face between my hands, told her she was wonderful but completely upside down. As I recounted to her the truths of the great Helmsmen she began to slowly trace my hair and my nose with her fingertips. For the first time in my life I wished I could pull off the face.

But I recognized it was a false moment. A surge of false emotion provoked by her beauty, the night, and my desire. I knew I was succumbing to it but I knew it would not be for long. When her fingers reached my lips I picked her up and sitting myself down on the rock filled her urgently with my mistaken impulse.

Just before I handed her over, she clung to me, her black eyes fixed on mine. I let her. Lifting her mouth to my ear she said, It is you who are wonderful but completely upside down. Please see the great evil it has all become. And if you see it you will not be able to endure it. Save yourself; save me.

The great Hornbill was awake when I returned. I knew I had taken far too long. He told me to get him and myself a shot of Ferment. When he had quaffed his, he said, The peerless archer always focuses on the eye of the bird, never on the bow or the arrow.

That night I slept not a moment and soon after midnight I began to run, scattering the beasts of the night, returning only when it was time to brew the vapours. It was the same the next night and the night after. And soon it became clear to me, the perils of the false moment. As always Aum was right. Sentimentality undid the best of men.

Nothing escaped the great Hornbill. Many weeks later he called me and embracing me, said, My tireless son, it's time for you to bring greater glory to the brotherhood.

THE PRAYING MANTIS

In the years that followed I became, in the words of the magnificent Captain of the Guard, one more glittering thread in the tapestry of our great purpose. There was no task allotted to me that I did not excel in. It was my resolve never to fail and the few times that I did not measure up to my own expectations I found myself torn with self-flagellation. I wanted every action of mine to be perfect. I wanted to be the greatest soldier in Aum's peerless army.

In my years at the Pass I did not allow a single animal, leave alone a man, to enter or exit the valley unless cleared by the captain. We always did duty in twos. Two Wafadars on the outside by the wet slit, ensuring nothing slipped through the rocks into our world. And two Wafadars on the inside where the passage opened onto the glory of our home – ensuring nothing slipped out. If, impossibly, anything living or dead did escape past one set – coming in or going out – there was no way it could do so past the second. Two Wafadars are a stone wall. Four are a veritable mountain.

I preferred to patrol the outside, where the greater threat lay. Our orders were clear. Anyone chancing near the wet slit had to be put to flight with a dose of terror that stopped their hearts and loosened their bowels. This I enjoyed. And to tell the truth I often found myself longing for the sight of a foolish man – or better still, men –

wandering up the path through the giant deodars, trailing their sheep or looking to collect firewood.

The captain said it used to be highly unusual to spot someone so high up but over the years it had become a regular occurrence. In the early years the Wafadars had patrolled only the insides, swiftly neutralizing the rare man who slipped through. To begin with the bodies were burnt in the valley. But then it became clear that unless the men out there found the carcasses of their dead they kept returning in endless waves of search parties. Aum as ever was right: these men lived in such fear of death that they paid more attention to the rites of the dead than to those of the living. So we began to leave the bodies where they were easily found and also stationed Wafadars on the outside.

Savages don't learn. Though we had terrorized hundreds and killed scores, new ones still kept blundering up. The captain said once there were only six small hamlets in the entire area, between us and the town many thousand feet below. But now there were five villages and more than a dozen hamlets with their profusion of cattle and children and women.

The cattle we often killed, taking away the meat so it appeared the work of a big cat. The children we frightened. My favourite trick was to hang from a tree by my toes, in the path of a meandering child, and then bare my teeth with a low growl. Their wails did not die out for weeks and could be heard deep into the nights, emanating from their stone and slate huts across the mountains. But it was their expressions that amused me the most. Men grow their children up full of such dread as no other animal can equal. If a child of the brotherhood found a beast hanging upside down and snarling at him he would take a stone and bash in its teeth.

Sometimes my brother and I played a game. We hung down at opposite ends of a forest path so whichever way the screaming child turned he found the same growling face waiting. In the villages it was whispered that there was not one djinn up there but an entire tribe.

The women we used. For pleasure and for the purpose. It was

mandated by the great Helmsmen. The Kiln was far and desire must never be allowed to become a distracting volcano. And by filling their wombs we were spreading ourselves. Occasionally when it seized us we would melt down to the hamlets, locate a worthy vessel and do the deed. For a Wafadar such a foray is as nothing, like a walk along the Jhinjheri; and the young women had long become used to being suddenly invaded by the djinns.

At this too – the harvesting – I earned much renown. I would be false if I said I gained the legend of the Wolf but I was among the finest. Each time an emergency requisition arrived for new bodies the captain would turn to me. I would pick two brothers from the guard and we would start to run, down the slopes, through the trees.

By now we had gone past the neighbouring hamlets and villages and were working the small towns. Sometimes when I entered them in the evening, so choked, so filthy, so noisy, I thought I would, given a chance, love to clean them up completely. These were not men, these were insects. Teeming, scurrying, jostling, chirring. Too many; too petty. They were fit to be nothing but training fodder for the pure.

But for the moment the orders were only to cull. No more than were needed. We all knew that there was a day in the future, for which we had been preparing for decades, when the pure would make a reckoning of fallen men everywhere.

Till then the keyword was caution. Mostly we moved after sundown, kept each other in our sights, and looked to isolate men who already seemed isolated. So we looked for bodies curled up under tattered blankets at the bus station, near the garbage dump, outside the shuttered shops of the bazaar. As we had them, the townsmen too had their savages: dark and wiry and full of rank smells, sleeping in thick clusters under tin sheds. You could take away as many of them as you could carry and the rest would wail and moan but never dare follow.

Accurate use of the chonch generally kept them comatose till we reached the valley. But sometimes a Wafadar erred, resulting in a noisy captive. We had orders then to dispose of them as we chose. I liked to throw them off a high cliff. To see the hysterical fear in their eyes and to hear how a man's voice peaks and falls as he plunges.

Let me say it was always upsetting when we failed to bring back someone robust. It left me in a temper for days. On the other hand, when we delivered the savages in good condition – ready for use, as once we used to receive them from other Wafadars – the sense of accomplishment was infinite.

One thing was more gratifying still: to play an angel. Once every year – seldom more – a brother who had lost his equilibrium ran away from the valley. It never happened on my watch and it was not always that the fugitive fled through the Pass. A deranged mind is capable of great excess. Some actually scaled the treacherous north slope where the gradient was not sheer but the snow ran loose, concealing crevasses so deep you could not hear a body fall. The chances of a man surviving that stretch were one in a thousand. That too with fingers and toes lost to frostbite.

The deranged mind is also capable of deceit. To our mortification, a few Wafadars – the purest of the pure – riding on the trust that was our right had walked through the wet Pass as if on a stroll and kept walking. So the hardest lesson of all had been learned. That no one, not even the finest, was beyond the reach of decay.

Recovering these lost brothers was not a task for every Wafadar. It was not merely about skill and strength. It demanded the wisdom of the Helmsmen and the sensitivity of the motherhood.

To pick the spoor of a runaway was easy. The painstaking work began once the trail had led us to a town. Then we had to lie low, merge into the walls and eaves, gather every floating whisper, and slowly smell out our brother.

There was one problem always: all of them tended to pull off their face. However, this was not as great an obstacle as it sounds. Bereft of the face their skin had the pallor of a lizard's belly while the apertures of their eyes were circled by a band of dark skin. We paid extra attention to men wearing caps and scarves and spectacles, and often pulled them off for a quick check.

Strangely, the most likely place to find them was either the bazaar or the Talkies. The bazaar it was possible to understand. There was food and cloth to purloin and masses of men to lose yourself amid. But the Talkies were a mystery. They were dank and full of foul odours and the noise inside was deafening. In the moonlight of the moving screen it was disgusting to see rows of grown men weep and whistle, shout and laugh like fools.

One time we recovered a brother who had been skulking at the Talkies for three months. His lunacy was by now complete. He was coated in grime and smelled rank. Yet he grinned with all his teeth and continually sang songs full of senseless words in a loud voice. No amount of persuasion would silence him. On the way back I had to break his jaw to keep him from destroying the peace of the high mountains.

It was morbid to see how degraded – and how quickly – my brothers became in the other world. I found one in a grimy hill town that was full of gaudy visitors come to dumbly worship at the feet of stone deities in a clutch of stone huts that ran up a slope. One look at the place – the mud churned by thousands of feet, mixed with the husk of coconuts, black peels of bananas, discarded plates of dried leaves, flecks of red-and-gold tinselly cloth, mucus and faeces – was enough to affirm the need to completely change this world.

Tragically, this lost brother had once been a Pathfinder. Now he sat on the washed-but-dirty stone floor at the entrance to these rock gods, his chest bare and striped with ribs, a white and orange cloth knotted around his groin, his head tonsured, paste marks on his forehead – the band around his eyes still faintly discernible – and he collected the shoes and slippers of the congregating fools – off their

very feet! – and handing them a token stored the footwear in a shelf
of little wooden boxes behind him.

When he caught my shoe I tightened my toes, making him
struggle. He looked up at me and immediately fell back with a cry on
to his shaky racks, sending the dusty footwear raining on his head.
We didn't know each other but I wore the face.

I could recognize him because I had been to the Mausoleum of Our
Egos before setting out. It was the large shed next to the one where
the old ustaad had measured me for the face. There was a new ustaad
there now, and his assistant had vanished into the endless rooms inside
the large shed and returned with the original face of the renegade.
Somewhere in there was mine too, and that of every brother.

I grabbed the ludicrous fellow by his shoulders as he sat aptly
garlanded with dirty slippers and shoes and shook him till his eyes
began to roll in his head. Then I picked him up and carried him into
the pine forest above the temples. There were scores of chanting–
swaying people milling around, but no one came to his rescue. They
merely muttered and whined and held each other. Animals are better
than these men, so bereft of courage and of consideration. No doubt,
before I had breasted the first line of trees they'd have run to their
stone gods pleading for help.

I set him against the scaly back of an old pine while my brother
stood at the treeline keeping an eye on the men and their gods
below. The Pathfinder's scalp gleamed with oil and he sat on his heels
cupping his ears.

I said, It's time to go back.

He said, There is nowhere for me to go now. This is the destination
of my life.

I said, This is filth and ignorance. This is what we were born to
annihilate.

He said, This is the abode of Shiva. It is where he rested before
destroying the world for its transgressions. He is still here in every
stone. Come with me tonight when the moonlight bathes them and
you will know it!

I said patiently, You are the child of Aum. You genuflect to no stone or tree. You are not of this world. This is a world you have to remake.

He suddenly looked up, his features snarled, and shouted, Shiva is the lord! Shiva is the truth! Shiva is the cosmos! Shiva is life and Shiva is death! Go away! My place is at the feet of Shiva! I am one with Shiva! I am one with the cosmos!

I slapped him so hard a tooth popped out. And with it a rain of tears. But he kept babbling his nonsense though in a softer voice.

Through his blood-flecked sobs he said, Come sit with me. Collect the shoes and slippers of Shiva's faithful. There is no greater joy in the universe. Shiva is love! Shiva is peace! Shiva is ecstasy! Shiva is the flute, the flute-player, and the music…

I said, Pathfinder, remember what you once learned and what you taught us!

He said, Forget it all! I was a fool! Come and collect shoes with me and the truth will be yours and all wisdom will be yours. This is what Aum too should have done…

I slapped him hard again and pulling him by his left ear began to briskly walk up the slope. Not one man from the temples had mustered the nerve to attempt a rescue. I had a sense of their ways by now. They would come a day later, solicitous about collecting the body.

Through his whelps of pain the fallen Pathfinder started to shout, Let me be or the great destroyer will destroy you with his cosmic dance! All of you! Even Aum!

His derangement was complete. I took the fourth chonch and before he could even register it pierced his skin in a dozen places.

When I handed him over to the captain, who would produce him before the great Helmsmen, he was chanting and swaying like the worst kind of stone-worshipper. It seems he did the same in the presence of our great guides. There was nowhere to send him to heal but down the chute into the Crater.

I kept waiting for a chance to visit the Crater. I assumed it inevitable that a sterling Wafadar would sooner or later be assigned duty there. It didn't happen. But I kept picking up snatches of information that fed my fascination. Down there it seems were brothers and sisters so twisted in the mind that it was difficult to believe they were born of us. Many of them were, singly, capable of spreading a venom that could poison the entire valley.

Apparently, in there was an old man who had been so fiery of speech as to make QT2's eloquence seem the grunting of a pig. When he was a mere twenty-two this arsonist had stood up in the congregation of the brotherhood and with his lightning tongue lit a fire of rebellion against the face.

Filled with ego, he had said perilous things. He was a believer but he wished to be himself, just as each brother should be. A nose was not an idea, and lips not principles. Men could be noble and joined in high thought without becoming copies of each other. The great Helmsmen let him speak. At the time it was thought the monthly congregation would bring out the best in the brothers. And so it was month after month with voice after voice bonding the flock in greater purpose. And then the arsonist stuck out his tongue of fire.

In a few months the arsonist began to contend the face could not be of Aum's ordaining. It was perhaps the idea of Ali or Alaiya or some other great master who imagined it to be the vision of the peerless one. For the truth was Aum had walked away from his world of men because it was filled with a growing decay, with men mirroring each other in weakness and in venality. He had sought to restore virtue to singularity. To find regeneration in the new. As his tongue flashed, a wave of nods coursed through the sitting heads.

It was then that the great Helmsmen understood how dangerous a man unaware of his boundaries can be. How exemplary things are brought to ruin not by men who know too little but by those who think they know too much. All men must have one sacred centre. Without it the world is a feast of beasts.

And then in the middle of one congregation, the torches burning bright, a gathering wind presaging a storm, the arsonist stood up, raised his arms, and flicking his tongue like lightning declared the time had come to shed the face. If men could not look at themselves and recognize who they were, they could never become who they wished to be.

Like a peal of thunder a great murmur shook the brothers. And then, before any hand of sanity could prevent it, the arsonist had ripped the face off, and in the whipped light of the torches the brothers were looking at a man they did not know. His skin was swarthy and the jaw firm. Beneath a long nose the mouth that spat fire was a graceful bow, befitting of a woman's promise. Each brother put his fingertips to his own face.

At that very moment, as if in fearsome reprisal, as if it were Aum's unhappy reproof, the storm broke and it was a storm the like of which the valley had never seen. Mighty trees were uprooted, roofs blown off, children lifted off their feet, big boulders set to rolling like small pebbles. And when the infernal gale broke the rain began to fall and for seven ceaseless days the skies vented themselves of their every drop and left not a single hair on any child, man, or woman dry. All was soaked and all was debris.

It took months for the valley to be restored to order. Each evening a great Helmsman came to counsel the flock. The world spun around itself like a top and floated in nothingness like a feather and sucked light from the sun like a child sucks milk from a mother's teat – all because there was a divine order. The poise of the universe rested on a million fulfilled promises. The luminous one had made a covenant with his people, on behalf of his people – and one of his own in a delirium of arrogance had broken it. The face was not just a symbol. It was us.

The monthly congregations were stopped. Free speech has no meaning when it sprouts without wisdom. The brotherhood did not need to interpret Aum; merely to heed him.

The lightning tongue was sliced and put to preserve in a jar. A reminder of words that spit and sizzle and can burn down the world.

The de-tongued arsonist was given back the face and sent to the Crater, to be resurrected in the image of the true one.

There was a woman down there, it was said, who had insidiously tracked the seven children born of her womb and gathering them one night in a moment of maternal insanity tried to flee the valley through the fatal northern slope where the snows were infirm like water. Her oldest boy, wise beyond his years at twelve, had informed the Pathfinders but by the time the Wafadars sighted her, two of her offspring had already slipped through crevices so deep their cries could not reach the surface.

In a display of profound evil the Wafadars had never seen before – and hoped never to again – they saw the demented mother push the trusting children one by one into the bottomless abyss. No proof more grotesque of the dangers of parental sentiment can be imagined. As the cries of the falling children faded, the Wafadars rushed in on insect feet to rescue the last remaining infant. Even as they reached her she'd wrung the neck of the baby and throwing it away leapt on them kicking and biting.

For weeks she was paraded through the valley so each one of the pure would know how terrifyingly close the impulse to impurity lurked. It was a reminder to every mother that the children born of their womb belonged not to them but to the flock. They were instruments of a greater purpose. To think otherwise was to tempt great perversion.

Because she continually wailed and flailed like a wounded animal, a tight cloth was run between her teeth and her wrists were tied behind her back. And though there could be no redemption for someone so evil she was sent to the Crater of Resurrections for the brotherhood lives ever in hope and wishes no violence on any of its people.

The most sinister man inside the Crater, it was said, was a tall thin brother known as the praying mantis. Unlike most renegades whose tongues flapped like leaves in the wind, his salient gift was stillness and silence. It was when I heard the story of the praying mantis that

I first discovered that far removed from the Wafadars there existed a highly clandestine class of brothers known as the Yodhas.

It took me a long time and many conversations to pull out their story. As it unfolded layer on layer I was humbled by the greatness of my people. All around me were ingenuity and excellence toiling silently for profound change.

The Yodhas were magnificent, the missionaries of the pure. They were our sleeping warriors in the outside world. Their task was to infiltrate the rotten structures out there, secure a perch, and wait for the moment. Just as the ancient Greeks had taken the impregnable city from inside the belly of a horse, the pure were relentlessly at work, positioning themselves to unleash the revolution from within the heart of the beast.

The Yodhas answered to no one but the Gentle Father and the great Helmsmen. I found it difficult to believe when I was told that there were more Yodhas out in the world than brothers inside the valley. The campaign had commenced at the time of the peerless one. It seems it was Aum himself who had decreed that the valley was not the goal. In itself it was a mere nursery. Its task was to craft the perfect saplings that were then to be planted through the waiting world.

Now I learned that the finishing fields of this nursery lay to the north of the highest terraces of the great Helmsmen. A place beyond bounds for all other brothers. It seems at that giddy height amid the snows there was tunnelled another pass into the other world. It was guarded not by men but by mountain wolves trained by the Yodhas. All these years it was their howling as they patrolled the nights that we had heard down the slopes. It was from there with a last instruction and benediction from the Gentle Father that the young Yodhas were sent out to penetrate the world.

Each new Yodha was sent to an older one who'd already insinuated himself into a crucial crevice. They instantly became bandhus, visceral comrades, entering a secret compact in which no one else could intrude: watching over each other, learning from each other, guarding each other. In time the younger Yodha would acquire his own junior bandhu, in a similar secret compact in which no one else could intrude. And so each Yodha out there was viscerally tied to two bandhus – an older and a younger, neither knowing the other.

Continually, ceaselessly, the capillaries of the comrades spread deep and wide, all connected and all independent. When called upon they could rise – within hours – like an interminable unfurling snake, full of menace and purpose; or if required each unit of three Yodhas could swiftly sacrifice itself without endangering the rest of the sleeping-preparing animal.

The Yodhas did not wear the face and they were not masters of combat like the Wafadars. They were skilled in subterfuge, the opposite of the rest of us brothers. They were masters of disguise, bahurupiyas, capable of donning a thousand faces. While Wafadars were shadows, Yodhas were actors.

It was now I learned that we had been scrupulously winnowed at the home and the barracks. Every moment they had been imparting us instruction, our Pathfinders had also been assessing us for our gifts. Each moment they had been – unknown to us – nudging us to wish to become what we were destined to be. I wanted to become a Wafadar because they made me want to become a Wafadar because they knew I was born to be a Wafadar.

It seems once you were in the know you could identify a Yodha anywhere in the world – but only if he wished you to recognize him. A Yodha's identity I was told lay in his eyes. At the moment he wished to reveal himself, or at the moment he became imbued with high emotion, his eyes acquired an intensity that clearly spoke his purity and his purpose. It was a gaze – it was said – that could still the heart and congeal the blood of ordinary men. What Wafadars did with their chonch a Yodha could do with his eyes.

A Yodha's only connect with the brotherhood were his two bandhus. One above, who had embraced him, and one below, who he had embraced. Every Yodha knew that through his two bandhus he was at all times connected – by a serpentine chain that ran through the entrails of this world all the way back to the valley – to the entire brotherhood.

Once a Yodha was sent into the world he was never to come back. He was to secure a good position and keep expanding it. Without fanfare, like a woodworm, his task was to further weaken the infirm framework of the hollow world. It was not a difficult task. What marked the valley were fixity, unity and selflessness. What marked men out there were whimsicality, divisiveness and selfishness. Using the cheap rhetoric of religion and money, power and possession, a Yodha could keep opening up fault lines down which the stupid men would hopelessly plunge.

There were outstanding Yodhas who with their hard work had managed to create vast pools of animus and discontent. Stoked the foolishness till men and community were pitted against each other. There were amazing Yodhas who had managed to spark widespread riots and mass killings.

There was a silver-tongued one – known as the dung beetle – who had gathered a bunch of curmudgeonly old men and persuaded them to unearth a symbol from the past – more than a thousand years old – and demand for it a fresh reverence. The symbol was a river, once sacred, once wilful and volatile, now dammed at its source to irrigate countless fields. The great dung beetle had made these cantankerous men start a movement to demolish the dam and allow the waters to flow unfettered as sacred waters should. The movement had found a million followers, each rabidly ranged against all logic. Protests had erupted all over the land. The war between reason and unreason had raged. As the peerless one had predicted, the world was full of fools who would in time tear each other up over scraps.

Through the old curmudgeons the splendid dung beetle had made the oafs of unreason march on the dam in a gathering whose size obscured the horizon. With typical arrogance the state had arrayed its guns. The hot screams of unreason and the cold iron of reason had mingled in a din that saw thousands dead, the dam breached, and scores of settlements swept away. Many years had passed and the rupture remained unfjorded. Blood ran continually; new wounds kept the memory of old wounds alive. The dung beetle, now dead, was a legend. A beacon for all other Yodhas. It took him a lifetime to construct his play, but what splendour he'd produced!

The praying mantis on the other hand had betrayed his life's covenant. He had turned on his brothers. It was said he was a victim of too much intellect and too little soul. It seems on the day he was being sent out the Gentle Father had said this boy would either bring great glory to the faithful or stick a dagger in their gut.

To begin with his success had been breathtaking. Using the perch of his senior bandhu – insinuated as a clerk in a government office – he had quickly opened up an array of friendships that allowed him to wend his way to the far-off capital where power bubbled all day like water on fire and crafty men sipped of it as one does of heady Ferment.

Soon he was treading the pathways of the outer domain of the minister of the interior. Already a master plotter he could guess the next ten moves of anyone, petty or powerful. At every step men reached out to his guile to help further their interests only to find that the thin, tall, brooding man – whose full sentences were rare as rainbows, whose hair parted in the middle and fell thickly on each side like the thatch on a hut – had leapfrogged much further.

It was not long before the minister discovered he had chanced on an uncut diamond. In his own profound cunning the minister knew he could polish this man till he would cut through glass and steel as was demanded of him. And this the praying mantis did.

Just as a Wafadar is schooled in strength and courage, a Yodha is trained in strategy and tactics. His lessons take him inside the minds of men. Not just their base instincts – their greed, their covetousness, their hatreds, their hedonism – but also their ostensible higher instincts – their twisted ideas of glory and honour, altruism and self-sacrifice.

As one counts numbers in arithmetic to get the desired result, a Yodha learns how to manipulate these many instincts – base and higher – to arrive at the answer he seeks. In this he is helped by the fact that these men imagine themselves to be highly complex beings – more philosophy than physics – whereas in truth they are nothing more than the simple sums of addition and subtraction, fundamentally enhanced and annihilated by the two basic principles of power and money. Some would add religion to it but a good Yodha knows religion too floats on the rafts of power and money.

Uniquely skilled, the praying mantis first became the minister's confidant, then his advisor, and then – crucially – his emissary. When a man earns the right to represent another he ascends to the highest rung of trust. The minister of the interior was nothing short of an overlord, a high-caste man, small of bone and sharp of feature and imbued with centuries of guile. On a daily basis he made and broke fortunes; incarcerated – under the law – irritants; and executed – outside the law – detractors. In doing all this he kept his hands scrupulously clean, as men who lead men in that world must always do.

Yodhas know in this world's destructive dance of money and power, hypocrisy is a key weapon. Only men who possess the ability to keep saying what they don't mean are able to keep dancing. The praying mantis became the minister's dirty hands, his unspoken but real voice.

Both his bandhus watched in awe. The praying mantis was a master. Word of his prowess rippled through the links of bandhus across the land. None had imagined a Yodha could achieve such success at such a speed. When the call came, this one brother alone would rip the heart out of this world – just as ZZ9 had done once with the challenge of QT2, exploding from within the closed circle of the naumukhi and tearing it to shreds.

Then the praying mantis ran into the maze of cleverness.

Instead of remaining the crucial thread through which all the beads around him passed, the praying mantis began to grow an ambition to become not the necklace but the wearer. He'd been infected by the most common disease of men, the one Aum had set out to erase. The urge to possess.

In a few years all that the minister heard, all that was heard from the minister – all that was heard about him – passed through one man. The stick insect should have held this pose, of control, indefinitely – as did his many Yodha brothers in different ways across the landscape. But no longer did he wish to be the brain that controlled the minister. Now he wished to be the minister himself.

In one single day of infernal noise he demolished the high-caste minister of the interior, a man of generations of wile, by passing on two brown files, tied by a thread, to his rivals. The papers inside the files spoke of the misconduct of other men, their lies and their purloining – little of it to do with the minister. It is the irony of these men, as they thrive by hypocrisy so they perish by it. The minister had done vaulting evil every day of his life but what he was crucified for was of no consequence.

Poised in profound stillness, the praying mantis spoke only a few words – each like a firefly, pulsing between light and dark, its precise location a shifting mystery. In consequence, the vendor of hypocrisy, the minister, trusted him; and the consumers of hypocrisy, the people, believed him. Soon the supreme leader sent for him. Men are addicted to advice. Often they do not know what to do and therefore seek it. Often they know what they have to do but wish someone to affirm it. The praying mantis did both with masterly ease – with a single nod, or a pregnant phrase.

There is a code between bandhus, of never breaking contact. No more than a week must pass between the sharing of information, the reassertion of solidarity. All the cells of the vast serpent must buzz in healthy harmony. Suddenly a week went by and the praying mantis could not be accessed by either of his bandhus. When they did meet him a few days later he was even more still and silent than he'd ever been. Their great enthusiasm at his ingenious positioning was dampened. But they corralled their anxieties, aware the stick insect was an extraordinary Yodha.

In the succeeding months the bandhus found themselves struggling to make an assignation with their brother. Entering the orbit of the supreme leader he seemed to have spun clear out of theirs. His house was a grand bungalow now studded with hairy old trees, guarded by men carrying quick-firing weapons; and his office sat in the deep womb of a formidable stone building that could easily repel cannonballs. They could not meet him any more unless he wished it.

This he did, but less and less, with fewer and fewer words. Now when he met them – in a tiny anteroom adjacent to his big office with a curiously whirling double-fan which had smaller blades mounted on its bigger blades – now when he met them he was constantly interrupted by his many phones and by men putting their head in through the curtains to ask for decisions. Now when the bandhus commented on the grotesque nature of the men around them the praying mantis said nothing.

Then one evening as they were reporting to him their news – the older still a clerk in a government office; the younger a policeman in the state constabulary – the praying mantis exploded, shouting at them for being dogs who understood nothing but the first lessons they had been taught. But I am not a dog, he declared, I am the one who makes men into dogs.

The bandhus were told they would henceforth be summoned for the meetings. No longer could they come to him of their own accord.

In six months they were called twice, and then that too stopped. As they read and heard about his growing influence they did not know what to make of it. Far more intelligent than they were, was he constructing a superior play that they did not understand, or had he actually become someone else, no longer their bandhu?

One Monday morning with the sun not yet up, the clerk went to the grand bungalow. It was the time of the weekly ritual set up by the praying mantis to meet petitioners. A great crowd of peasants jostled at the gate. Stern securitymen checked the folds of their clothes for hidden weapons and let them in. In a lawn at the side, they sat on rich green grass, and as the sun came up drank water in steel tumblers, running it from a big plastic jug set on a table. At the head was a single big chair and when the praying mantis came and sat on it he looked like a thin long shoot growing out of a thick root. By his side stood two men – one fat, one thin – putting order to the seekers, shushing the out-of-turn speakers, peeling the desperate peasants off the praying mantis's ankles, interpreting his nods and single words and making notes of them.

Cross-legged the clerk sat in the middle of the jumble trying to read the signs. The loose unresponsive body, the half-closed eyes – was he still one of the pure or was he now one of them? When his turn came, he stood in front of the chair, bowed at the waist, hands folded together, while the thin man and the fat man urged him to speak his plea by poking his shoulder.

The clerk said one word, the very first sound of the universe, befitting of who he was, the very first of everything. Aum! The praying mantis jerked his head up and in that moment the clerk knew that the man in front of him was no longer a bandhu, no longer a Yodha. The light had gone out of his eyes.

A few weeks later the clerk's throat was slit to his spine in front of his house. No motive could be located for his killing. Soon after the policeman was put away in a solitary cell for being an enemy agent. As evidence it was pointed out that the man lacked any antecedents. No family, no village, nowhere that he came from.

With the natural cruelty of the men he was now one of, the praying mantis had the young Yodha's nails pulled and his bones broken. He wanted to know the next and next and next links in the unending chain of bandhus. In the private meetings of the state he began to declare there was a sinister giant serpent growing in their midst and it ought to be of the utmost priority to locate it and annihilate it. The supreme leader gave him his ear and his permission.

So I was told.

I learned all this in bits and pieces. My head ached with the complication of it all. And yet I pursued the captain to know more and more. Often I would lie awake at night trying to visualize it all – the treacherous world of the men out there, and the great courage of the Yodhas. At such times I was glad I was a Wafadar, a declared warrior, uncontaminated by subterfuge, not constrained to live in the dishonest world out there.

The captain and I were sitting outside our shed just above the Pass, drinking our day's Ferment. The valley lay bathed silvery-blue by a fat moon. The captain's face – which was also my face – shone with a recent polish. He took more pride in his face than most of us and had it touched up every few months. I had not been to the ustaad's shed in two years and the bridge of my nose and the tip of my jaw had lost their sheen.

The captain was a big man – the biggest I had ever seen – and could simultaneously crush two men under his armpits till their ribs cracked and their heart exploded. His hands were giant paws. He could hold the entire fist of a man in them and crush it like a lemon till the juice ran out of the mashed bones. On Judgment Days I had seen him do all of it – to savages and irredeemable renegades – and been filled with pride.

Had he not been such a formidable warrior the captain could have been a Pathfinder, so well did he think and speak. Everyone knew he was destined for the higher slopes – to be a great Helmsman, and perhaps even, one day, the Gentle Father. Now I asked him to finish for me the story of the praying mantis.

Draining his snifter the captain said it had been a time of unprecedented peril and the future of the pure had hung in the balance. The unblemished one had always said a faithless brother was more dangerous than a hundred enemies. It is easy to best a man who sees your body, tough to combat one who reads your soul. No Yodha uttered a traitorous word but with his dangerous mind the praying mantis began to hunt down the bandhus. Each time one was snared and brought to his presence he identified him by looking into his eyes.

The Yodhas are bahurupiyas, unrivalled actors, capable of a thousand faces, and now the entire serpent tried to turn, disintegrate, disappear – become a thousand different faces. But by now the praying mantis had drummed up a scare, sown suspicion in every mind. Neighbours watched neighbours, workers other workers. In every locality across the vast land foolish men were sniffing for Yodhas like dogs for meat. Decades of silent hard work by the pure was being threatened with utter ruin.

The praying mantis – ruthless now as his adopted world – had also dispatched armed missions to the mountains to assault our valley. The founding fathers in their infinite wisdom had foreseen such a day. Aware of the low seductions of the other world they had put in place a protocol that ensured every new Yodha left for the outer world wearing a blindfold. The cloth was only removed at the town by the lake that lies many hours below us and eddies with changing crowds every day of the year. It was here, on the edge of the flats where they play their foolish ball, under a gigantic pine, a Yodha would wait to take his new bandhu into the heart of his purpose.

It was from here that the praying mantis sent his armed soldiers up in every direction. But our mountains are not a sport of ball. A thousand men can spend a thousand years and still not find the hamlet they seek. In any event these mercenaries were little more than beasts of burden, paid to fight, moving in dread. To muddle their navigation, pairs of Wafadars, for months, ambushed them in different places, slashing through their ranks like high mountain sleet. As it is with the men of that world, the leader's resolve was not theirs. Not one uniformed fool managed to climb high enough to even come close to the wet slash that opens up the Pass of All Hope.

By then a team of eight Wafadars – led by none other than our present Gentle Father – had been dispatched to the far-off capital. The praying mantis's time was up. It was a long journey. Only one of the eight had ever been that far. The capital was a gigantic anthill gone mad. One man is a foolishness; many, a lunacy. The octet could see when the time came taking these people apart would be a walk in the woods.

The praying mantis had retreated deep inside five layers of cordon.

He had never known a Wafadar but he knew of them. Inside his office, inside his bedroom, he sat with a black gun, three black dogs with long snouts and sharp incisors splayed at his feet. At every door and every window, uniformed mercenaries stood like statues, pointing their firearms at any intruder. Surely, not even a Wafadar from the distant high mountains, untutored in the ways of this world, could pierce this armour.

To kill the stick insect would have been easy. But the octet was here to take him back alive. He was after all a brother and deserving of a chance at rehabilitation. Only four of the warriors went in, in the hour after midnight, flowing past the mercenaries like water through grass. The other four waited around the vast bungalow, invisible bats in the big old trees, a second line of attack if needed. The canines were dead even as they started, their growls dying in their twisted throats.

Opening his eyes the praying mantis could see nothing, but he knew the dark was full of menace. With one hand on his firearm he threw the switch of the lamp and on each side of his bed, staring down at him, was the face. Before a sound could leave his mouth, four pairs of chonch had pierced his skin, silencing his mind and stilling his body.

In the morning there was pandemonium. There were three dogs with broken necks but no sign of the man they guarded. The mercenaries swore they had seen nothing enter or leave. A frantic search rippled out in every direction. Above the false roof, on slim wooden beams, motionless as statues, sat the four Wafadars, the fallen Yodha laid out between them. So they stayed for three days, by when the search parties had moved deep into the countryside. It was typical of these men, to look afar for what lay at their doorstep.

On the fourth night, rolling their comatose brother in a sheet like a corpse the eight Wafadars began their journey back. Many weeks later when the praying mantis came to his full senses in the assembly of the great Helmsmen he howled like a jackal, declaring what a significant man he was in the world of real men, and the doom that awaited the valley if he were not returned forthwith.

With the grace that is always owed to a brother – even such a disgraced one – the praying mantis was cast into the Crater. Before being sent down, all his teeth were pulled out, barring two front ones above and two below. This was done to keep him from thoughts of conspiracy. For more than twenty-five years now he had spent all his time nibbling on food. With every year he'd become more of a stick insect, motionless, wordless, cured of the sickness of power and pelf.

The world he had been so infatuated with forgot him in no time. With customary suspicion the men around him concluded he had run away to another land to where he had siphoned off his illicit gains. To drape an honest cloak on his disgrace, they named a small street after him. In a few years those who walked the street had no idea who the praying mantis was. The great serpent of the bandhus settled once more and each Yodha went back to quietly clamping his tentacles as wide and deep as he could, preparing for the moment when the alarum would be rung.

So I was told.

A FAT MAN SINGS

I have been telling you my story as I lived it, and felt it.

Were I to decorate it with the embroidery of hindsight, with the new knowledge of new things, it would be another story, and I another man. I know men everywhere tend to do this: make their lives, in the recounting, what they wish them to be rather than what they were. They do it not from vanity alone, but also in a quest for solace. When the light of a man's life starts to dim he grasps for some reassurance that it has not been all in vain. But if I were to do so, such meaning as there may be in my life would be lost. My life then might count for a lie in the living, and in the telling.

And in the great pharmacy of the world's stories it would be no more than a spurious pill, producing distress instead of succour.

I never forgot her.

That is the truth. Let me be truer. I thought of her every single day. Yes, I did not acknowledge this even to myself and I never gave it any words. Had any brother asked me – as I lay on my back looking at the sky – what was on my mind, it would never have occurred to me to admit – even to myself – that it was her. Yet her black hair and black eyes – flashing – were always with me.

I did not think of her consciously. Never. I knew it was not right for me to think of her. She was just with me. I cannot say it better. It has to be understood. Like a presence. Undeclared, but always there. Each time, day or night, that I shut my eyes I saw her standing at the barred window looking out at the moonlit slopes while I watched from behind the pine tree. Or I found myself applying unguents and poultices to her luminous skin. Or holding her face and falling into her bottomless eyes. Often I also saw myself – I can say it now – wrenching the great Hornbill away from her inert body and flinging him into the raging fire. Yet when I opened my eyes I refused to recall anything.

Each time I went to the Kiln to burn off my body I found myself looking for one with black eyes and black hair, bony shoulders and plum breasts. I would go from room to room carefully checking out the new entrants, quite sure it was only a matter of time before she was moved for a while from birthing to pleasuring. Of course it was not a quest I admitted to. It just existed – unacknowledged, unarticulated.

But she never showed up.

Let it not seem like I was in some state of acute ache. My days and years were devoted to the glory of the brotherhood. Every instant I was aware my life was being lived in the service of a great cause. As I learned of the Yodhas and grew older, I also understood that the great transformation – the final move – would not come in my lifetime, just as it had not in the time of Aum. And yet my labours were crucial. Without my daily toil the magical hour would never come. The splendid captain spoke to us of these things all the time and once every month we assembled at the foot of the higher terraces to be showered with the wisdom of the great Helmsmen.

The great Hornbill had passed over many years ago – and I had sat in quiet memory and meditation on hearing the news. Among his effulgent peers the one who now inspired me the most was the great Tragopan, the youngest of the great Helmsmen. He was short with a booming voice and when he spoke he moved his hands as if he was carving animals out of the air. Unlike many of the great Helmsmen he had never been a Wafadar. He'd risen to the higher terraces by being a Pathfinder who, each time he spoke, made the hair on the body of every student stir. He articulated Aum with a rare passion and was a stunning inquisitor and explicator at the truth and purity trials. The Gentle Father in calling him up had said, His words are even more powerful in the service of the brotherhood than the chonch of the Wafadars.

I for one agreed with this fully. When I heard the great Tragopan speak, his eyes on fire, his hands cutting the air into beautiful shapes, I felt wings sprout on my shoulders and my heart expand till it was big enough to contain the world. I knew, as with all things of worth, his journey had been a long and arduous one. For a long time – before he ascended to the higher terraces – he had been kept under a scrupulous watch. The memory of the arsonist and his tongue of fire had never ceased to haunt the flock. Words could light up the world, and words could burn it down.

But this young Pathfinder had proved to be a brother without a flaw, his surpassing intellect and words committed to nothing but the cause of the pure. In less than fifteen years as a Pathfinder he had sniffed out and handed over more than a score of fallen brothers, a few of them fellow Pathfinders who had lost the meaning of the message even as they were passing it on. And when the purification trials were held in the presence of the great Helmsmen, he had been relentless and brilliant in exposing the lies and failures of the betrayers and the traitors.

The legend was he was so skilled in the cleansing inquisition that he could snare every dangerous thought inside the mind of his brothers – no matter how deep and hidden – and drag it out into the light. Brothers who began their trial denying every charge of deceit and failure were by the end found weeping in apology and in contrition. Many were forced to admit he had discovered a canker in their souls that they themselves had not been aware of. He had a manner. When he finished and the fallen brother had nowhere to go but to the Crater, he would turn to each of the great Helmsmen and bowing to them say, May Aum gift me wisdom, and the great Helmsmen purity.

Arrogance undoes the best. Its absence saw this Pathfinder become the great Tragopan while he was still a young man. Just as ZZ9, the great Serpent Eagle, was called upon to face down physical challenges, the great Tragopan was summoned when the august council wished to decode, in the light of new developments, the profound thoughts of the timeless one. And like ZZ9 he never failed. Always he could find the answer and outline the path that satisfied everyone and was true to the spirit of the eternal father.

Early in his ascension the great Tragopan sought and was granted permission to journey through the other world. He did this in the company of the great Tree Pie who for twenty-two years had travelled alone from coast to coast bringing back news and information of the continuing degradation of men's lives, of the spread of squalor and disease, the worship of stones and bricks, the mindless march of the machines, the cult of possession and greed, the culture of lies, deceptions, cruel hierarchies and organized violence. Each time he returned from his travels, the great Helmsmen spent days absorbing the fresh inputs and making their plans.

Many great Helmsmen made these journeys with the great Tree Pie. This was something they could choose to do, in preparation for the responsibilities that lay ahead. Not all felt the need to do so; a few did. But it was whispered that one could not transcend into the Gentle Father unless one had known the other world while being a master of our own.

Without ego the great Tragopan followed the great Tree Pie, eyes and ears wide open. Each time he returned from a journey he spoke to us at the foot of the higher terraces. We waited for these moments. Sculpting the air at high speed he gave us hellfire descriptions of the chaos, misery and despair he had encountered. Nothing was sacred out there. Men bartered in everything including god. In inventing money they had found all meaning. Its pursuit filled their waking hours. For it they could guiltlessly slit throats and pull out entrails. The love of it divided brother and brother. Some had so much of it they could not run through it in a thousand years; some not enough to get to the end of the day.

The peerless one had been right: possession, ego, greed. If we did not act on his vision to rescue the world, its demise was certain.

The returning traveller also never forgot to remind us of the great resolve of the Yodhas. It required a heart of boundless purity and purpose to live among those men and not have one's soul infected. While brothers in the valley were surrounded by their own, each Yodha had only two bandhus as his anchors in a sea of debasement.

Over the years I saw the great Tragopan become not only the voice of the great Helmsmen but also their executing hand. A time came when he ceased to travel and the entire affairs of the valley came under his watch. All day from distant ends of our home brothers came to him to report their progress and take fresh instruction. At the Pass we heard stories of how firm and stentorian he was: the perfect great Helmsman, marrying humility with an unbending will. No slack was given to those who fell short. The world could hardly be changed by men who lacked a grip on themselves.

His surpassing triumph lay in not sparing even a great Helmsman. In a purification trial that lasted weeks – and shook up every brother in the valley – the great Tragopan arraigned the great Horned Owl, who had once been a Wafadar of phenomenal valour and often been mentioned as a future Gentle Father. It was said he could run backwards as fast as he did forward, and could stun any adversary, man or beast, by banging them with his forehead. He spoke little, knew no fear, and was admired by all.

Then the great Tragopan revealed he had broken the faith by forging a dishonest relationship with a madonna at the Kiln. He named her, and we knew her to be of a stout build, older in years, sought by few. The great Horned Owl was charged with converting pleasure into possession and for using his hallowed position to keep her at the Kiln long after she should have been sent back. In the purification trial every attempt by the Horned Owl to clear himself was torn to pieces as the great Tragopan systematically bared the tragic betrayal of the vision of the taintless one by a brother enjoined to protect it.

We knew all brothers tended to return to their chosen madonnas, but that was in pursuit of ephemeral, idiosyncratic gratification. But this, the great Tragopan argued, was a case of shameful attachment. For three years the Horned Owl had visited only this madonna, and had ensured she was not moved to the Serai, the motherhood, or any other place. If each of the pure did the same it would be the end of the brotherhood and of the glorious quest.

The transgression stood multiplied because it emanated from a great Helmsman, a bearer of the torch. It was in the order of things that the chastisement meted out be in equal proportion.

The Horned Owl offered a defence. So we were told. But it was so feeble that the great men of the council were forced to look away in shame and dejection. The great Tragopan then proceeded to extricate a chain of lapses that had marked the life of the Horned Owl. So skilled was his interrogation that he dragged out terrible offences of thought dating all the way back to the barracks. By the time the trial was done, it had been revealed that there had been occasions in the childhood of the Horned Owl when he had doubted the immaculate one and his pristine message.

Each day at the Pass we waited to hear the news. The Horned Owl had been one of us, a great Wafadar: we wanted him to emerge unblemished. But as the weeks rolled by the shame settled on us. And at the end we were relieved when he confessed he had often been unworthy and was ready for penance. He was banished to the family garden at the very end of the valley – the eternal resting place of all brothers, the final symbol of our abiding equality. Here he was to live out the rest of his life in speechless atonement, daily digging holes in the ground in which the brothers he had wronged would forever lie.

It was then this most glorious of brothers, the great Tragopan, who sent for me. Waving me off, my valiant captain said it was possible I was being chosen to honour myself with greater service to the pure. For an entire day my heart hammered with an excitement I had last known more than twenty-five years ago when I had first been summoned to meet with ZZ9, the great Serpent Eagle.

As I stood in front of him, trembling, the great Tragopan slowly cut the air into beautiful shapes. I had been picked after meticulous screening for greater responsibility. No longer was I to just guard the frontiers of the pure. The time had come for me to work inside the valley, to monitor the inner workings of the flock. As much as the strength of my limbs it was time for the robustness of my spirit to be tested. The debacle of the Horned Owl had alerted us to the perils of complacence. No one was impervious to temptation. It was constant vigilance that kept the pure pure. It would be our duty – mine, and three other brothers', shepherded by the great Tragopan – to ensure the flock remained spotless beyond compare.

We were given a shed on the second terrace just above where I had first slept all those years ago. The two brothers who had housed me then were gone, their places taken by others. Of the four chosen I was the only Wafadar. The other three were Pathfinders, also handpicked by the great Tragopan for their attributes of head and heart. I could see they were fascinated by me. A Wafadar is a mythic being. I say this without any ego. He is fashioned to do things ordinary brothers can barely imagine. Inside the shed and outside they waited for me to take the lead. I was careful to not let it bloat my head. We were brothers; we were equals; and that is how it had to appear always.

The first task given unto us was to visit the very granary where I had once erased my ego washing mountains of dishes. This was one of nine granaries in the valley, home to brothers who tilled the soil and maintained the livestock. Since my time the brothers here had been honoured by the Gentle Father with a new nomenclature. They were now known as Foodgivers – nourishing the bodies of the pure, no less than the Pathfinders who did the same for the mind.

The granary was as I recalled it, only bigger. The broken shed at the back of the cookhouse where I had first been assailed by corruptions of the flesh was gone. In its place were three large sheds extending all the way into the forest which had been pushed back at least thirty trees deep. Walking along the new line of the fence I tried to locate some of the ancient trees I had known, but they were gone – a clear sign the brotherhood was growing and flourishing.

I recognized the brother from the cookhouse who had most tormented me by the twitch in his right shoulder. He had developed a slight stoop and walked with a shuffle. He was now the First Foodgiver, the guiding hand of this granary. There was no way he could recognize me but he hosted us with the respect brothers arriving from the higher terraces deserve.

On the first night, while the Pathfinders ate with the Foodgivers in the dining hall – much bigger now, with two wings – I became a shadow around the complex. We were on a routine inspection but we had some information that the germ of song and music had been spotted in these parts. I found nothing except two brothers burning through themselves in a bunk.

For the next few weeks we did what the Foodgivers did. We went to the fields, we reaped and sowed corn and vegetables; we worked at the animal sheds, feeding and milking; we slaughtered at the abattoir. At the appointed time we bathed and slept, meditated and marched, and on the weekend when the preceptor came we sat and listened to the stirring stories of Aum and Ali and Alaiya and drank in the wisdom that was our inheritance.

The Serai in this granary was set in the middle of open fields. It ensured you could spot from hundreds of metres all who went in and out. The Foodgivers went there in batches, twice every week. We went too. I had forgotten how beastly vigorous the brothers of the granary could be. The madonnas who came here were done with motherhood or incapable of it. Most of them were robust and admirable in their ability to serve up pleasure at all hours to such a demanding cast of brothers.

I only watched while the Pathfinders chose to burn themselves calm. When the madonnas discovered I was from the higher terraces they pursued me for information on the beauty and skills of the madonnas up there. Without uttering any obvious lies I assured these rough women they were in no way inferior to the those in the Kiln. They also inquired about possible companions from childhood but I was of no help for I had always transited through the Kiln at functional speed, paying little attention to individual stories and details.

In turn I asked them about a mother with hair black as night and fire in her eyes. They speculated on many such – exclaiming with descriptions – but not one of them sounded like her.

At the end of the third week we bid farewell to the Foodgivers and with the sun rising above the peaks we left the granary. An hour later we were in the forest and when we were deep in it I broke step and finding the smooth trunk of an old plane sat down against it. The Pathfinders' queries I waved away. They were my brothers but by now I knew they were made of much weaker clay.

All day I slept as only a Wafadar can, sitting up, still, conserving all energy. I could sense the other three circling, talking, exploring, but I did not let it intrude on me. I rose after night had fallen and told them to follow me. At the edge of the granary I gestured to them to wait. They were Pathfinders: I could not trust them to negotiate the dark.

Not a body stirred anywhere as I went through the sheds and dining halls like a wraith. But my ears had picked up something. A low, long, unbroken wail. It was emitting from the very last shed – a new large one, beyond the small one in which I had once lived. The shed sat in a finger-like clearing embraced by the forest, pale light limning the chinks in its logs. All the windows were barred and I could see from the gap under the door many feet braced against it. The wail rose and fell and was a sound unlike any I had heard before. It was accompanied by a rhythmic thudding, of something being hammered.

In a moment I was up at the high windows and what I beheld chilled my soul. The shed was filled to bursting with Foodgivers. They were sitting layer on layer, in concentric circles, wedged into each other, limbs intertwined, their arms a sheen of sweat. In the light of a dozen lamps hung from the rafters I noticed, for the first time, that most of the faces were in a state of disrepair, in desperate need of replacement or a fresh coat. Some eyes were closed in seeming meditation; all the others were focused on the brother at the centre, from whose wide open maw issued the terrible wail.

He was terrifyingly fat – the exact opposite of the eternal one. I could see the ustaad would have struggled to fit him his face – it was so corpulent, with big jowls and a high dome. His belly fell around him like a gown covering his legs and feet, and his short fat arm with short fat fingers was raised high, chopping the air jerkily as he wailed.

Like some kind of demon he could push his voice up higher and higher till it trembled the pine planks, and each time he did this the Foodgivers burst into hurrahs and claps and swayed against each other like rustling ears of corn. Then, demonically he would drop his voice to a mere whisper, to the silence of a walking ant, and every shameful renegade in the room would go still and soundless, slavishly following the fat brother's lead.

Above his belly he had big mammaries and his monstrous frame was like some kind of a bestial barrel for the creation of all kinds of sounds. As I watched horrified he produced them without pause – high and low, fast and slow, low and loud, words and no-words – and the Foodgivers swayed to him as if he were a sorcerer. Here was clear evidence if any had ever been needed of the wisdom of strictly proscribing all song and music. I scanned the hall carefully. There was not a brother who was not entrapped.

Suddenly the terrible corpulence picked up his voice, louder and faster, with the brother behind him tapping his wood-flat in a new tempo. At this a short thin Foodgiver leapt up from the front row and broke into a hectic dance, his arms flailing the air, his eyes closed and his mouth open. Everyone cheered. Then another jumped in. And another, and another...

That was enough for me. When I kicked in the door the brothers standing against it went flying. Several of the others roared in anger and turned towards me. Quicker than the eye could see I had five of them on the floor writhing in pain. In the light of the high lamps I saw the rest of them cower, shrink into each other and the walls. Those near the doorway tried to edge out and run. It didn't matter. There was no getting away now.

In the centre of the shed the fat one had barely struggled to his feet. I slapped him so hard his face cracked and he fell to the floor, and tried to curl up on his side. I kicked him in his buttocks and it was like hitting a sack of corn. He had wrapped his fat arms around his broken face and was mewling like an injured animal.

Every man in the room had dropped to his knees. I wanted to slap each face till it splintered. The Foodgiver who'd been beating the wood-flat was slowly backing away on his knees, trying to melt in with the others. I pulled him up by his shoulder, caught his chin, and with a snap turned his face all the way around. He fell on his stomach with a thud, the face staring up at the rafters. As Wafadars are taught, an example always speaks louder than a thousand words.

How right the great Tragopan had been. Not only had these brothers shamelessly fallen they had also found in themselves a dangerous cunning. I slowly turned on the balls of my feet, looking at their chipped and discoloured faces. The weeds would have to be pulled out; the poison drained. Order would have to be restored.

And it was – with the strength, speed and grace that were the great Tragopan's signature. The trials were swift and the Foodgivers full of contrition. As it is with the pure they were allowed to name their own penance. Two of them opted for Just demise and six declared that they deserved to be flung down the Crater. Most of the older brothers embraced maun – total silence – for a year and were then scattered among the stone quarries and timber yards. Each time they erred by speaking they would extend their maun by another year. The younger Foodgivers were distributed among the other granaries after being marked with a burning brand to remind them of their trespass. The fallen granary was reconstituted with a new family of brothers drawn from all over.

Many of the madonnas wept in repentance. For having kept quiet when they had known. Most of these chose the infirmary at the motherhood for their reparation, endlessly washing and cleaning the offal of the babies. The rest went away to the coarser houses at the sites of new constructions and digs.

It was a stirring sight to behold. Day after day, one by one, each of the fallen would come in front of the council and, transfixed by the unblinking eye of the great Tragopan, start to sob their atonement. Without a querying word from the council they would confess their transgressions and name their own penitence. Mostly it would be too harsh and the great Helmsmen would lighten it. It was an inspiring exhibition of the humility and grace of the pure and I felt privileged to witness it.

As the details of the scandal emerged, the valley was nonplussed. The fat man who wanted to sing had gathered around himself an audience. At first deep in the forest where no one else could hear him. Like a virulent scabies his song had swiftly infected more and more of the Foodgivers. Soon not a brother in the granary remained pure.

At the trial each one said it had been sorcery. They had been caught in a spell and could not break out of it. Every evening they would finish their tasks and rush to the shed that intruded like a finger into the forest. The fat man's magic was so powerful that on occasion the entire night would pass in a trance and when morning came they would find themselves slumbering on the floor all around him.

The inevitable descent into deception had followed. They had built a hut for the fat man in the forest where he was kept hidden when visitors arrived. Every new Foodgiver was first subjected to the hypnotism of the voice; then sworn to secrecy. This had gone on for so many years that some brothers were diseased beyond redemption. One of them, during his trial, began to speak of the exalting nature of song, calling it the quickest pathway to Aum. It turned out he was the one who had first brought the fat man to the granary. He said the fat man's voice was a manifestation of god. Prejudice had killed our senses – else we would see not a fat man singing but divinity unfurling. It was horrible. For the first time I heard the great Helmsmen shout out in dismay. The deposition had to be cut short and the wretch executed before he uttered another profanity.

The fat man was kept for the last. He proved to be a troubling curiosity. It was baffling how he had been allowed to become so fat – it was a sacrilege among the pure. Our abiding ideal was Aum's bamboo frame: the body a mere bow to propel the arrow of the spirit. Anyone going to fat was made to strive and starve till his weight was no longer a burden on land or soul. The fat man could have become so monstrous only by being hidden away for years and years from concerned eyes.

While his sorry past was being traced he was kept alone in a small room. It had stone walls so thick they could stop a herd of broad-browed mountain goats. But they could not hold back his voice. His keepers had to tie his hands and muffle his mouth. He would try and hum through the cloth and each time it was removed for him to eat and drink he would instantly start to sing. It was, thus, arriving to query him that I discovered his secret. His keepers had just given him his food and removed his restraining gag and immediately he had burst into song.

The song filling the room and bursting the stone walls was about a mother waiting for her young son to return from foreign lands. He has gone to work his fortune and he has been gone many years. Each day of his absence, the mother laments, has been an aeon. She lists the tasks that line her day. They have been unchanging for thirty years since she was married as a young girl. The only difference is her missing son. Her eyes are sore from scanning the horizon; her spirit leaden with sorrow. Is he well? Does he have a roof over his head? A bed to sleep on? Food in his stomach? Are strangers kind to him? Do they recognize the beauty of his soul? Even her husband, she says, is a conquistador laying claim to her body and heart. But her son is herself, carved from her flesh, blood of her blood, bone of her bone. The song ends with a final moment of doubt. Has he been perchance annexed by another woman's love? Is it possible he no longer belongs to her? It cannot be. It cannot be. It cannot be.

The refrain in the song went:

> My days are too long; these mountains too high,
> Will your feet find their way back before I die.

Bhima!

Plump Bhima with the fleshy hands and moist eyes. Humming-rhyming-singing Bhima. My companion at the home. With a girl's breasts and sagging buttocks. Bhima who imagined he saw his father by the Jhinjheri. Bhima who had been taken away by the menacing men with glinting sickles while I hid breathless in the grass in the grove of horse chestnuts. Bhima who had never been found.

How could I have recognized him – he had become a mountain of flesh. It was impossible any more to see the boy in him. When I went in he was singing more than eating and I had to shout his name twice before he stopped and stared at me.

His face was still cracked where I had slapped him. The fissure ran from the corner of his right eye to his mouth and it looked like a congealed tear.

Closing the door behind me I said, I am ashamed of you my brother, and he began to cry, the half-chewed morsel still in his mouth, the water running from his nose and eyes. The worst of us never change, I thought.

But I was not here to philosophize on his life. I was here on a mission. The council wished to know if this fat man was part of a larger conspiracy. Every abysmal man in the world was someone's son, brother, father or friend. These were not ties that ought to have any meaning. That I had known him intimately at the home was a stroke of fortune. It would make it easier for me to find out all I needed.

I waited for him to stop weeping and to finish swallowing his bite. He pushed the rest of the uneaten food away. I said I was happy to wait. He said it was not important: as it were he ate sparingly. I thought if not gluttony this monstrous body must spring from some other grossness of spirit.

As if intuiting my thoughts he said his huge frame had nothing to do with food. It was merely a vessel for sound. If he had been ordained to run he would have been given powerful legs; if to make beautiful things then supple fingers; and if to think great thoughts then a strong head. But the divine had wanted him to sing, with abandon, without pause – therefore he was blessed with this big drum that was good for little else but producing sound.

I could read his trickery. A sinister modesty and beneath it a cunning determination. This is how he must have disarmed the gullible Foodgivers before casting his spell on them. It was how he was in the home too. Pretending to a helplessness while conniving to act. How easily with his whimpering he had coerced me into accompanying him to find his father! He was dangerous from the start. One had to be careful to hear not his words but what was actually meant.

And so I listened to his words and knew them to be false. He said after he was dragged away by the three men brandishing sickles he was presented in front of two sombre brothers at the granary. They patted his head gently and asked the man who was his father to tell him that he was not. Bhima protested. His father turned him around to face the window and clapping his hands on both sides of Bhima's head lifted him straight off the ground. The ears pulled excruciatingly and he cried out in pain. His father said, Tell me, can you see your father anywhere? I can't.

With tears streaming down his cheeks Bhima had to admit he too could not see his father anywhere.

The two brothers then ordered him taken to the end of the valley – by the brittle rock face, farthest from the higher terraces of the great Helmsmen. Here was a compound called the Nest for the Unabled. At the entrance gate was written: all children are equal but they need to be prepared for unequal tasks. At this the fat boy was elated. It was clear to him he had been chosen to be groomed to make music.

This was not how it turned out. He was put to physical labour and that is how he spent the rest of his childhood years. There was the breaking of stones, the logging of wood, the picking of fruit, the work in the scullery of different kitchens. Each day as he set out to work with the other special children, one of the brothers in charge of the Nest would clap his hands on his ears and lift him up and ask him if he could see his father and when he had said no – with tears filling his eyes – he would be put down. In a few years he'd become too fat to be lifted and then the brother would merely press his ears and ask the question and he would give the right answer.

That he was being punished for seeking out his father proved a blessing. It left him free to keep singing. And this he did without pause, while breaking stone, chopping timber, picking fruit, washing the kitchenware. The Nest brothers tried to dissuade him but eventually gave up since there seemed to be no way to stop him except by pulling out his tongue. In any case at the Nest many norms of the valley were incapable of being applied. Also they discovered it helped their labours: in the night in the sleeping shed the fat boy's singing voice helped keep the special children, who tended to howl and rage, reasonably calm.

The more he sang the more song came to him. And the more song came to him the more the aches of his body and heart fell away. And he grew fatter and fatter and he knew he was fat only with the sound. For he did not eat more and he did not wish to eat more. He knew then that he would have to open his mouth and keep it open all his life so that the sound could keep escaping out into the world and not bloat his being till it burst.

And here was the miracle. Now when he sang he felt he was one with Aum. No longer was he fat Bhima pulled up by his ears. He was now the slim, tall, effulgent, singular, eternal, matchless, peerless one!

So he said to me: the stupid, foolish, grotesque man. I thought, He is more doomed than anyone I've ever known. Were I not on a mission to gather information I would have instantly cracked his head like an eggshell. With the infinite tolerance of a Wafadar, I reached into myself and leashed my pounding rage and asked him to continue.

There was a brother at the Nest who loved his song. As often as he could he kept him from labouring on stone and wood. He would instead take him into the forest at the edge of the brittle cliffs and urge him to soar free. Far from the heart of the valley, far from the higher terraces, the brother said he had gained clarity. There was no question that Aum was the timeless one but they were wrong in imagining that the path to him could not run through song.

When this brother was moved to a granary he arranged to take the fat man along to work at the scullery. Here, one Foodgiver at a time, this brother seduced everyone to listen to him – first the men of the kitchen, then the men of the fields, and then the men of the orchards. Carrying flagons of Ferment he would take them deep into the forest behind the cooking sheds and ask Bhima to sing. And when the songs were done and the flagon was done and the night was done he would ask each one, what was the more intoxicating, and always the answer was: the song. That is how a time came when the entire granary became tightly roped together in the secret of the song.

No more was he asked to do any work – in the scullery or the field. Other brothers shouldered his tasks, and beyond the last shed, well beyond the enclosing boundary, safely inside the forest, a small hut was built for him. Each time there was a visitor, in a moment he was driven to this hut, where he lay humming, till the granary had been once again rendered safe. For the valley he did not exist. For the Foodgivers of his granary he was the sound of every night.

The shed in which I had snared them was built by the brothers for this purpose alone, for the frenzy of these nocturnal revels. The weeks we – the three Pathfinders and I – spent there had been very trying for them. Never had they gone so many days without song. And singing with a clenched mouth inside his hut in the forest the fat man had thought he would burst if he could not soon open his mouth wide and empty the sound ballooning inside him.

To say I felt a fire scorch my brain would be mild. Here was frightening evidence of every horror we had been tutored against. The pitfall of softness; the perils of song; the danger of one weak brother making an entire brotherhood weak. If I had broken his neck that instant or pulled out his heart, it would not have been held against me. But I knew this mountain of decadence had more secrets to reveal. The great council would want them all extracted before they were done with him.

I asked him if he had ceased seeking for his father. He said it had ceased to be of consequence. He had gone beyond mundane quests. He knew now that his father and his mother, his tutor and his god were all merely the song. I asked him if he knew what his transgressions were and what lay in store for him. He smiled like a fool and said, Anyone who has drowned himself in the river of song has left the fears of men on the banks.

How right the timeless one was. Men lived by fantasies that ought not sustain a worm.

When I left him he was beginning to sing again. It was a rumble of a sound as of a distant thunder and then, as I stepped away from the stone cell, it grew and grew and became like the noise of the Jhinjheri when it first blasts through the rocks, weeping and raging and sweeping all before it.

In the inquisition his defilements were revealed to be so grotesque they put him beyond the justice of a simple execution. The council concluded he needed to be preserved and observed: all his deformities catalogued before he was finally put away.

The great Helmsmen took this task upon themselves. At the narrow end of the eighth terrace – below the Gentle Father and above the keeper – a small stone hut was built and a chain with a hook hung outside its door. Every evening, once his labours were done, some great Helmsman or the other would take the chain off the hook, stand at the open door and study him.

Since he could never staunch his throat, each time the door was opened his terrible wail would float out and hang over the terraces, trembling. With the fascination that men have for deformity the great Helmsmen would examine him for hours.

The Gentle Father himself came by often. And on days he could not, the fat man was made to heave himself up to the highest terrace so the greatest of the great Helmsmen could make his own observations. Sometimes others from the council would join him, and sitting together sipping their Ferment and eating their food they would provoke the perverse man to display all the perversions of his voice so they could further hone their fine sense of distinction between the terrible and the worse.

PURIFICATION RITES

The terrible. And the worse.

As I say it, it sounds to me like the last sermon of a diabolic prophet. But let me not start to look down the vista of the past with the eyes of the present. Let me keep walking the path as I truly walked it. My tale is as nothing if it is not told without all decoration.

Finally it all began to come apart when the fat man was gutted by the great Tragopan.

He took me along for the task. He was after all a man of the word; I of the hands. It was the pit of the night and the monstrosity lay on his back – a vast bale of hay – humming even in his sleep. With characteristic foolishness he showed no fear when he was roused. Perhaps he had become inured to the great Helmsmen arriving to observe him hum at all hours of the day and night. His face was still cracked where I had slapped it so long ago. In the moonlight the tear that never stopped running seemed thicker than before.

The great Tragopan said, You have been trying to practise your sorcery on the elders?

The fat man said, in rhythm, I do nothing – I only look for this sound inside me.

He was drumming his thick fingers on his vast belly.

The great Tragopan said, Do you know why Aum forbade song?

Instead of replying, the fat man kept making a hum in his throat like the buzz of bees and shook his head from side to side. I wanted to put my hand in his mouth and rip his tongue out.

The great Tragopan said, Tell me, rare monstrosity, would you care to be anybody but yourself?

The fat man opened his mouth and unloosed a low long wail that tore open the night sky. I clamped his nose tight so he had to stop. When I released him he took a few loud gulps and then instantly began to hum again, shaking his head. I twisted his ear, and said, Answer! Would you?

Real tears sprang up in his eyes. The fool.

He said, No. I am only what my sound makes me.

The great Tragopan said, Does your sound make you many things?

The fat man said through the hum in his throat, Yes many things. It is the gift of the sound. It can make me light as a butterfly and heavy as a boar; frisky as a wagtail and thoughtful as an owl...

The great Tragopan said, And have you ever thought, mighty corpulence, what would happen to the brotherhood if all brothers became many things? Would there be purpose? Would there be courage? Would the vision of Aum find its final bloom? Would the world of men find salvation at the hands of the pure? Or would everything just fracture in a chaos of many things?

I leaned into his fat face and said, Did you learn nothing at the home, abominable beast? The pure must not succumb to tears or laughter, sorrow or joy. These are illusions. They distract and diminish. They make us the animals you mentioned, boars and wagtails, butterflies and owls...

The great Tragopan said, Fixity of purpose. That is the mark of the pure. Not many things. Not anything that makes the pure into many things.

The fat man said, his throat vibrating like a hundred bowstrings, I am light as a butterfly. My great master said, You are simply as gaudy and perishable as one.

He looked me in the eye and I began to break the drumming fingers. They were short and fleshy but they cracked tidily. Through it all the great Tragopan spoke to the fallen fool. His profound error, he explained, was not that he sang but that he had made it a canker for all his brothers. It was the problem with idle afflictions: song, dance, laughter, games. They spread like pollen, draining men of intent and resolve.

With much regret the great Tragopan said he hoped the fat man could now see his misdeeds and was in agreement with the punishment being meted out to him.

By now I had pushed the sixth chonch into his chest, driving it smoothly through the layers of lard. The first thick smudge of red was beginning to power through. He was crying in waves, holding up his unhinged fingers. To my tired ear this too sounded like some attempt at song. I pushed the third chonch into the side of his huge neck. How battered his face – which was, alas, also mine – looked. It had not been touched up in years and it now shone with wetness.

The great Tragopan said, All is not waste. Go knowing your story will serve as a warning for generations of brothers.

I pushed the fourth chonch into the other side of his neck. The first one was creating a small pool of blood by his head. Turning his big head to me, he said, still in a singing voice, It's your stories that should serve as a warning. If you want to know what you really are, go to where I come from… and weep. I am happy to go where I can sing forever…

In quick succession I punctured him with the seventh, eighth and ninth chonch, from the thick pipe in his throat to the thick ones in his chest and he burst all over, his heart going silent along with his infernal voice.

After he had been buried in a cavernous hole in the terrace below – he was too gigantic to be carted to the family garden – I was witness to some astounding developments. It was nothing I could talk about and no one would have believed me if I had.

Ten days after being rid of the fat man – his wail still hanging over the terraces – the great Tragopan called me to his room and said the central moment of my life was at hand. Everything I had prepared for, everything I had lived for, the very truth of my belief in Aum was about to be tested. He was sitting on the floor, in the lotus pose, thumbs and forefingers touching. I kneeled in front of him and opened my palms, ready to receive his benediction.

The great Tragopan said the enlightened one's teachings were clear: no one was infallible, not even the masters. And the duty of every warrior of the pure was to always and ever be true to the truth of the master, and not the master. As he spoke, slowly beginning to lift his hands and sculpt the air, I felt the hair on my body rise. He said just as we had learned to reject our fathers and our mothers so that we could reach for the higher verities it sometimes became necessary for us to reject our masters so that we could preserve their truth.

I said I was the warrior of Aum and none else.

He said, Stand corrected, my brother! Not of Aum, but of the truth of Aum!

I said, shamed, Yes, not of Aum but of the truth of Aum.

He said, Would you drain my blood for the truth of Aum?

I said, Great Helmsman I would drain your blood for the truth of Aum.

He said, Would you drain the blood of Aum for the truth of Aum?

I looked into his face which was my face and saw his eyes were clear of guile.

I said, I would drain the blood of Aum but for nothing else save the truth of Aum.

He said, carving the air, You are a true son of Aum. In years to come the faithful will recount your legend. And legions of Wafadars will hold you as their exemplar.

Standing up he put his hand on my head and told me what lay ahead of us, what we had to do. I was astonished and moved. I could think of no other brother in the valley, no other son of Aum, who was blessed with the clarity and the courage of the great Tragopan. Ever since the purging of the first granary and the capture of the fat man, over a year ago, he had stirred a frenzy of purification through the valley. With my team of Pathfinders I had visited granary after granary, lauding devotion and detecting deviation. Even the finest sword, to stay shining and sharp, needs to be regularly slapped against stone. And as we had found, the rust was beginning to catch everywhere.

As we had toiled, something remarkable and inspiring had happened. Slowly, starting as a trickle, information had begun to flow to us from all corners of the valley of the faithful who had strayed from the path and lost their way.

The pure are schooled to know neither tears nor laughter: both are cheap excesses that distract the spirit. The pure forever live in a state of unlaughing joy: blessed in who they are, rapt in the exertions of their extraordinary destiny. But now like weed after rain, across the valley these dreadful things were beginning to sprout.

As my great master said, The challenge always is to start the cycle of good – once you do, it keeps moving. This is what the luminous one did.

Each week an honest brother, a disturbed brother, would bring us news of more rust and each week I would dispatch a team of the best whetters to go and rub it out. By now, instructed by the great Tragopan, I had assembled a platoon of twenty-four brothers who floated through the valley like bats of the night, unseen but seeing.

For months the great council conducted the inquisitions, and it was moving to see my errant brothers confess to their derangements and seek atonement. The Pathfinders on my team prepared each case with scrupulous care but I was the only one permitted inside the council room. In fact I had to be present at all times for there would be the rare brother who, even at this hour, had failed to complete his self-scrutiny and was inclined to be rambunctious.

I had to break the neck of one who leapt on the Gentle Father. He was a small fellow – a mere morsel for any Wafadar – and he had been found in the granary under the slope of silver oaks pretending to teach the gospel of Aum. For weeks one of my bats had observed him closely. What he was really doing was breeding disaffection among his brothers. He claimed to know the nine books and perhaps he did. But he understood them not. He spoke to fill his brothers with unrest and to turn them against their brothers and even against the great dwellers of the higher terraces.

It was when I saw him screaming at the council that I realized how wise our great Helmsmen had been to prohibit the preaching of Aum's doctrine by any brother except the ones ordained. In the hands of a child a sickle is a hazardous thing. The true meaning of Aum came only to a few and it was their duty to hold fast its purities.

So I was there when the unimaginable occurred. I was expecting something; I did not know what. In the morning the great Tragopan had told me to steel my heart for unsentimental action. The call to glory was at hand. As always I was standing by the jamb of the door, motionless as the mountains. The council sat in the formation of a horseshoe, awaiting the next fallen brother. It was late in the afternoon and there was time only to process the atonement of another two.

Suddenly the great Tragopan rose – from the end of the horseshoe, from whence he had been prosecuting the fallen – and ordered me to latch the door. Then, turning to his great brothers, he began to speak in soaring words of the splendour of Aum. It was a story whose every word we knew but he told it with such an eloquence that I could see even the great Helmsmen smooth the rising hair on their arms.

It was not possible to tell what the great Tragopan was leading up to but so mesmeric was his narration of the birth of the pure, of the ambidextrous Ali and the beauteous Alaiya, of the great march over the high peaks, of the miracle of the valley, of the glory of being the chosen, of the honour of the face, of the unsung labours in exile of the Yodhas and the continual courage of the Wafadars, that no one broke in with a single word. Sculpting the air into breathtaking beauty, reminding us of our singular destiny, the great Tragopan finally brought us to the monstrous deviations of the fat man.

The fat man, he said, was nothing more than the darkest symbol of all our failures. For, as the past one year had revealed, in granary after granary, in every nook of our great valley, failure and flaw had found purchase. When a man's legs walk him to transgression or his hands reach out to sin, the fault is never of the limbs but always of the mind. To punish the limbs is an act of deception. It is the mind that must be addressed. It is the mind that must be brought to account.

The great brothers assembled in this room, he said – now chiselling the air into the coruscating image of Aum – had been enjoined by the faithful to be their Helmsmen. The destiny of the pure lay on our shoulders, the fulfilments of its great tasks in our hands. And had we managed to do honour to it?

It was clear as daylight that the brotherhood had been let down. The rot was everywhere. Would Aum have forgiven Ali for such a betrayal? Would he have hesitated to bring Alaiya to a reckoning? Was anyone in this room more luminous than either?

There was rot, and yes, it had touched many brothers. But most brothers were still without a taint. These pristine sons of Aum were looking for a sign. That the order of the pure was even now the order of the equal. That the keepers of the true were even now followers of the true.

Standing by the door I was in a daze. I knew I was being witness to something I was not worthy of. The great Tragopan's voice by now seemed detached from his person: it was coming down from the rafters and off the walls. The great Helmsmen sat frozen, their eyes still as stones.

Grief was never the path of the pure, said the great Tragopan. Action was. Yet grasping for an answer he found himself touched by grief. Could one be angry with Ali? Could one be angry with Alaiya? Could one be angry with the great men in this room? And yet as he spoke he found himself being hurled into anger. Even though anger was not the path of the pure. Action was.

What is a great man who ceases to be great for his people? What is the sun if it does not shine on the world?

Should good brothers embrace darkness because their sun has lost its way? Or were they right in seeking the light of another sun?

Is not the hope of light almost as great as the light itself?

In this hour of crisis, what were the great men of this room? The hope of light, light itself, or nothing of either?

And what is light itself? Is it the man? Or is it the idea?

The body of Aum has been long disintegrated. The idea of Aum grows sinews by the day.

Men are significant only for the idea they emblazon. It is glorious that men should perish so the idea may live.

All the collected greatness in this high room – and here he looked each great Helmsman in the eye – is little more than a humble offering at the altar of the idea.

I had no clue where the great man was leading us. Now he was shaving and shaping the air very slowly and some of his pauses were so long they left you thirsting for the next word. It was clear we were on the brink of something momentous. The great Tragopan was filling the room with heavy – and heavier – words and there could be no doubt that soon their pressure would blow out the windows and the walls.

There was a fat man, he continued, who had ruptured our rippleless peace with his infernal voice. He had unleashed forbidden seductions on hapless brothers. The dauntless warriors of Aum – and he waved towards me – had brought him to his knees. And we – he cut the air in an arc to take in all the great Helmsmen – and we had placed him in the armpit of these high terraces where only greatness may come!

And each day, we, the keepers of the faith had exposed ourselves to this fiend's sorcery. Soiled our souls while pretending we were studying the soiling of our souls! Such trickery with oneself! As men practise in the world out there!

Here in this high room with every door and casement barred was it possible for anyone to speak in the name of the peerless one and claim that the fat man's voice had not led us unto deceit?

Anyone?

In the granary, for a similar transgression, much lesser men had served themselves up for severe penitence. In this high room, for months the great council had brandished the scourge to remind the pure of a timeless covenant. Brother after brother had been arraigned. Yet that was not the lesson of Aum. The taintless one believed men could be tamed by the scourge but they were made glorious by the example alone.

By now the great Tragopan had gone from eloquence to rage. From the end of the horseshoe he had walked into its heart and was slaughtering the air like a butcher at the abattoir. The great Helmsmen were all sitting back, their arms folded across their chests.

A sign! – raged the master, cutting the air's throat – a sign! That is what the valley was looking for. A sign that justice was just, that equality was equal! That brothers were truly brothers and purity was truly pure! That no shadow had fallen across the path of the faithful! That no shadow would be allowed to fall!

And now the great Tragopan stabbed himself in the chest and said, A sign! It is what I have been waiting for. A sign that we are great by our greatness, not by the elevation of our terraces! A sign that we can still look in the mirror and see the face that is never me but always us! Each time I heard the fat man sing so that one of my great brothers could observe I knew the mirror was fast clouding so we could no longer see.

Standing at the door I knew I was witness to an extraordinary moment in the life of an extraordinary great Helmsman. I was in a state of perfect poise as Wafadars assume when they know action may be at hand. I had no idea what might unfurl but I was prepared to deal with anything that the spirit of Aum might decree.

Suddenly the great Tragopan threw up his hands splitting the air in two and said, I would this instant slit my throat if it restored the faithful to the straight and narrow! But what manner of sign would the death of a man like me be? The moment calls for something more worthy, more becoming of the glory of the brotherhood. We know from the teachings of the boundless one that right conduct must never be choked by love or ties. There is the true path, and it often cuts through the heart of our desires and our affections; and the challenge for the pure is never to break step no matter what it cleaves.

And with this my master pulled down his hands and only I – a Wafadar – saw clasped in his right the small dagger which with a single step he plunged into the throat of the Gentle Father, making him gurgle blood. No one moved as my master pulled out the stained blade and holding the dying head gently kissed its hairless scalp again and again, tears streaming from his eyes.

Then stepping back, choking, he said, Is Aum our eternal quest or the truth of Aum?

In an echo came the collective whisper of the greatest men among us, The truth of Aum.

Still choking, my master said, Is it the Gentle Father we revere or the truth of the Gentle Father?

In a stronger whisper the greatest men of our time said, The truth of the Gentle Father.

Placing the stained dagger in the darkening pool next to the fallen head, my sorrowing master said, I would sooner have carved out my own heart than done what I have done, and I would do so even now if the great Helmsmen of the pure so deem fit. None have cherished the Father more than I have; none worked harder to speak his glory. That is, until the fat man cast his spell. Even so I would have much sooner looked away, and it is what I long did, for he was my Father before he was anyone else's. It was he who brought me here and honoured me with the tasks of a great Helmsman. It was he who taught me that the truth of the brotherhood is always greater than the brotherhood. And in putting my dagger through his throat it is his very words that I have bowed to. For I saw him crave the fat man's voice; and when I had stilled it – with the help of this noble Wafadar – I saw him grieve. I knew then to be true what the wind had been whispering across the valley for months. He was no longer the Father we revered. No longer was he worthy of helming the pure.

Standing against the door, ready to quell any dissent, I was moved. The great Tragopan was sculpting the air again, his voice once again strong, rid of the tremble of grief.

We know, he said, what honour demands us to do. There must be no more deceit, no more lies. We have the sign. Take it to the faithful. Let them know there is none who can ever claim to be above the idea. Among the children of Aum, justice is always just, equality always equal, and purity always pure. I leave it to this council of great Helmsmen – all of whom are wiser than I can ever hope to be – to decide if the faithful should know it was I who stuck the dagger into the Father's faltering flesh or it was the great council that meted out justice. To me it is as nothing. I would do the true bidding of Aum even if all the worlds were set against me.

In one voice the great brothers said, The council has given a sign. Let it be known to the pure that the council speaks as one, and speaks against all who stray from the path, even if it be the Father himself.

Less than a month later, the great Golden Oriole was anointed the Gentle Father. For many weeks before the glorious purge my master had been meeting with him each day. The great Golden Oriole was a former Wafadar who seldom spoke. At the meetings of the council I would see him slowly flicking his eyes across the horseshoe as his great brothers deliberated.

One evening, after a meeting, the great Tragopan had asked me what I thought of him.

I said I knew he was a great Wafadar and a great Helmsman but beyond that it was very difficult to tell for he never said a thing.

That is his abiding virtue, said my master, as we slowly walked up the terraces, the blue light of night beginning to press down across the mountain peaks.

Following at his heel I said I did not understand.

He said, Sometimes the faithful need not more words, not more sermons, but a wordless assurance: the deity of stone that we can fill with the meaning already given unto us. Aum's flock know his words. The Gentle Father is merely a constant reminder of them. He does not need to mouth them or mend them.

At the time I did not understand but I held my tongue. Later, when the great Golden Oriole had been named our Gentle Father I understood much. And as the months rolled by, each day that my master visited the Gentle Father and emerged to give new directions to the brotherhood I understood more and more.

The great Tragopan was not such a soaring master for nothing. What we understood as words he knew as praxis. What was important was the truth of the Gentle Father, not the Gentle Father. And this truth existed outside and above the Gentle Father. The less the Gentle Father spoke the less likely he was to muddy the great truths that were the glory of our people.

By speaking for him, by keeping him away from the direct line of words, my master opened up just enough space for correction and reinterpretation. Even great Helmsmen cannot always be right – though they always are. But the Gentle Father can simply never be wrong. Now, between the eloquence of the great Tragopan and the silence of the Gentle Father, there existed just enough room for amendment and repair.

So my master had become like Ali and Alaiya, the voice of the one. And though the Gentle Father could not ever be Aum, he was for the faithful the embodiment of the truth of Aum, and it was imperative that the terrible wound the fat man had inflicted on this truth was quickly healed and never ever risked again.

The great Tragopan brought back a briskness and purpose to the flock. No longer did the great Helmsmen only meditate, deliberate and practise their poems. Now each one descended from the higher terraces and fell into a routine of travelling the valley to assess, inspire and monitor the brotherhood.

Speaking for the Gentle Father my master said the time had come for the pure to shed all sloth. One by one a combing of each of the granaries commenced – to identify Foodgivers who were capable of more than just tilling the ground. They were then taken to camps beneath the high terraces where they were tested for a physical, mental and emotional prowess far greater than any they'd had to summon so far in their lives.

More warriors, more warriors, chanted the great Tragopan. We need more warriors – more Wafadars, more Yodhas! The pure will not change the world by growing corn!

I was often sent to assess the progress and I have to say I was initially filled with dismay. The flab and the breathlessness would be gone in a few months. What bothered me was the absence of passion. Everything seemed to be a task, not the very meaning of life.

But then my great master began to address them every week – chiselling the air into images of apocalyptic transformation – and I saw the mood change. It was visible not in the way the novitiates moved their limbs. It could be seen in their eyes. The surest way to recognize the pure, and the purest of the pure, is to look into their eyes.

In a few months it became clear to the selected Foodgivers that destiny had finally picked them for glory. All traces of the idle banter that I had spied in the granaries vanished. Beyond the shallows of joy and grief, leisure and labour, they began to become one with the boundless depths of Aum, rich with an unwavering sense of transcendent purpose, of the greatest good of the greatest number.

The beautiful thing to observe was that as each brother honed himself he became less and less indulgent of the shortcomings of his other brothers. What Wafadars know every moment of their lives, what Yodhas know every moment of their lives, now became a verity for these reapers and tillers too: men overlook the failings of other men so their own may be overlooked in turn: this is the prescription for a shabby world: such as Aum turned his back on. It requires real courage to not forgive, to not condone, for it indicates you would seek no such abject charity yourself.

The world becomes splendid only when men demand the most out of each other, mercilessly.

It was heartening to see the tillers and reapers, week on week, ascend above the petty ties of comradeship and conversation, flesh and memories, bread and billets, to the higher allegiances of purpose and purity, the sheer beauty of Aum, the truth of Aum.

A time came when each day I saw the tillers and reapers come to the door of the great Tragopan – where I mostly hovered – with urgent news of brothers who were failing to rise to the glory of the flock. Once my master had ascertained a tragic failure, I – with my tireless squad – was sent off to do the culling.

This wave of cleansing turned out to be much smoother and quicker than the earlier inquisitions that had followed the terrible outrage of the fat man. By now the illustrious council and the Gentle Father trusted the great Tragopan to do the perfect thing, no less perfectly than they would have. And in turn my master trusted me to do the right thing, no less rightly than he would have.

And I in turn dug deep into the truth of myself to ensure I – and my team – acted with speed and precision, and with no taint to the lustre of the pure. Every erring brother was given a chance to explain his conduct. I left the querying to one of my Pathfinders, a tiny brother with the teeth of a rabbit whose voice was smooth as silk but filled with words that cut like glass. I admiringly called him my rabbitwolf.

As he talked to prise open the falsehoods of the arraigned brothers I quietly watched their hands and eyes. I knew by now it was the surest way to spot guilt. Working with the great Tragopan had made me an astute student of my own brothers. Duplicity in the heart would become a tremor in the fingers; deceit in the brain could be seen as a flicker of the eyelash. By the time the rabbitwolf finished his questioning I had my sentence ready. Since we were all brothers I never pronounced it till I had carried out a consultation with my squad.

That my methods were foolproof was clear from the fact that almost never was there anything but full consensus. If someone felt there was cause for ambiguity I had the rabbitwolf carry out a second round of querying. No matter what arguments were proffered the hands and eyes could not fool me twice.

Since it is a covenant amongst the pure that wayward brothers must be given enough opportunity to recognize their failings and to confess to them, we sent each one to the Room of Inner Truths. Actually there was not one room but four that had been built close to the oak forest, a hundred feet apart. These were more robust than the ones we had known in our childhood. Each was five feet by five feet, fifteen feet high, and built of mature red cedar logs. There was no door and no window. The final logs were hammered in once the brother was inside. Food, air and water went in through a six-inch aperture just under the roof.

The understanding that a brother who has lost sight of his inner truths needs to be taken away from all distraction so he may relocate them is a sound one. It never ceased to amaze me how swiftly an erring brother saw the light once all clutter was removed from his life. Aum always said that all our answers lie within ourselves and it is no wonder then that in that magical room, left alone to peer into himself, each brother was able to swiftly find his inner truth.

Sometimes this happened within hours. Mostly it took about a day or two. When an errant brother cried out in a fever of illumination we would sidle up to the logs and ask him to speak. Some brothers were so moved by their moment of re-awakening they would sob as they spoke. Once they had confessed their shame we would ask them to prescribe their own atonement. It was a tribute to the integrity of the pure that the brothers tended to punish themselves more harshly than we ever would have.

The rabbitwolf called it the spirit of self-correction. He said it hid quietly in the solar plexus, happy to sleep. To rouse it you had to go beyond assaulting the mind. He said his style of questioning was aimed at putting his hand through the brain and stroking the heart so it was stirred awake.

Some brothers experienced such an intense awakening that they prescribed for themselves the harsh punishment of the Crater. Some went further, asking for the ultimate penitence. Just demise.

I could see the rabbitwolf's stirring of the solar plexus and the epiphanies of the Room of Inner Truths were often producing an excessive self-flagellation in the brothers. But I held my hand. There was no room for sentimentality. The soft virtues of the tongue are always protected by the hard cage of the teeth. In strength there must be no place for weakness.

And in any case there is no such thing as too much justice.

In a few years, under the guidance of the Gentle Father, under the guidance of the great Tragopan, we had cleansed all the granaries. The best of the Foodgivers were on their way to becoming warriors – Wafadars and Yodhas – and those who'd lost their way had been brought back to the path.

Other reforms had swept the valley. My master – following the wishes of the Gentle Father – had decreed the holding of a weekly Sermon of Aum that every one of the pure was obliged to attend. No one was exempt. No reaper, tiller, logger, mason, butcher, cook, Pathfinder, Wafadar, Yodha, child, madonna or mother. Not even the great Helmsmen or the benighted souls in the Crater.

The sermons lasted two hours on Sunday mornings and were delivered by a new group of brothers created by the great Tragopan. They were called Bhaktas and they were tasked to distil the life and teachings of the peerless one and feed it in a steady and continual dose to the chosen. The outrage of the fat man, the subsequent discovery of drift, the martyrdom of the Gentle Father – all of it had revealed to the great council that virtue could never be taken for granted. Like a good fruit tree it needed constant pruning and watering and manuring.

The Bhaktas were trained by a tall Pathfinder handpicked by my master. His throat had a big walnut that moved up and down when he spoke. It riveted me as much as the deep baritone it produced.

He had a way of speaking – unlike my master, but no less mesmeric
– with very long pauses and unmoving hands that took you straight
back to the pilgrim fathers. He knew more stories about them than
I had ever imagined existed. Each one illuminated the glory of their
lives and the sheer beauty of their vision. I could listen to him for
hours and was never anything but deeply moved and filled with
gratitude for the unique inheritance that was mine.

All the Bhaktas he trained were no less, in their knowledge or in
their eloquence. It appealed to me that they often referred to Aum
as the Paigamber, the prophet. It meant he was not just the first of
everything but also the foreteller of the last of everything. It meant
everything there was to know and learn lay safely vested in him.

I also thought it appropriate that the timeless one should be
known by numberless names. Ordinary men are known by a single
name. But one who encompasses all things, all knowledge, all
wisdom, the dead, the living and the unborn, the world here and
the world hereafter – such a luminous spirit is like nature itself,
deserving of many descriptions and many names, all of which attest
to his singular glory.

In the beginning my squad and I would travel inconspicuously
through the valley to check if all the brothers were attending the
sermon of Aum. But soon we discovered it was unnecessary. Not only
was everyone arriving for the weekly session, there were many who
were now seeking out the Bhaktas for sermons all days of the week.

Seeing this my master decreed that in every corner of the valley the
oldest deodar tree be marked as a sermon tree. Around each a stone
platform was constructed from where the Bhakta could preach. And
then in a stroke of vaulting inspiration – the kind he was famed for
– the great Tragopan one morning summoned the ustaad and asked
him to make a mask of Aum. It was to be the greatest undertaking
of his life. No matter how much he excelled, it was destined to
fall short.

To be honest, for the first time I was assailed by doubt. Was it not
diminishing to give form to the formless one? But when I saw the

ustaad's artistry I was overwhelmed. As always my master had been right. The image of Aum – with its all-seeing eyes, the serene beard, the halo of long hair, the high forehead, the noble nose – the image radiated unparalleled beauty and power and truth. I felt strong in its presence. I wanted to genuflect to it.

Not surprisingly every brother felt the same. As the ustaad carved copies and they went up one by one on the broad trunks of the sermon trees above the stone platforms it became commonplace to see the pure all hours of the day and night prostrate before them.

It became clear that making the face would no longer be the ustaad's primary concern: it would now be the task of his deputies. The ustaad himself for the rest of his days would be doing nothing but carving icons of the timeless one. For soon there arose a clamour from every shed and barrack and dining hall for one more image, and one more image and one more image – the pure wanted to see him keeping an eye on them every moment of their lives.

It brought a new sense of purpose to the valley. By just bathing himself in the gaze of Aum a brother could stave off any weakening of the flesh or spirit. For the first time stories came to us of infirm brothers who'd found in themselves the strength to attempt becoming Wafadars and Yodhas merely by sitting close to the image.

Though I did not have any more doubts that my master had done the right thing, one evening I took it upon myself to seek a deeper understanding. We were in my master's shed but we were not alone. The young intern – who was absorbing the faith from the great Tragopan as I once had from the great Hornbill – was rubbing perfumed oils into the master's skin. It was a heart-warming sight. The boy was astride the great Helmsman – who lay on his stomach – sliding on his body, his smooth sinews soaked with the oil that he was caressing into the master's skin. Each time the intern grunted with effort the master grunted in relief. I knew – because I had often done it for him – that he liked the base of his neck rubbed hard. It was all the hard thinking, it knotted up the stem of his brain.

I was squatting against the wall, looking at the two of them and beyond them to a big image of the shoreless one – a truly ethereal representation the ustaad had crafted for this greatest of Helmsmen.

I said, I know we have done the right thing and the evidence of it is everywhere, but tell me, great Tragopan, why did Aum not wish it so?

His eyes squeezed tight by the pleasure of the kneading fingers, he said, It's a good question and it has several possible answers. The first is we cannot be sure he did not wish it so. There is nothing written, in the nine books or any of the original parchments, that asserts this clearly. The second – and this is most likely – is he may have waved such decorations away. He was Aum, he was the Paigamber, he was the first and last of everything – the word, the law and the prophet. The glory of the faithful lay in being able to apprehend him in all his fullness. It was not possible for him – in his infinite grace – to instruct his people on how they must do this. The sun simply shines: it does not tell those it warms and illuminates how they must address it. How adequately they do it is a measure of their gratitude and character.

It made perfect sense and I became suddenly aware that I had not done enough to celebrate the luminosity of the great Tragopan. I had neglected telling my brothers how blessed they were to live in his time. I often forgot it myself. That is how men are. They underestimate the sun as long as it is shining. And only judge its value when it is gone.

I said, I now see the light itself – not just all that the light allows me to see.

The young intern began to press down hard with his oily knuckles on the master's lower back and buttocks, forcing from him a series of moans. Go easy, I wanted to say, here too is a light. As if he had heard my thought, the young brother dismounted and went away to brew some vapours.

The great Tragopan sat up slowly, his bony body glistening, and pointing to the beautiful image of Aum said, Look at him! Does not just looking at him make you purer? Imagine then the brothers in the fields and in the sheds, in the workshops and the orchards, in the slaughterhouse and the kitchens; imagine the Pathfinders and the Wafadars, the Yodhas and the Bhaktas; imagine the mothers and the madonnas; imagine our seed in the home and in the barracks – try and imagine then what the armies of the pure desperately require as they toil at our great purpose. Not just the words of Aum, not just the memory of Aum, not just the spirit of Aum – but Aum himself, made visible! As we know, even the chosen may flag, their faith grow thin, their resolve turn weak. One glance at Aum, radiating the truth, is all the resuscitation they need. Today I know that if I could give each one of the chosen an image of Aum in their own hands they would never again know doubt or fear or confusion. And this I shall do before my time is done.

Like everything else he did, it worked to perfection.

Using a fine brush of mongoose hair and a dark dye from crushed stone the ustaad mastered the art of making, with a few strokes, a compelling likeness of Aum. This he taught to his assistants, who created a hard papyrus of pulped reeds on which they could draw. These were then secured against rain and ravage by a thin veneer of bee's wax.

Every one of the pure had the right to acquire one. And I need not say it: everyone made a rush for it. Each assistant could turn out dozens in a day but that was far from enough. An order had to be established, and then to avoid a crush at the workshop a system of delivery – especially to the distant corners of the valley – had to be evolved.

It was astonishing to watch. A new kind of fervour swept the flock. Passing a thread through the hard papyrus, some tied the icon to their wrist, others to their upper arm. But most chose to hang it around their neck so it nestled close to their heart. Soon it was not uncommon to see everywhere brothers and madonnas kissing the icon tethered to their bodies even as they mouthed the catechism of the pure.

When I mentioned this to the great Tragopan, he said, Men of learning make the mistake of thinking nothing is more powerful than the word. For too long the great Helmsmen have assumed the word is enough to fire up the faithful. But now you can see that the image has the power of ten thousand words. See how the pure clasp Aum's icon to themselves. It is true that in the beginning is always the word. But it is truer still that in the end there is always and only the image.

My master's triumph did not come without opposition. For weeks the council had debated the creation of the icon. The Gentle Father had held his opinion – as his stature deemed – whereas every other great Helmsman had resisted the idea.

Aum had never wished it.

It was against the tenets of his beliefs.

To cast him into an image was to shrink his vastness.

The great Tragopan was as ZZ9 in his battle against QT2, deploying the kachchua, moving his words like the great warrior's steel blades, at such blistering speed that everything was deflected.

What was being essayed here was the apotheosis of the truth, an image of the pure.

Is it not obvious that even the unequalled one would not demand that he be genuflected to! It is the test of his followers that they choose to.

And what was this new spirit of hubris in the great council? Was it possible for anyone to shrink or expand the immensity of the limitless one? In fact the order of things was, in case it had slipped the august council, the other way around. It was Aum alone who could diminish or grow the faithful! That, verily, was the meaning of the icon. The very sight of the luminous one would swell each of the pure to their true size, and beyond.

Listening at the door I could not see how anyone could possibly fault my master's logic. And yet – blasphemously – the great

Helmsmen persisted. It was like throwing spears of grass at a big cat. It was inevitable that sooner or later the beast would spring, not out of injury but from outrage.

The Gentle Father finally cast his voice behind the great Tragopan, and that night when the moon had grown faint I walked behind my master, up and down the higher terraces, opening up the thick pipe in the throats of four of the nine members of the great council. As I waited, the tip of the chonch ready to break flesh, hand clamping mouth shut, my master gave each of them a last oration on their betrayals, calling them his great brothers and calling this the most difficult task of his life.

Next morning the Gentle Father announced to the flock that he had ordered with a heavy heart the Just demise of his great brothers for they had fallen from their greatness. If a ploughman could be brought to penitence for the sin of the ego so could a great Helmsman. As it were, as it should be, each of them had offered up their atonement when confronted with their failure. For the record, their names stood besmirched only for their last days: the lustre of their early endeavours was to remain undimmed.

And with this, he said, the purges were at an end. The pure were once again without a blemish.

And it was then that he declared his decision to make available the icon for all.

A wave of pride coursed through the valley.

That night – the night after the cleansing of the great council – the great Tragopan summoned me to his shed and told me two things that were to overturn my life forever. The first sent the blood rushing to my head. He said he had begun to think that I was destined to be a great Helmsman and soon he was going to make me one.

The second I did not hear till it was repeated several times, for the blood was pounding so loud in my ears. And when I finally heard it, it seemed utterly prosaic in comparison to what had been said before.

There was a last task to be carried out before he started the process of elevating me to the higher terraces. He wanted me to undertake a complete clean-up of the Crater of Resurrections and the Nest of the Unabled.

Given the large-scale cleansing I had carried out over the years this sounded like a walk in the woods. I said his will would be done but I did not think I was worthy of being a great Helmsman. In this life, or the next. And I meant it.

He clapped the shoulder of the young intern who was sitting at his feet, slowly pulling at his toes, cracking them for relief. When he had left, the great Tragopan said the task was not as easy as it seemed. Both of us – he and I – would have to steel ourselves against foolish sentimentality. The proposition was simple.

Would we eat a fruit that had turned rotten?

Would we keep alive an animal that had lost its limbs?

Would an army forsake the battle by tending to its dying rather than fighting?

Would Aum have aborted the great march because a few of the flock were unable to carry on?

I looked at his face which was my face and his eyes were calm and still, not as they usually were, passionate and dancing. His hands too were unmoving.

He said, from this unusual posture of stillness, For longer than you and I have lived the noble brothers of the council have been confronted with this question – even as the answer has sat facing them. And always they have looked away. I do not wish to demean the great men who have gone before us but this much I know that we can no longer afford to look away. We must not look away.

I said, We will not look away. Thy will be done.

Some days later eight of us – handpicked for stoutness of heart – left for the other side of the valley. As we were leaving, the great Tragopan said to us, Remember the way of the slaughterhouse: never look into the eye of the beast. When the butcher swings the chopper he holds his head high and talks to his brothers as if they were holding a palaver in the cookhouse.

Our first destination was the Nest of the Unabled. Once we were done there, the Crater would be easy. It was fine weather to walk, the middle of the year, with the sun overhead. The trees were in thick leaf, and yellow, purple and pink flowers were everywhere. The rushes and bushes were hectic with the bustle of birds, and the hum of insects hunting nectar filled the ears. We walked along the Jhinjheri, taking a dip in its sparkling waters each time the sun made us too hot.

Every moment I thought of what my master had said. I was worthy of being a great Helmsman! It was a difficult thought to hold. I re-played my life year on year. At no point did I find myself imagining such eminence. All I had wished for was to be a Wafadar. I looked at myself in the trembling waters of the Jhinjheri. I could still see the boy I once was. Short, lacking real breadth of shoulder, and not blessed with a word of the eloquence the Pathfinders – and now the Bhaktas – possessed. I had another face then – the false one, of ego and vanity – but I could not recall it any more. All I remembered was a big black mole on my right cheek with two hair sticking out of it, a small ant with its antennae.

The great Tragopan had erred. I was not worthy.

I did not doubt my intellect or my commitment or my courage, but I did not think I had it in me to take on the big questions of the flock, to conduct myself with the sweeping confidence I had seen displayed by ZZ9 and the great Hornbill. Just witnessing the martyrdom of the Gentle Father was a heart-stopping affair. One could not even imagine conceiving or essaying such an act.

As the Jhinjheri flowed my face like water I decided I would finish the tasks my master had set me and when I returned I would tell him that I was unequal to the high plans he had made for me. My place was to be forever the sword, never the arm.

It was getting to night two days later when we reached the other end of the valley where the rock face is desperately brittle and large pieces continually break off and crash into the woods below. I had never been to this corner before. There was nothing here except the Nest of the Unabled.

I was surprised by the air of desolation. The entire area by the cliff bore a bruised look, with trees damaged and flattened by the boulders, which sat fatly among them like pebbles amid grass. The hospices of the Nest were set a little distance away from the cliffs, though it was clear that every now and then a big rock did bounce all the way into the playing yard.

I had to rattle the timber gate hard before a stout brother came waddling out of a nearby shed, went rushing back in, and came rushing out again. By the time he let us in, three more had emerged from the same shed and they all now stood at attention, trembling and straightening their clothes. I could see the food bellies on them and smell the Ferment on their breath. From the corner of my Wafadar's eye I saw another one scuttle out from a door at the far side, hustling two boys ahead of him. They vanished into the trees in the dark.

And then just as I was about to ask a question I heard an infernal howl. It was low and long, like no animal's I had ever heard, and it slashed open the night as a knife does skin. And barely had it died than there came another – different from the first but again unlike any I had heard any animal utter. I am a man without fear – as were the brothers by my side – yet we all felt a cold hand clutch at our hearts.

And then there was another and another and soon the whole night was ripped apart by a beastly howling that seemed to come from no beast we had ever known. I was sure it would shrapnel the mountains behind us and soon we would hear the crash of boulders. By now three of the brothers, on a signal from the fourth, had raced off into the dark.

The remaining one could read the questions written on our faces. He said, You never get used to it. One of them starts, and then like maddened demons they all join in. And they never stop on their own. If we don't go and shut them down they will be at it till the sun rises.

I said, Why do they not listen?

He said, They do when they choose to.

I said, That's an unacceptable state of affairs.

He said, It is.

I said, You know why we are here?

He said, Yes we heard. To close things down.

I said, Do you approve of it?

He said nothing, merely looked at the ground.

I said, Brother, do you?

Without looking up he said, These are big questions, to be answered by great Helmsmen. I do as I am told.

I could see why I had been sent here. Clearly there was something so beastly happening in this place that it needed to be permanently stopped.

I said, First food and lodging for my men. Then come and tell me all you know and all you do.

Three weeks – a literal lifetime – later I made a run for it.

I did not head back into the valley. Given who I was it would have been easy for me to have walked quietly out through the Pass and down the forest of giant deodars and on to the mountain track below, down to the road that led to the village and further to the town where the last buses came. I was no longer a young man but I was still a Wafadar. I could have done it in six hours from the Pass and by the time they came in pursuit I would have fled further.

I did not head back into the valley because I did not wish to encounter anyone I knew. I wanted nothing to weaken my resolve. In particular I was terrified of running into the great Tragopan. In his mesmeric presence I would become a reed, bending whichever way the gale of his words blew me.

I just wanted to run, without looking back.

A kind of knowing had undone me. There was nothing to do but flee.

Marshalling all I had ever mastered of mind and body, as the moon rose, I scaled the crumbling mountain, feeling pieces of rock break off in my hands. I knew the legend: no one had ever climbed this face and reached the top alive. But I was not afraid to come down with a loose boulder and be crushed. What I was afraid of lay within me.

When I crested the top my fingers were bleeding. In front of me the ranges of the highest mountains known to man rolled away in endless stacks. Out there a thousand paths led to a thousand places in the world. One of those would welcome my feet, carry them to a distant place, any place, that would harbour my spirit and my grief. I still had some years left in me. I needed to spend them looking at myself, making a reckoning of a life of masks.

Far far down below were rallying shouts. The ground still smouldered and the air still burned. Pinpricks of burning torches could be seen at the bottom of the cliff. They must have discovered my escape. I knew it could end terribly for me. But then it already had. There was nothing more to lose. For the first time in my life I had done something that was not about following an order. Even in the midst of my despair it made me feel newly born. It also made me feel heedless of consequence.

A high mountain blackbird squawked just above my head, announcing approaching daylight. I pulled my laces tighter, tucked the flaps of my tunic in and, with a last look back at the valley that was my home, I began to run.

THE LAST SECRET

I put down my mug of tea, click the machine shut, and stretch myself. I ought to be grateful. The night has gone better than I had expected. My story winds to its close and I have had the immeasurable joy of hearing the 2 o'clock train whistle its way in. It was late tonight, and as if to make up – as if to signal the last pleasure of my life – the driver blew and blew the whistle till every wagon wheel had clacked past.

The beauty of that sound in the heart of night! I cannot imagine anything comparable.

To tell the truth I am surprised they haven't moved in yet. It's not like them to play games. They are warriors, unsmiling, unrelenting, filled with purpose. After all these years I am almost curious to once again feel the fervour that radiates from their bodies, to once again see the face. As it once was: everywhere I turn, the unchanging face.

I remember when I first took it off. I had been running for weeks, tracking my way down the mountains, passing swiftly through villages and circling towns, trying to avoid suspicion or leaving a spoor. I knew before setting off my pursuers would have been to the Mausoleum of Our Egos and studied the face I was born with.

As I fled, moving night and day, one evening by the roadside I came upon a man singing and urinating. A small man, like a rat, with two upper teeth sticking out over his lower lip, he gave me a ride on his truck. He was chewing on tobacco and I was relieved that he spoke without waiting for a reply.

His truck was an old creaking machine and he was carrying stones in it. This was making him laugh. He said the fantasies of rich men were converting stone into gold. Next they will pay me for bringing leaves from trees, he said, and laughed. And a little later: and next they will pay me for air from air: and he laughed. It was more laughter already than I had heard in my entire life.

He was driving slowly but the truck lurched from side to side, its one eye wildly flinging its light this way and that, against the mountain face and into the abyss. Often I looked out of my window and the precipice was only a few feet away. This brought on more laughter. He said, chuckling, At least you will die before me! That's the best one can hope for – that one will die last! One cannot hope never to die!

Then he began to comment on my skin. How smooth it was. How it glowed. I looked like an older man but my skin was that of a boy. The cream, he wanted to know the name of the cream I used. Then he reached out and ran his fingertips over my cheeks. Like marble, he said. Extraordinary!

That night as he slept under the truck I sat inside the cabin, turned on the light, and took off the face. When I looked into the small narrow mirror I saw someone I had never seen before. I did not sleep for a moment that night. Again and again I twisted this way and that, tracing my fingers over my nose and mouth and eyebrows and cheeks, able to see myself only in small slices, the strange features, the mole, the roughness, the indentation of skin and bristle. It felt as if I had peeled off dead skin and found a living one underneath.

This was me. Alone and unique in the universe. Priceless not because I was like everyone else but because there wasn't another like me anywhere. Ten thousand men over millennia had seeded ten thousand women to create the uniqueness that was me. No ustaad, no god, could ever match that. Something heady powered through me. When dawn came I was still looking into the narrow mirror and the tiny naked light in the truck was pulsing with heat and smelling of burn.

So often over the years I have felt I should have saved the face. As a reminder of who, and where, I had been. But at that moment I was so filled with loathing for it that I threw it on the ground and slammed it with my feet and when it was cracked along the nose and the eyes I went to the edge of the road and flung it out as far as I could, watching it catch the wind and sail in a slow whistling arc down into the abyss.

Now I am appalled at myself that a part of me is eager to once again see the face, to feel the energy of the pure. Is it possible that I am still afflicted? Is it possible that I am somewhat like the drain inspector – against the sewer and for the sewer at the same time? An absurd mash of detestation and desire.

Is it possible that a part of me still believes in the brotherhood? In the peerless glory of Aum?

It cannot be. I will not allow it to be.

Yet it is true that I have spent more hours thinking of the flock since I fled it than I did in all the years when I was of it. Each moment – while sculpting Zubair's wooden figurines, while hearing Parvati's steady bustle, while reading and reading and listening and listening, while visiting the Talkies and the bazaars, while drinking with the drain inspector and watching the night uncurl – each moment I have thought of my people and my life.

As in a diffusing morning mist so many things I could not see have slowly become clear to me. Great anger and regret have rocked my being. Like the drain inspector I have felt like ranting and raging – against the very scheme of things, against the way the world has ordered itself, against the life it had led me into. Like the drain inspector I have felt like rushing out and burning the world down: my world, of the valley, of the pure.

And yet, and yet, so often the darkness of my spirit has been illuminated by flashes of lightning that once again reveal to me the rare virtues of the flock, the nobility of its vision, the beauty of its purpose, the unflinching strength of its resolve. At such a moment I am struck by terror. Have I erred? Have I, in a final reckoning, merely fallen prey to the very failings that the peerless one taught us to fight?

Then the flare of lightning passes and I know its light is false and fleeting, limning the world into shapes it does not actually possess. Without saying it aloud I know that the drain inspector, with his excesses of the dark rum, with the smell of the gutter sticking to his skin, with his frothing determination to seize the world for his sewermen, with his continual beating and loving of his lame wife, I know that the drain inspector carries more virtue in him than any great Helmsman.

He takes on the terrible imperfections of the world with his own imperfections.

He knows – or intuits – a great secret.

That more than anything else men must fear the quest for perfection.

He looks at himself in the mirror. The bloodshot eyes, the twisting fury, the rank odours, and he knows he is the man for the job. To fight injustice, to fight oppression. He knows those pristine men in the temples – bathed in incense, with their poison-soaked pieties and calculating eyes – will not, and cannot, do it. Their hearts are cold with correctness. They listen to just one god. They listen to just one music.

The music. Without talking of it I know that my cross-legged master in the kiosk, with his red fragrant fingers folding green leaves at a breathtaking pace and his unstained knuckles pulling out crisp cigarettes and his incarnadine mouth ceaseless in its hum, I know the cross-legged master carries more virtue in him than any great Helmsman. He takes on the sorrows of the world with his soaring music. He knows it is hubris to imagine the world can be fixed. And wisdom to understand that it must simply be endured. The music makes it possible – balm and blaze, tears and laughter, the instant and eternity.

It is the great secret he knows. In the fecund womb of music waits the perfect moment. And anyone can have it.

I have seen it at the kiosk. Men arrive with fret heavy on their foreheads. And as he fills and folds the wet leaves with a hundred fragrances he hums a few bars – often closing his eyes and raising his hands in reverence – and by the time they leave, mouths working the juice, they have lost their cares and entered the womb of the perfect moment.

In this world it is what I have embraced above all. The music. I cannot describe the excitement I feel when I return to this room and prepare to tear the cellophane and crack the glass case inside which sit new sounds sold to me by the cross-legged master. Look at the shelf on the wall! It is overladen with the treasure. I fill with pride when the drain inspector – taking pause from his fulminations – examines the new acquisitions and nods with approval. Then he feeds it to the machine and we both enter the perfect moment.

If there is one thing I would take to the high mountains, to that vast valley full of high purpose, it would be this shelf. The fat man – the companion of my childhood, whom I calmly gutted one night – knew something profound. Today I know he was the most valuable man across the length and breadth of my land.

Even as I have rushed tonight to finish my offering to the pharmacy of the world's tales I have not been so full of panic as to ignore my last few magic moments. In between the telling of the last of my story there is fresh cellophane that I have ripped. This one is a maestro from the heart of the burning plains. The picture on the jacket shows him to be round-faced, bald and with caste marks on his forehead. His right arm is raised and his mouth is open. My cross-legged tutor says he heard him in person once, at night, in the eternal city by the holy river, the lights dancing on its timeless waters. Opening his eyes wide, he says, While I thought I had died and gone to heaven, a hundred million dead souls rose on either bank to hear that voice!

I have just heard it and when my tale is done – which it will be, moments from now – I will put it to play again. I like the thought of my brothers arriving to claim me as the maestro's voice seizes the air and commands to attention the spirits of the night. I know it will not, but I hope perhaps it will infect my brothers too. Make an incision in their carapace through which some emotion may intrude. I like the thought of the maestro's voice opening up my pores even as the chonch open up my pipes.

I like the thought of entering the womb of the perfect moment even as I exit the doors of this life.

A shadow moves in the upper buttresses of the semul, just where the streetlight stops and the dark begins. It is so subtle that even the horned owl perched on the last finger is not stirred. Only a man like me, once a Wafadar, could possibly sense it. I wonder what the Angels are waiting for. How many of them have come. Do they fear my old reputation and would rather take me when I am drowsy with sleep? Or is it that the great Tragopan, in the anger of betrayal, has asked for me to be taken back alive?

That I shall not allow.

I fear that in the valley of the pure, in the presence of the great Tragopan – as he carves beauty out of the air – I may once again find myself overwhelmed. Today I know the truth of myself. I have had many years to look at my real face in the mirror, so soft and pasty.

Clearly I am not a man who seizes the world or bends it. I am a follower. A man who enables other men to unleash their will. Of the horrors that result, I would like to be absolved. But today I know the truth: this cannot be. Without my compliant limbs their will would be as nothing.

She was not like me. Her will was her own.

It was she who made me unnaturally brave – that one time.

Enabled me to climb out of my mask, to scale the brittle cliffs. Were it not for her unbending will I would even now be carrying out inquisitions in the valley, listening to the Bhaktas, brutally cleansing my brothers.

Her eyes were still black as a moonless night but her hair was now flecked with the grey of a summer twilight. I had no idea she was at the Nest. That first night when the infernal howling tore up the skies and would not stop I asked the brother who was showing us our quarters to take me to its source. He was reluctant. They would soon bring the din to a close. The morning was a better hour to reconnoitre. I insisted.

The large shed he led me into had so many beds – each a double, the one above low and tight on the one below – it reminded me of the sheep corral at the granary. In each lay an unabled child or a man-child writhing and screaming. Bearing lanterns the three brothers we had met at the gate were weaving themselves through the inferno. They were slapping down each unabled who was sitting up, and tying a bandanna across the mouth of each one screaming without pause.

Most of them did not have the face – they had become garbage before its time had come.

As I walked through the narrow aisle dazed by the howling I could see many of these creatures were chained by their ankles to their beds. Several of them were reaching out to claw us and we had to parry them and dodge them. Some seemed old – almost men – but there were many who could not have been more than six or seven years of age. But they were beasts no less – screaming with wide open eyes and maws, thrashing their arms and legs – demanding a gag and a tether. I saw many were beyond all polite restraint and the struggling brothers had to concuss them into silence with hard blows to their temples. I was tempted to bang a few heads myself.

When I emerged into the night at the other end I had to sit down to settle my nerves.

A brother said, You never get fully used to it.

I said, Is this how it always is?

He said, No, it can be better, and worse. You never know what stirs them.

It was then that I realized there was howling in the air that did not emanate from the shed we had just walked through.

The brother said, There are more. Many more. At one time the Nest needed a new shed every fifteen years. Now we build a new one every few years. There are eight already, all smaller than this one. But mercifully in two of them these cursed ones are unable to even howl – they merely moan and drool, wetting the beds on which they lie.

I did not know what to say. I had not been prepared for this. We all knew the Nest was an enclave of dysfunction. But the flock did not – was not supposed to – talk about it. After all, it was an area of our shame. It was where the failures of the motherhood were housed. It was a crude reminder that blemishes could be forced even on to the pure. Yet I had no idea of the scale of the stain. When the fat man had talked of his time at the Nest he had only spoken of the delirium of his song and nothing of the ruinous taint.

I now understood why the great Tragopan had sent me here, why he had been full of gloomy contemplation as he spelled out my task. I saw how heavy the burden of greatness is: to undertake the unpleasant, which ordinary men will slyly turn their backs on.

The brother said, Would you see the rest tonight or shall we leave them for the morrow? I was still sitting, the howls still ringing in my ears, and my first impulse was to say, yes, the morrow, but then I remembered I was here on a crucial mission – a dark, difficult one – and with me were my sterling brothers and it would not behove us to be sluggish in spirit or in action. When training to be Wafadars we had been taught, in battle, to first go for the most fearsome adversary. Once the biggest devil was felled the rest were easy.

I said, Tonight, my brother, tonight. Let us continue. All eight of them – even if it means we meet the sun before we finally repair.

It remains to this day the longest night of my life – far longer than the one I am living through as I tell the last of my tale. Some things I have learned must never be given utterance for they become even more fearful to behold. And so I have kept it for the last and even now I struggle to put words to it.

As the brother led me from shed to shed – each in a clearing removed from the trees, each packed tight with double beds, atop one another, each made visible in the spectral light of shaking lanterns – as I went from shed to shed I saw sights that still come to me each time I shut my eyes.

An army of the mangled and the maimed, from infancy to middle age, writhing in their bunks like upturned insects, twisted arms and legs jerking the air in spasms of uncoordination.

Open mouths with lips loose like the jowls of cattle, askew and trailing drool. The stench of unwash and the refuse of the body thick in the air like fog in winter.

And uncurling everywhere infernal howls – as if entrails were being pulled out of bodies, slowly, inch by inch.

And underlying it all a stream of wordless moans, the speech of suffering animals; and the clanking of shackles, anchoring this insanity down.

I struggled to look and to not look. In a single line behind me walked the brothers of my squad, doing the same, absorbing the shape and scale of the task at hand. Not a word was said, not a gesture made. At the end of every shed I sat down on the ground and looked at the stars and at the face of every brother that was also my face.

This was the offal of the valley: much more than any of us could have imagined. It had to be cleaned up. I was not sure how. I needed to get all this howling and moaning out of my ears before I could think clearly.

In the last two sheds were confined the distaff of this refuse. It was no different, the howling and moaning and drooling and the ripping of the air. I can never forget the moment. I went into the first and there was a girl sitting on top of a bunk tearing at her bared breasts and screaming for her mother. Maaaaaaaaaaaaa! She had a long nose and bottomless lungs and did not once break for breath. Our host brothers caught her by the head and chin and banged her teeth together several times but to no avail. After each bang the Maaaaaaa came out even shriller. One of them then bunched her quilt and smothered her with it, leaning an elbow with all his weight onto her face. The Maaaaaa still quavered through.

I decided I'd seen enough.

When we were in the shed prepared for us I sent for the Bhakta allotted to the Nest. He'd already fallen asleep and came in wondering what it was that could not wait till the morning. It took him no time to realize who I was.

His report gave muscle to the great Tragopan's plans. The months he had been here, the Bhakta said, had been the most harrowing of his life. His training lay in taking forth the life and lessons of Aum – the Paigamber, the prophet, the peerless one – to the flock. He had been taught by the great Bhakta – the one with the big walnut in his throat – that the task of the Bhakta was to keep the pure spotlessly pure. In time even pristine water sullies if left unrefreshed. The word of Aum was the water of the Jhinjheri, chaste, heady, lifegiving. Each day the Bhakta carried it to the faithful, rinsing out all doubt, making fresh the belief.

But what was the uncontaminated word to swine? Here were animals, beyond the lines of doubt and belief. He spoke each day and it was as dust in the air – greeted by howls and moans and drools that even beasts eschew. At night he drank more Ferment than was good for him, somehow to shut out the failures of his day.

Even now I could smell it on him. I told him what our great Helmsman had been forced to consider.

He said, The great Tragopan is never wrong. We look to him to know our path.

I said, Tell me, Bhakta, what would Aum have done?

He said, It is not for us to say what the limitless one would do. We can only speak for what he would have us do.

I said, And would it be what our great Helmsman suggests?

He said, There can be no doubt that when the great Tragopan speaks he speaks the word of the prophet.

As I pause at the many tiny black holes that are the ears of the machine, a soft mewl breaks the silence. I leap up in alarm. In the frenzy of finishing my story I have forgotten my most important responsibility for the night. Without scrabbling for my slippers, on bare feet, I rush down the stairs.

A lone yellow bulb shines in the kitchen and a block of its light slants out into the small dining room. On top of the low bureau against the wall – inside which are stacked colourful plates and glasses: set out on special occasions, when the drain inspector visits – amid porcelain figurines and plastic flowers sits a brown cardboard box bearing the faded markings of strawberry jam.

I open the interlaced lid and the kitten inside is propped against the side like a climber starting on an impossible wall. I pick it up with soft fingers and it is the size of my palm. Right now its mewl is larger than its size, but it has reason to complain. I stroke it with one finger and its protests grow quieter.

I am grateful Parvati has not woken. She sleeps like a bear in winter but this baby's wail always manages to drag her awake. I carefully place it in the pocket of my frayed jacket and go to the kitchen, closing the door behind me. It takes me less than a minute to heat four spoons of milk, which I mix with four spoons of water. I test it with the tip of my tongue, then swirl the pan to cool it some more.

The kitten has begun to mewl aggressively again and I can feel it scratching at the lining of my coat. I rinse the plastic syringe a few times, then suck it full of the watery milk. I hold the baby against my chest and slide the blunt nozzle into its mouth. Immediately it grips my fingers with its disproportionately large paws. Each time I am surprised by their size. They seem to belong to a fully grown cat. I joke with Parvati that we do not know what we are nurturing. One

day we will come down the stairs and find a large jungle cat waiting
for us.

Parvati found this one two weeks ago. In the morning she opened
the door at the back of the kitchen to check on the debris of the feast
she lays out every night and there were these five wriggling babies all
in a pile. They were faintly pink, their coat of brown-grey spots and
striations still merely a suggestion.

I was woken and dispatched to get a discarded cardboard box from
the grocer and some syringes from the chemist. When I returned
Parvati was wiping the orphans with the softest cloth she could find
in her cupboard, dipped in disinfectant. Each infant was the size of
my middle finger and she handled each one as if it had emerged from
her own womb.

I was ordered to learn to do it too. Especially in case the drain
inspector showed up. He was bound to rant, berating his mother-in-
law for cosseting animals while ignoring the misery of men trawling
the sewers. Parvati could answer to that but she would not dream of
crossing words with her son-in-law.

By the night – even as we fed them half a syringe every two hours
– one of the five was dead. In the dark I dug a six-inch hole by the
road and buried it. In the morning I dug another hole next to the
first and buried a second. I earmarked this one – who now grabs at
the syringe – to be the next to go. It was the most sluggish, its eyes
barely open.

My nocturnal vigils – the telling of my story – served our nursing
schedule well. Parvati looked after them during the day and I took
over once she fell asleep. Now, since my time is done, since I have set
out to say it all, I must confess that the nocturnal nurturing has given
me the most gratifying moments of my life. Sometimes I think I was
set on the path of telling my story only so I would be awake at night
to tend to this fragile life blooming in our dining room.

As I picked each child, holding it close to my chest, feeding it till
its stomach bulged dangerously, I felt an emotion I cannot describe.
Happiness, love, contentment, gratitude – I truly cannot tell.

As mysterious was the grief that overcame me when I was woken four days later by a sad Parvati. Opening the box she had found two of the infants stiffly dead, tiny legs up in the air. When I had buried them next to their siblings I could not go back to sleep.

I sat on my chair in the small room as the first rays of the sun broke through the many arms and fingers of the semul, held my head in my hands and for the first time in my life I wept. They had been fully alive just a few hours ago when I had tucked them in among the rags in the box. I could feel their paws – too big for their bodies – grasping at my fingers, their trusting eyes looking at me. I could feel the immensity of life beating in their tiny bodies. Now they were dead without a reason. Dead before they had started. Dead because I had failed to do something right.

I was crying for them, and yet I felt I was not crying for them alone, but for myself, and for everyone I had ever known and would not know again. When Parvati brought me tea there were tears running down my cheeks salting the corners of my mouth. With her wordless wisdom – that I have come to adore – she said nothing, just held my head close, and left. There can be no questioning – or understanding – of the springs of sorrow.

The sadness stayed with for me for days – centred on an image, of them buried by the roadside, their tiny eyes and whiskers still. Life was just beginning to stretch their beautiful bodies. It was difficult to believe how – and why – it had suddenly left them.

Against all logic, against all odds, this one – who I had thought would die first – survived. Parvati said there was a lesson in it. I could see many.

She named it Chand, the moon. She said if it turned out to be a girl she would change it to Chandni, moonlight. True to its name it sleeps during the day and stays awake at night. At times these last days when I have struggled with finding the words for my story I have gone down, taken it out of its box and played with it, a kind of slapping game, its two outsized paws against my two hands. It is feisty and knows no fear. Already its talons move in and out of its skin with the menace of a predator.

In a move of convenience Parvati has given it an androgynous name but it is nothing like the moon or the moonlight. It is gray black, almost a dirty colour, with striations on its head and neck and legs, and spots on its back. A bit of tiger and a bit of leopard. What is beautiful about it, I think, is its will to live; its round eyes, full of curiosity and of challenge.

When I tire of slapping with it I give it Parvati's thick hairband. It bats it across the room, chases it down, tosses it over its head, then leaves it unmoving on the red oxide floor – a black curled quarry – as it stalks it from all sides. It is pure frolic, such as I have never known in my entire life.

Soon it tires, and curls its tiny body and looks at me. I pick it up, hold it close to my chest, and feed it one last syringe.

But tonight there is no time to watch it at its sport. I have already seen a shadow caress the semul. Some power whose shape I do not know has kept me alive long enough to let me finish my tale. Fifteen minutes more is all I need. I know an unfinished story is no story. It is a pill the world's pharmacy of tales will reject. It will succour no one.

I put it back inside the box, prising open its claws that are dug into my jacket. Then I pick it back up and rub my face against its grey pelt and kiss its small head.

Before I race back upstairs I go into the kitchen, turn off the light and peep out the rear window. The feast is on, a joy of working maws and scrabbling paws.

There can be no doubt. If there is a law of karma, Parvati will be born a queen in her next life.

By the time she came to see me, two full days had gone by and like the Bhakta I too was drinking too much Ferment. I was a Wafadar who feared nothing but after the inspection of the first night I had not found in myself the courage to go back into those sheds. As you can see I dread the memory too and have kept its telling at bay till all has been said and I cannot keep from it any more.

For two days I made myself purposeful by summoning and questioning every single brother who manned the Nest. It was not necessary but I felt the need to be assured that what we had to do was what everyone felt we had to do. I also hoped someone would suggest how it could be done and would also undertake to have it done.

If I was looking for some quick solace it was not offered to me. Each brother arrived malodorous with drink and then proceeded to talk in circles. If there was a hell anywhere, this was it. There could be no burden heavier than this, the failures of the motherhood. The great Helmsmen had to be praised for casting their eye in this direction. It was the valour of the great Tragopan that he had ordered a move that should have been made a long time ago. And it was his great wisdom that he had sent illustrious brothers from the high terraces to do what had to be done. This was after all no task for ordinary brothers.

All the while as the brothers talked, spraying their rank breath, the demonic wails floated in the air. Did they never cease? It was the way of the unabled, the brothers said. They rose and rested without any human pattern and whenever they woke they cried out to the skies. The moment a brother left, the moment I was alone, I pressed rolled balls of cloth deep into my ears.

In the middle of the day when the sun was high I saw some of the older unabled led into the yard, to take in the fresh air and to move their gnarled limbs. It was a daunting sight but I did not pull my eyes away. I had to understand what I had to deal with.

I must say it as I felt it. They were like insects. Their limbs seemed as if they had been broken into pieces and put together again by a blind child. Most of them seemed to have their arms screwed on the wrong way and their necks twisted in different directions. Some of them came out crawling on their limbs, not walking on them.

One was like a spider, his face close to the ground, his arms and legs spread all around him, just about keeping his body from being scraped. Each time he encountered a rock he lifted his torso with a huge effort to make his way over it.

There was another whose lower jaw was out of line with his upper, leaving his mouth permanently open. He was continually blowing bubbles of spit through it, big ones. As each filled his mouth he tried to catch it but his limbs were so poorly coordinated he ended up slapping his face.

I looked at them from the window and if one of them looked back I stepped away. For some reason I did not wish to have them see me see them.

They wheeled and crawled around the yard, raising dust, and when they went close to the forest, the brothers of the Nest gently beat them back with a switch. Two of the unabled had their legs and arms firmly lashed together at the ankles and the elbows. They hobbled around like a strange two-headed beast, their long tongues lolling down their chins. The Bhakta – who stood by my side, holding his head – said they were twins and inclined to violence. When the fury came upon them they had to be dragged out and tied to the penitence pole where they were free to claw at each other till the fit had passed. I could see the rips on their face and neck and the gashed ears that had suffered bites.

What a sorry sight it was. Every creature in that yard seemed to bear lacerations on its skin. Each one's clothes were soiled and tattered and damp with ceaseless drool. I could not smell them from where I stood but the revolting odours of the first night still clung to my nostrils. If I needed affirmation of the necessity of what needed to be done, it crawled in front of me in unsightly abundance.

There appeared to be one exception. A creature who looked quite old, his face heavy with whiskers, though his scalp was closely tonsured. The Bhakta said he was known as the disciple. He sat in the middle of the yard, his eyes bulging, his gap-toothed mouth open, with a soft unbroken invocation streaming out – Auummmmm! His legs appeared to be without bones and he had tossed them over his shoulders, the ankles meeting behind his neck. The Bhakta said he'd been uttering the eternal name since he was nine and no one recalled the breath in his chest ever running out. The brothers of the Nest always handled him with care.

As I looked I thought, There has to be a simple way.

I could see it was both a task and a test. Was I ready for bigger things? Could I carry not just myself but also my brothers to our destiny? Was I ripe to lead, to set aside personal desire and distress for the greater good? This was my hour of reckoning, at this distant Nest, this fiendish commune of mangled and forsaken creatures. What I did here in the next few days would leave me primed for glory or consigned forever to a deserved smallness.

The Bhakta said, They are crying for deliverance. You must give unto them deliverance.

I thought, There has to be a simple way.

A simple, clean, quick, effective way.

I was lying on my back, working to empty my head till it had reached a point of perfect stillness, when the knock came. Twice, without hesitation. It was well past the midnight hour and the brothers – of the Nest and of my squad – had left only ten minutes ago, after finishing several flagons of Ferment in between narrating stories of the unabled that ranged from the pathetic to the grotesque.

We had not discussed the way.

We were still talking the talk that would prepare us for what had to be done.

Because it was dark, because I was not expecting her, because too many years had passed, because there was a gale beginning to blow outside, because my mind had almost become a white sheet without a single ripple, because she was wearing the face, I looked at her blankly when I opened the door.

Saying nothing she pushed past me and finding a nail on the rafter above hung the lantern she was carrying and pushed up its wick. The face makes us all one beyond vanity and ego but it does not change our eyes.

In that instant of recognition my mind became a frantically flapping sheet and all I could say was, Aum be the truth! You!

She said, Your legend fills the valley. They say you rise up the terraces every year. They say there is only one Wafadar the great Helmsmen ask for when they want something arduous done. They say there is no greater enforcer of the faith. You are steadfast and constant, all will and purpose, unblemished by feeling or sentiment.

Another place, another person saying these things would have filled me to a fullness. But now I felt small, and empty.

Before I could consider a reply she said, Some say you will one day be a great Helmsman yourself, maybe even the Gentle Father. And that is why you are here. It is here, at the Nest where the unabled huddle, you will do what none have been able to do and make your undying myth.

Nothing, I could see, had changed in her eyes. They were still full of fire, saying more than her words, giving to her words the edge of a dagger. I felt something strange happening to me. Instead of being perturbed by her tone I was filled with an urge to rip off her face and see her once again as I had known her.

She said, standing hard and straight as a pine, What is it about power that makes men so blind? Every year I thought, surely now he will see it, surely now he will raise a voice that will shatter the silence.

I was scarcely listening to her. I had plunged into a pool of memory I had carefully skirted every day of my life. I could smell the hair, the skin, the warm breath that was sweet when she fell to sleep and miraculously sweet when she woke. In my hands swelled plum breasts and I was held by strong limbs in a place I never wanted to leave. My heart was beating in a way it had never before and would never again and as I lay naked, my body was painted with long lines of black hair. She was talking, even in the depths of the pool, she was talking. But in a sweet whisper and in words that filled me with so much sentiment that I should have been ashamed of being a brother, leave alone a Wafadar. And then I was walking down the high terraces on a moonless night and there was the pad of a big beast in the deodars and there was a hand in mine that I never wanted to let go of. And then she was sitting on a rock and holding my face and tracing my nose and my lips, and for the first time in my life I wished I could pull it off and feel her fingers directly on my skin. And then I had picked her up and sat down on the rock and found a moment of frenzy and stillness that I was to never find again. And then there was the escort from the motherhood waiting for her, and she'd put her arms around me and her mouth to my ear, and more than twenty years later the words were the same: It is you who are wonderful but completely upside down. Please see the great evil it has all become. And if you see it you will not be able to endure it. Save yourself and save me. I'll wait for you. I love…

She did not leave till the night had become morning but nor did she lie in my arms. She did what she did best – no less well than the great Tragopan. She talked, with flashing eyes and chopping hands. But her words were different. My great master's words were soft and wet mud, which could be sculpted and re-sculpted by his hands into different and beautiful shapes. Her words, on the other hand, were flint, hard stone, only to be shaped once and designed to spark fire.

To say I was burnt by them would be an understatement. I was charred, devastated. I heard things that night I could never have imagined. It was as if I'd been picked up and skinned inside out and had boiling oil poured over me, slowly, mug on mug.

I wanted to disbelieve every word she said.

I wanted her to just hold me, close, very close, and then leave.

I knew every word she was saying could condemn her – even without the formality of an inquisition – to the Room of Inner Truths. Heard in its entirety her rant could plunge her down the Crater of Resurrections for all time and beyond.

I sat on the edge of the bed and she on a shaky wooden chair. Along with the howling of the wind could be heard the moaning and howling of the unabled.

She was heavy with seed by the time she returned from her initiation in the higher terraces at the hands of the great Hornbill. She was settled into the motherhood and some months after she had delivered her first fruit she was sent off to the Serai, a madonna ready to be ploughed with seed again.

As she had always been, she was full of guile at the Serai, and it was a rare brother who could find his way into her limbs. When any did manage to she deployed her cunning to keep them from spilling in her. There was no question, she was a disgrace. While everyone around her returned to the motherhood with smooth regularity, their wombs full with new soldiers of the pure, she remained as thin as a bamboo and as hollow within.

Barren cows invite attention. Once again after so many years she found herself in the presence of the small, powerful mother whose voice was four times her size. The mother remembered the girl with black hair and black flashing eyes. The girl remembered the blinding slaps that had felled her to the ground and the Room of Inner Truths whose walls were tight and smooth and high.

In the presence of the mother she was held down firmly and filled with seed again. And when she had swelled and delivered with honour she was sent back to the Serai where once again she crossed her legs and clung to the shadows. But now she was being watched and it was not long before she was recalled by the stentorian mother and rendered fecund once more.

She was filled with darkness. So she said to me. For a time she contemplated taking a leaf of the aboba to liquefy her womb, drain it of all that was not just hers. But the leaf often does other things, blinds the eyes, freezes the joints, bloats the tongue. Then she thought of putting the spice stick into her egg and cracking it open. She found she couldn't. Its brutality baulked her for she found she had already developed a kinship with the life forming inside her.

It was dark, very dark – and she knew of at least two madonnas who had done away with themselves, so filled were they with the grief of being parted from their infants. But she was never one for the easy way.

And did she ever think of her time at the great Hornbill's? The days and the nights. The play of breath and the weight of unsaid words.

Every single day. Each time she had a moment to herself. Each time she wished to yearn for something that would bring warmth to her soul.

I rose and poured out two glasses of Ferment and gave one to her. She quaffed it at one go. I did the same.

She kept hearing of him. The Wafadar who had the complete trust of the great Tragopan. Who ranged the valley with his handpicked squad, monitoring the flock. She hoped he would one day show up at the Serai, or she would somehow be dispatched to the Kiln – which was the rightful place for a great Wafadar like him. But the Kiln demanded madonnas of exceeding allure – for a Wafadar must be tested against the greatest temptations – and though her beauty was exquisite and widely acknowledged, her conduct placed her in a low position.

She thought of sending him an epistle, a word, through other madonnas who were destined for the Kiln. But there were none she could wholly trust. Loyalty amongst the faithful was always to higher things, never to each other. Also the stories she heard about him did not fill her with much hope.

When she had been ploughed successfully and reaped for the fifth time and the mewling infant taken away and she was once again being prepared for the Serai, she entered a tunnel of terrible darkness out of which she emerged one day by slashing the slopes of her breasts and the planes of her thighs.

She worked the knife in a wide expanse of crosshatching lines, driving the tip deep so the marks that arose would be permanent. It proved heady. The ugliness liberated her, made her happy. The doors of the Serai were now closed to her forever. And by now the motherhood had concluded she was unfit for further harvesting.

She parted her tunic and pulled up the layers of her shirts and I would have wept if I'd known how to. All these years I had lived with the memory of her plum breasts and flawless skin. Now all I could see was an elaborate embroidery of thick welts. They were like small serpents wriggling up the slopes to suckle at the black peaks – which I remembered pink as sunset.

She was proud of what she had done. As I watched transfixed she put the fingers of her right hand amid the serpents and caressed them slowly. In horror I felt something stir deep in me. But then abruptly she pulled down her clothes and closed her tunic. I looked back into her hard shining eyes and I knew I must not ask why, and I knew this terrible mutilation was not the climax of her story, and I knew she was taking me someplace terrible I ought to stay far away from.

Outside, the wind had dropped and the only howling came from the sheds of the unabled. This is where I finally came, she said. To begin with, having become a field no brother wished to plough, she was fixed with the face and sent to the cradle. Here, along with a dozen others, all wearing the face, she had to play universal mother, hugging the children in rows, clipping their nails and cleaning their ears, playing with each for an equal amount of time, never focusing on the same child two days running, watching over them even as older mothers watched over her.

None of it interested her. Her focus lay elsewhere. She had been making inquiries. It helped to be ugly and fallow. She could move in the shadows with greater ease. She soon gained knowledge of two things. The Nest of the Unabled, where failed children went; and the Mausoleum of our Egos, where everyone's original face was stored and the chronicles of every child were maintained. The brotherhood harboured distaste for sentiment but not for the maintenance of records.

It took her more than a year of cunning cringing to have herself moved to the scullery of the Mausoleum. It took another year of

posturing – a continual display of eager foolishness – to gain a foot
in the inner chambers. It proved a revelation. The sense of order in
there was astonishing. In room after room, inside aromatic deodar
bureaus, meticulously catalogued, month on month, year on year,
were housed the original faces of thousands of brothers.

In there buried and hidden lay our individual truths, who each
one of us really was.

Each day news came from different parts of the valley of changes
in the life and station of brothers and these were duly entered into
the catalogue of their lives. The quarters of the fourteen egokeepers
girded the Mausoleum like a belt. They were fully aware of the value
of what they curated, and in vigilance or in word they never faltered.

She scrubbed and cleaned and muttered and mumbled foolishly
for another year before she was allowed to wander freely inside
the Mausoleum in the service of the egokeepers. It would take her
another year before she could find all she was looking for. She could
not be cautious enough. She knew if she raised a hair of suspicion she
would be instantly ejected and never allowed back in again.

I said, What were you looking for?

Many hours had passed and I was mesmerized by her tale. It
seemed like the story of a deranged mind.

She said, For the truth.

I said, Of what?

She said, Of us.

The first bell of the morning rang in the cookhouse at the other
end of the yard. She jumped up and made for the door. As she flung
it open a fresh round of wailing filled the air. It was still dark outside
but a light grey was invading the black.

I asked, Why?

She said, the black eyes flashing, The truth needs no why. It is the
end of all things. Did not Aum say that!

The door that she banged shut shook the entire room.

I spent the day in a haze. Not for lack of sleep, for a Wafadar can do without it for days, but because my mind would not still. I would scarcely smooth it into a spotless white sheet than it would ruffle up with a hundred agitating thoughts, with images and questions. For most of the day the sheet looked like the thick embroidery on her breasts.

Steering clear of the sheds of the unabled I wandered off into the thin forest that surrounded the Nest, the infernal howls trailing me wherever I wandered. On one side, just beyond the trees, rose the straight brittle cliffs; on the other side stretched the valley. Here, at the end of the tree-line, I discovered a hidden trench overgrown at the edges with bushes and weeds. It was deep enough to take in a tall man and much too wide to leap. At its bottom lay bushes of bramble and thorn. I followed its winding path and found myself at the bottom of the cliffs. Clearly it girded the entire Nest and was meant to keep out the wild animals.

Till the sun died I sat on a boulder and stared at the sheer wall. I felt impelled to just dig my fingers into the first crevice I could find and start to climb it. The rock was brittle and deceptive and rose several hundred feet but I felt I could do it. In fact it was all I wanted to do: something that so absorbed every cell of mine that it pushed out the mad clamour inside my head.

I was experiencing something strange and upsetting. Never in my life had my mind been a house to battling thoughts. I'd always given thought to how to do things. Never to what, or why. I felt she'd put her hand inside my head and squeezed and pulped my brain like a tangerine. Its juices had run out and no longer could I feel its clear shape.

When I went back, long after the sun had died, the brothers were waiting for me. From the door of my shed I could see the twins lashed to the penitence pole, snarling and clawing at each other. I was told a fit had come upon them and by morning they would be spent and then they would lie on their backs for a week till the injuries had healed. The sounds they were emitting were reminiscent of the savages we used to hunt while training to become Wafadars.

The brothers had been drinking, all of them. I looked at each face which was my face and at their heavy eyes which were their own and I knew it was not possible to last here without the Ferment. There were many things I wanted to ask them – the ditch, the unabled, the past, the present – but I knew the answers I would get were not what I wanted to hear. I wished they would leave, and she would come. I dreaded what she would say when she arrived, and I could not wait to hear it.

So we sat silently and quaffed. Then the Bhakta arrived and began to tell a tale of the boundless faith of Alaiya and Ali. It was a new one. A brother contracted a frightful fever. His body burned like the midday sun and it bloated up like that of a dead man in water. Carbuncles burst all over his body like weeds in the rain. None dared go near his hut. Merely to look at him was torment. His food was pushed in with a stick, and he was spoken to through the walls. When the peerless one heard of it, he turned to Alaiya and asked her to go and bed with the afflicted wretch. This she did without a query while everyone else recoiled. When the morning came, the brother emerged as he'd once been, all fevers gone, so smooth of skin. Now Alaiya lay there, unsightly with bloating and carbuncles, her body on fire. The following evening the boundless one summoned a distraught Ali and asked him to go lie with Alaiya. In the morning Alaiya was once again pristine while Ali was beyond all witnessing. Now Ali lay alone in the hut, food pushed in with a stick, spoken through the walls. Some days later the luminous one asked for a volunteer who would take away Ali's blight. The first to rise was Alaiya. But when she reached the hut Ali refused to let her in. He was not willing to give her his sickness.

The door opened and another brother came in. Each time the door was opened the beastly howls filled the room. Everyone waited for the Bhakta to finish the story but he had poured himself six fingers of the Ferment and was sipping it.

Finally I said, Does anyone have an idea how we should do it?

They all looked away, none catching another's eye.

I said, Does everyone agree we have to do it?

Each of them nodded.

I said, How can we be sure this is what Aum would have us do?

The Bhakta said, Who speaks his voice most clearly in the valley?

A brother said, softly, The Gentle Father.

And who speaks the word of the Gentle Father?

The great Tragopan.

And on whose instruction are you here?

I drained my glass. It's what I'd wanted to hear – one more time. I liked this kind of clarity. It allowed a man to act, as men must, with speed and with purpose. I hated what she did to me. Set me to war with myself.

Tonight we had affirmed we had to.

Tomorrow we would decide how to.

When everyone was at the door, a brother said, What happened to Ali?

The Bhakta, who'd been waiting to be asked – it is how they told their stories – said, One week later as evening fell the taintless one went to the hut – outside which Alaiya sat importuning Ali – and calling upon his greatest follower – fevered and defaced with monstrous carbuncles – embraced him. In that instant, in the arms of the Paigamber, Ali was restored to his angelic beauty.

The brother who ran the Nest gave a long belch and said, It is in the fullness of faith that we become beautiful.

So it's the embrace of faith that does it? she said mockingly when I'd finished telling her the Bhakta's story.

I'd waited for her, untouched by a single finger of drowsiness, and she had come in past midnight, when soaked in the Ferment all the brothers were asleep, beyond any waking by moan or by howl. Tonight she sat on the bed, and I on the chair.

I said, It was the embrace of Aum.

She said, Maybe you ought to try it too, as a great soldier of Aum. You can take your pick. We have shedfuls here waiting to be embraced.

I wondered how she now looked, beneath the face. I remembered the smooth, fair skin, the sharp nose, the full lips, and my fingers gliding over them every chance I got. I had tried to hug her the moment she entered my room, to relive what I had once known, but she had pushed me away firmly, saying, It just cannot be.

I said, What did you look for in the Mausoleum? What did you find?

She said, You. You've never looked for anything in your life and you've never found anything. Yet such power you possess. Over lives and deaths.

I did not reply. I did not wish for an argument. After a day of being badly ruffled the white sheet of my mind was smooth again. I felt quiet in myself. Through the agitation she was trying to sow I could feel an understanding growing in me.

I said, Tell me.

She said, her eyes flashing, And will you even know it when you are told it?

Before I could answer she got up and grabbed my hand and pulled me out the door. The moon was more than half, its light strong on the snowline beyond the trees. She led me past all the sheds, slowly, forcing me to take in the insane medley of moans and wails roiling the night air.

I tried to push her to walk faster. I hated the inhuman sounds. But she kept it slow and measured. We crossed the last shed and kept walking. At the tree-line she sat down on the stump of a sawed-off pine. I remembered the last time I saw her face by moonlight, more than twenty years back. Less than a finger's breadth away as I wedged her into me one final time on the rock. I had to admit not a day had passed since that I had not relived that moment.

How did she look now, beneath the face?

She said, in a voice colder than the night, You know what they are?

I kept quiet for a long time.

She waited, her eyes on me.

I said softly, The mistakes of the motherhood.

Her body, which she had been holding hard as a stone, suddenly went slack. The fire went out of her eyes and she said in a voice softer than mine, You still see the world upside down. I waste my breath.

I said, I am not here out of free will.

She said, Mighty Wafadar, no one is – barring me.

I said, You were at the Mausoleum when you last spoke to me.

She said, And long was I there, Wafadar. Convincing the egokeepers I was nothing but of the faith. Working the records to know what all born unto life need to know. Who am I? Where do I come from? And who do I leave behind?

In one of the sheds the chanting girl went into a mad crescendo. Maaaaaaaaa! Maaaaaaaaaaaaaaa!

She said, Who my mother is… And who my child…

Immediately the memory of a slim woman with sharp collarbones filled my heart with howling winds. I remembered the sweet smell of her skin, the texture of her thick black hair, and the sound of her voice crooning in my ears as she pressed me and released me and I clung to her as one would to a raft in a shoreless sea. I remembered how she would press me in so tight that my cheek would get a dent from her sharp collarbones and my breath would stop and how I was happy to have my breath stop as long as she did not stop holding me.

I saw myself as a small boy, four years old, in the bathroom, naked, alone, looking at the bucket of unmoving ice-cold water, about to bathe, and I heard a sob break the night air between us. I looked at her in surprise and realized it was my throat that was moving in thick lumps and my eyes that were wet and there was salt in my nostrils though I could not feel the tears running over my unfeeling face.

Turning away from her I said, And what did you find?

She said, That my mother was a slim woman with sharp collarbones and thick black hair and she died as her womb was being reaped for the ninth time. I was her eighth reaping. Her first had become a great warrior of the pure.

I sank to my haunches, my head empty of all understanding, my heart colder than the water in the bucket of my childhood.

There was no way that girl would not find her mother. By now her cries were surely tearing up the heavens. Maaaaaaaaaaaaaaaaaaaa aaaaaaaaaaaaa!

The next night she walked me slowly through the sheds.

For the first time in my life, all day, I had lain in bed, unwilling to move, unable to move. I wanted to be dead. I wanted no thought in my head. The brothers who came seeking me had been dismissed with a sharp wave. In the evening the Bhakta, smelling of Ferment, had come and put a testing hand on my neck and I had squeezed it so hard his eyes had watered as he yelped.

She held the lantern in a steady hand and stopped every few steps so I could look around and take in each one of the unabled. In the long shadows one could almost imagine they were not so mangled. I have to confess I would not have dared look so closely had I not been searching for something.

She had told me too many things. She had stuck every chonch in the valley into my skin and bled out all the meaning from my being. I was a husk, empty air inside me, and in it floated feathery, hollow words. They were familiar but each time I caught one I could not feel its weight or shape.

Straining in the lantern light, every few steps, I pointed to an unabled who had black hair or firmer limbs, or who was not moaning like a beast in distress. Each time she shook her head and walked on. When all the sheds were done I had still not found him. She had warned me it would not be easy but I had insisted.

When she'd manipulated, in her pursuit of him, to move here from the Mausoleum – easily done, since the Nest was a blight everyone wished to turn away from – she too had failed to spot him. She had to hunt him out, but once she did, she knew he was hers as clearly as day is day and night is night.

The air was cold and I held her at my side, close, but different from how I had ever held her before. Strangely it did not feel worse, or lesser. In fact it created a warmth in me I had never known before. Beyond the many-throated howling of the unabled, an owl was making some sharp holes in the dark. First light was on its way.

On my urging we went back in. I wanted to try one more time. Did he look more like her or like me? He would be a young man now. How maimed was he by a twisted desire? Could he tell who she was? Would he reach for me if I reached for him? Was he one of those fitfully asleep? Or was he pulling at his hair and howling like a wolf? When the last shed was done I had still not found him.

The lantern had run low and the sky was lighter. I hugged her to my side one more time. Suddenly she seemed smaller and frailer than ever before.

It was not the motherhood. These blemished fruit were the heedless sowings of the brotherhood.

This was a nest of gnarled love.

This was a world of men gone mad.

And hidden in these sheds, their horrific refuse.

Four days later they set fire to the Nest. As everything is with the pure it was done neatly and without error. As always trust had been married with surveillance. For all his belief in me the great Tragopan had also put on me an eye. What needed to be done would be done even if I would not do it.

At midday when the sun was high and the burn would not show, a line of fire was put to lick all along the inside of the winding ditch. Eating up bush and tree to feed its growing hunger it reached the heart of the Nest many hours later as the unabled lay locked in the sheds in their afternoon slumber.

When I rushed out, its many mouths were already all around me, torching the air and swallowing up everything in their path. I felt the heat but what I saw was her. She was lashed to the penitence pole, her mouth bound shut and her pipes expertly opened by two score chonch as only a Wafadar can wield.

I held her head close to my chest and put my face in her hair and she was limp in my arms and I was wet with her blood. I lifted her mouth to mine and she whispered, For the love of Aum, go! And then she was still. I put her on the ground and took off her face. She was no longer the smooth-skinned girl who had once snared my nights. But she was beautiful. More beautiful than all the ideas that had filled my life.

I held her face to my face as long as I could, drinking in her beauty, knowing now that beauty comes in many ways though it rarely comes, and to not see it and to not esteem it is to miss the meaning of this thing called life.

And as I drank of her beauty the flames took the sheds and the screams of the unabled were louder than the raging tongues of the fire. I rushed to the third shed where he would have lain on the low bed, fourth row from the door. But even a Wafadar – even a father – cannot walk in fire.

I tried. He must have too. But even if there was the slimmest hope, of all the mangled children of Aum, he was the least likely to have made it.

The last howls rose above the wall of fire and I tried frantically to look through its burn to see him one last time, for though I knew him only for three days and a half, he was no less gloriously beautiful than she was.

She brought him to me on the night that followed the night I could not spot him. I had stayed in my room all day and had shut out any brother coming by.

I was still a Wafadar – my training was vast – but I could no longer keep my mind a smooth sheet. The hands of two questions kept rumpling it all up.

How did it all come to this?

What should I do?

When I heard her tread I rose from my bed. There was also the sound of other feet following her. I immediately strapped on my belt of chonch and merged into the shadows at the far corner of the room.

I did not see him when she first entered the room. Then she stood aside and he crawled in carefully, lifting his torso over the steps and the sill of the door with a great effort. It was the spider from the yard, his face close to the ground, his arms and legs spread all around him, just about keeping his belly from being scraped. His head was held up on a stretched neck as he tried to see where his mother had brought him.

I dropped to the floor and went to him on my knees. His hair like everyone else's was cropped to his scalp, making his ears look big. Then I went lower, onto my elbows, so he would not have to crane his neck. That made him smile. His eyes were curious and kind. They held no anger in them.

His mother said, I told you he would come.

He said, in a voice so slow that it slowed down time and the world and my blood, The fur of the fox is made up of rocks.

After a long time, in a voice as slow as his, I said, The beak of the crow melts in snow.

He gurgled, his eyes dancing, and I put my hand on his face and it was warm and alive. He said, To eat a duck's egg use your back leg.

I said, The Bhakta's arse is made up of grass.

At that he rolled over on his back and waved his spider limbs in the air.

I did the same, and his happy sounds filled the room.

I looked up at her and her face was wet.

The next three days and a half I was with him as much as I could, making of my sentences a rhyme as he did, lying prostrate on the floor so I could hold his face and look into his eyes, carrying him on my back – his twisted limbs securely clamped around me – into the forest and to the cliffs. His gurgles filled the air and rose to the skies and were heard across the valley, all the way up the higher terraces.

Aum's very best are the children of the Nest.

The horned owl has suddenly taken wing.

Did it sense something? Are there more shadows in the semul now? I make a quick trip to see Parvati and the kitten one more time. Both are sleeping the sleep of the blameless. Before I go back up with one last glass of tea I write a note for the drain inspector and place it where it will be swiftly found, on the television set. In it I direct him to my story. I wish I could tell him how much I admire him but it is tough to do so on a scribbled piece of paper. I hope when he hears my narration he will know.

Strangely now I feel grateful to my pursuers. They have allowed me to get to the end of my story, and the story of my people. As my blood drains out I can be content that my little pill will find a place in the pharmacy of the world's tales.

I can hope many a seeker – and this is my learning, that seekers alone redeem the world – will come to it, and in it find some succour.

That they will stand warned of the preparations of the pure.

That they will be able to identify the Yodhas amongst them by the look in their eye.

That they will learn to tell the difference between ideas and men; between god and his image; between Aum and his Helmsmen.

Between the word and its meaning.

I am ready. My Wafadar's eyes tell me the skies have begun to lighten at the end of the horizon. I look at the maestro from the heart of the burning plains, round-faced, bald, his right arm raised, his mouth open, and I slip his voice into the black box and close my eyes.

I like the thought of my brothers arriving to claim me as the maestro's voice seizes the air and commands the last spirits of the night and the first of the morning, and I feel I am by the holy river that I have never seen, the lights dancing on its timeless waters, a hundred million dead souls by my side, stirring to attention.

I like the thought of the maestro's voice opening up my pores even as the chonch open up my pipes. I like the thought of entering the womb of the perfect moment even as I exit the doors of this life.

The maestro's voice begins to climb. It scales the semul and reaches for the heavens. Darkness and light hang in its quavering balance. I think, perhaps it will transform my marauding brothers too. Make an incision in their carapace, give them pause. Perhaps sow in them the one word, possibly, greater than music or love.

Doubt.

That should forever alternate with faith as day does with night.